THE HATAK WITCHES

T0163473

Volume 88

Sun Tracks

An American Indian Literary Series

THE HATAK WITCHES

DEVON A. MIHESUAH

THE UNIVERSITY OF
ARIZONA PRESS

TUCSON

The University of Arizona Press
www.uapress.arizona.edu

ISBN-13: 978-0-8165-4118-8 (paperback)

Cover design by Leigh McDonald
Cover art by JR Korpa/Unsplash
Designed and typeset by Leigh McDonald in Adobe Jenson Pro 10.25/15 and Telmoss WF
(display)

Publication of this book is made possible in part by the proceeds of a permanent endowment created with the assistance of a Challenge Grant from the National Endowment for the Humanities,
a federal agency.

Library of Congress Cataloging-in-Publication Data
Names: Mihesuah, Devon A., 1957– author.
Title: The Hatak witches / Devon A. Mihesuah.
Other titles: Sun tracks ; v. 88.
Description: Tucson : University of Arizona Press, 2021. | Series: Sun tracks: an American Indian
      literary series; volume 88
Identifiers: LCCN 2020017310 | ISBN 9780816541188 (paperback)
Subjects: LCSH: Choctaw Indians—Oklahoma—Fiction. | Witches—Oklahoma—Fiction. |
      LCGFT: Detective and mystery fiction.
Classification: LCC PS3563.I371535 H38 2021 | DDC 813/.6—dc23
LC record available at https://lccn.loc.gov/2020017310

Printed in the United States of America
♾ This paper meets the requirements of ANSI/NISO Z39.48-1992 (Permanence of Paper).

If an Indian was suspected of being a witch or devil
he was killed by the other Indians.

—ELIZABETH WITCHER, APRIL 18, 1938,
MCALESTER, OKLAHOMA

THE HATAK WITCHES

I

CHALAKWA RANCH, EAST OF ADA, OKLAHOMA

The hollow is damp, dark, and smells of decay. Poison ivy and skunk cabbage dominate the sodden stream banks. Thorny creepers, thin as green barbed wire, twist around gnarled tree trunks and weave through the underbrush.

Rainwater runs downhill toward the hollow through the sunlit grass and disappears into the dense tangle of growth, where it turns malodorous and sluggish. After making its way through the twists and turns of the myriad tannin-dark and clay-filled waterways, the water drifts out of the forest in thick brown rivulets. Over time, a few small oxbow ponds evolved into shallow, mossy bogs.

Squirrels, hawks, opossums, raccoons, mice, and other varmints typical of Oklahoma make the hollow their home. The foliage is almost impenetrable in some areas, creating hiding places for the smallest of them. The bobcats and coyotes that wander the meadows occasionally venture into the darkness as well. Time slows in this thick forest at the three-acre heart of Andrew Tubbee's ranch.

A large population of tarantulas live in the grassy portions of the ranch, so many that Andrew considered naming his place Chulhką̓n Land until he heard there already is a ranch in Texas named Rancho de Tarantula. He'd once thought to name his allotment Sinti Lusa Land, after the cottonmouth water moccasins, thick as branches, that haunt the creeks and bogs. Instead, he named the five-hundred-acre property Chalakwa Ranch after the light-brown copperheads that blend into the ground foliage as smoothly as a white polar bear does in snow. The ranch is also home to coral snakes—those red, yellow, and black serpents that need to chew to inject their venom. "Red touch black, good for Jack," Andrew's mother taught him so he could distinguish them from the similar-looking but nonpoisonous king snakes. When he entered the hollow, however, the last ditty of his mother's refrain sounded loud and clear: "Red touch yellow, kill a fellow."

Large wild hogs that Choctaws call *shukhusi* also roam the humid jungle. Some weigh six hundred pounds and eat whatever they can find or bring down. The intelligent and prolific descendants of Spanish boars and domesticated pigs destroy crops, upend fences and cemetery headstones, and dine on small wildlife, including fawns. In the past two years Andrew had shot more than a hundred of the *shukhusi* he found rooting around his property. After the arduous task of gutting and quartering the animals, he donated the meat to the food bank, needy families, and the big cat sanctuary in Wynnewood.

"No more of those damned things!" His wife, Sistina, admonished him from the kitchen window last summer after he brought home a litter of dead piglets along with their two-hundred-pound mother. The sow had rooted up his tomato garden and mangled his squashes, corn, beans, peppers, okra, and amaranth. He unleashed his fury and blasted the lot of them with his Browning ShorTrac Hog Stalker. The .308s trashed the piglets and blew the head off their long-legged momma. The impoverished Woodsbury family would welcome the meat since Mr. Woodsbury had lost his job a few months prior. Andrew felt a twinge of regret

after shooting the cute, spotted piglets, but he also knew they would rap-
idly grow into four-legged engines of destruction. He chained the hefty
female's back legs to the ATV and dragged her to his house.

"The freezers are full," Sistina continued. "And the one you kilt last time
got into some bad acorns or something. The meat's bitter." She moved closer
to the screen and saw the piglets. "And those're ruint."

"I know. I'll bury them down where I buried the others," he told her as
he headed to the detached carport for a shovel.

"We're gonna have to rename the ranch 'The Pig Cemetery,'" she called
after him. "Not cool!"

The lush foliage of the hollow blocks sunlight and turns day into perpetual dusk. Condensation on leaves reflects moonlight as if fairies are
dancing in the darkness. The nights are almost completely black, and the
air always feels thick—like a storm is approaching. Animals can hide easily. Hunting in the gloomy, mucky hollow is challenging and potentially
dangerous.

Andrew does not allow many hunters onto his land, the exceptions
being pig hunters, whom he follows around in his ATV to make sure they
behave, and his cousin Dustin Peters, whom he trusts. His land means
everything to him, and not just because the allotments are home to a
variety of game animals and trees that he values as resources. The Tubbee
family lives on side-by-side allotments. Andrew bought a section from
his aunt Jerrilynn when she moved to Albuquerque twenty years ago and
another from his sixty-year-old cousin, Wyatt, who decided he preferred
working as a fishing guide in Florida to farming his family's land. Andrew
was lucky to get the land, and he knew it.

He had inherited the other allotment twenty years ago from his
father. His grandmother Bertha had inherited that parcel from her
mother, Mary Wilson Blue, when she died two years after receiving
the allotment from the government at the turn of the century. Many
Choctaws sold their allotments for quick cash and spent the money so

fast they had no time to consider how their decision would affect future generations. Now their lands are gone, more often than not in the hands of white Oklahomans with oil wells that chug out enough black crude to make a tidy sum.

Andrew carefully manages his animals, and his attention to conservation makes his property even more valuable. Poachers manage to take an occasional deer or turkey on the allotment's periphery, but most have no interest in the center of Chalakwa Ranch.

On this warm fall evening Dustin Peters and his fifteen-year-old son, Zach, sweated and panted as they trekked through the muck on the first day of bow season. Their new hats, shirts, jackets, and pants—in Cabela's Mossy Oak Break-up camouflage design—were already filthy, and their green boots (treated with Scent-Lok to curtail foot odor) looked like last year's models.

The two had been awake since 4 a.m., eager to reach Andrew's ranch before sunrise. "There's Sirius," Dustin had told his son as he drove with one hand on the wheel and the other pointing to the southeast. "The bright star. You see Orion there, right? You can tell it's Orion because of the three stars that make up his belt. Follow those and it's almost a straight line to Sirius."

"Is it named for Sirius Black, Harry Potter's godfather?"

"Uh, I dunno," Dustin said. "Maybe."

"Well Sirius was the son of Orion Black, so it must be where the star's name comes from."

"Hmmm. Okay." Dustin wasn't sure who named stars and didn't much care. "Eat something, Zach. It's gonna be a long day."

"Not hungry."

"You will be. At least have some trail mix. And drink some juice."

He heard Zach crinkling wrappers. "Gimme that sandwich if you're not gonna eat it."

Sirius was the last thing on their minds when they reached the gate to Andrew's land. They had to move quickly to situate themselves in their stands before dawn. Once there, they sat for two hours with not a deer in sight, although a 'possum and a raccoon wandered by. Dustin thought an owl glided by overhead, too, but he couldn't tell for certain in the dark. It was big, whatever it was.

The two grew weary and butt-sore from perching on the small seats. Once it got light, they lowered their bows to the ground with haul lines, climbed down, and went to look for sign along the creek. After several fruitless hours, they returned to the camper for food and a nap. Surely they'd have better luck if they returned to the hollow around dusk.

And so they did. Dustin touched Zach lightly on the arm when he spotted the twelve-point white-tailed buck grazing on the moss at the edge of the creek twenty-four yards away. Zach quietly drew a black carbon arrow from the leather quiver his grandmother had given him on his tenth birthday. He fit the notched end into the bowstring then slowly pulled it back. His father had offered to buy Zach a compound bow for his birthday, but Zach preferred his old longbow, a special gift from his grandpa. Besides, after his football workouts, with some extra attention paid to his shoulders and back, Zach could hold the pull even longer than he was able to last spring.

Zach aimed for the chest, hoping for a shot through the heart that would also perforate both lungs. Quick and clean. He inhaled, then, slowly exhaling, let his fingers release the string. The arrow hit the buck in the side behind its front leg. The deer huffed then bolted in a last burst of adrenaline-powered fear.

"I got him!" Zach yelled. "I got him, Dad!"

Dustin smiled and swigged from his water bottle. "Yup. Lung shot, for sure. Heart too, probably. Let's go find him, son. He can't go far."

Dustin knew that Zach would hang the buck's mounted head over his Little League trophy shelf with the stuffed pheasant he'd killed last summer. Dustin salivated as he thought of venison backstrap grilled with peppers. Or maybe a roast cooked in the crockpot with vegetables. Sweet corn and watermelon from the garden, too. He could already taste the melted butter on the cob. Maybe some okra . . .

"Dad," Zach said behind him.

Dustin jerked his attention back to the present.

"That buck took off," Zach said. "I don't see where he went."

"He couldn't have gone far. That buck is dead, son." He was annoyed that he hadn't been watching when the buck disappeared into the gloom.

"Yeah, but he could be anywhere in here."

"True enough," Dustin muttered. "And it'll be dark before long." He looked at his watch: 7:12. He'd already turned on the LED light on his hat. Complete darkness would settle soon, and he knew they had to hurry. He didn't relish the thought of being in the hollow after dark. Zach walked ahead of his father as fast as he could with muck sucking at his feet. He lifted his knees high to clear the mire and clinging ground vines. Dustin could dress the animal quickly, and the buck would be lighter once relieved of his guts, but dragging the animal through the darkness and thick undergrowth would still be difficult and time-consuming.

An owl hooted, deep and loud, from a branch just above him. Dustin stopped and looked up to see a huge bird silhouetted against the fading light, tufts of feathers sticking up on top of his head like Batman's ears. Family stories said that owls were omens of bad luck to Choctaws. The great horned owls, called *ishkitini*, could change themselves into men with birdlike faces and ornery dispositions. Dustin, a good Christian, didn't think he believed that. He was pretty sure that owls were just stupid birds that preyed on mice and other little scampering animals. Besides, even if *ishkitini* were evil, and their little screech owl friends, the *ofunlo*, the bringers of bad news, were here in the hollow, his faith in God would protect him. Still, his heart raced at the sound. Better to be safe and skedaddle before the sun disappeared altogether.

Zach, also watching the owl, almost tripped on a tree root but kept his footing. They were nearing the edge of the hollow. His heart sank at the thought of going down there. Behind the owl's head he could see the twinkling of a few stars through the thick foliage of the tall cottonwoods. Between treetops in the canopy he saw three meteors streak across the sky. He gasped.

"Dad!" Zach yelled in fear, taking off at a run.

"Slow down, son," Dustin called to Zach. "Stop! Take a deep breath, Zach. We need to keep checking the ground for tracks. Shine your light. Did he stay on this game trail?"

"Stars just ran across the sky! Did you see them?" Zach panted.

"Son," Dustin said as he looked up again. The big owl had followed them. It sat on a limb and watched, big yellow eyes unblinking. "Those weren't stars," he said as he eyed the large bird. "They were meteors. Stars don't fall."

Why is it following us? Dustin wondered. Every owl he had ever seen had seemed eager to avoid him.

"Uncle Leroy says witches are out when the stars run," Zach said.

"There aren't any witches, son, and those weren't stars."

"How do you know, Dad? You know that for sure?"

The owl hooted again. It sounded like a laugh. "We gotta find that buck," Dustin said as calmly as he could manage. "Help me look," he repeated. "The tracks have to be here."

Zach wiped his nose with his sleeve and shined his beam downward. Meteors scared him. He was also concerned about the giant pigs that ran through the forest on quiet feet. Andrew had told him that if one knocked you down, it might come at your face or try to eviscerate you with its tusks. Zach was not yet too worried because the huge pigs he saw made a lot of noise. He also knew that his father packed a Colt .45 in the holster at his waist.

Dustin looked up again. No more stars twinkling through the thick branches. "That buck could be anywhere."

"Even in a tree?" Zach asked sarcastically.

"Just keep going, son." Dustin put his hand over his mouth and nose. The loamy smell grew worse at night.

Zach shined the light in front of them. "Hey, look here! I see them. The deer's tracks go off the trail into the scrub." Zach headed into the tangled bushes, knowing his heavy pants would protect him. Dustin followed his son, trying to avoid the backlash from the branches Zach pushed through.

"How did that deer get through here?" Dustin panted.

Zach shined his light to his left and saw the buck. It was lying on its right side between two cottonwood trees strangled by poison oak.

"Here," Zach said. He looked closer then inhaled sharply. "Dad? Dad! Look at him!"

Dustin stepped forward and aimed his headlamp at the carcass. Zach's arrow stuck out from behind the buck's front leg just as he expected, the green and blue feathers still bright. What he hadn't expected to see was the buck's legs, broken and bent the wrong ways at the joints. Intestines from the eviscerated carcass stretched out into the darkness like glistening strands of a spider's web. The antlers had been sawed off close to the skull, and the left eye was gone.

Dustin pulled out his Colt and looked behind him. "Shine that light on the ground in front of the buck. In front of his head."

Zach was crying softly. "Pigs? Was it pigs?" He leaned his bow against a creeper-wrapped tree and pulled out a bandana to wipe his nose again.

"I don't think so. No tracks. And they don't break bones like that. Or carry saws," he added dryly. "Shine the light on his side." Dustin gasped. The backstrap had been removed. The skin had been cut, pulled back, and the meat excised cleanly.

"My God," he whispered. "Now shine it behind his rump." He and Zach circled the animal and saw nothing on the ground except for the buck's hoof prints. Dustin tried to swallow, his mouth suddenly bone dry. "I don't understand. No tracks besides the deer's, but someone sawed off those antlers and took the meat. And whoever did it, did it quick." He pushed his hat back on his head and wiped his sweaty forehead with his arm.

"I didn't hear anything," Zach sniffed. "Pigs are loud when they kill, right?"

"Well, they snort and squeal some. We didn't hear any of that." Both looked around. "We better go."

"What got his eye?"

"Maybe a crow or raven," Dustin answered.

"You told me they sleep at night."

"So I did." Dustin felt more comfortable with the weight of the Colt in his hand, but in order to hit a target he had to see it. His heart pounded.

Zach looked regretfully at his ruined buck. "Wait. What's that on his head?" Zach moved closer. A cluster of feathers wound together by a piece of buffalo grass lay atop the congealing blood. "Brown feathers. Looks like an owl's."

At Zach's comment, a flurry of noise shook the leaves above them. The air was suddenly filled with brown wings that beat at their heads and talons that clawed at their faces.

"Come on!" Dustin grabbed Zach's arm and pulled him back in the direction they'd come. The attack subsided as Dustin and Zach reached a stand of thick oaks. After a chorus of hoots, the birds disappeared.

The thick forest remained silent a few seconds. Then a crashing and rending of branches sounded nearby. Bullfrogs bellowed and a wildcat screamed. The hollow had begun its nightly song. The hoots sounded again.

"Here they come, son. Run!"

"My bow!" Zach yelled as he tried to break free of his father's grip.

"I'll get it tomorrow! Move!"

Dustin leaped a narrow stream and pulled his son through sticky mud. His headlamp beam danced wildly in front of them as branches tore at their clothes and scratched their faces.

A tidal wave of wails and shrieks—of pigs, birds, and bobcats mixed with unidentifiable voices that laughed and moaned—pushed them from behind. After a terrifying ten minutes, Dustin and Zach climbed out of the hollow to reach solid footing.

"Almost there, Zach," Dustin gasped. "Keep going."

The pair sprinted to the truck. Dustin dug the key from his pants pocket as he pushed Zach through the driver's side door ahead of him. Dustin missed the ignition hole and tried again. "Come on!" he yelled.

"Dad. We're OK. Calm down."

Dustin took a deep breath, and the key hit the mark.

Then something large hit the top of the vehicle in three rhythmic *whomps.*

"What is *that?*" Zach cried.

"I don't know," Dustin whispered.

The engine roared. Dustin forced himself to keep from breaking off the shifter while putting it in gear. He noticed that Venus shined brightly, but he had no time to admire the Evening Star. They sped over the rocky and bumpy dirt road to the gate with the wooden sign that read CHALAKWA RANCH.

Dustin put the truck in park and jumped out to open the chain-link gate. "Drive it through the gate," he told Zach, who moved to the driver's seat. Gasping and shaking, Dustin hesitated as his son maneuvered the truck through the gate, wondering if it was really necessary to close and lock the gate behind him. After a high-pitched laugh sounded in a nearby bois d'arc tree, Dustin decided it wasn't. He pushed Zach into the passenger seat and climbed back in.

"Andrew is going to be pissed, Dad."

"He'll get over it."

Dustin gunned the engine. The two bounced in their seats as the 2015 GMC Sierra 1500 careened down the potholed dirt road, unaware of the yellow eyes that watched them.

2

Leroy Bear Red Ears awoke in a coughing fit. He felt as if something had crawled into his mouth and down his throat. A gnat or a small spider was in there, all right. He took two gulps of lemonade from the Pioneer Woman tumbler on the bedside table. The ice had melted, but the lemonade remained cold and refreshing.

The old man coughed a few more times. White curtains billowed from the open window. Light from the waxing gibbous moon shined through the sheer material, allowing him to see the details of his room. Leroy's dresser stood next to the window, the white poppy mallows and yellow meadow parsnips he had picked in his yard yesterday still bright in the clay pot his granddaughter Tupelo had made for him when she was in third grade. Another gift, the misshapen sculpted horse painted psychedelic colors, sat next to the pot. Tupelo was in high school now and no longer made crafts for her grandfather.

He heard something off in the distance—a rumble, like thunder. He picked up the iPhone charging on the bedside table and clicked on his weather app. The radar showed no clouds, no storm. He typed his zip code into the National Weather Service website and discovered the skies were clear for five hundred miles in all directions. Another sound, a distant scream, grew louder as it flew into his room on the breeze and then dissipated. He put down the phone. His cat, Lorraine, lay curled behind Leroy's knees, her eyes wide as she listened.

The stillness did not fool Leroy. Something powerful and purposeful moved outside in the darkness. He felt the evil presence as sure as he felt the gentle spirit of his long-dead wife. Leroy closed his eyes and listened. He heard only crickets and a single late-season cicada.

Unlike his deceased brother Strong Bull, who suffered back injuries in a car wreck several decades before and stood bent at the waist as if he intended to pick something up off the ground, Leroy is a virile seventy-something with straight posture and refuses to submit to the decrepitude of age. He walks briskly every morning and performs yoga with the lady instructor on an early-morning television show. Hard work in the garden keeps him fit, especially in spring when he carries compost, breaks up the soil, and repairs fencing.

The gardening is essential because Leroy prefers the traditional Choctaw diet. He makes large batches of the old corn dishes *banaha*, which resemble tamales, and *tamfula*, corn mush with hickory oil, pecans, and turkey instead of squirrel, on Sundays so he has enough for the week. Leroy used to make his own cornmeal and hominy, but pounding corn is hard work, and soaking it in wood lye ash too time consuming. Now he gets his cornmeal from a younger, more vigorous neighbor or buys it from a health food store in Oklahoma City. His hunting friends and family bring him deer and elk roasts in the fall and turkeys year round, enough to keep his freezer full. He admires much in American culture, but that does not include the greasy, salty, sugary foods that cause heart disease and diabetes. Nature would have to work hard to defeat him.

An owl hooted in the cottonwood tree by the creek. Leroy sat up straighter, cocking his head. Another owl, maybe a quarter mile away, answered. Then another to the east. He slowed his breathing, waiting. Lorraine, now sprawled across his legs, lay still as a stone, her ears perked.

A coyote yipped and then howled, a curious high-pitched yodel that sounded forlorn, lost, and afraid. He waited for a response from another coyote, but none came. He was not surprised. Coyotes respond only to their own kind. Lorraine growled and opened her mouth to hiss but made no sound.

Chahta medicine man Leroy Bear Red Ears moved Lorraine on to the soft quilt, then swung his legs to the side of the bed and planted his feet on the floor. He sighed and began preparing himself for what he knew would be a long day.

3

Oklahoma is beautiful in autumn. The trees and bushes that remain green stand in muted contrast to the intense red, orange, and yellow leaves. Hot days begin with cool, still mornings. The sun rises later and sets earlier. Black-eyed Susans form bright yellow carpets along the roads and in ungrazed meadows. Monarch and swallowtail butterflies flit amid the last of the milkweed and Queen Anne's lace. Pecans and walnuts begin to drop.

Monique Blue Hawk glanced at the bedside clock and smiled at accurately predicting it was 5:50 a.m. She lay still for a few more minutes, enjoying the warmth of her husband, Steve, in the fresh morning air. She got up slowly so not to disturb him and their homely cat, Foogly, who slept next to him. Monique took an Ibuprofen and a long drink from her water bottle, then padded down the hall to their thirteen-year-old son's room. The glow of the dim blue aquarium light illuminated Robbie's face. The languid movements of the small neon tetras calmed her, though they should not be swimming in green water. She needed to remind Robbie to clean the tank. She stood at her son's doorway a few more seconds and watched the comforter rise and fall with his breathing.

After running and lifting weights for twelve days out of the last four-teen Monique wasn't in the mood to exercise. But it was such a glorious morning. She decided that four or five miles before breakfast would do it. Although the days were warm enough for T-shirts, the mornings some-times required tights and perhaps a hoodie. She dressed quickly in the guest room where she kept her clothes, attached the iPhone to her upper arm, put in her earbuds, and turned on a Harry Bosch audio book. She went to the back door, laced her shoes, and whistled. Rover dashed out from under the deck like a bullet from a gun. "Wanna run, girl?" Monique asked.

Rover jumped up and down enthusiastically on stubby back legs. Monique jerked her collar as she tried to attach the leash to the squirming dog. "Stand still, Rover! Stop." To her surprise, the bowlegged little dog had proved a good running partner. Monique had wanted to take home a dozen dogs from the crowded shelter two years ago. But then she spotted Rover bouncing up and down on her back legs like a dancing bear. Her previous owner had beaten her so badly she'd lost an eye. Monique had seen Rover's diminished eyesight hinder her only once, when she chased a stick and ran face-first into a tree.

Once Monique had Rover under control, they started on a slow jog down the leaf-blown street. The morning felt too balmy for tights after all, and she wished she had worn a tank top instead of a long-sleeved T-shirt. The trees that sheltered her neighborhood were magnificent in their fall colors. Her yard would soon be covered with pecan, oak, and maple leaves. Winter ice storms and spring winds would break branches. Today, though, she enjoyed the dark, clear, and quiet morning.

A road construction truck motored past her, and the driver put his toast in his mouth and waved. Another neighbor sat in her garage reading her Kindle. She was out there every morning in her recliner. The garage door remained wide open even in winter, the lady covered with blankets. Monique figured she had insomnia, or maybe she just wanted some space from an undesirable spouse.

Off in the distance, an owl hooted. Night birds gave a few last calls in the tall pecans. Monique caught a glimpse of an animal with a long tail streaking across the street a few houses in front of her. Too gray for a fox—probably a small coyote.

After a mile of warm-up, Monique and Rover sped up a bit. Another animal darted across a yard, this time an early-morning rabbit. Unable to resist, Rover swerved to the right, jerking Monique's arm and almost tripping her. "Rover! Damn it. No!" Not that yelling does any good when a dog is after a fast, furry creature. Which is why Foogly stays in, and Rover stays out.

After fifty minutes, they returned home. She smiled at the red and pink geraniums still blooming in colorful pots on her front porch. The backyard okra and pepper plants were still producing, the tomato plants had dozens of blossoms, and she crossed her fingers for weather warm enough to produce more fruit. She might have a dozen large pumpkins for Halloween if the squash bugs didn't get them.

Monique added kibble to Rover's bowl before beginning the next part of her workout. The dog gulped her food then ran outside to the fence and began barking at the neighbor's Labradoodle. The two sprinted back and forth the length of the fence, yapping and gasping. Monique took off her shoes, hopped on the trampoline, and did front and back flips until she felt dizzy. Then she watered her garden and popped a few cherry tomatoes and a sweet banana pepper into her mouth. As Monique savored the sweet, earthy flavors, her cell phone vibrated. She swallowed and answered, "Blue Hawk."

"Good morning, Detective."

"Captain Hardaway," she said in surprise. "Good morning." This was unusual. Calls normally came from dispatch, and Hardaway did not come in to work until eight. She moved toward the house, anticipating what he would probably say.

"A security guard was assaulted at the Children's Museum. Another guard is missing. We just got word. Get over there." She looked down and barely missed stepping on a woolly bear caterpillar on the cement porch. Its orange segments were wider than the black ones. That meant a mild winter.

"Anyone dead?" She strode through the door and into the mudroom.

"Not yet, but he might be soon. The incident took place in the basement, apparently outside one of the offices."

"Does Chris know?" As she walked through the kitchen, she plugged in the panini press and noticed that Steve had pinto beans soaking in the spaghetti pot.

"Dispatch is calling him now."

"I can be there in twenty."

She entered her bathroom—the one in the guest room—turned on the shower, dropped the armband and phone onto the counter, and stripped. She pinned up her long hair before she stepped into the lukewarm cascade. A quick face wash with apricot scrub and a few twirls in the sharp spray, and she was done. Her clothes lay on the bed where she'd put them the night before. Her earrings and watch lay in an ass's-ear abalone shell on the dresser. Monique had learned early on that having to hunt for clean and pressed clothing in the mornings would ruin her day. If she forgot to put things out the night before, she would be forced to wear yesterday's shirt or to break out the iron. Steve appreciated the arrangement because it gave him a few more minutes' sleep in the mornings. The added bonus of having her own bathroom and closet is that it eliminated the stress of arguing with Steve about her job.

Monique's black, slightly flared stretch slacks hid the Beretta Pico in her ankle holster. She considered leaving off her bulletproof vest but decided to wear it. Usually she dropped it in the passenger seat, but this morning she was headed into an unknown situation, and she was not one to take unnecessary chances. She donned a stretchy off-white button-down blouse and an expensive fitted jacket that covered her .40 Glock semi-automatic. She quickly put in two pairs of stud earrings, one set of turquoise and another tinier set of mother-of-pearl, then tied back her long hair into a low ponytail and twisted it into a tight bun secured with bobby pins.

Now dressed, she walked into the master bedroom to see if Steve was awake. Steve sat up in bed and watched Monique button her jacket. Foogly stretched and purred.

"Morning," he said. "I gotta get going, too. There's a big point-to-point rally coming up, and drivers have been driving me crazy for tune-ups and parts." Monique's husband owned an auto parts store, and his vast knowledge about cars and trucks was in great demand. Local auto racers had discovered that Steve knew more about scratch-building than they did. He quickly found an extra income boost from the drag, sprint, and rally racers who sought his advice. The big Pawnee tried to keep up with weight lifting and biking, but as his business prospered, his workouts diminished.

"Why're you going in so early?" Steve tucked his hair behind his ears.

"Trouble at the Children's Museum."

"What, kids paint the naked lady?" He meant the transparent woman whose June Cleaver voice told giggling schoolchildren about her innards. As she named and described each organ, the part in question flashed a bright light. Monique thought it funny that the see-through woman only briefly discussed the large intestine and did not describe anything lower than her navel.

"No. A guard was assaulted. Although a painted naked lady would be more fun." She smiled in an attempt to disarm him before he got riled up. He hated her job. She had not worked patrol in ten years and now solved cases instead of confronting miscreants. Nevertheless, they still argued about the potential dangers of law enforcement. He maintained that family was more important than her risking her life for strangers. Monique countered that detectives like her kept families safe. They would not resolve the old argument.

"What the heck?"

"Steve. Don't worry. It's probably just a robbery."

He picked up Foogly and put her on a pillow, then stood and started toward Monique.

"I gotta motor," she said as she hurried out the door to avoid further discussion.

Monique hustled to the kitchen, where she took a glass container out of the refrigerator and inspected the contents. "There's some turkey and chile burritos left," she called to him as she placed one in the panini press and closed it. While it warmed, she stood in front of the hall mirror and applied the mascara she kept in the pencil holder. The mirror showed a few crow's feet around her eyes.

Steve walked up behind her and kissed her neck. "How long will you be gone?"

She snuggled into his chest briefly before slipping away into the kitchen. "You ask me that every day, and every day I tell you I have no idea. I'll leave this plugged in." She took the burrito out of the press and wrapped it in a paper towel.

"Morning, Mom."

Monique turned and smiled at her sleepy-eyed son. Robbie at thirteen was the mirror image of herself at that age—slender, with dark brown hair and eyes and tawny skin. Too skinny after his latest growth spurt, she thought, but he'd make that up quickly. It remained to be seen if he would fill out like his high school football star father. She didn't like to think of her baby playing football.

"Morning, Robbie. The aquarium needs cleaning. The fish are getting a little hard to see in the murk." She gave him a quick peck and hurried to the garage, throwing back a quick "Love you."

Monique put the burrito on the dash through the open car window then bent to slip on the New Balance walking shoes she left next to the car every day when she got home so she could slide into them on her way to work. The trunk of her unmarked Crown Victoria held extra clothes and shoes in case she had to deal with a messy crime scene. She grabbed her Thermoflask of ice water from the garage fridge and set it in the drink holder. Her sunglasses were hooked onto the rearview mirror, the keys hung from the wiper arm, and her small purse lay under her seat where she'd left it the night before. Ready to roll.

"Bye, Mom," Robbie yelled out the kitchen door.

"Bye, sweetie, Love you," she answered as the garage door opened. "Have a good day at school. Learn something."

"Always do."

4

As she drove out into the brilliant October morning, Monique wished they had moved back to Oklahoma sooner. Steve never tired of reminding her that he had not wanted to move to Moose City in the first place. The Northwest was too damned cold. The mild summer temperatures in the mountains were nice, but the lake waters were uncomfortably cool for swimming. The cold spring winds often kept Monique from running, and fall in Moose City felt more like an Oklahoma December. Plowing the long driveway twice a day in the heart of snowy winters and cleaning up the ashy mess around the wood-burning stove quickly became unpleasant duties that they both resented. But the higher detective salary for Monique combined with the promise of elk in their backyard and groomed cross-country skiing trails were enough incentive for them to give it a shot.

Steve planned on finding work as a diesel mechanic, but shortly after they arrived in Moose City, a neighbor's father put his auto-parts store, Ma's and Pa's Parts, up for sale. Steve wasted no time in wrangling a loan to buy it. He changed the name to Auto Parts 'N More, and the enterprise proved successful, as had Monique's career.

But nine murder cases in three years had left her emotionally and physically exhausted. Worse, the violent cases and her long hours away from home threatened to shake her relationship with Steve, and she was tired of missing Robbie's track meets. The last bitingly cold winter had been the final straw. Monique secured a position as a detective in Norman, packed up her family in early spring, and arrived in time to see the red-buds blossom. Steve sold his building, shipped his inventory, and opened a shop on the outskirts of Norman, miles from another auto-parts store, Walmart, or any other competitor. He paid off his loan in less than a year. Both were happier for the move, and it did not take long to settle back into the comfortable rhythms of the Okie seasons.

Absorbed in the beauty of the fall colors, Monique was shocked to realize she was going almost fifty as she approached the school zone. Although she had turned on her lights and siren, she braked to thirty as she scanned the area for runners. It was too early for school, but the cross-country teams began the first of their two-a-day workouts before classes, and the boys' soccer team occasionally ran before morning practice. The only pedestrians she spotted were two women walking their dogs.

She remembered her burrito and took a large bite. "Dang. Forgot the salsa."

As she got closer to the museum, she noticed Halloween decorations in store windows and a few driveways with lopsided orange leaf bags made to look like giant pumpkins. Robbie hadn't mentioned a Halloween costume yet. Monique smiled at memories of Robbie's yearly concern about his costumes. In middle school he put on round black glasses and looked like a tawny Harry Potter. Then he matured and no longer looked anything like him. The next year Robbie wore khakis, a coiled rope over his shoulder, and an Indiana Jones hat. The last time he trick-or-treated, he preferred the anonymity of a ninja costume. Now in eighth grade, Robbie had no more interest in dressing up. Monique's mouth turned down at the thought that he might have outgrown it.

Monique reached the Norman Children's Museum of Science and History in less than eight minutes. She had once known this museum well. As a child, she'd confidently walked the halls of the large, old enterprise, aware of the exact locations of the T-Rex and triceratops skeletons, the twelve-ton iron meteorite in the Hall of Minerals, the fearsome Japanese samurai, and the stuffed red-assed baboon that looked a bit more flea-bitten each year.

The museum also held vast collections of preserved flora and fauna specimens and supposedly housed an archive of items created by Indigenous peoples from around the world. She knew there were also skeletal remains somewhere in the bowels of the museum, but it had been almost twenty years since museum officials succumbed to complaints and pulled the last display of Native American skulls. The museum board was never specific about how many items—or what items, for that matter—the museum possessed, much to the dismay of Natives who try to keep track of such things.

Monique approached the museum from the south, where the Omni Theatre rose just higher than the Noble Planetarium dome on the west wing—though neither was as tall as the central dome of the museum foyer. Monique had once watched the "Oklahoma Sky" orrery programs at the Noble. The seats had headrests and tilted back to allow the audience to see the entire sky. In the center of the planetarium, a large metal ball dotted with tiny holes rendered constellations on the dark ceiling. She recalled with special fondness the Friday midnight "Laser Magic" shows set to the music of Pink Floyd. As teenagers she and her girlfriends had smoked weed in her blue Vega before the shows. They giggled as they leaned back in the Planetarium seats and looked up, stoned and mesmerized, at the lights set to psychedelic riffs. She had wanted to relive that warm memory with Steve after they met, but it didn't go quite as planned. She coughed and gagged at the first toke on the joint she had acquired from a bust a month prior, and the light show gave her a headache. Steve complained that the seats were uncomfortable. Some things should stay in the past, she thought.

Monique parked her car in the museum's front lot next to Detective Chris Pierson's white Chevy Caprice. She felt slightly annoyed that her partner had arrived first. Ambulance and fire personnel were already there as well.

She touched her weapons and checked her mascara in the rearview mirror before getting out of the car. Her vest was already constricting her movements, and she debated taking it off. Caution won. She inhaled deeply, exhaled slowly with her eyes closed, then exited the car.

"Howdy, Chris," she said to the lanky red-haired man who walked up to meet her. In some ways her partner of two years reminded her of her Moose City partner, who looked like a surfer dude but had a profound southern twang. Chris spoke with a strong Northeast accent, but like her old partner he could disarm most people with his charm. As usual, he wore cheap shoes, a wrinkled suit, and a shirt with unidentifiable stains on the front. Forty years old, Chris was newly divorced and had no kids. Monique knew he could afford to buy a new shirt every now and then, or at least to send the old ones to the cleaners. "Nice shirt."

Chris looked down at the stain and pulled his jacket across his shirt. He was used to her sarcasm. "Uh, morning. What have you heard about this?"

"Same as you, probably. Hardaway told me a security guard was injured by an intruder in the office area in the basement." She took a tube of Blistex from her pocket and swiped some across her mouth. "And they can't locate the other guard."

"Who are 'they'?"

"Don't know their names. Hardaway said 'security guards.'"

"No, I mean who called it in?"

"I guess another security guard who found him. Let's find out."

Chris followed Monique as they walked quickly to the museum entrance, simultaneously wary of what they might find and eager to get started. Monique eyed the two sets of double-paned entry doors ahead, each with a heavy metal bar set horizontally across the frames. They didn't show obvious signs of tampering. The gray front wall stones were bumpy, and large-leafed ivy had been bent to the left and right once it had reached the gutters at the top. The east wing addition built ten years prior stuck out awkwardly and looked like it had been constructed with maroon Legos. The new design disappointed her.

"Why would someone break in?" Chris asked.

"Lots to steal."

"Pots?" Chris asked. "Someone wanted pots?"

"Maybe," she answered. "There are some rare artifacts here. Pottery for sure, also animal hides, gemstones, megalodon teeth, a samurai sword, human skeletal remains."

"Megalodon teeth?"

"Big shark teeth are valuable. A serrated one bigger than six inches is worth well over a thousand dollars. I saw one online for eight thousand."

"You're kidding."

"I found a four-incher in North Carolina when I was a kid, perfectly symmetrical and serrated, and saw one on a shark teeth page just like it for six twenty-five. I keep it in the gun safe."

"I didn't know people buy teeth."

"Yup. If you find an undamaged seven-incher, you could buy a new wardrobe. And a new car," she teased.

"I'll keep my eyes open next time I go fishing."

"Biggest ones you'll catch around here are alligator gars."

"So, this maybe was a botched theft?" he said, getting back on the subject.

"Botched for sure," she answered. "If it was indeed a theft, thieves could have been after any number of things: The cash register in the gift shop. Maybe a painting or an old saddle. The exhibits have probably been rearranged since I was a kid, so I don't know what's here anymore."

"Things worth injuring someone for, though."

Monique shrugged. "People hurt and kill other people all the time just for the hell of it." In the back of her mind she hoped that this break-in had nothing to do with the museum's collection of skeletons.

They walked past the pond at the entrance and watched the ducks swim through the fountain spray, quacking joyously and wagging their tail feathers.

"I came here a lot when I was a kid," Monique said. "Some of the exhibits had Indian masks and skulls. They're gone now, and I don't miss them. They should never have been on public display."

"How come?"

"Would you want your ancestor's bones on display?"

"Yeah, okay. I mean, no. I see what you mean."

A tall, burly security guard with an impressive handlebar moustache watched them approach the entry. His ebony skin contrasted with the tufts of white hair sticking out from under his Texas Rangers ball cap. Monique increased her speed and got to the door first.

"Officers?" he asked in a deep, shaky voice. He was out of breath, as if he was excited or had been walking fast. Maybe both. Monique noticed dark stains on his right brown shoe. There were blood spots on the back of his hands and on his uniform shirt.

Monique moved her jacket to the side so he could see her badge. "I'm Detective Monique Blue Hawk, and this is Detective Chris Pierson."

He nodded. "I'm Lester Martin. Follow me."

"This door locks behind us, correct?"

"Yes, ma'am."

Monique took off her sunglasses and exchanged them for the black-framed eyeglasses in the case attached to her belt. Steve said they made her look like a scary, but sexy, librarian.

"I take it that you've been to the scene, Mr. Martin?" she said.

"Yes, ma'am. I'm the one who found him."

She gestured at his hands and shirt. "Are you injured?"

He looked at his hands then rubbed them together. "No. It's Ethan's blood."

The two followed Martin through the doorway and into the building. The distinctive smell of a museum, the lighting focused on old display items that might once have been important in someone's life, and the spirits of dead things swirling about her put Monique in a melancholy mood. Life come and gone. Anticipation of the job that she and Chris faced intensified her feeling.

"What can you tell us, Mr. Martin?" she asked as they walked.

"Not a lot," he started in his deep voice. Monique tried to place his accent. Louisiana, perhaps. Not all Okies sound alike. Some have southern accents so strong they're difficult to understand.

"I came in for my shift," he continued, "which starts at seven-thirty. Normally, another guard comes in at the same time, but he had his appendix out and another is on vacation, so it's just me this week. I didn't see Samuel Rector or Ethan Lewis. We relieve them every morning. Both of their cars were in the lot. I thought they'd be in some other part of the building, and I went on my rounds as usual." He looked at his hands again.

"I found Ethan outside the office suite on the basement floor. He was unconscious with a big gash on his head. I tried to stop the bleeding with some paper towels from the coffee tray. Didn't help any. I looked for a towel and couldn't find one, but there was a sweater hanging on the rack. It had been there for months like it didn't belong to nobody, so I wrapped it around his head. Then I walked down the halls in case whoever did it was still here, you know?"

"You didn't see or hear anything?" Monique asked.

"No, ma'am. Nothing. Then I called 911 and told the dispatcher about Ethan. The ambulance got here ten, maybe twelve minutes later. Right before the firemen. I ran up here to let them in and took them downstairs. Stayed there about five minutes or so and came back up to meet the po-leece, and here you are." He hiccupped and took in a big breath.

"You did the right things," Monique said.

"Thank you, ma'am."

Her words had the desired effect. Still, he should not have scouted the hallway before calling 911. It might have cost the injured guard his life.

The detectives followed Martin through displays of dinosaur skeletons, rocks, dioramas of people and animals, old radios and televisions, and Conestoga wagon wheels from pioneer days. He led the pair down a passage that Monique remembered used to be called the Hall of Insects and had displays with large tarantulas from South America, huge black scorpions from somewhere in Africa, and vinegaroons from Texas, those odd insects that look like a cross between a crawdaddy and a scorpion. A few live snakes had occupied the last five habitats.

The insects and reptiles were gone now, replaced with displays of weapons from around the world. Stuffed birds sat atop cabinets of bows, guns, spears, and knives: A dusty Emperor penguin. A bald eagle and a red-tailed hawk, their wings spread and talons grasping crooked branches. Exotic parrots that could have been alive except for their marble-eyed stares, a clean-headed turkey vulture, and a large pileated woodpecker.

After passing through the hall of weapons and dead birds they reached the gift shop, which displayed wares on both sides of the hall. Colorful stuffed toy animals and plush tweety birds, educational games, and random toys sat alongside hats, T-shirts, and books. A dried and slightly curled anaconda skin at least thirty feet long was mounted on stained wood and nailed high on the wall.

Chris pointed to it. "Glad we're not facing one of those. What do those things eat?"

"Anything they can squeeze and fit in their mouths, I expect," Monique said. "That skin is old. It was up there when I was a kid."

The three arrived at the huge foyer, its domed roof curved above them like the Biosphere. An indoor moat lined with tropical plants surrounded the central hall. Shiny orange Japanese koi filled one side of the moat, and alligator-like caimans floated in the other. The humid room smelled of reptile excrement and musky soil. They crossed the marble floor inlaid with an intricate map of the world. A Kodiak bear and a mountain lion with bared teeth stood menacingly on the west side of the great hall next to the winding ramp that led up to the second-floor planetarium.

"How bad is he?" Chris asked as they passed into the tearoom café bordered by vending machines. Through the windows they could see the open-air courtyard where a peacock strutted amid the prairie dog holes and small owl burrows.

"Hard to tell," Martin answered. "I got a wrist pulse while I was calling it in on my cell phone. Luckily Dr. Adams came in, and he had a towel in his office. That sweater was soaked."

"Who's Dr. Adams?"

"The head of the Anthropology Department."

"Where's the other guard? You said his name was Samuel?" Monique asked.

"Haven't seen Sam. I called him on the museum transceiver and his cell phone, but he didn't answer."

Chris turned and looked over his left shoulder, then his right, as if he expected to see Sam standing amid shadows of the mounted animals.

They passed through the unexciting re-creations of a 1880s dentist's office and schoolhouse classroom. As they passed by a side room, Chris asked, "What's that big red hollow log?"

"I think it's supposed to be an artery," Martin said.

The next area featured a life-sized display of four men in animal skins trepanning the skull of another. The stricken man lay face down, his hands bound behind his back. One member of the group had opened the prone man's skull with a flint scraper to reveal a pink brain. Another stood back a few paces, feathered rattles in his hands. The display read "The History of Medicine," and the short description revealed that the unfortunate individual suffered from a headache. The wild-haired shaman oversaw the expulsion of whatever it was that ailed him.

Martin led them to a heavy door marked PERSONNEL ONLY where he punched in a code on a keypad entry lock.

"We'll need that code," Monique said.

"Not hard to remember," Martin said as he pushed open the door. "Eleven sixteen nineteen zero seven."

"That's very patriotic."

Chris looked puzzled. "The date of Oklahoma statehood," she explained.

They walked down a stairway and hallway where over Martin's shoulder Monique could see the paramedics working on the injured man. She smelled the blood before actually seeing that it oozed in several directions around the fallen guard. Red, gummy footprints meandered all over the floor. The towel, sweater, and paper towels lay in a sodden red heap. A pair of city policemen leaned against the wall, and a woman stood next to the receptionist's desk, out of the way of the emergency crew but close enough to gawk.

Chris took a roll of yellow police tape from his pocket. He motioned to an unmarked door by the stairs door. "I'll string this from that doorknob to the reception desk."

Monique nodded and focused on the man lying on the ground. She stepped around the pool of blood and squatted by his head. A deep cut extended from his left ear, across the temple, and horizontally across his forehead. His heels tried to dig into the floor as he moaned something incomprehensible. Head wounds bleed profusely, and Monique hoped his problem looked worse than it actually was. The paramedics worked to wrap the guard's head with sterile padding and gauze. Blood quickly soaked the dressing, and they added another layer.

"How's he doing?" Monique quietly asked an enormous dark-haired firefighter whose nametag read ROSE. He wore bloody latex gloves. He stood, and she estimated him at almost seven feet tall. People probably asked him if he had played basketball in school.

"He's lost a lot of blood," Rose answered. "They're going to get a drip going to bring his heart rate down."

"Has he spoken?"

"Nothing coherent. And it looks like he got hit on his left temple."

"It's hard to tell exactly how bad it is," a stout female paramedic with multiple ear piercings said. "The blow could have cracked his skull. I'd say he has a concussion, at least."

"Like someone went caveman on him," Chris said.

"I'd say so," answered Rose.

"All right. Thanks for your work," Monique said.

Rose nodded and turned to leave, and Monique turned her attention to the woman who stood next to the neat reception desk with a nameplate that read LILA WILLIS. Behind her was a door marked PHYSICAL ANTHROPOLOGY. Lila wore her white hair sixties style in a backcombed and shellacked helmet. Her hip orange-and-brown-framed glasses clashed with her faux-pearl necklace, lavender dress suit, and pink rouge.

"Hello," Monique said as she stepped toward the woman.

Mrs. Willis saw the badges on the detectives' belts. "Oh thank goodness you're here," Mrs. Willis said in a shaky voice. "Let me tell Dr. Adams."

She turned and knocked on the door behind her, opening it at the same time. "Dr. Adams, another policeman is here. And his assistant."

One of the firefighters coughed. "Actually, I'm Detective Monique Blue Hawk," Monique corrected her. "This is Detective Chris Pierson."

"That's nice, dear," answered Mrs. Willis, oblivious to the insult.

An older man dressed in gray pants, white Oxford shirt, and gray sweater emerged from the office. With his white hair, bushy gray eyebrows, and bifocals, he looked like everybody's grandpa. His shirt had blood on the cuffs, and blood spotted the knees of his pants. When he looked Monique up and down, she saw thick hair in his nostrils. He seemed surprised to see a female officer. He walked toward her with his hand out. "Dr. Lloyd Adams," he said. "Head of Anthropology."

"Detective Monique Blue Hawk. This is Detective Chris Pierson."

Adams looked over at the fallen guard and shook his head. "Poor man," he said. "Shocking."

"When did you arrive this morning, Dr. Adams?"

"About fifteen minutes ago."

Monique looked at Lester Martin, who nodded. "That's right. He held that towel on Ethan's head for me." Martin pointed to the bloody pile next to the wall. "The police and firemen arrived right after that, shortly before the ambulance got here. You two got here five minutes after that."

"Have you seen the other guard?" she asked Adams. "The one Martin came to relieve?"

"Sam," Martin interjected.

"I know Sam. No," Adams said. "I didn't see anyone until I got down here and saw Lester with his hand on Ethan's head. Wait, I take that back—I saw Clarence in the parking lot."

"Who's Clarence?" Monique asked.

"Our ornithologist. He may not be in the building yet. He was sitting in his car reading the paper. He does that most mornings."

"We need to get a few more of our people here," she said to Chris. "This museum is big, and we have to look through the place." She did not recognize either of the police officers who stood nearby with their thumbs stuck in their belts. "Gentlemen," she said loudly. They snapped their heads up and walked over.

The blond thirty-year-old with acne scars and bright blue eyes wore a nametag that said WEISER. Monique was sure that his nickname would be Bud. Weiser's beer belly stretched his shirt, and he smacked his gum with his mouth open. The button above his belt had popped off, revealing a roll below his bulletproof vest.

The older, dark-skinned officer, Blount, had a shaved head and a slight smile on his full, sensuous lips. He folded his arms across his chest and stared at her insolently. Monique did not miss his body language.

"As I'm sure you know, a security guard is missing," Monique told them. "So is the perp who assaulted this one. There may be more than one."

The paramedics lifted the wounded guard onto the stretcher and started rolling down the hall toward the elevators.

Monique paused to watch, then looked back at Blount. "We need at least two armed officers to look through the building."

"Yeah," Weiser said.

"We know," Blount said, turning to go.

"Wait. Just a moment, please." The men stopped and turned back. Blount rolled his eyes. Monique took a step toward him and looked directly into his eyes—or tried to. Blount averted his gaze and looked over her right shoulder, then at her chin, then settled on her left earlobe. Chris watched, fascinated. Weiser squirmed.

Blount finally met her gaze, and his head moved back an inch. He swallowed and tucked his hands in his waistband.

"And we probably need some tape across the doors," she said quietly, so he would have pay close attention. She continued to look at him. "No one else should come into the museum."

Blount cleared his throat. "All right," he said, glancing back at her left shoulder.

Monique smiled. "Good."

"Excuse me, but the museum is due to open in two and a half hours," Adams said.

Still looking at Blount, Monique said, "The museum will have to be closed today, Dr. Adams. We need to cordon off the building."

"If anyone goes out, the alarm will sound," Martin added.

"Fine," she answered. Then she looked back at Weiser, who had crossed his arms and was looking at the floor. "You two stay in touch with us. Every five minutes call in to Martin. We don't know who we're dealing with, and they could be hiding anywhere in the building." She looked over Weiser's shoulder at the group around the gurney. "Maybe one perp. Maybe more." She looked back at Weiser. "No telling with sort of weapons they have."

She cocked her head, then shouted at the group by the elevator. "Wait!" She looked back to the two officers. "Go up in the elevator with them and keep watch. They shouldn't leave here without an escort. After they're out, then start your search."

Martin gave them his cell phone number since the officers did not have portable transceivers. "It's easy to get turned around in here," he told the two officers. "If you think you're lost, call me right away. There're maps at the front entry way in case you want one."

"Uh, okay," said Weiser, now looking nervous. Blount said nothing.

"Lotsa places to hide in this building," Martin said, "so be cautious."

"Yes," Weiser agreed.

"It may seem like a good idea to split up to cover more ground," Monique said in a low voice.

"But staying together decreases the chance of getting lost or ambushed," Weiser finished the sentence for her. "They could come up behind us."

"Exactly."

Blount swallowed. The smirk was gone from his face.

Chris watched the exchange. Monique knew when to get to the point and when to offer a subtle suggestion. She did both with confidence, which she had in plenty. A good officer had to be savvy, too. You never know when someone might pull out a gun and all your knowledge and self-defense skills go right down the toilet. Monique, he knew, had learned that the hard way. She'd been shot in the arm three years ago while answering a robbery-in-progress call. The liquor store owner got his money back, and Monique got seven weeks of physical therapy to regain the full range of motion in her left elbow. Her wound left with a nasty scar and a barometer that could predict rain.

Weiser and Blount looked at each other and turned to leave, jogging toward the elevator. Monique stared after them as she took off her glasses and wiped the lenses with her jacket. Chris watched her, trying to figure out what it was about her that commanded respect. The sexist men she often had to work with did not intimidate her. She had presence. Standing five-eleven in flats, she equaled Chris in height, if not in weight. She told him once that she was 145 pounds, and he could not believe it. On the other hand, he knew she lifted weights. Muscle weighs more than fat, so that might account for it.

Lloyd Adams was also observing her. Tall, broad-shouldered, and attractive, she looked like a dark Patricia Neal. When she raised her voice, it resonated through the hall with confident Lauren Bacall power. His wife, Fran, had also once been quite a catch, with her Veronica Lake waves and tiny waist, but now she was reaping the rewards of consuming biscuits and gravy five days a week.

"Mr. Martin," she said gently to the guard.

"Yes?" He didn't take his eyes from the group at the end of the hall waiting for the elevator.

"I'd like you to stay here and make sure no one gets closer." Then she leaned in closer and added, "First, go wash your hands and get cleaned up. You'll feel better."

He nodded and wiped away a tear. "I've known him fifteen years. Ethan's got little ones at home."

"It happens. It's a risk all of you take."

Turning her attention to Chris, Monique voiced her thoughts. "So, the doors were locked when Martin got here. You need a code to enter. But you can push it open to leave. Or they could have found a hiding place. We have to figure out which." There was a real possibility that one or more violent men or women could emerge from a hiding place and attack again.

"It's a big museum," Adams said.

"What about that elevator?" she asked him. "Is that the only one in the building?"

"Yes."

"Is there a way to open the ceiling and get on top of it?"

"Not anymore. These elevators are new, and the only way to open the hatch is with a key. Firefighters have them, but no one else would carry one."

"All right. Good to know. We need more people here, Chris," she reminded her partner.

"I'll call it in," he said as he poked at his phone.

As the elevator doors opened, Ethan Lewis began thrashing around on the gurney, yelling, "Stop! Stop!" His head bandages started to slip. Lewis struggled to sit up and motioned in the general direction of the reception desk. "He's in there! He's in there! The Room of Secrets!" Then he jabbered a few indecipherable words, fell back, and was quiet. His chest heaved from the exertion.

Chris and Monique ran toward the stretcher.

"Who's in where?" Chris asked.

"He meant the other guard, I think." Monique answered. "Lewis pointed to that door at the end of the hall. What did he call it? Room of Secrets?"

The paramedics worked quickly to stem the new blood flow.

"He's hallucinating," Blount said.

Monique stood over the bleeding man. "Mr. Lewis? Can you hear me?"

"Passed out," Rose said.

"He said 'Room of Secrets,'" Weiser said. "I heard him."

"Rose, we need you and the fire personnel to stay until we have more officers here," Monique said. "The ambulance crew needs to go." She nodded to the impatient paramedics, who quickly pushed the gurney into the elevator. "Weiser, Blount, go with them. And Chris, call Captain Hardaway and see if we can have an officer stationed outside Lewis's room at the hospital. I want to know as soon as he can be questioned."

Monique noticed that Blount had his hand on his Glock. "Rose, bring that medical kit with you." She stopped. "Does that elevator go to a door where they can exit quickly? Or do they have to go through the building?"

"It's right next to an exit," Rose answered.

"All right." She turned and hurried back to Adams's office.

Rose carried the metal medical kit. Two other men came with him. One, a young, short, muscular man who looked like he spent his spare time lifting with Rose, came up and stuck out his hand.

"Name's Connor MacLeod. Glad to meet you." Except it came out sounding like "A'm gled tae meet ye."

"Connor MacLeod?"

"From the Clan MacLeod," he said in a thick Scottish brogue, "to my great sorrow." MacLeod's hair was as long as the Fire Department allowed, and his ears were pierced.

"No shit." She looked at his small nametag. It did indeed say MACLEOD. She wondered if his parents also had a daughter named Elspeth.

"Ah lass," he said, warming to his theme. "Were that I was not."

Rose rolled his eyes.

That did not make much sense, but Monique realized he got a lot of mileage from the movie *Highlander*.

"Well, MacLeod, I hope the Kurgan isn't hiding around here someplace."

MacLeod beamed. "Aye, the Kurgan is the scourge—"

"All right," Monique interrupted him. "That security guard said 'Room of Secrets.' Agreed?"

"Yeah," said a young firefighter with MARLOW on his nametag and blood on his arms and face. "I heard him clearly. Room of Secrets."

"Sure did," agreed Rose. "What's that mean? Where is it?"

"Oh, dear," Adams said.

Monique followed Adams's line of sight to the door across the hallway from the reception area. The door looked to be made of metal, not wood like the other doors in the hallway. "What's in there?"

"Skeletal remains," Adams answered. "Maybe some burial items like pots."

"Remains," Monique repeated. "Human remains?"

"Yes." He looked at Monique, who was considering him the same way his wife did after he farted.

A loud cough echoed in the stairwell next to Mrs. Willis's station. The door opened, and a tall, pear-shaped man with thick hair and round glasses emerged. A small woman wearing a blue sundress came in behind him. They ducked under the tape then stopped a few feet in front of Monique.

The woman was looking at the blood on the floor. The man was looking down the scalloped neckline of the woman's dress. The woman noticed and elbowed him in the ribs. "What happened here?" he asked, grimacing.

"Detectives," Adams said, "this is Dr. Clarence Wright, our museum ornithologist, and Dr. Janice Rice, the museum's head curator."

Monique nodded, and they nodded back, although Wright kept his eyes on her chest longer than he should have. He smelled of coffee and an everything bagel.

"How did you get in?" Monique asked.

"Through the Omni door. The other doors have police tape on them."

"I'll take care of it," Chris said. "Back in a minute." He turned and hurried toward the stairwell door.

"You need to stand back, please," Monique said to Wright and Rice. "Stay right here. The assailants might still be in the building."

Janice Rice gasped. "Assailants? Here?"

"We don't know. Where is your office?" Monique asked.

Rice pointed at a door down the hallway that led to the elevator. She kept her eyes on the blood on the floor. "My God! Is someone dead?"

"Dr. Rice," Monique said. "Please go into your office and shut the door. It's not safe to be in the building right now."

Rice nodded, wide-eyed.

"Mr. Martin," she said to the sad security guard, who had reemerged from the bathroom. "Please escort Doctors Rice and Wright to their offices."

"Will do."

"Can't I stay here and watch?" Wright asked.

"No, sir," Monique answered. "You may not. Mr. Martin?"

"Dr. Wright," Martin said. "Come on."

"Oh, man," Wright whined like a frustrated teenager.

"Is there someplace where you can wait that's more protected, Mrs. Willis?" Monique asked the pale, nervous receptionist.

"I can wait in the lounge, dear. It's just down the hall, and there's a television."

"That will be fine. Now," she said, turning back to Adams and pointing at the metal door, "if you'd open the door, please."

"Well, all right," he said hesitantly. He brought a heavy key ring from his pocket and fingered the keys—at least twenty of them. Monique watched him fumble through them.

"Aren't the keys marked?" she asked.

"Well, the ones I use every day are. These others look alike."

Monique stared at him, her expression deadpan.

"I got it. I think." Adams held up a key.

Monique motioned toward the door with an arched eyebrow. As they moved to the locked door, the stairwell door flew open and crashed into the wall. Chris emerged, breathing hard.

"Geez," Monique said, her hand on the butt of her pistol. "Chris! Jesus. Don't do that!"

"Sorry," Chris said. "I wasn't expecting it to open so easily. Are we going in?" He drew his Smith and Wesson M&P 19. Monique already had her Glock out.

"Do it," she told Adams.

Adams swallowed and turned the key in the lock. Monique took hold of his sleeve with her left hand to stop him before he could open the door.

"Step back."

"Surely," the clearly relieved anthropologist said as he took two long steps sideways into the hall.

"Where's the light switch?" Chris asked.

"On the left as you go in," Adams answered.

Chris glanced at Monique, who nodded. Holding his pistol in his right hand, he pushed down on the metal lever handle with his left then opened the door with his hip. The heavy door swung open a bit and immediately began to close. Chris kicked it open again and quickly entered the room, moving to the left while Monique entered and went right. Chris found four light switches and flipped them on.

The warm air that flowed toward them felt heavy and oppressive, like thick, acrid breath. Bright overhead lights revealed an immense cavern the size of a high school gym. It was filled with shelves holding hundreds of boxes. Monique gasped and hoped that Chris and the firefighters could not hear her.

"Holy shit," Clarence Wright exclaimed as he kicked an old chock of wood under the door.

Monique did a double take. She had not seen him approach behind them.

"Get back, Dr. Wright," Monique said to him over her shoulder. "Go to your office, sir."

The shelves stretched more than a hundred feet to the end of the huge room, which looked like a smaller version of the warehouse at the end of *Raiders of the Lost Ark*. Boxes of all sizes were stacked on the shelves like blocks. Ladders with rollers at the bottom leaned against rails on the top shelves.

But Monique's eyes were focused downward on the body of a man clad in shredded pants and shirt. His neck was deeply cut, and his ears and scalp were gone. The ruined body sprawled inside a wide circle of red just out of reach of the old bones and empty boxes strewn across the floor. The guard was Caucasian, but massive blood loss had wiped any hint of pink from his skin. He looked like an ivory sculpture against the gray cement floor.

"Oh, hell," Lester Martin said from the doorway. He must have followed Dr. Wright out of his office. "It's Samuel."

"Mr. Martin," Monique said, "return Dr. Wright to his office, then please call Weiser and Blount and tell them what we found." Her eyes scanned the wall of boxes as she spoke. "Tell them to be cautious and to keep searching. Chris, I'll go along this wall and look down each aisle as I pass. You go to the opposite wall and do the same. Then we'll go down each aisle together as we return."

They quickly moved down the nine rows of boxes, their weapons at the ready, each detective looking up and down the tall piles as they swept the rows.

"There are no footprints in the dust," Monique said when they reached the far wall.

"Man, oh man," Chris said. "There're thousands of boxes. Look at this side—they're stacked at least ten deep and a dozen high on each shelf."

"I don't like all these shelves," she said. "More than a few people could be hidden behind the boxes. We'll go down these rows together. I'll go first. Look left, and I'll look right."

She moved ten feet into the first row, giving each stack a cursory inspection. The largest boxes, which looked big enough to accommodate computers, sat on the bottom with several layers of smaller boxes sitting on top of them. The smallest were the size of Kleenex containers.

"They're packed in here so tightly there's no way anyone can fit between them," Chris said.

They completed their hasty sweep of the aisles. Somewhat assured that the room held only five live humans amid hundreds of boxes of dead ones and the unfortunate guard, they made their way back to the body.

"Is he . . . scalped?" Chris asked.

"Yes," she answered. Her first thought was that a disgruntled Native might be involved. This room was filled with bones of long-dead Indigenous people, so that seemed a logical assumption. She knew that body mutilation, including scalping, was often symbolic. Many people believe that Indians invented scalping. Others say it was the Dutch, who at first offered bounties on entire Indian heads. When carrying around heads proved too cumbersome, the Dutch agents settled for the lighter load of skin and hair. Others say Mexicans started the scalping tradition when they offered money for the scalps of Apaches. That also became a problem when eager scalp hunters saw no reason why they could not just take scalps from other tribes or from Mexicans and say it was Apache.

Monique chastised herself for immediately thinking that an Indian had done this. *Could have been a wacko from any group.* But considering that the other guard also had a serious scalp laceration, she would keep her first idea on the front burner.

And where scalping often involved taking only a circle of hair from the top of the head, this was different. This scalper took everything from the nape of the neck to the eyelids. Monique envisioned the killer cutting, then tugging and twisting the scalp and pulling away all the vessels and tendons that held the tissue to bone. She fervently hoped the guard was dead beforehand.

5

ndrew Tubbee had been awake since 2:30 a.m., which was odd for
him. Normally he slept soundly—too soundly, according to Sistina,
who wore earplugs to block out his snoring. She claimed he was as
noisy as a bull buffalo. Not that she'd ever heard a bull buffalo snore,
but she had heard one pass gas over at the Wichita Mountain Wildlife
Refuge.

He had managed to go to sleep after Dustin's call last night, but he
was worried. The uneasy Choctaw poured his third cup of hot chicory
and coffee. Both upset his guts. He added a sprinkle of cayenne pepper,
another of cinnamon, and a pack of stevia. He stirred his drink and took
a sip, following it with a chaser of three Tums. He'd heard that chicory
reduced cholesterol, and he needed caffeine to wake up, so he dutifully
drank a whole pot every morning despite the stomach upset. A vicious
circle.

An easy breeze moved through the kitchen window. The air still felt
warm, but that would change in a few weeks. By the end of the month
it might even sleet. Fewer hummingbirds had been visiting his feeders.
He hadn't seen the purple martins around their miniature apartments

atop swaying metal poles for a month, which meant they were migrating southward. He missed their distinctive chirps and clatters.

Andrew looked through the screen at his garden, a small but integral part of Chalakwa Ranch. The tomatoes that survived the hog rampage had already turned orange and in a few days would turn red. These fruits would be the last of his garden, along with a few banana peppers and the pumpkins that grew up the fence. His Seminole buddy Gene Cudjo had given him some of his grandma's pumpkin seeds from her Everglades garden. Andrew took pride in growing and cultivating the heritage squash. Sistina made his favorite dish—agave-squash casserole—from the sweet fruits. Like other gardeners, he hoped the pumpkins would continue to grow until the Halloween frost. A dozen were already the size of volleyballs.

To the east and eight hundred yards past his garden stood a line of tall pecan trees with massive trunks and strong branches. Andrew imagined they were sentries. Beyond the pecans stood cottonwoods that were just as tall as the pecan trees, but they grew out of the slope leading into the hollow, and he could only see their tops. From his vantage point in his kitchen, he thought that the garden and trees bordering the hollow looked like a postcard.

Every morning he looked out toward the hollow. Nothing that happened in the dark tangle of vines, branches, and muck could be seen from his house, but he heard plenty. Especially the nightly screams, which had grown alarmingly louder of late. Andrew sat in his back porch Adirondack chair each evening to hear the first yells—usually a coyote started it. Then came a few crow caws, then the cats and other shrieking creatures he had never identified. Visitors who had never heard the nightly chorus were by that time horrified. But then the real screams started. All the mammals, birds, and insects out there seemed to join in. His wife hated the sounds and turned up the television or the fan to block out the noise that she said came from hell.

The cacophony lasted about ten minutes then faded to nothing, as if the entities involved had released their frustrations, finished their hunting, or just worn themselves out. During the night, though, lone cries, howls, and burps sounded through the darkness and roused Andrew's imagination. Did these creatures stand or sit side by side and make their noises? Did they kill each other? Andrew had lived on this allotment his entire life and had been in the hollow only twice during the din. The sound both thrilled and repelled him. He simultaneously loved the hollow and was frightened by it.

This morning Andrew watched the trees expectantly. Yesterday afternoon while gathering some pecans he'd realized that the tangle of forest in the hollow had become quiet. He heard none of the usual chirps. No insects buzzing. Nothing. Even though he saw nothing unusual, his stomach knotted. At the edge of his vision, he perceived a dark shape with flapping wings. He turned to watch it pass over the tops of the trees, hover a few seconds, and then, with a strange squawk, sink into the green canopy. "What the holy hell?" Andrew said aloud. Whatever it was, its wingspan was wider than an eagle's and the head looked much larger. He turned and ran back to his ATV. He sped back over the meadow, heedless of the bumps and the nuts falling out of his bag. When he got home, he felt foolish for running away like that, but he also knew he had seen something vile.

Andrew tried to distract himself with a *McSweeney* story on his iPad—something about cultural appropriation, white women, and pumpkin spice—before the two Benadryl knocked him out around midnight. Then he suddenly jerked awake less than three hours later. He looked at Sistina, who held her small pillow over her head to drown out his snoring. Andrew did not know what had awakened him in the middle of the night, although he guessed it could have been a wildcat or a maybe one of the pigs. He thought he heard the faint hooting of owls, then all became quiet. After dozing on and off until six-thirty, he gave up and went into his office to read the news online.

An hour later Andrew stood sipping his bitter drink as he watched the trees. Sistina had started a load of laundry. He heard water running through the pipes, then the old washer churned and vibrated the walls. She would be in to make breakfast soon. Maybe some of her thick oatmeal corn pancakes topped with sulfured molasses would settle his stomach.

He debated filling his cup again and decided a glass of juice would be a better idea. As he set his mug down in the sink, he looked out the window and saw a black cloud rise from the hollow. He stared at the black mass for a second then picked up the binoculars he kept on the windowsill in time to see hundreds of birds fly upward from the trees and separate in all directions. Loud crow caws and panicked chirps of scissortail flycatchers, blue jays, sparrows, robins, and dozens of other songbirds filled the air. Never in his entire life had Andrew seen so many birds in one place.

His dogs sleeping under the shade of the willow jumped up at the commotion. Hot Shot, the black Lab, looked around, yipped, then peed. The obese basset hound that originally was christened Laredo and now goes by Lardo howled and barked.

"What the hell?" Andrew said.

"What the hell what?" Sistina asked behind him.

"Get your binocs off the table and look."

She picked up her small Bushnells and joined him at the window.

"Oh, my God. What am I looking at?"

"Everything is leaving the hollow."

"Do they sense an earthquake? There's more of them around here 'cause of that fracking. Maybe—"

Before she could finish, what appeared to be another dark cloud suddenly appeared in front of the pecan trees. The mass grew larger as it approached Andrew's house.

"Andrew?" Sistina quavered.

"I don't know, but it's coming this way. Get away from the window."

As the cloud grew near, it gave off a droning noise, as if millions of insects had joined forces in one monstrous mass. To his dismay, the black ball flew closer to the garden and then obscured it from view. The two dogs bolted for their doggie door. Andrew heard their frantic bays echo in the garage.

The cloud entity approached the window as if it were a living being. It was indeed millions of flies, mosquitoes, wasps, bees, dirt daubers, and butterflies. They careened into the side of the house and into the kitchen window screen. Sistina cried out and dropped to the kitchen floor, covering her ears. Those insects that did not splatter against his windows and bricks buzzed away in zigzags, leaving Andrew with tears in his eyes and the knowledge that the foul presence he'd sensed in the trees the day before had also been sensed by others. And they were trying to escape.

6

onique could handle many situations with equanimity. Flat tires, her son's broken bones, big hypodermic needles. She even set her own thumb after she dislocated it falling off her mountain bike. A month ago she'd hauled her neighbor's poodle to the vet after a Doberman grabbed the little dog by the head and ripped off its right ear. She could handle gruesome crime scenes, too, but she was always haunted by the fear that she might miss something or make a mistake that would allow the perpetrator to go free.

"What you got in here?" young Marlow asked. The energetic, curly-headed man stood in the doorway, trying to see around her.

"Just one step in. No more," Monique told him. Marlow put his right foot inside and looked at the fallen guard. The young man gasped and his face paled. He leaned over and put his hands on his knees as if he was winded. Or about to vomit.

"Hey," Monique said. Marlow looked up at her. He appeared to be about twenty-five. Marlow was a firefighter and an EMT, so he had probably seen some bad injuries in his time, but from his expression she figured he had never before witnessed how badly humans treat each other.

"You can be sick, Marlow," she told him matter-of-factly. "This is how it goes." He nodded then his eyes widened. He slapped his hand over his mouth, and sprinted for the men's room. Monique watched him go. She had been witness to the worst of human nature and had long since passed the urge to toss her cookies.

The lofty Rose and Highlander MacLeod looked into the room and stared silently, but neither looked ill. Monique turned her attention back to the floor. "I'm going to take some pics before the others get here," she said as she started towards the body. She snapped a dozen shots from various angles. "Okay. Chris, look at the prints in the dust between the door and Mr. Rector."

The dusty floor looked as if no one had cleaned it in years, and numerous shuffling footprints and blood splatters could be seen clearly. "Looks like someone has been dancing," Chris said. Trying to tiptoe between the rivulets of blood to get a better look at the fallen man, he lost his balance and put his left foot into a thick puddle of red. "Shit! Damn it!" He left his foot in the thick red pool then leaned down and put two fingers on the man's neck in hopes of finding a pulse. He shook his head and backed out of the blood. He took off his shoes and left them next to the puddle.

Rose gracefully avoided the blood to double-check the dead man. "Yup. Gone beaver."

"What?" Monique asked.

"Dead."

"Right. Let's clear the room," Monique said loudly. "Mr. Martin, stay by the door and make certain no one else comes in. Rose and MacLeod, stand here next to him." She turned to Chris. "You can get a pair of my Merrells out of the trunk when we're done here."

"I wear eleven and a half," he countered. "That translates to a woman's twelve."

"I'm aware of that," she answered.

Chris glanced at her feet and said nothing.

Monique figured Marlow was still in the men's room. The museum employees who were supposed to be in their offices watched the proceedings through the open door.

"How in the world could that happen?" Clarence Wright asked from the hallway in a loud voice.

"Sir," Rose said, "you must return to your office."

"God, that's gross," Wright continued, ignoring him.

"Get him out of here, Chris," Monique said.

The crime scene was getting out of hand. Normally, the museum personnel would be segregated from each other and sitting quietly while the detectives asked questions. But there were not enough police. Monique echoed Rose as she walked out the door and into the comparatively fresh air of the hallway. "Everyone, listen. All of you need to return to your offices and—"

"How'd someone get in here?" Wright interrupted. "This room is always locked."

A small, wiry man who had been standing behind Dr. Wright stepped forward. He looked to be Japanese American. "Bob Shimura," he raised his hand by way of introduction. His accent was thick New York, and his rapid-fire talk sounded odd in contrast to the slower Oklahoma twangs. Rose took two steps forward and towered over him. The diminutive man looked up but did not stop talking. "Nothing can get through that metal door without a key or fire ax," he continued. "In the eight years I've worked at the museum, I've never seen anyone enter or exit." He craned his neck to get a look inside. "Guess that's why we all call it the Room of Secrets. Or the Room for short. I have never been in there."

"You're a paleontologist, Bob, so there's no reason for you to enter it." Lloyd Adams said. "There aren't any fossils there. But you made the point. Someone had to have a key to get in." He looked at the assembled museum employees in turn. "Maybe that someone is standing here."

"I doubt that," Janice Rice said as she folded her arms.

"Oh, really?" Adams answered. He folded his arms, too.

"Stop it," Monique interjected. "How did you get in the building?" she asked Shimura.

"Through the atrium. The other doors are all guarded."

"Do all of you have keys to every entrance?"

They all nodded. Adams said, "And the number to the keypad on the basement door."

"Great," Monique sighed. "Everyone. All of you. Please move to your offices. The ambulance and crime scene personnel need to get in here."

"All the rooms containing human remains and cultural objects stay locked," Adams said, disregarding her request. "Security is tight throughout the museum, and no one but authorized personnel are even allowed in the hallways behind the exhibits. No one without a key could get into any of those areas."

"None of us would take anything, Lloyd, if that's what you're implying," Shimura said loudly. "It had to be an outsider."

Monique saw over Adams's shoulder that Officers Weiser and Blount had returned from searching the museum. She motioned them to come in. "You need to see what's in there. It's bad."

"Blood doesn't bother me," Weiser said.

"I guess that makes you special." She inclined her head, telling him to go in.

He smirked as he strutted toward the door. He took a step inside, stopped, and then turned around, his face pale. Blount looked in and stood up straighter. He backed out slowly then leaned against the wall, his head down.

Monique ignored their reactions but noted that Rose looked satisfied.

"All right," she said louder to the group. "Museum security is going to check your offices. Mr. Martin will go through each one." He nodded in agreement. "Weiser and Blount," she said, "are you certain that you looked everyplace?"

"We went everywhere," Blount said. Monique felt pleased that he was sweating and that Weiser looked faint.

Marlow finally emerged from the bathroom, his hair wet and finger-combed. Monique knew better than to ask how he felt.

"You, Rose, and MacLeod won't need to stay much longer," Monique told him. "As soon as more officers get here you can get back to your station."

She looked to Weiser and Blount. "Let's get going."

Weiser shuffled his feet. "Uh . . ."

"What?" she asked.

"We looked everyplace," he said again, looking sideways at Blount.

"Do it again."

Weiser hesitated. Blount nudged him along.

The elevator dinged as the two men made their way toward it.

Rachel Martinez, the forensics investigator, stepped out followed by her assistant, Louie Jameson, and Officer Ned Leung.

Monique said a quick hello. "Good to see you, Ned. Rachel. Louie."

"Monique," Ned answered. Ned and Steve Blue Hawk were old friends who fished together, and she saw him at least once a month in his weekend clothes. He could look either Black or Chinese, depending on the angle and lighting.

Louie gave the peace sign and said, "Howdy." His spiked hair and multiple piercings were deceptive. Louie might look like a punk rocker, but he had a genius IQ.

"*Halito*, Lighthorseman," said Rachel, who looked like the schoolteacher version of Salma Hayek.

Monique smiled and nodded. "*Ola. Halito.*"

Monique and Rachel had known each other for five years and occasionally went out to lunch. Rachel had been an accomplished rock climber until she lost two fingers to frostbite during an ice climb in the Tetons. Her right cheek bore a deep scar from a rockslide in Sedona, the same rockfall that had crushed her boyfriend's head. She had not climbed or dated since, but she recently had begun assuring Monique that she was almost ready to socialize again. Meanwhile, she spent hours in the weight room and pool. Her chiseled body bore witness to that. Monique teased her that she should model as an anatomy chart.

Monique had once told her about the Choctaw Lighthorsemen, the Nanulhtoka, the men who were charged to enforce Choctaw tribal law after the 1820 Treaty of Doak's Stand. They rode throughout the Choctaw Nation, settling disputes among neighbors in addition to arresting, judging, and punishing violators, especially those who imported liquor. The entire Indian Territory was shockingly violent in those days. Marauders lurked on every road and in every town in Indian Territory. From 1834 to 1861, the Choctaw Lighthorsemen were the only law enforcement in the Choctaw Nation.

The mounted Lighthorsemen no longer exist, and there never were any women in the old companies, but Rachel insisted that Monique would have been a great one and always addressed her as such.

Chris managed a nervous "Hi" that Monique thought was a little too loud for a guy who was trying to act cool around a woman he'd been crushing on for two years.

Rachel smirked and looked back to Monique. "Ambulance is right behind us. What you got?"

"Come with me." She led them to the Room. "This," she made a wide gesture with her right arm, "is the Room of Secrets."

The three newcomers took in the bloody and ruined body, the scattered bones, and the overturned boxes.

"Anthropological archives. No shit," replied Rachel. "Even without that poor guy on the floor, I'd say it's the Room of Death."

"That it is."

Rachel, Louie, and Ned cautiously stepped into the Room. "Whoa," Rachel ordered. "This floor is dusty. Any person who came in here left prints. Let's not mess them up any more than they already have been."

"Yes," Monique agreed. "The only ones who've been in here are me, Chris, and the two firemen, Rose and MacLeod. We went to the back of the room and up each aisle."

"All right. We'll need your shoes before you leave."

"Fine. You'll need to look at Chris's socks, too, since he took his shoes off. They're next to the body. Ned, watch the place while they work, please," Monique said. "Call if you need me. Chris, get another pair of shoes." She tossed him the keys to her car.

Monique walked out the door to where Lloyd Adams stood. "Your colleagues say they never come in here, so who does have keys?"

"Me. The guards. You'll be able to tell who came in and out. There's a video recorder focused on that door nights and weekends."

She looked up at the ceiling and tried to find a surveillance camera. If there was one, it blended in well. "Where's the camera? I don't see it."

"It's at the base of the light. There's also a motion detector inside. If something as small as a mouse moves around inside, the motion detector is tripped. I assume that's why Samuel went in there."

She spotted the small camera lens peeking out from under the old light fixture. "Oh, I see it. Pretty small." Her eyes moved to the door of the Room.

"It's set on that door? And the other doors don't have cameras?"

"Yes and no. Just on that door."

"Valuable things are in there?"

"There are valuable things everywhere in this museum."

"But you keep that door locked all the time and a camera on it."

"No one needs to go in there."

"Don't people use the items to study?"

"No. Never."

"So, why have this archive if no one uses it?"

He heaved an impatient sigh. She spoke before he did to avoid a confrontation that she did not intend to start. "How do we access the tape?"

He paused for a second, evidently glad that she did not press him about the usefulness of the Room. "Easy."

"Then let's do it."

Adams walked behind the counter, took out a key, and unlocked and opened a cabinet to reveal a DVR player. He pressed the STOP button and removed an SD card. Stacks of tiny SD cards in plastic cases were placed next to the black player. Each had a sticker on it telling the date it was made. "Is there a surveillance camera inside the room?" Monique asked.

"No. Just on the outside."

"Why not on the inside?"

"Because the camera tells us who goes in. Why have the camera on the inside?"

"But what if they got into the room from another entrance?"

"There isn't another entrance."

"Windows, the ceiling, through a thin wall?" she suggested.

"No. The walls are cinder blocks. There are no windows, and the ceiling doesn't have a crawl space. No attic. The planetarium is directly above the Room."

"And we can watch the video of this area in your office?"

"Yes. On my big monitor."

"We want to do that. But first," Monique motioned to the door of the Room with her head, "come with me." She led him to the entrance. "You know there is a body on the floor?" He nodded. "There also are a lot of bones strewn around. I want you to look at the bones and the overturned boxes and tell me if you can, from the doorway, what you think these people were after."

Adams started to walk in. Monique held up her arm across his chest. "Not yet. Forensics has to give the okay for you to enter."

He took in the dreadful scene from the doorway. "Well, uh. I can't really tell from here. That skull over there is clearly very old." He looked at the body again, then at the boxes.

"Anything else?"

"You have eight overturned boxes and a lot of bones. From here looks like hands and feet—lots of little bones. It may take a while to get all the bones back into the right boxes. Then we can determine what's missing." His eyes went to the butchered guard again.

Chris returned, wearing Monique's shoes. "They fit great," he announced.

"Uh, what's that?" Adams pointed toward the nearest bottom shelf. "That gray thing in front of the shelf."

Monique squinted. "You mean that wad of dust?" From where she stood, it appeared to be a small oblong ball of gray twine. "Looks like a dust bunny."

"Rachel, there's a dust ball or something over there in front of that shelf."

"I see it." She walked over to the wad, bent over, and pushed it with her pen. It seemed firm. Not like dust. She left it alone.

"All right, so, we've looked all above us. Is there anything below us?" Monique asked Adams.

"Yes. A small library."

"You mean there are more rooms down there?"

"Well, yes. Several offices, two labs, and a storage area."

Monique sighed and clenched her jaw.

"Where's the door?"

He pointed toward the elevators. "At the end of the hall. On the other side of those boxes."

Monique's eyes followed his extended arm. Boxes were stacked almost to the ceiling on the far side of the elevators.

"I don't see a door."

"Can't see it from here. It's hidden behind the boxes."

"Crap. Chris, call the others and tell them to get down there and look."

"I'm on it." He left the office, fingers dancing over his cell phone.

"That door stays locked as well," Adams said.

"Is there another entry?" Monique asked.

"No. I have the keys to that door and to the labs. So do the guards."

Blount and Weiser, both sweaty and winded, returned from their abbreviated search.

"Nothing?" Chris asked.

"Nada," Weiser answered.

"Okay, guys," Monique said. "Just found out there's another story below."

Blount leaned over and put his hands on his knees. Weiser panted and looked at the ceiling.

"Gotta hop to it. The space isn't as big as this floor. Right, Dr. Adams?"

"Less than half. Mainly large labs."

She pointed to the elevators and held out her other hand for the keys, then handed them to Weiser. "Here's the keys, and the door is at the end of the hall. If you're not back in fifteen, we're coming down."

"Fuck this," she thought she heard Blount say.

Monique walked to him, tapped his chest with a finger. "Take a breath," she said quietly. "Drink some water and move it."

Weiser grabbed him by the arm and pulled. Both men jogged down the hall. Monique waited until she heard the door slam, then turned back to Chris and Dr. Adams.

"All right. What about air ducts?"

"In the walls."

"Let's look at the video, then."

Monique and Chris followed Adams into his office, a large room that looked smaller than it was because of the paintings, carvings, books, and specimens Adams had crammed into it. He was apparently particularly fond of big-horn beetles and skulls of small animals with large incisors. There was no window, but numerous lamps gave the room a warm glow.

Monique and Chris removed their jackets before settling into uncomfortable chairs behind the desk. They sat side by side, facing the monitor. "Okay," Monique said. "Before we start, what's in the Secret Room? Specifically. And do people really call it that?"

"You mean the Room of Secrets. And yes, some people call it that because no one ever goes in it, and they're curious about it. I think it's a ridiculous name, frankly."

"Go on."

"All right. Skeletal pieces. Some cultural items. I can't be more specific. I've been in the room maybe three times in three years. It's been almost a year since the last time."

"You haven't been in there for twelve months prior to today?"

"Uh, yes. That's right. Until this morning."

"Why so long?"

"The materials aren't of use to me and haven't been for some time."

Monique paused, her hand under her chin. Her eyes lasered in on Adams. "I find it hard to believe that the director of Anthropology hasn't entered one of his rooms in a year."

Adams tried to swallow and coughed instead.

She let him off the hook again. "Tell me once more why this is called the 'Room of Secrets.'"

"Well, because in many respects what is actually in there is a mystery. There are a lot of old items, bits and pieces, that have been stored in there over the years. We don't use items in the Room for research. I don't know that anyone has ever even looked through the entire room, much less catalogued the things in it."

"You haven't?"

"No, just parts of it. There are hundreds of boxes in there. You saw for yourself. Perhaps thousands. Most of them contain items that were donated to the museum and lack proper documentation, so they aren't all that useful for research."

"All right. Go ahead."

The video started. They watched a few seconds of static, then the door appeared followed by a few more lines of static for four minutes.

"This doesn't operate by motion? This records even when nothing is moving?"

"We need to upgrade."

Monique sighed. "Can you start this at closing time last night?"

"That's what you're seeing. I always start recording at 5:30 p.m. and turn it off when I arrive in the mornings. Except today."

"Does this run during the day?"

"No need. Except on the weekends."

"What about surveillance in the rest of the museum?"

"There are multiple cameras in the building, and they feed to a central locale. That office is upstairs by the planetarium."

"Do they film like this one?"

"I think so. Except when the building is closed. Then they record only when they detect motion."

"We need to see those films from the day before."

"Hundreds of people came through yesterday. Very crowded. It was museum day for the Edmund schools."

Monique sighed and thought a moment. "Fast-forward it," she ordered.

They watched for ten minutes and saw nothing but the door. It was as boring as the movies Steve had made of Robbie sleeping when he was an infant.

"What time is it?" she asked.

Adams clicked the TIME button on the remote and it showed 8:30 p.m.

"This is fast forward, right?"

"As fast as it goes."

They looked at the screen for twenty minutes more and still saw only the door.

"What's the time now?"

"Four-thirty a.m."

Chris sighed. "Dang. Are all the videos like this?"

"I guess," Adams said absently. "I've never had reason to look at all of them. Nothing ever happens here."

"Let's keep going, then," Monique said.

After another few minutes of fast forward, the security guard Samuel Rector rushed to the door and unlocked it.

"Stop. Go back."

Adams rewound until they saw Samuel Rector appear. He was moving quickly, holding his transceiver. He put it back onto his belt, unlocked the door, and went in, then the door closed behind him. Monique flinched at seeing that he had thick, dark hair and a full Tom Selleck moustache.

"Looks like Rector called someone before he went in," Chris said.

"Probably Ethan," Adams answered.

"Mark the time," she reminded Chris. He wrote down 6:22 a.m. on his notepad.

At 6:26 Ethan Lewis appeared onscreen, and he, too, unlocked the door. He entered the room and the door closed behind him. After less than a minute, the door opened, and Lewis staggered out, his head bleeding. He then moved out of camera range.

"What time was this?" she asked.

Adams pressed the button. The screen said 6:31 a.m.

"About thirty minutes before Martin came in for work at seven," Monique observed.

"That poor guy lay there bleeding for half an hour?" Chris asked.

"Obviously," Monique said. "Hopefully the transfusions didn't come too late. We should be hearing something about his condition pretty soon. Speed it up again."

They watched until Lester Martin appeared. He looked frantic then moved out of the frame. "Stop. All right. Let's go through this logically. Why did Rector rush into the room?"

"The motion detector went off," Adams said.

"Yes," Monique agreed. "Which means someone was in the room. But the tape shows no one going in other than Rector and Lewis, and no one leaving but Lewis. But it must have went off because that's the only reason Rector would go in there," she said.

"And the other guard, Ethan, got word from Samuel, so he followed him inside," Adams added.

"Why didn't it go off when we went in there?" Chris asked.

"It should have," Adams said. "I guess I didn't think about it."

"Then maybe it was disabled or malfunctioned."

"I suppose so."

"How do you disable it?" Monique asked.

"I don't really know," Adams answered. "It's only five feet above the ground in a box next to the door, so it's easy to reach. But I've never messed with it."

Monique rubbed her neck and thought. "There has to be another entrance."

"There isn't," Adams insisted.

"I don't buy that," Chris said. "Someone got in there and murdered a guard. There's another way in."

"Nope. No attic, no basement, no closets."

"There's another way." Chris was adamant.

"Could someone have tampered with the recording? Martin, maybe?" Monique asked.

"What?" Adams was surprised. "Why do you think that?"

"Sometimes an unlikely suspect is the culprit."

Monique heard clicking of footsteps in the hallway. She opened to the door to see Blount and Weiser at the desk looking around.

"I'm here," she said as she opened the door to let them in. "Anything?"

"Fossils, dinosaur skeletons, and lab stuff," Weiser said, slightly out of breath. "Several closets with more animal bones. Big shells. Things like that. No other entry that we could see." He handed the keys back to her.

"All right. Good work."

"If they are still here, they're dug in," Weiser said.

"But they have to try to get out at some point, and we'd see them, right?" Blount asked.

"Dunno," Monique said. "Still, there's something eating at me. There's something we haven't found yet, or something we've seen but haven't recognized."

"What I was saying," Adams continued when Monique reentered the office with Weiser and Blount in tow. "Is no. Absolutely not. Lester and Ethan were friends. Lester has six kids, and his oldest girl babysits Ethan's little boy. They've known each other for fifteen years. Besides, what's his motive?"

"Maybe his wife was seeing Lewis," Chris suggested.

"Impossible. Lester's wife died four years ago."

"Okay," Chris conceded.

Good detectives looked for the obvious first, then worked from there. However, Monique and Chris also understood that the obvious might not always be easy to discern.

"What about yesterday, or even the day before?" he asked. "Maybe someone went in twenty-four or more hours before the guards were attacked—"

"And they waited until this morning to leave," Monique finished. "Could be. Let's find out."

Adams sighed as he loaded the previous day's recording.

Monique looked to the two officers. "Weiser, you and Blount take a break. Go to the concession upstairs until we're done here. Get something to drink from the machines. Okay?"

"Yeah," Weiser said. "A cold one sounds good." He elbowed Blount in the arm, and the men strode down the hall.

"When you're done, take another look on that floor," she said to their backs.

They both slowed, and she knew they heard her, but neither turned their head as they exited through the heavy basement door.

After half an hour of watching nothing happen on the tape, Monique stood and stretched. "So, we're back to where we were. We need to talk to forensics. Lloyd, go ahead and look one more day ahead."

"Pretty unlikely someone got in there two days ahead of time," Chris said.

"You never know, partner," she said before walking out.

7

eroy Bear Red Ears had a reputation for being tolerant. He never
turned away non-Indian scholars who wanted to interview him for
their research projects. When his intuition told him he was dealing
with an insensitive writer, he just launched into Chahta anumpa. He
could sense when an academic planned to use information to further his
or her career and not to assist the tribe. If a researcher wanted to record
the interviews for later translation, just for fun he switched to the old style
understood completely only by him and a few other elders, including his
late younger brother Strong Bull and Strong Bull's wife, Ninah.

Both brothers originally had their father's name, Strong Bull. When
they reached adulthood, Leroy decided to take their mother's family
name, Nita Haksobish Humma, translated roughly as Bear Red Ears.
Like many Natives of other tribes, his brother never used a first name,
just their father's name. Ninah was also a medicine person, a rare situation
since normally a family produced only one spiritual leader in a generation.
Well into her nineties now, Ninah kept secrets only spiritual leaders knew
about the tribe's history. Fortunately, the two powerful Chahtas never got

in each other's way except to bicker over mundane issues such as whose turn it was to do dishes.

Ninah was no housewife. She did not formally serve on the Tribal Council, but her constant campaigning for tribal rights, health care, and educational services influenced the thinking of the members. She planted a half-acre *tamfuller* garden each spring and lovingly tended it. Like Leroy, who also kept a roasting ear garden, Ninah believed the lazy American way of living had killed too many of her tribespeople.

Strong Bull had been highly respected by the tribe, and many people came to him and Ninah for counsel. But Strong Bull had died from a stroke ten years ago while filling his hummingbird feeders early one morning. Ninah found him dead on the porch.

"Hummingbirds swarmed all around him, right here, like they're doing now," she told relatives as the tiny birds buzzed around the porch feeders at the after-funeral meal, "If I were an Aztec, I'd say they looked like tiny warriors. Maybe his spirit is inside the cranky one there with the red throat. See how he dive-bombs the others?"

Strong Bull's funeral service was simple, a combination of tribal tradition and prayers offered by a local Methodist minister. Strong Bull was fascinated by the stories of the Bible and by the possibilities of Christianity, but he believed it a religion ruined by interest groups that interpreted the Holy Book for their own selfish purposes. Still, he told his friends that Christian prayers were welcome in his home, "Just in case."

Members of the tribe who understand such things called Leroy and Ninah *alikchi*—doctors. Leroy only finished ninth grade and Ninah fifth, but to those who believed in tribal traditions, they were wise doctors nonetheless. They were taught by the Little People, the Kowi Annukasha, who took potential *alikchis* into the woods to live when they were teenagers to teach them how to use traditional medicines and how to behave as *alikchis* should. Monique and other relatives had stopped trying to explain the Little People to outsiders a long time ago and instead told friends that Leroy and Ninah were doctors and left it at that. Non-Indians usually thought that tribal cosmology stories and the fantastic beings who lived alongside humans were nothing more than entertaining myths. Traditionalists generally went on allowing them to believe that so they wouldn't be bothered by opportunistic writers or spiritual hucksters.

This morning Leroy dressed in his usual jeans and soft denim shirt, then finger combed his hair into a ponytail and secured it with a purple rubber band. As he watched his breakfast of frozen fruit, yogurt, and whey protein powder churn in the blender, he thought about how oppressive the air had become lately and wondered if he should call Ninah. He was reluctant. She would be packed for her Disneyland and Sea World vacation. He did not want her to cancel her trip again. Last year a young man in high school came to her complaining that a witch had put snakes in his legs so that he wouldn't be able to play football that year. He was too good a quarterback to sit out a season. Ninah spent an entire week preparing to remove the snakes—which only took an hour once she got to work—and missed her San Diego trip. No, Leroy would handle this situation on his own. He was not sure what it was yet, but he was certain he could manage any trouble that came along.

Lorraine meowed as she rubbed against his ankles.

"I just fed you," Leroy reminded her.

The cat looked up at him and stretched her front legs up his calf and mewled, asking to be held.

"What's wrong with you?" Leroy asked. He turned off the blender and picked her up. Faint taps sounded on the screen. Lorraine turned her head to look out the kitchen window. She opened her mouth wide and hissed. The taps turned into beats. Lorraine jumped out of Leroy's arms, ran to the sofa in the den, leaped up on the back, and looked out the window. And then she howled.

More whacks hit the windows, and now it sounded like a hailstorm assaulting the house from the west. Leroy could only see a cloud of dark specks coming at him. Finally, the window screen was completely blacked out. He went to the den, and those screens were also covered. The sounds stopped.

Leroy opened the front door and saw only a few dead grasshoppers and beetles on the porch. The door faced east, away from the onslaught. He stepped outside and walked around to the west-facing kitchen and den windows. He gasped at the sight of piles of dead and dying insects that had careened into not just the windows but into the side of the brick house.

The chickens emerged from their coop and hopped around their yard, wings beating madly as they chased injured insects. His turkeys were running and jumping after the sudden bonanza as well. Scissortail fly-catchers, bluebirds, and other bug-eating birds swooped and dived after the unexpected snacks.

Leroy stood still, thinking. He looked to the west, toward Andrew Tubbee's place. Lorraine, who had followed him out, meowed and wound figure eights around Leroy's feet.

"You're right, Lorraine," he said. "Maybe I can't handle it."

8

A new set of ambulance personnel waited outside the Room for the crime scene team to finish.

Monique stood at the doorway and looked in at Rachel and Louie, who had deferred to Melinda Batters, the newly arrived medical examiner. Blood from the injured guard remained on the floor, and everyone walked around the congealing mess. She had not heard Melinda's footsteps in the hall, nor did she see her enter the Room. "Sneaky little thing," Monique muttered fondly to herself. She watched as the smallest women she had ever met went about her business. Melinda was at least forty years old, stood about four foot ten, and could not weigh more than ninety pounds. She wore her frosted hair in spikes and used no makeup. Monique used to wonder about Melinda's sexual orientation until she met her six-foot-two husband, Milt, the county recorder. Both of them loved the outdoors and traveled to Alaska at least once a year to hunt bears and moose.

"He's measured?" Melinda asked Louie.

"Yes."

"You got pictures?"

"Yup." He patted the camera in his pocket.

"Hey, Melinda," Monique said through the doorway, "how're you?"

"Monique," Melinda said without smiling or standing. She never answered when Monique asked that question. She took off her gloves and dropped them into a plastic bag. "How're you?"

"This is a tough one," Monique answered. She always ignored the question, too. They had played this game many times. Someday one of them would slip and answer it.

"The cause of death *seems* obvious, but I'm not so sure," Melinda said. "Rigor has set in. His body temperature is eighty-nine. I'd say he's been dead around three and a half, maybe four hours. Cement floor's cold." Melinda spoke slowly and paused between words, as if she were trying to keep from stuttering.

Monique looked at her watch. Ten o'clock already. Melinda hit the time of death dead on, so to speak.

"Quite a mess," Melinda continued.

"And quite a mystery," Monique added. "We don't know how the perps got in here."

Melinda looked up. "Uh, the door?"

"Hey, we never thought of that. But no."

"Just trying to help. Attic? Window? Trapdoor?"

"No, no, and no."

"Through the looking glass or wardrobe? Came up through the well or down the beanstalk?"

"Nope."

"Well then," Melinda shrugged. "It's obvious."

"Impress me."

Melinda leaned in and whispered, "The secret passageway."

"I do believe you missed your calling. To hell with pathology. Come join us."

Melinda snickered and turned her gaze back to the dead man. "Tough way to go out. How are *you* thinking this went down?"

Monique shrugged. "There's no other entry into this room, but according to the video camera aimed at the door, no intruder entered or left. Gotta be the secret passageway."

"Okay to take him," Melinda told the paramedics. The two men and one woman brought in the gurney. Everyone looked appropriately solemn.

The detectives and crime scene team watched as the paramedics lifted the bloody body into the bag and loaded it onto the stretcher.

"Call if you need us," Rose said over his shoulder.

"See ye efter, Lassie," Connor said with a bright smile and a wave.

Monique looked at Rose and rolled her eyes.

"Who in heck is that?" Melinda asked.

"Connor MacLeod. From Clan MacLeod."

Melinda laughed. "No shit? Cute for a nerd."

Melinda finished packing her bag and straightened. She considered the blood pool. A good portion of Samuel Rector had flowed out onto the cement floor. "Cause of death might be the cut to his neck. Went all the way through to his spine. That of course, would be immediately fatal. It's hard to tell if he was scalped before or after death. His upper lip is also gone. Can't tell if he had a moustache."

"He did," Monique said. "I saw him on the video."

Melinda nodded. "At any rate, I'll know more after the autopsy. He could have died from something else. I'm curious as to why his esophagus is ripped."

"What do you mean?"

"A knife or something cut his throat, but part of the esophagus is up in his mouth. That's one of the things I'll look at."

"That would have happened after death, right?"

"I certainly hope so." Melinda picked up her bag. She looked around at the vast room of boxes, the bones on the floor, and the blood congealed at their feet. "Looks like you have a long day ahead of you. But I have great faith that you'll locate that secret passage."

Melinda paused for a few seconds, eyeing the bones that had spilled across the floor. "I spy a tib, a fib, and a rib."

"Gee, thanks," Monique said.

"You're welcome," Melinda said as she walked out the door.

Rachel and Louie both stood, hands on their hips. "I'm stumped," Rachel admitted.

"I can't imagine why. Tell me."

"There aren't any footprints with blood on them besides Ethan Lewis's and Chris's. Rector didn't get up after he fell. I didn't see any particles on the body, but maybe Melinda will find something."

"Did you find his clothes?" Chris asked. "He's missing his shoes, socks, belt, gun, part of his shirt, and all of his jacket including his badge. And whatever he may have had in his pants pockets."

Louie shook his head. "Haven't seen them. I did a quick walk up and down the aisles and didn't see anything on or under the shelves. At least those I could see, that is."

"Maybe they put his clothes in one of these boxes," Monique suggested, "although I'll be damned if I know why they would have." She had no desire to look through hundreds of bone containers. "Or they could have taken them."

"We need a K9 team," Chris said. "Maybe a dog could find them."

"Yeah. Call in the request. And Rachel, get prints from those bones on the floor, the door handle, and the whole door." She looked around the room again. "What else? From here, I only see boxes and metal shelves. Maybe look for prints along the shelves where those boxes overturned?"

"Can Dr. Adams come in and take a look at the boxes now?" Chris asked Rachel.

"As long as he doesn't touch anything," Rachel said.

Monique called him in. Carefully avoiding the ring of blood, the anthropologist approached the bones and overturned containers. He walked hesitantly to the middle of the front row and stopped in front of a jumble of opened boxes. A yellowed tibia, a fibula, and some metatarsals lay scattered across the floor. A skull with only a few teeth and some vertebrae lay a few feet away. He focused on one of the box tops. "Oh, yes," he murmured. "Just as I thought when I looked in from the door."

"Oh, yes, what?" Monique asked.

"These are old Native American bones. Very old."

"You mean white native American or Native?"

"What do you mean?"

"The term 'Native American' can refer to anyone born in this country—white, Black, whomever. Native used alone refers to the original inhabitants. As does Indigenous."

Adams sighed. "I mean American Indian bones."

"I prefer 'Indigenous' myself," Monique said. "Sometimes 'Native.'"

Rachel snickered from a few rows away. Monique always won an argument over the politics of naming.

"And which one of those do you prefer I use?" Adams asked slowly and sarcastically.

"Let's go with Native for now. Anyway, whose remains are these?"

"Unidentified ones."

"Then how do you know they're Native?"

"They all are in here," he said.

"Then why did you act surprised?"

"I didn't know I looked surprised. I guess I flinched because these are so old and fragile."

Monique crouched down to see that the shelf extended back six feet. The boxes sat three to four deep and stacked two to three high. Now that she looked closer, she realized there really might be a thousand boxes.

"Looks like the perps pushed boxes out of the way in order to get what was in the middle of the shelf," she said. "What's on this aisle?"

"Those boxes are pretty much forgotten," Adams admitted. "I'm not certain what's in them."

"You mean *who's* in them?"

He evaded the question. "Some of the boxes might contain pots. Or pot sherds."

Monique stood and considered the tumped-over boxes. She used the end of her pen to lift the tops so she could read their labels. Then she looked at the labels on the boxes stacked next to the disturbed ones. Rachel gently pushed some out of the way so she could read labels of the back boxes.

"It appears that the last two digits on this group of boxes are identical. And they're placed together on this shelf."

Chris glanced up from boxes ten feet down the aisle. "These are definitely of the same group. This one says 4-MI-23. This other one is 2-MI-23. Does the 23 mean 1923?"

"No," Lloyd said, "1823."

"They were stolen in 1823?" Monique asked.

"No. They were first catalogued in 1823. They could have been, uh, excavated much earlier than that. There's no way of knowing unless there's documentation."

"What sort of documentation?"

"In the early 1800s it was usually a handwritten paper or letter describing where the items were found. There weren't any real archaeological excavations. I mean, not like those today. Back then, pothunters and arrowhead collectors who found bones often didn't record the environment or exact location where they found them. Sometimes they destroyed an entire site. I'm sorry to say the same is sometimes true today. Collectors don't always record the latitude, longitude, soil strata, where the artifacts are in relation to one another, that sort of thing. They take what they want and often leave other items behind that are crucial for context. Knowledge is lost. Some pottery, pipe bags, and skeletal remains are in good condition and quite beautiful. But we know nothing about them, so they're useless, really, for research. The same is true for many of the bones in this room."

"Where would letters with information be? In the boxes with the artifacts?"

"No. They're kept in separate files."

"So, anyone could have dug up the bones that are in here, right?"

"Pretty much."

"Do you have items from the trails?" Monique asked him.

"What trails?"

"The removal trails. The Trails Where They Cried. All the tribes had a name for them."

"You mean the Trail of Tears, I suppose?"

"That's one of them. There were many trails. The Five Tribes—the Cherokees, Choctaws, Muscogees—also known as Creeks, Chickasaws, and Seminoles—all had them. Thousands died. The elders tell us that many of them were left on the trail in shallow graves or in creek banks because the ground was frozen. It didn't take much rain to wash them away."

"I don't know if we have any of those," Adams answered.

"Why do people dig up buried bones anyway?" Chris asked.

"People have always loved to collect Native artifacts and remains," Monique said. "Thomas Jefferson is a good example. He was fascinated by the original inhabitants of North America. He studied Native cultures, and he filled his house with artifacts. He considered them a noble people. Native remains and artifacts were a big deal to white people in his time. They were a crucial part of forming the American identity."

Adams exhaled heavily through his nose.

"How could digging do that?" Chris asked.

"Diggers could imagine the lives of those who had come before them," she continued. "Were they superior, inferior?"

Adams pushed his glasses up the bridge of his nose. "You have a theory about digging?"

She squatted down to look more closely at the boxes. "Winners create history. The losers' voices are pushed aside, and their cultures are appropriated. So are their cultural articles and their bodies. If the culture had vanished, then the people who disappeared were believed to be inferior to those who found their remains."

"Now, wait a minute," Adams objected.

Monique looked around the room as she spoke. "And the finders were free to speculate about where these dead people had come from. Tribes have creation stories that have been passed down through the generations for thousands of years. By ignoring the tribes' beliefs that they emerged from this continent, the invaders could justify their land grabbing. They're still doing it." She cleared her throat, signifying that was all she planned to say about the matter.

Adams did not respond.

"How did all these remains get here?" Chris asked him, gesturing at the boxes.

"Well, these items could have been stored in someone's home then later given to a museum, perhaps the Army Medical Museum in Washington. After this museum opened in 1938, some items were shipped here. Other museums like the Peabody in Massachusetts and the Smithsonian have many more remains and burial objects than we have. We've also received skeletal goods from the Southeast and from small museums and collectors from around here and Texas."

"Why would the other museums give them up?"

"Didn't need them. Couldn't identify them. I don't know. Ran out of room, maybe. All the information we have should be on the matching cards in the file. In that cabinet in the corner over there." He pointed to an old oak filing cabinet that stood beneath a vent high on the wall.

"That cabinet will tell us where the bones were found?" Monique asked.

"Maybe. I mean, the general area at least."

"How old is that thing?" Chris asked. The scarred and dried out cabinet looked like an antique.

"At least a hundred years," Adams said. "I don't know for sure."

"We may as well dive in," Monique said. "We need to get in that cabinet and find out what the murderer was after. Rachel, can y'all dust this cabinet now?"

"Right away," her voice rang out from three aisles over.

Monique put her hands on her hips and spoke as she studied the old cabinet. "The people who used the trails started out with their possessions. Some brought pianos, china sets, jewelry. When their horses and draft animals dropped dead or their wagon wheels broke, they abandoned what they couldn't carry. They left a stream of wagons, dead animals, and all kinds of valuable items on the roads behind them. Scavengers and thieves who followed the marchers picked up many of the items. Maybe they kept the items for themselves or gave them to relatives."

"Or sold them for profit?" Chris commented.

"Yes."

"Pianos, huh? I thought the Indians were too poor for that sort of stuff."

"Some were wealthy. . . . I need some water. This dust is getting to me." Monique walked out and drank from the water fountain in the hall. Her phone rang mid-swallow. She pulled her phone from her pocket and saw Robbie's name on the caller ID. She walked back inside the Room as she answered. "Hi, honey. Is everything okay? Are you at school?" No answer. "Hello?" The line had disconnected. "Huh." She walked back through the door and dialed Robbie.

"Hello," he answered. "What happened?"

"No reception in the room I was in. Go ahead."

"Yeah, I'm at school. Can I have a snapping turtle? I found one on the way to school and Dad took him home and put him in the wading pool."

"Robbie. Little snappers are cute, but they get as big as you. And they eat fingers that look like worms. And they make a mess in their tank."

"I'll clean it."

"Robbie. Be happy with your snake."

"How about a chameleon? They're on sale."

"A chameleon?" Monique sighed.

"Yeah. Cages and lights are on sale too. Pleeese."

"God. All right. But no more."

"Thanks, Mom! Love you." He hung up.

"Love you, too," she said to the dead line.

Monique took a few more swallows of cold water and wiped her mouth with her hand as she walked back into the Room. "Some Natives were wealthy, Chris. They used Black slaves before and after they settled in Indian Territory. Some were highly educated with PhDs or law degrees. The Cherokees had the female and male seminaries that offered chemistry and French. Hundreds of members of the Five Tribes were Christians and spoke nothing but English."

"I didn't know that. But what about the Indian Indians? You know, the real ones?"

Monique stared at her partner. "Chris."

"Sorry. Well, you know what I mean."

"Not really."

"Uh, I . . ."

"Do you mean the ones with tipis and feathers?"

"I guess I did."

"So, you did not mean the majority of Indigenous peoples. The ones who did not use tipis, wear braids, or eat bison. The ones who were not in *Dances with Wolves*."

His face reddened.

"A lot of their bones and burial goods are in museums, too. Or in the homes of private collectors."

In an attempt to wade out of the shit pile he had created, he deflected. "So, did the removed people take remains of those who died with them?"

"No. They were buried in shallow dirt because the ground was frozen, or their families looked for soft dirt in a stream bank and put them there. Some bodies were wedged high up in between tree branches so wolves wouldn't get them."

"So what you're saying is that the bodies could get washed away with a heavy rain, and the ones buried on the trail could have been easily dug up? And bodies in the trees just probably fell out."

"Yes. Some bone collectors knew they could probably sell them and may have labeled the bones as to where they were found. Approximately, that is."

"God. How horrible."

"True again."

"How terrible that some people had to leave members of their families behind in unsecured graves," Rachel said from one aisle over.

"You had family die on the trail?" Chris asked Monique.

She stiffened. "Yes. We all did. You should talk to my Uncle Leroy sometime. He carries the family stories."

"Sorry," he muttered.

"Chris, look around you." She made a sweeping motion with her arm. "Look at all these boxes. And this is a small archive compared to what other museums have. If you think that a dead Native American, American Indian, or First Nations person is secure underground, then you better think again."

9

Jenn Baker considered how she could die. Before they came to her again.

Her left temple was bruised and scabbed from repeatedly hitting her head on the wooden posts. Her nails were torn from trying to tear apart the ropes that held the posts together so she could make a noose. She had tried to cut her wrists with a rock. Then they cleaned out her cage, and she no longer had access to anything sharp enough to tear her flesh.

If she could tie pant legs together and throw one end over a tree branch or rafter, she could hang herself. But there were no long pants. Yesterday she'd worn a skirt, and this morning they gave her shorts. If she had scissors she might cut her long blonde hair and braid it into a rope, but she didn't. And there were no rafters or trees above her.

Jenn now understood her mistake. She should not have traveled by herself. After graduating from University of Texas with her degree in fashion merchandising, her parents bought her a new silver Lexus. Her plan was to drive from Austin to Oklahoma City to meet friends, and they would then fly together to Cabo San Lucas for a week. The last time she called her mother was eight days ago when she was shopping at the

Galleria in Dallas. She knew she should have turned on her GPS tracker, but she didn't want her mother asking questions about every place she went. Her parents and friends would have missed her by now, and she continued to hope that police would burst in at any moment to save her.

The men had taken her and her Lexus at the rest stop on I-35 outside of Denton. She did not know what the men looked like. One had put a blanket over her head as she washed her hands in the ladies' room. She fell asleep after inhaling a smelly rag. She vaguely recalled being carried through a humid place that reminded her of a zoo. No doubt they'd ditched her car or hidden it well.

They put her in a cage in the dark. Although she was still woozy, she explored it on her hands and knees. She seemed to be in a cage about ten by ten feet with walls of wooden poles. There was haze of light in the far distance, but not enough to allow her to clearly see details of the surroundings. A stinky man with a deep, hoarse voice brought her food and told her she could turn on the lantern only when he said to. And that was after he moved far away enough that she couldn't see him.

As soon as she flipped on the light it was clear that she was not in a house or barn but in a cave. The ceiling was not high, maybe fourteen feet in most places, and because of the draft, she guessed it stretched back a good way.

The first night, Jenn sat in the dark and whimpered as she wondered what they had planned for her. She heard a coyote howl, loud and clear, then another and another. They sounded close. A bird, maybe a hawk or eagle, screeched, followed by dozens of other birds at ear-splitting decibels. Other sounds joined the assault: one deep voice sounded like a howling werewolf and another could have been a mountain lion. Pigs squealed and grunted. She sobbed until she could hardly breathe through her swollen sinuses. Then, suddenly, the night was quiet again. This sound explosion had happened at least eight times, so she knew she had been held captive for more than a week. They always came after the sounds died down.

Two things were certain: the men reeked, and they spoke a foreign language when not addressing her. She refused to eat for a few days, but she realized that if an opportunity to escape arose, she better be healthy to take advantage of it. So, she asked for even more food, and they seemed pleased to bring it. Once she asked for pizza, and they gave her a large one along with a plastic container of Wet Wipes and a six-pack of cold Diet Pepsi. They would have known she drank that because her cooler in the car was full of them. The next morning she asked for scrambled eggs and green tea, and they provided that as well. Even the peach and mango smoothie she wanted was cold, as if they had made it in an adjoining room. The little child's potty in the corner was emptied and cleaned twice a day. She had fresh clothes brought to her each morning, but never long pants.

Jenn tried to make herself as unattractive as possible. She rubbed dirt from the floor over her body, ripped her clothes, and refused to clean herself after using the pot. But the three men didn't care what she looked or smelled like. They came anyway.

10

larence Wright opened his office door as Monique passed. "Hey, can I come out now?"

"No." She took hold of the knob and pulled the door closed.

"All done," Rachel said from the door of the Room. "No new prints on that cabinet. As you saw for yourself, it's covered in dust. It's been a very long time since someone touched that thing."

"Thanks," Monique said.

"But there's a problem." Rachel continued.

"What?"

"We looked at everyone's shoes. There aren't any tracks in this room that we can't account for."

"Explain."

"There's nothing to explain. No one else has been in here. Or at least no one else has walked on the dusty floor."

"Obviously, someone else was in here," Monique said.

"Maybe he was killed in the hall and thrown inside," Chris suggested.

Rachel shook her head. "Nope. No evidence of him skidding or rolling to where he was found. It's more than ten feet from the door to here. Couldn't have happened."

"And it's not on the video, Chris," Monique reminded him.

"Oh, right. Uh, cables from the ceiling?" He looked up.

"No way to attach them," Lloyd Adams said from the doorway.

Monique sighed. There was no containing him. She pushed a wayward strand of hair off her face.

Rachel waved her hand toward the shelves. "I'll work through here some more while you figure out those files. And maybe how someone got in here."

"But there's no way in here besides that front door," Chris said firmly. "I thought we all agreed on that."

Monique shook her head. "There has to be another way in. Louie is walking the room perimeter again." She pulled latex gloves from her pocket and put them on as she went to the old cabinet, then pulled out a drawer in the middle. It was packed with recipe-sized cards. Her heart sank. Maybe this wouldn't be as easy as she'd hoped. "There're hundreds of cards in here."

"There are a lot of items in the room," Adams said. "Not just bones. I already said probably pots and pot fragments."

"Are those valuable?" Chris asked. "Monetarily speaking."

"Not if they're not documented. As I already said, we can't use them as study tools if we don't know their provenance."

"Then why keep them?" Monique asked as she glanced around the room again in hopes of finding some overlooked passageway.

"Where are they supposed to go, Detective?"

"Some say that the remains and burial objects should go back in the ground."

Adams did not respond.

Monique opened the next drawer and saw just as many faded old cards. She pulled one out and tried to make sense of the many numbers and abbreviations and descriptions of the box contents. One card read: *Mandible. Northern Tucson. Site unknown. Tribe unknown. Gift of Wallace Petterson, Yuma. 1898.*

"This says a gift," she said. "How could a mandible be a gift? Why would the museum keep something like this?"

"I didn't make the decision," Adams said defensively. "The first museum board took in almost everything that came in. Our policy is that we don't give items away, and we rarely sell them, although we do sometimes trade items with other museums. Actually, it's the policy of the American Association of Museums. Whenever someone donates an item to the museum, the intent is that it becomes a part of the public domain. You can only sell items under certain circumstances."

"Such as?"

"Like if you need to upgrade a collection. A museum can lose accreditation if it doesn't dispose of items properly."

"The laws of NAGPRA are a bit different," she said. "As I'm sure you know."

"What's that?" Chris interrupted.

"Native American Graves Protection and Repatriation Act. The short version is that organizations that receive federal funds are required to return skeletal remains and cultural objects to tribes."

"Obviously you can't sell skeletal remains through public auction," Adams said. "Or sell them, period."

"People do it all the time," Monique corrected.

"I mean public auction. Not private ones. And museums can't auction items, either. Moreover, if a tribe can't establish descendency or relation to an item, then they can't have it."

"Of course not," Monique replied sarcastically.

"Would you want to be responsible for taking care of thousands of bones that don't belong to your tribe?"

"No. But some tribes are willing to. Many Natives argue that remains should be buried even if we don't know who they are."

"Point taken." It was not, really. But it had become clear to Adams that Detective Blue Hawk had a personal interest in this case. Adams was stubborn, and Blue Hawk was going to get the information she wanted only by playing nice. Conversely, if he was to get out of this mess, he would have to play nice, too.

"Chris," Monique said in a voice that echoed through the huge room, "what's the number on the lid by your foot?"

Chris called out, "6-MI-35," and walked back to the catalogue.

She found the corresponding drawer and looked through four inches of cards until she located the one that matched the box. "Great, they link to the boxes. We should find information about all of them." Monique hoped they could figure this out before her medium-sized headache blossomed into a migraine. "Is that right, Dr. Adams?"

"Should be," he wheezed.

"But it looks like there are a lot more cards than there are boxes," Chris observed.

Adams took off his glasses and wiped off nervous perspiration. "A lot of the boxes on the top shelves are small."

"Swell," Monique said. "More hands or feet. Let's get the numbers from the boxes on the shelf where the overturned remains were."

After spending a few minutes writing down the numbers on the box labels, they rummaged through the filing cabinet to find the corresponding cards that would reveal what was in the disturbed containers.

"Maybe this is a useful one," Chris said, holding up a yellowed card that matched one of the larger boxes.

"Lots of cards for lots of bones," said Louie. He had been standing behind them, listening. "You got eight overturned boxes that need to be filled. What's that card say?"

"Uh, *two femurs, two tibias, two fibulas, two patellae, left and right foot metatarsals and phalanges.*"

"Two legs," Adams clarified.

"Two legs," Monique repeated. "And feet."

"That's sixty bones," Adams said.

"Why are there only legs in a box?" Chris asked. "Where's the rest of him? Her?"

Monique talked over him. "Okay. The box number on the card is 6, and there it is on the floor. And there is only one pair of bones on the floor, so . . ."

"Thanks," Adams said sardonically. He headed for the bones with the intention of setting them back into the appropriate box.

"Nope," Louie said. "Don't touch."

Adams held up his hands. "Sorry."

Chris cleared his throat. "Could the perp have stood on the boxes and killed the guard? That would explain why there're no footprints."

"No way," Louie answered. "These boxes are cardboard. And they're old. They couldn't support any weight."

Monique returned to the card file and looked for the rest of the cards that matched the boxes.

"And another thing," Louie said. He motioned to the boxes. "There's nothing here. No one put a hand on these. The boxes are dusty on the sides. They're clear on the bottoms and tops where another box sat on them. We can take these into the lab for a better look."

"No smudges where fingers could have pulled or pushed them over?" Monique asked.

"None that we can see."

"All right, in the meantime, we need to sort these bones," Monique said.

"Go ahead. Just don't touch them," Rachel repeated Louie's order.

The detectives and Dr. Adams took notes, identified the boxes, and after an hour had almost all the bones on the floor assigned to the correct boxes. Mentally, that is, because they couldn't handle them. Each box held only parts of a skeleton: the humerus, ulna, radius, wrist bones of one arm, along with the phalanges that made up its hand; half a rib cage with scapula, clavicle, and cervical vertebrae of a person cut in half lengthwise then in half horizontally, minus the head.

Another box held four skulls. No box held an entire skeleton. Even boxes next to each other contained disarticulated skeletons. "Why aren't there any full skeletons here?" Monique asked Adams.

"There probably are some," Adams said, "but a lot of collectors went after only parts. Skulls were popular. Some collectors were destructive when they dug, and in the process of getting a few bones or sacred items buried with the body, they broke or crushed the others and left them behind."

"I know about the destruction. Skulls are popular in Oklahoma. Grave robbers steal them then sell them at gun shows or on the black market. The Corps of Engineers in Texas and Missouri find historic grave sites torn up from dynamite and backhoes."

"That's disgusting," Chris said.

"It's a business," Monique said. "I'm aware of almost a dozen cases in the past four years in which grave robbers were either caught in the process of desecrating a gravesite or arrested at gun shows with skeletal remains. And true to the form of the Oklahoma legal system, all those cases were dismissed. In half of the situations, the judges also were prominent collectors of Native artifacts."

"Anthropologists don't blast gravesites," Adams said.

"That's decent of you," Monique answered.

"We study them. The reason you see so many parts here is because after the Indian wars in the last part of the 1800s, a lot of Indians killed in battle were dismembered for study. Thousands of bones were sent to the Army Medical Museum in Washington."

"Yes, I know."

"How come a person would want items that were sacred to tribes?" Chris asked. "Hell, if I got a hold of a medicine bundle or something like that then I'd worry about where it belonged. I wouldn't be able to get rid of it fast enough. Who would want their bones to end up like this?"

"Plenty of people leave their bodies to science," Adams pointed out.

Chris saw Monique's jaw clench. He decided to keep his mouth shut.

The group completed the matching process for six of the seven boxes and had accounted for all the bones on the floor. That left one box, number 7, empty. The card for that box was different from the others.

"All it says here on the card for box 7 is 'See Doc. 7514,'" Monique said. "What does that mean? All the other cards have information listing the specific items in the boxes."

Adams waved his hand in dismissal. "I really don't know. Perhaps the items in box 7 were loaned to another museum. Or they were older specimens that no one bothered to catalogue. The document referred to is probably the donation letter or form. They aren't of interest."

"Were they ever?"

"I can't tell you that." He realized how that sounded and tried again. "I don't know. Maybe to the early museologists."

"Well, where can we find this Document 7514," Chris asked. "Is it in this cabinet with the index cards?"

Adams shook his head. "No. It would be in another office. The box probably contained just a few skeletal pieces like the others. There's no real use for the items we can't name, but we can't throw them away. So they get stored in this room."

"You need to know what was taken," Monique reminded him. "Someone was after the contents of a box in the back of the shelf—this box, most likely, since it's empty."

Adams shrugged and pushed his glasses up his nose. "Could have been random. Maybe they wanted to take something old. You know, nothing in particular."

"You really think someone broke in here and murdered a guard because they wanted to steal just any old thing? Don't be ridiculous." She thought for a moment. "On the other hand, if the remains aren't identified, then they aren't listed. And if they aren't listed, then tribes won't try to claim them. Unidentified remains stay in the collection forever. Am I right?"

"Yes. I've explained that." Adams turned back to his cards.

"How would someone not a part of this museum know what's in the boxes if the contents aren't identified?"

"I don't know."

"But if the cards do identify the items," Chris speculated, "then it's possible that a descendant of the people who took the remains in the first place wants the bones or pots back."

"That seems unlikely," Adams countered. "It's more feasible that Indians would want them back than the descendants of white people who took them."

Although Monique figured Adams might be right about that, she was not going to say so.

"When will you finish dusting these bones?" she asked Rachel and Louie.

"Another hour or so," Louie answered.

"Well, then." She tried to swallow, but the dust in her throat choked her. "Where are those other files?" she asked Adams before stepping over the old bones and waiting for Adams and Chris to follow her out the door. "Y'all coming?" she asked through a cough.

II

When they reached the reception desk, Adams said he needed to make a phone call and went into his office and shut the door. Monique was annoyed but not surprised to find Mrs. Willis at her desk as well. No one seemed able to stay put in this place. When Monique asked what she was doing there, she explained quickly that she had just come back to get her sweater because the lounge was cold.

Monique coughed again, unable to clear the dust from her throat.

"You want some juice, dear?" Mrs. Willis asked. "I have some apple juice right here in my little cooler."

"Thanks. I'd appreciate it," Monique said gratefully.

"You look pale," Chris told her. "Well, not really pale. You're still dark, but . . ."

"I know what you mean, Chris. I feel pale."

Mrs. Willis got a small juice carton from her fridge and handed it to Monique, who stuck the straw in the box and sucked down the contents, musing again that she would have to visit her uncle Leroy Bear Red Ears for cleansing after being around dead people. But that would have to wait. For the moment, she needed to grit her teeth to get through this case.

Unfortunately, she was gritting her teeth quite literally, which made her back molar hurt. Maybe she had cracked it. She also needed a headache pill. She felt around in her jacket pocket and found two Ibuprofen tablets. She tossed the two bitter tablets in her mouth. She couldn't swallow.

Mrs. Willis watched her. "Those taste like hell, don't they, dearie?" she said sweetly. "Drink this." She handed Monique a Juice Monster can labeled "Mango Loco." "This will make you feel even better."

Monique popped the top and sniffed. "Smells good. Cheers," she said before chugging half the bottle. She coughed and gasped. "My God! What's in this?"

"Oh, just some juice. And 152 milligrams of caffeine. It's better than coffee when you need a boost," Mrs. Willis said.

Chris looked over her shoulder. "Ah, reinforcements at last. Joe and Linda are here."

Indeed, Officers Joe May and Linda Hudson were hurrying down the hall toward the reception desk. With Linda, as always, was her K9 partner, Taz. Linda was tall and skinny with dark blonde hair. Joe was a short, muscular man with thick black hair slicked back with shiny hair gel. Taz, short for Tasmanian Devil, was a four-year-old female long-haired German shepherd. Like all canine officers, the big black-and-brown dog was all business when on duty. The other officers knew better than to try to pet her.

"Hi, guys. Hello, Taz," Monique said, already feeling jittery from the caffeine jolt. The aloof Taz turned her head, signaling that she found the cinder-block wall more interesting.

Monique quickly apprised Linda and Joe of the details of the assaults. "We need to find the dead guard's missing clothing," Monique told them, "as well as find any leads on where the perps went or how they got in. There are three others searching through the museum. One is a museum security guard named Lester Martin. He has on a uniform and a red-and-blue Rangers gimme cap. Officers Weiser and Blount are out there somewhere, too."

"Ah, yes," Linda said with an eye roll. "Toby Blount and Bud Weiser."

"Toby and Bud?" Monique started to laugh.

"They're okay. Well, Bud's kind of a sexist. Just don't try and socialize."

"Hadn't planned on it."

"Bud has women issues," she continued.

"Yes, I caught that," Monique said. "Look around the building first, then we have to check out all the offices."

"How many perps?" Joe asked.

"We're not sure yet. The surveillance video doesn't show anyone going into the room other than the two security guards. It recorded all night. All we know—or think we know—is that someone else besides the two guards was in that room, and they didn't come in or out through the door for twenty-four hours prior to this morning's assault."

"A window?" asked Linda.

"None in there."

"Through the ceiling?"

"Nope. Solid. The planetarium is directly above."

"And a box of bones is gone, too," Chris said.

"Not the box," Monique corrected. "Just what was in it, although it was almost certainly bones. Some of the boxes we've seen in there have bones for only a single body part in them." She pointed over her shoulder with her thumb to the Room. "Some have more than a few."

"And how old are these bones?" Joe asked with a concerned look. "They aren't, you know, like, fresh, are they?"

Monique shook her head. Nobody wanted to handle bones with tissue on them. "No, no. Old, dry bones. Again, we aren't exactly sure what we're looking for," she repeated. "While you're looking for the perp, look for anything odd."

"Odd?" Linda repeated with a smirk. "No problem. It's not like I never run into anything odd. Once I found a moose calf and an alligator inside the apartment of a man who had been eaten by rats. The moose and the alligator went to the Tulsa Zoo, and the rats were poisoned by an exterminator, which set off an uproar among animal activists."

"Yes, I recall that."

"And there was the time we found a woman so huge she had grown around her lounge chair. You should have seen the medics try to—"

Monique cut her off. "Taz needs a scent. Let's take her in."

Taz obediently walked into the Room at Linda's side. Monique observed the dog as she walked slowly around the blood ring. Taz kept her nose to the ground but did not touch the drying liquid. Once she got the smell, Taz backed up and whined. She pulled Linda hard to the empty bone box, sat on her haunches, and howled.

"Taz? What is it, girl?" Linda said.

Taz growled at the box. Then she suddenly cocked her head and stared at the east wall. The big dog stood and pulled Linda toward it, then dragged her up and down the length of the cinder-block wall.

"What have you got, Taz?" Linda repeated. "Monique, do you know what's behind this wall?"

"Part of it may back up to the elevator shaft. I need to check," Monique said from the doorway.

"Well, she sure is interested in it," Linda said. "Taz got a good whiff of the blood, but she did not like that box. And she was interested in the east wall."

"So I noticed." Monique looked again at the gray-painted, unadorned, and apparently impenetrable cinder-block wall. She focused again on the small air vent in the wall three feet below the twenty-foot ceiling. "Linda, take Taz out and see if she finds something else."

Once outside the Room, Taz barked again and started to pull Linda down the hall, like her own Rover pulled her when she was ready to run, Monique thought. Taz, though, could pull a shoulder out of joint.

"Taz! Heel!" Linda ordered. Taz slowed and whined.

Lloyd Adams came out of his office wiping his glasses with a white handkerchief. His eyes got big at seeing more law enforcement and a large dog.

Monique motioned toward Adams with her chin. "Look in his office first. It won't take long."

Adams looked back at his office, and his shoulders slumped.

"Dr. Adams, if you have nothing in there, you've got nothing to worry about. Besides, you want to be cleared, right?"

"Very well." He seemed to have aged since this morning.

"Look in his briefcase while you're at it," Monique said to Linda as she moved toward the door.

Adams gritted his teeth but did not argue. "Do you want to look in the other room for the files with the document now?"

Monique did not want to search the other room, but it had to be done. She glanced down the hall and saw Dr. Janice Rice standing in the hall in front of her office, wearing a long sweater over her sundress. She had her arms wrapped tightly around her, and she smacked her gum so furiously Monique heard her from twenty paces.

"Not yet. I'll talk to Dr. Rice first," Monique said.

"Yeah, we should," Chris agreed. They needed a break from bones.

"I'll be in the lounge down the hall, then," Adams said, "until they're finished searching my things."

"That's fine. We'll let you know when you can leave."

Linda, Joe, and Taz entered Adams's office, and the detectives heard chairs being moved around.

Janet Rice had turned away and was about to enter her office.

"Dr. Rice!" Monique said loudly, as she hurried down the hall. "We need to speak with you for a moment."

"Oh, sure," she answered. "Come on in."

"Native Martha Stewart Living," Monique said under her breath when she saw the interior.

"What?" Chris asked.

"Nothing."

The light maroon walls provided a backdrop for the mission oak furniture. Wood-framed paintings of landscapes, animals, and profiles of

Plains Natives hung at eye level. The books on the bookshelves had gold-stamped spines. Small plaster casts of bears, eagles, wolves, and other western animals decorated the shelves in front of the books. Woven table runners in Navajo designs draped the desk and computer table. A Diet Pepsi looked distinctly out of place next to the heavy wood frame with thunder symbols that held a photo of a brown-haired man wearing eyeglasses. Cheap dream catchers with colored turkey feathers hung in the windows. A large Hopi Kachina posed on top of a filing cabinet. A bowl of potpourri next to it gave off a holiday odor that battled with the spring-fresh scent of the bouquet of flowers on the desk. If she bought flowers like that once a week, Monique thought, then Dr. Rice ran up a heck of a tab. Monique couldn't help but wonder if Rice's décor was meant to impress visitors or to simply please herself.

"Please sit." Rice motioned to the chairs in front of her desk upholstered in a Navajo pattern. "Want a drink?" She reached under her computer table where a small refrigerator hummed and pulled out another Diet Pepsi. All the offices apparently had the same small cooler.

Chris took it, but Monique waved her hand. "No thanks, Dr. Rice. I'm good." The caffeine from the Monster drink still surged through her system. She felt giddy. "How long have you worked here?"

"About six years. I taught anthropology and archival studies at the University of Michigan a few years and decided I didn't like academia. When this job announcement appeared, I came after it."

"Do you like it here?"

"For the most part. We get a lot of donations, and I stay busy enough to keep me interested."

"What do you do?"

"I'm the head curator, which means I look at the donated items and consult with the other departments in order to assess their value to the museum. Then I consult with the museum board to decide if we want them. Then I assist the departments in creating a display for whatever the item is."

"That's a neat dinosaur exhibit by the entrance," Chris said.

She smiled. "Thanks. I didn't put those bones together, of course. Bob Shimura does that kind of thing. But I helped design the display. I had nightmares for several months after working with that tyrannosaur. His teeth are longer than my foot."

"Yeah, pretty cool." Chris grinned.

"I also manage the museum's website," Rice continued.

"How many other departments are there?" Monique asked. "Can you give us an idea of how many people each employs and what time they open?"

"Let's see. The gift shop has four or five rotating workers and one manager. It opens at ten o'clock when the museum does. The two employees in School Services deals with school tours and classes. The café opens at eleven. The Omni Theatre opens at two, and the planetarium at noon. I'm not sure how many people work there. The custodians work after hours, and the admissions people arrive about five minutes before ten. They don't have a lot to do to get ready to sell tickets."

"Custodians? How late do they stay?"

"It depends. They start cleaning before the museum closes, and unless there's a mess someplace involving spilled sodas, I imagine they're done before midnight. The day shift custodians tend to the café and the restrooms so the trash doesn't get out of hand."

Monique looked to Chris. "Custodians," she said thoughtfully. She turned to Rice. "They go everywhere in the museum?"

"I don't think they have access to every room and exhibit," Rice said, "or at least not unsupervised."

"We'll check that. What about the displays like the schoolhouse and the dentist's office?"

"I manage those. We don't really need a historian here to figure that stuff out. We got an old dentist's chair from a donor, then I bought some other cheap items to create an office based on old photographs. Not everything in the museum is completely authentic. Most of the items in the schoolroom are things I found at garage sales. That exhibit is for the children. They don't know the difference between an authentic book and a replica."

"How many people help with curation?"

"It varies. I often use students majoring in museum studies at the University of Oklahoma, although some come from Tulsa and Stillwater. Oh, and the photographic archives and library. Those departments are open to the public Monday, Wednesday, and Friday, although researchers can look at photos at other times. By appointment only."

"Is the photo archive in any way connected to the other archives? The ones with remains, I mean."

"Not directly, I think. If someone is looking at a certain point in time, then maybe some connection could be made. There may be some photos of people from tribes that have remains and objects in the boxes."

"You don't mean the archive has photos of the people who are now in the collection as bones, right?"

She hedged. "Well, it's possible, I guess. I don't know of any photo—bone connections."

"But there might be a photograph of the person whose bones were in the missing box?" Monique pressed.

"You can't know. No one can unless everything is identified and labeled. Anyway, the older bones and other items wouldn't have definitive photos to go with them. It just wasn't done that way back then. The archivists don't know what person belongs to what tribe. It's a real pain for researchers because the archivists can't help them much. One of the two people who run that department is mainly interested in photos of old mining camps and the other deals with historic photos and sketches of plants and animals."

"It's worth checking, though. When do the photography workers come in?"

"Nine or nine-thirty, I think."

"Anyone else who may be in the museum off hours?"

"The café people may come in early to get food ready. I don't know much about that. They sell mostly cold sandwiches and salads. No hot food except for coffee and hot dogs and sometimes soups on the weekend."

"When did you get here this morning?"

"Right when you saw me. I walked in with Clarence."

"Do you ride to work with him?"

"God, no." She crinkled her nose. "No way. Clarence is . . . well. Just, no. Normally, I get here after Lloyd and Clarence and I don't walk past the reception desk the way I did today. I come down the stairs at the other end of the hall because the lounge is there. I get coffee before coming to my office, and I carry it with me. The first person I see most days is Grumpy Lloyd."

"Grumpy Lloyd?"

"Oh, yes," Rice said. "He rarely speaks to me."

"Why is that?"

"Mainly because I enjoy tormenting him with pro-repatriation talk."

"So you're a curator and pro-repatriation?"

"I don't display skeletal remains or sacred cultural items except for items donated by tribes. And there are precious few of those." She changed the subject abruptly. "What tribe are you?"

"Choctaw."

"You look Plains. Well, I'm not. Not even part Cherokee."

Monique laughed. "Thanks for admitting it."

"Almost every white person says they have a Cherokee ancestor, right? Well, I'm 100 percent white trash and proud of it."

Chris fidgeted in his seat.

"Even so," Rice continued. "Some people can hang around the dead and not be bothered. But I'm not one of them. My job is to categorize pots and baskets. The first thing I do when I receive an item is to try and assess whether or not it had been part of a burial. I would refuse to display funerary objects and the museum board knows better than to accept them. But sometimes they slip through as part of a larger collection."

"Do donations arrive with descriptions?"

"Sometimes. Grave robbers who try to sell cultural items to private buyers sometimes lie about where they got them. If the tag says a Mescalero burial, then how are buyers who aren't versed in the things they collect going to know if it's really a Mescalero or Kiowa item? Buyers aren't always discriminating because they figure they can turn around and sell items to others. Small museums and private collectors also might buy them. We certainly don't."

"So a lot of items are mislabeled?"

"Donations from the public often are. They come in from well-meaning donors. They say they found a pot while out hiking and that's all the information they can give us. A lot of times, of course, they've dug where they shouldn't have and lie about it."

"And what else do you have to assess about the items you get?"

"If tribes have reported the item stolen. The list of stolen items from various tribes is a very long one. Masks, fetishes, medicine bundles, pipe bags, lances, jewelry. Many of those come from graves. The chances that the tribes will get those things returned are slim. Anyway, if I can't ascertain enough about the items, I contact the tribe in the vicinity of the gravesite and see if a rep from the tribal cultural preservation office can identify them. I rarely walk among the old boxes holding body parts because not only do I believe it's wrong to desecrate the graves of any race, regardless of age, I get queasy."

"You must feel queasy a lot around here," Chris said.

She laughed. "Well, a lot of the remains are in the Room of Secrets, and I never go in there. Full skeletons are housed in the two large rooms below us. I don't go down there either."

Monique sat up straight. "More bones? There are more bones than the ones in the Room?"

"Oh, yes, the ones the anthropologists are actively studying are kept in the labs."

Monique looked at Chris. Weiser only mentioned fossils and shells.

"How many anthropologists are in this building?" she asked.

"Lloyd's the department head. Roger Murcule comes in three times a week. He's at the University of Oklahoma. He does dental analyses on skulls."

"All the items in the museum are on a list someplace?"

"Each department is supposed to have an inventory of its items."

"And do they?"

"Probably not for everything, no. There are files on various acquisitions in the Room."

"We've seen those. That's quite the index system."

"Probably very old. The newer system is pretty much the same, actually. Just not as dusty and it's downstairs. The National Museum of the American Indian Act ordered museums to inventory their holdings in 1989. Lloyd should have a copy of that."

"Lloyd told us he hasn't been in the Room of Secrets for six months."

Rice shook her head. "That's not true. I saw him coming out of there about two months ago."

"Are you certain?" Monique asked.

"Absolutely."

"What do you think he was doing?" Chris asked.

"I have no idea. Maybe he was working on identifying some of the bones in there so they could be repatriated to the proper tribe." She swigged some soda.

"What'll happen to the remains in the Room?" Chris asked.

"Probably nothing. Prior to the passage of NAGPRA, this museum held almost three thousand full human skeletons and countless skeletal pieces. A lot of those have been repatriated now. This whole country is one big tribal burial ground, you know, and pothunters and grave robbers will be very happy to pilfer Indian graves until they're all gone. Unless tribes can positively identify skeletal remains and cultural objects as belonging to their community, those items will remain in the archives."

"Forever?"

"Maybe. Some museums will not return a bone to Natives if they don't have to."

"Museums like this one?" Monique asked.

She grinned. "Exactly like this one."

"Do you think someone would break in here to steal a few bones?" Chris asked. "Why one set and not another?"

Rice shook her head. "Maybe they believe they're related to the deceased."

"What if they wanted the bones to study?"

"They can simply ask permission. We've had lots of researchers, but I'm not aware that anyone has asked about the bones in that room."

"Do you think Lloyd could have taken the ones that are missing from the box?" Monique asked.

"I don't know why he would. I mean, he has access to them at any time."

"He suggested that one of you might have stolen them," Chris said.

"Listen, Detective," Rice leaned forward. "Lloyd is paranoid about thieves. Not only does he get all worried about archival items disappearing and turning up in art shops, he gets nervous over the prospect of renegade Indians appearing up in his office armed with bows and rifles to demand their stuff. Lloyd and his cronies don't believe that all the Indians who want remains really deserve to have them. Nevertheless, like a good boy, he adheres to NAGPRA for the most part."

"For the most part?"

"I can't prove anything, mind you. But I don't think he's honest on all the NAGPRA requests. That's just my speculation."

"Is it easy to be dishonest?"

"Ha!" she snorted. "There are so many museums in this country with remains that there's no way the people enforcing NAGPRA could possibly check every one. Smithsonian's Native American Repatriation Review Committee only has a few members, and they usually have full-time jobs of their own. They come together periodically to review what's been given back, reported, and inventoried."

"Have they been here?"

"Once that I know of. About four years ago. They evidently found out what they needed to know and left."

"This is really surprising to me. I used to visit this museum as a kid and had no idea so many remains were here."

"Some museums have a lot more than we do. Like the University of Texas at Austin, University of Nebraska, the Smithsonian. The Peabody at Harvard has literally thousands of remains and tens of thousands of burial objects, and it can barely keep up with the demand for repatriation of those things. There are thousands of smaller museums throughout the country with millions of partial body part remains and cultural items. It would take several armies to see what's in all of them. Oklahoma and Texas are dotted with small museums that have bones. It's probably easy to hide them whenever someone comes to check on them. Anthropologists make careers of studying Indians, but very little of their research benefits tribes. Whenever I say something like that to Lloyd, he just says that I sound like the activists who make his life hell."

"And Lloyd gets hit with protests?"

"Sometimes. Not as many as twenty years ago."

"So, how do Natives get their property back?"

"Well, I can tell you that being charmingly persuasive doesn't work," Rice smiled, "and most of them aren't in the mood to be charming anyway."

"Which leaves only two ways to get what they want, right?" Chris asked. "One is the legal route."

"And the other is stealing," Monique added.

"No Indian would do that," Rice countered. She seemed affronted by the idea that Indians might have stolen something. Even worse, perhaps would even kill for it.

"Maybe you're not aware of what some of them are capable of doing." Monique stated.

Rice shook her head. "What I meant is I don't think there are many Indians willing to go into that room—or any room with remains. The only ones who do go around the dead are the spiritual leaders, or those who know they have access to a medicine man so they can be cleansed right away."

This brought Monique back to thinking that she needed to get to her uncle Leroy Bear Red Ears, and fast.

12

tanding outside the west entrance with Chris, Monique called the hospital to check on the injured guard, Ethan Lewis, and found that he was in surgery. Monique closed her eyes, face to the sun, and breathed deeply. Chris had a granola bar in one hand and a Pepsi in the other. The Norman afternoon had warmed to a comfortable and windless 73 degrees—T-shirts, shorts, and sandals weather. This was the time of year that Monique loved: calm, peaceful weather with an occasional ribbon of cool breeze sliding across the landscape to remind her that winter approached.

"So, is Adams keeping remains illegally?" Chris asked in between bites.

"Doubtful." Monique put on her sunglasses.

"Maybe he keeps items in the Room that he wants for himself?"

"Maybe."

"Should we detain him?"

"No. Let him stew. I can't see how Adams's research would have any bearing on this murder. Besides, we don't know that what Rice said is true. She's only speculating. We need to focus on the fact that someone wanted something in that room and killed to get it. If Adams wanted an item from the Room, he could just walked in and take it anytime. Why would he do it in the wee hours of the morning?"

"Maybe the object is too big to sneak out. Or maybe he thought he could take it out and hide it someplace else in the museum?"

"How big of an *it* are you talking about? The femur is the largest bone. A skull or pelvis might be the most cumbersome. If it was bones he wanted, he could just put them in a briefcase or gym bag."

"Yeah," Chris sighed. "You're right."

"If Adams wanted to steal something, that is. Plus, we still don't know what was stolen. It could have been a few teeth or an entire skeleton, or even a pot of some kind." She shook her head. "I think we have to consider that the person or people who did this are Indians. On the other hand, if a Native person is going to bother to steal and commit murder, then going to a medicine man would be unnecessary."

"Why?"

"Most tribes have spiritual leaders, and most spiritual leaders are healers who try to do what is best for the welfare of their people. But not all medicine men and women focus on good things. And that's what scares me." Monique turned her back on the sun and went back into the air-conditioned foyer. She stopped at the water fountain for another drink, still unable to get the dust out of her throat. The cold water ran down her chin and dripped onto her white shirt. She rubbed some on her neck. The museum atmosphere pressed in on her at once, however, and she felt compelled to go back outside and sit with the ducks.

Chris tossed his wrapper in the waste can then unwrapped a piece of gum. "Man, this is a weird, truly weird case."

"Yup."

Monique looked down at the koi swimming in their clean, safe water. Always fed, no fear of predators. Except maybe for kids wanting to win a bet that they could catch one.

"I want to talk to the other people in this hall," she said, straightening her back and pushing away wayward strands of hair. "Bob Shimura and the tall guy. Dr. Wright?"

"Yeah. The bird man."

"Lead the way."

They wound through the now-familiar exhibits. They double-timed it down the stairs to the basement, their footfalls and breathing the only sounds in the stairwell.

Chris stopped in front of an office and read the nameplate. "Here's Bob Shimura's office. Want to see him first?"

Monique nodded and Chris knocked. Bob Shimura opened the door almost immediately. He wore glasses and had rolled up the sleeves of his checkered cotton shirt.

"We need to talk to you, Dr. Shimura." She was not asking. Despite the break and the cold water, her headache was back in force.

Shimura backed up a step. "Certainly," he said in his rich, deep voice. "Come in."

Whereas Janice Rice had covered or filled every square inch of the walls and surfaces of her office, Bob Shimura had opted for a no-clutter, Zenlike environment. The walls were painted pine-bark brown. Two framed pictures sat atop a blue-and-gold desk runner in a Japanese pattern. A cup of tea steamed on a cork coaster. Monique spotted the electric kettle on the wooden cabinet against the wall underneath a stunning gold-and-black painting of Godzilla in a bronze frame.

The shelves were full of neatly arranged books interspersed with human heads carved out of wood and marble. One face had a pointy chin, thin moustache, exaggerated high cheekbones, and arched eyebrows— Satan. The marble head next to it was hollow-cheeked with deep-set eyes and a vile smirk, another depiction of evil. Across the room on a wall shelf stood matching gold-leafed demons, their wings unfurled and talons extended. Monique considered the artwork and wondered why anyone would feel compelled to create these things, much less to decorate with them.

Chris found the statuettes disturbing. His eyebrows knitted together almost into a unibrow as his eyes went from one to the next and finally settled on Satan.

"I'm not a Satanist, Detective," Shimura said, clearly aware of Chris's thoughts. "I just find his face interesting."

"You think this is what he looks like?"

"What do *you* think he looks like?"

Chris shrugged. "Those faces are as good as any."

The office felt overly warm to Monique, as if the paleontologist kept a personal heater under his desk. Or was she having a hot flash? Wasn't she too young for menopause?

Shimura's computer sat on a table against the wall, and classical music wafted from its speakers. The obligatory dorm-room mini-fridge sat under the window. There was only one chair in front of his desk. He opened a small closet next to the bookcase and took out another folding one. She and Chris sat while Shimura scurried around to his seat.

"Well, how may I help you?" he asked.

He looked to Monique to be in his late thirties, a few years younger than her. On the other hand, lots of people said she looked younger than forty-four, so maybe he looked younger, too. He moved like an old man—quickly but hunched over, as if his joints ached. He seemed nice enough, but she knew that deception could take a variety of shapes.

Monique started. "What time did you arrive this morning?"

He reached to his computer and turned off the music. "After everyone else. I had to help with my daughter's basketball demonstration team this morning. Tossie's on the City Dribblers," he added proudly.

"Tossie?"

"Yeah. It's short for Trent." He noticed the puzzled expressions. "I mean, when she was little, she couldn't say Trent, so she said Tossie."

"I see," Monique replied. He named his daughter Trent?

"Anyway, they do halftime exhibitions at the high school games. You know, fancy dribbling, twirling the ball on their forefinger, trick shots. She has a demonstration tonight, and on game days, we have early morning practices."

Shimura's surname and appearance made him of Japanese descent, but Chris thought he looked at least part Caucasian as well. Maybe a Japanese father and American mother, Chris figured. He couldn't remember the term for a second-generation Japanese American. *Issei*, maybe? *Nissai*?

"What is your position here at the museum?" Monique asked Shimura.

"I'm the chief paleontologist. I specialize in the Late Jurassic. My research is on archaeopteryx specifically, but I look at all the fossils that come in."

"Late Jurassic being when?"

"A hundred and fifty million years ago."

She paused. "Why is your office here in the anthropology department?"

"Access to the paleontology lab, that large room at the end of the hall across from the elevator. That's where the fossils are kept. I used to have an office upstairs across from the *T. rex*, but I was constantly up and down those stairs. Being here makes more sense. Plus, it's really loud up there, particularly on days the elementary school children visit."

"Is your office door open or closed most of the time?"

"Well, I sometimes prop it open a crack." He pointed to what looked to Monique like a large rock until she saw that it was a shell.

"What's that?" Chris asked.

"*Duouvilleiceras*. It's an ammonite." He looked at them to see if they recognized the name. He tried again. "A fossilized cephalopod—a creature related to squid and octopus—probably from the Cretaceous period. Notice that it's broken. If it was in good shape I wouldn't put it there where someone could take it. A good specimen could fetch almost three hundred dollars."

"Looks heavy," Chris said.

"You sell specimens?" Monique asked.

Alarmed, Bob said, "Oh, no. What I meant is that someone might take it because they could sell it. If it were a better specimen, it would be in the lab or on display."

Monique nodded.

"Anyway, it's heavy and makes a good doorstop. Five pounds. A related species from that period was almost six feet in diameter."

Monique could look up cephalopod factoids later. "Your door?" She prompted.

"Ah, yes. It's locked whenever I'm in the lab. I have four assistants who come and go in here as well."

"Assistants," she repeated. "Where are they this morning?"

"Two are doctoral students at the university. They teach morning classes, so they don't come in until the afternoon. The other two only work three days a week because they're finishing their dissertations. All of them leave when I do."

"Do they have keys to the building?"

"No. And just the ABDs have the door code and keys to the lab."

"ABDs?" Monique asked.

"Stands for 'all but dissertation.' They've passed their oral and written exams but haven't finished writing their dissertations. Jessica Linder and Evan Flowers. They have their research projects in the lab, but they write at home."

"If their research projects are in the museum, then why don't they write here?"

"We only have two computers in the lab, and we need them for data analysis. Even if they have laptops, there are no offices for students. The lab gets really noisy. Middle school and older kids come in on field trips every week or so to see the bones and the dinosaurs we're assembling. It's not an atmosphere conducive to writing."

"Does Lloyd have assistants?"

"Same as me. They come and go each year, sometimes each semester. He's got two anthropology students now. They come in on Tuesdays and Thursdays. I think they're still taking classes, and for now they just talk to him. I don't know their areas of interests."

"I'd like to look in the lab, please."

"Sure." He started to stand.

"In a moment."

He sat.

"Tell me about your coworkers."

"You mean my students?"

"No. Lloyd, Janice, Clarence, Mrs. Willis."

"I wouldn't really call them coworkers. I mean, I see them every day, but we don't interact much. Maybe at holiday time, but that's it. I see Mrs. Willis more than I see anyone. She's friendly, does her job, and goes home. She's probably aware of everything that goes on here. You know how some secretaries are. A lot of them pretty much run the business or department they work for. Mrs. Willis is like the resident grandma who wants to make sure we're all healthy and take our vitamins."

"Are you aware of the others' comings and goings?"

"Sometimes. I like to come in early to write if Tossie doesn't have practice. Lloyd gets here before me most days. Janice's office is on one side of me and Clarence's is on the other, so I hear them come in if I get here first. I'd say we all get to work around the same time, between eight fifteen and eight forty-five, and leave between four thirty and five o'clock."

"When did you leave yesterday?"

"Four fifteen. I had to get groceries and pick up the kids since my wife is out of town."

"What about the security guards? Do you ever see them?"

"I see Lester most mornings because usually by the time my tea is brewed he's on his second round through this hall."

"Have you ever seen anyone go into or come out of the Room?"

"No. Never."

"Have you ever been in there?"

He shook his head. "No need. Janice told me there are human skeletons inside, and I have no interest in that."

Monique nodded. "Would Janice or Clarence have reason to go into the Room?"

"I don't think so. Clarence studies crows and ravens, not humans." Then he averted his eyes. "And other things."

"Such as?"

Shimura hesitated. "Well, you know, weird animals. Legends and imaginary creatures. Clarence has never worked in a university."

"Crows and ravens aren't unusual."

"No, but he likes, well, uh, Bigfoot. Aliens. He's calls himself a cryptozoologist." Shimura laughed. "He studies things that don't really exist."

"Bigfoot? Really?" Chris asked.

"Yes. Evidently there are all sorts of Bigfoot groups across the country, people on the lookout for him. Or it. Or her. I don't know much about the creature. Anyway, he's here because he's an ornithologist, but most of us think he's crazy. Certainly we don't have much respect for his research."

"Wait. You mean there might really be a Bigfoot?" Chris seemed enchanted at the idea.

"I don't, no. But Clarence will give you a different opinion."

"Why is his office in this hall?" Monique asked.

"His lab is downstairs next to the other archive that has skeletons and pots and things. There isn't an office down there. This is the closest he can get."

"Do you have a key to the Room?"

The sound of Taz's panting drifted into the office as the K9 team jogged past Shimura's office door.

"Who was that?" Shimura asked.

"Linda, Joe, and Taz," Chris said.

Monique tapped on the desk. "You didn't answer my question, Dr. Shimura. Do you have a key to the Room of Secrets?"

"No." He held up his key ring and named each key: "Front entrance, back entrance, my office, my lab, and the lounge."

"Okay. Let's take a look at the lab now."

Shimura opened the door of his lab and turned on its lights, revealing a spacious and airy room with half a dozen tables piled with bones of various sizes and shapes. Three-ring binders and tattered books packed the bookshelves that lined the walls, and colorful cardboard dinosaurs hung from the ceiling. The smell of plaster and wet earth permeated the air. In one corner was a large reconstruction of a strange creature.

"What's that?" Monique asked.

"Archelon, a turtle that lived during the Mesozoic era. Almost thirteen feet long. He looks odd right now because there's no shell. We're putting a plesiosaur together over there." He pointed to the four heavy-legged, eight-foot-long tables pushed together to hold enormous bones. The three-foot skull was mostly intact.

"And a plesiosaur is?"

"A marine predator. This one is only a partial specimen, but they grew to almost fifty feet long."

"Dang!" Chris exclaimed. "Fifty feet!"

"There was one in the *Jurassic World* movie."

"The one that jumped up and ate the shark?"

"Yes."

Chris walked around the tables, as delighted as a child on Christmas morning.

"And you deal with . . . what did you tell us?"

"Archaeopteryx. The first bird. She lived a hundred and fifty million years ago. Although she really was a flesh-eating dinosaur. Birds evolved from dinosaurs, you know. Archaeopteryx is descended from small, bird-like dinosaurs called maniraptorans. She had clawed fingers, sharp teeth, and a tail. And feathers. Perhaps you've seen this picture." He pointed to the iconic picture of the fossil of the dinosaur bird, which clearly was a predator. Its neck was arched backward in the awkward pose many animals assume in death.

"Archaeopteryx was small. But some extinct flightless birds were much larger than a man. Very scary and efficient predators. If you've ever seen an angry ostrich or cassowary, you know what I mean. They can eviscerate a person with one kick. Multiply that size bird tenfold, and you have a *Phorusrhacus inflatus*." He pointed to a poster of an especially wicked-looking monster bird with a huge beak and legs with enormous thigh muscles designed to race down prey. "Note the tibia-to-femur ratio. A very fast runner."

"Hey, Monique," Chris said. She turned and saw him looking a glass case.

"Is this a megalodon tooth?"

She peered into the case and saw a gray, triangular tooth almost five inches long.

"Yes."

"*Carcharocles megalodon*, actually," Shimura corrected. "It's extinct, of course. That animal could have been up to a hundred feet long. That's considerably bigger than the modern great white." Shimura chuckled. "Clarence, of course, will tell you that they still exist."

"No way," Chris said.

"If a megalodon did exist, there would be more than one, and we would not have the large sea mammals we have today."

"Monique has a tooth," Chris blurted.

"Really? How big."

Monique shrugged. "It's a bit larger than that one."

"Oh!" Shimura explained. "I'd love to see it."

"Maybe I'll bring it by someday," Monique said. "This is all we need from you for now. Go back to your office until it's searched, please, then you can leave for the day."

"Sure. I need to take a few notes home with me. Call me if you need to. And let me know when you can bring in that tooth." He gathered his papers while the detectives walked back down the hall to ask a few questions of Dr. Clarence Wright, cryptozoologist.

13

The K9 team checked in as Monique and Chris were about to knock on Clarence Wright's office door. All the other rooms on the first floor had been searched and nothing unusual had been found—at least nothing pertaining to the murder.

Linda and Joe took turns telling Monique and Chris about the odd collections they had discovered in some of the offices, including the pine-cones favored by the out-of-town herpetologist who specialized in South American venomous snakes. Her office also contained hundreds of cones from around the world, ranging in size from tiny Canadian hemlocks to enormous sugar cones from a Northwest forest. The brown cones were heaped in baskets and hung from the ceiling by fishing wire like a snow-flake display.

The office belonging to the assistant curator who primarily dealt with the westward movement featured drawings of complicated sexual posi-tions from India on the walls and an impressive collection of Kama Sutra oils on the shelves. Monique felt lucky that he, too, was out of town, and she did not have to meet him.

Clarence Wright's door stood open and he was playing a game on his computer. His trash basket overflowed with Kleenex, Mountain Dew cans, and candy wrappers. Books and files obscured the desktop. Bird specimens floated in formalhyde-filled bottles on the bookshelves. Wright was officially the museum's ornithologist, but Monique saw no evidence that he studied ravens and crows. Posters of strange animals covered the walls. One striped creature with an enormous mouth looked to be half hyena and half wolf. Other posters featured the Loch Ness Monster, UFOs of various shapes and sizes, gargoyles, and peculiar animal hybrids.

A strange painting in a heavy carved-wood frame caught Monique's eye. It was a robed, winged woman. She was screechingly ugly, and by the look of her arched eyebrows, very angry. Bird Woman appeared to be yelling as she flew through the air on tattered wings.

Wright had no chairs besides the one he sat in. That did not surprise the detectives.

"Dr. Wright, we need to ask some questions," Monique said.

"They already searched my office," he answered in a bland monotone.

"We know. You can go when we're through talking. When did you arrive this morning?" She already knew the answer but wanted to hear it from him.

"Right after you did. You saw me come in."

"Is that when you always get here?"

"Usually. Between seven-thirty and eight."

"And what do you do here? After you come in?" She looked at his computer screen and saw fast-moving colorful shapes streaking randomly around the screen. He clicked his mouse to turn it off, revealing his screen-saver. A robust snake with two small horns above its nostrils stared out at Monique. She stared back.

"Pretty, huh?"

"I guess so."

"It's a gaboon viper. *Bitis gabonica*. From Africa. Two-inch fangs and totally lethal venom. Awesome animal."

"Impressive. Though, I think our rattlers and cottonmouths are enough to deal with, thanks. Tell us what you do, Dr. Wright."

"I'm an ornithologist. I study birds."

"Yes, I know that. What do you do here in the museum, exactly?" she repeated.

"I look at the animal specimens that come in. I lead kids on tours. I'm kind of a community resource, too. People ask me to identify birds that flew into their windows or are in their yard." He shrugged. "I got a call to catch a screech owl that came down a lady's chimney last month. It got soot all over her house. You wouldn't believe the damage that little sucker did!" He snorted with laughter. "Flew through the house knocking over stuff on shelves and tables, then slammed chest first into a wine rack on top of the refrigerator. Ten bottles of Merlot crashed down and broke on her new wood floor. I caught him in the kid's bathroom and set him on the back porch. He flew away and never looked back."

"Exciting times," Monique said.

"Sure was."

"Are you connected with the university?"

"No." He broke eye contact.

"Have you ever worked at a university?"

"No."

"What else do you study?"

"What do you mean?"

She pointed to a framed picture of Bigfoot.

"You study birds."

"And Bigfoot sightings."

"There's more than just them, you know," Monique said. "Natives have many stories about giants."

"You Indian?"

"Yes. Choctaw."

"Your people have a story about them. They call them Shampes." Wright pronounced it as rhyming with lamps.

"Shampes," Monique corrected, pronouncing it Shamp-eh. "You know of them?"

"Of course. That's probably where the Bigfoot legend comes from. At least the Bigfoot from around here. There are Bigfoots all over the country."

"Not Bigfeet?" Chris asked.

"No. They're not like Blackfeet people, Blackfeet Rez, Blackfoot Nation."

"I'll say they're not," Monique said.

Wright cleared his throat. "Uh, well, anyway, some people say they stayed in Mississippi and didn't come west over the removal trail when the Choctaws did." He looked at Monique. "You believe that?"

Monique did not answer.

"See! You don't believe it. You think they're west of the Mississippi. Down in the Kiamichi Mountains, right?"

Monique's eyebrows rose. "Maybe." Like much of the tribal lore she had learned from her relatives, she wasn't sure whether she believed it or not.

"Maybe my ass. There's a group called the Oklahoma Monkey Chasers who record sightings of all kinds of things. Bigfoot is one of them. Your Shampe is tall and hairy, right? Smells bad?"

"So I've been told."

"Hey, people have seen him. I bet someone in your family has, too. Am I right?"

Monique opened her mouth to speak but then shut it.

"Ha! See? I told you. There's a place not far from here where Bigfoot hangs out. It's on a ranch named after a snake. I dunno how to pronounce it. I've always wanted to look in there, but the owner won't let anyone in."

Monique kept her mouth shut. The last thing she wanted right now was for Wright to know that Andrew Tubbee was a friend.

"You believe in UFOs?" Chris asked him.

"Of course. There's no way that we're the only life in this vast universe."

"What's cryptozoology?" Chris asked.

"The study of animals that you don't normally see. We call them cryptids."

THE HATAK WITCHES | 119

"You mean because they're cryptic, hidden?"

"Actually, yes. Mysterious. There are animals out there that the world of science doesn't accept as real."

"Like Bigfoot." Chris said.

"Of course. And other things. Birdmen, dire wolves, giant reptiles, the kraken. There are dinosaurs in South America and Africa, you know. And I got a call this week from a lady who saw the Ozark Howler in the hot tub out on her deck."

Chris started to ask about the Howler, but Monique held up her hand. "Look, Dr. Wright. We need to ask you some questions about the museum." She then posed the same queries she had asked Janice Rice and Bob Shimura. His answers were useful only because they revealed that he knew nothing about who entered the Room of Secrets.

"No, I've never been in there," he answered. "No need for me to go in there. Hell, I don't know why anyone would want to. I don't have a key to that room, anyway. Only Lloyd does."

Monique paused and looked at Wright for a few heartbeats. To give him time to change his mind if he was lying.

"Are there many visitors in this part of the museum? Do other researchers come down here to visit with you?"

He leaned back and laced his fingers on top of his large belly. "I don't get a lot of visitors, no. There aren't all that many of us. Most of the people who come down here want to talk to Lloyd or Janice. They look like anthropologists."

Monique bit her cheek to hide her smile. "And what do anthropologists look like?"

Wright took a few jellybeans from the jar on his desk and threw them into his mouth. "Well, now, let's see. Beards—the men, that is—man purses, jeans, T-shirts or cotton shirts with Indian patterns, ponchos, running shoes. The younger ones always look like they're about to go camping."

"Anyone other than anthropologists?"

"Bob is usually putting a dinosaur together or he brings kids and retirees down here on tours of his lab. Janice has people in her office a lot. But I think those people are interested in topics besides Indian stuff."

"How do you know that?"

"She always takes them to the other side of the building where the displays are. I never see her go downstairs or hang around this floor much. Last week some people wanted her to create an exhibit on how the military has changed through the years. You know, anal patriotic types who collect war memorabilia and participate in Civil War reenactments."

"No one else then? No one unusual? No one has caught your attention?"

Wright burped and stroked his chin. "Uh, there were some Indians here about two months ago."

"Indians? How do you know they were Indians?"

Clarence looked at her oddly. "Um, they looked like Indians?" It was Monique's experience that most people thought Indians had long braids and wore feathers and paint. And lived only in the past—dead and buried. Or in the case of this museum, dead and unburied.

"Were they scholars?"

Clarence laughed. "Doubtful."

"Why do you say that?"

"They didn't dress like academics. They had long hair, one guy had braids, one carried a feather fan, and were pissed off about something."

"Pissed off?"

"Look, I didn't hear what was said. I just heard them at the end of the hall yelling at Lloyd. And Lloyd yelled back. They were mad."

"How many were there?"

"Seven. Maybe eight. One woman had really long hair—down to the back of her knees."

"Had you seen them here before?"

"Not them. Course, it's not the first time angry Indians have been here. Until Lloyd took skulls and some masks off display, they used to come in pretty regularly to protest."

"I remember a protest twenty years ago about a Ghost Dance shirt and an Iroquois False Face mask," Monique said.

"That was a biggie, I hear. Before my time." He snorted. "The museum may have acquiesced and removed them from display, but they're still hidden around here someplace."

"Maybe we're sitting just a room away from sacred items?" Chris offered.

"Probably," Wright agreed.

"What were they protesting this last time?" Monique asked.

He shrugged. "Don't know. There isn't anything offensive on display right now that I know about. If there were, Lloyd would be strategizing about how to make the Indians happy." He chuckled at that.

"What's funny?"

"Lloyd always goes berserk when he has to deal with Indians. He thinks they're a pain in the ass and that they should leave their remains to science. You a body donor?"

Monique's nostrils flared. Chris quickly jumped in. "Do you socialize with Lloyd or Janice?"

Wright seemed oblivious to Monique's posture. "Nope. Never. I see them throughout the day, depending on who's walking past my office or who's in the lounge at the same time I am. Sometimes I don't see them at all because they're in a lab or Janice is working on an exhibit."

Monique fumed, but she knew it would not serve a purpose to argue with him. Her shoulders slumped as she realized the difficulty of finding the people that Wright mentioned.

"We need better descriptions of these people." She took out her note-pad and started flinging questions at Wright, who fidgeted through half an hour of questioning about the appearance of the mystery protestors. And at the end of the hour she had little more than his original descrip-tion of them. Some people have no eye for details.

"Here's my card in case you think of anything else," Monique said.

"Yeah, okay. And here's mine." He winked. "Call anytime."

She could not imagine why she would need to call Dr. Clarence Wright, but she took his card anyway.

14

"Why didn't Adams tell us about those protesters?" Chris asked as they marched toward the lounge. "That's something he should have mentioned right away."

"He's hiding something," Monique said. "Otherwise he would have told us."

Chris knocked twice on Lloyd Adams's door and opened it without waiting for an answer. Adams appeared disappointed to see the detectives. Some classical music gently wafted through his room. The computer screen showed he was looking at Facebook. Adams's office had already been searched, and he was waiting for Monique to tell him to leave.

Instead of telling him he was free to go, Monique came at him with an angry question. "You had an encounter with some Natives in the past few months," she said. "What was that about?"

He looked surprised.

"Clarence told us," Chris added.

Adams looked distinctly uncomfortable. "Yes, I had forgotten about that."

"You forgot about a dozen pissed-off Indians yelling at you?" Chris asked.

Adams shrugged again, clearly stalling for time. "I don't think there were a dozen of them."

"Let's see what you can remember. Tell us about it," Monique said. "What did they want?"

"Nothing unusual. It happens fairly often. There were some displays they didn't like. Three skulls, which I explained were plastic. They also wanted a Ghost Dance shirt and a False Face mask from one of the displays. One man said the mask belonged to his people. One of the others said the shirt belonged with his tribe. So I gave them up." He looked longingly at the briefcase and hat on his desk. He sounded tired.

"You handed them over just like that?" Monique asked. "Did you verify their identities? How did you know the mask and shirt belonged to them?"

"I just knew."

"So they took the shirt and mask and left? That was the end of it?"

"Yes. That was the end of it. I haven't seen them since."

"You at least have their names, right?"

"Yes, of course."

"Let's have them."

"The list is on my computer."

Monique motioned for him to proceed.

Adams clicked the keyboard while Chris and Monique waited in silence. The printer whirred. He stood and handed two pages to Monique without meeting her eyes. "Here."

Monique read the first page. "Edwin Left Hand. Ginger Wastannee. Lin Short Horn. Bryan Smith. Billy Longhair. Jake Lynx. No tribes listed. No addresses."

Adams shrugged. "That's all I have."

"Sit down," she ordered. Adams sat while Chris and Monique stood. "There is something mighty odd about this, Dr. Adams." She held the papers up and crumpled them a bit to make her point. "You gave some Indians who you didn't even positively identify some items from the museum? Is this policy? NAGPRA requires paperwork. Investigation."

"Yes, yes, I know all that," he said with irritation.

"You just handed over a False Face mask and a Ghost Dance shirt?" She was almost yelling. "What about museum policies? Did your Board of Trustees approve this? These people could have turned around and sold them to someone else. Natives do that, you know."

Chris looked at her, alarmed at her tone and even more surprised that she admitted Indians might do that sort of thing.

She continued. "And why were they on display? I thought you removed those items decades ago."

Adams looked very nervous now. "Some influential patrons requested they be put back," he whined. "The museum board approved."

Monique stared. "The museum board?"

"Yes. The board okayed the displays."

"Why did you not mention this? We're looking for murder suspects—people who stole relics from the archives—and you didn't think this might be important?"

Adams rocked back and forth in his chair. "Look. Those Indians—they were forceful."

"Forceful how? Did they threaten you?"

"They always threaten."

"Always?"

"Every time they've been here, they've threatened me."

"How many times have they been here?"

"Four times that I remember."

"What did they say?"

"Nothing."

"They said nothing," she repeated after him. "But they also threatened?"

"They showed me."

"Showed you what?"

"They had . . . power. Well, one did. One of them touched my shoulder, and I fell against the wall."

"Touched you how? Pushed you, you mean?"

"Just touched me."

Monique sighed. "Explain."

"One touched me with a fan. A feather fan."

"A man touched you with a feather fan, and you fell?" Chris asked, clearly perplexed.

"That's exactly what happened. Except it wasn't a man. It was a woman."

"This Ginger . . ." Monique looked at the paper again, "Wastannee?"

"That's what she said her name was."

"What did she look like?"

"Hard to describe. Young and old both. That is to say, she could have been thirty-three or sixty-three. No lines on her face, but her eyes looked old."

Monique let him talk instead of prompting. It would have been easy for her to suggest brown eyes, dark hair, and dark skin, but not all Natives are dark-skinned, and not all of them have brown eyes or black hair.

"I remember her eyes best. They were dark. Her hair was brown, not black, and it was really long. Her skin was kind of tan. Not dark. You know?"

She shrugged. "What did the others look like?"

"One of the men was dark and had a scar across his cheek." He made a motion across his right cheekbone. "Another was short and had a small nose. Another was my height with short black hair and crooked teeth. The all looked rugged and mad. They might be on the video."

The pounding in her temple stopped for a few seconds. "From the camera outside the Room, you mean?"

"I have six months' worth. It should be in there." He twirled in his chair and opened the cabinet. "Let's see." He rummaged through the top layer and set a neat stack on the floor. He looked through the second tier while Monique drummed her fingers on his desk. "This might be it," he held up a small plastic case. "Here it is—August 14. It was right before the museum closed. I had just turned on the recorder and those Indians demanded to see me."

"That's pretty specific," Monique said. Adams did not look at her. "Let's see," Monique ordered.

Adams pressed play, and they hit pay dirt. The three watched as Adams stood by the Room of Secrets door and several others, obviously Natives, walked in and out of the frame. One man approached Adams, then moved nose to nose with him and began yelling. He had straight, shoulder-length hair and wore a T-shirt. Since the film was black-and-white, it was impossible to tell what color.

"Who's that?"

"The Iroquois. He wanted the mask."

"What tribe? Mohawk? Onondaga? Oneida? Tuscarora? Seneca?"

Lloyd shrugged.

"Never mind. What did he say?"

"The usual. That I had no right to keep things that belong to others. That the mask is sacred, and the tribe needed it for ceremonies. The other man said pretty much the same thing. The Ghost Dance shirt was needed within the week for some ceremonial observance. Or something to that effect."

On the tape, another man, shorter and rounder, stepped next to the tall one. His hair was cut short, and he wore a triple-strand necklace of dentalium shells.

"My kingdom for audio," said Chris.

Then all three men moved out of the frame, and the three viewers were left with only the Room door again.

"Speed up," she said.

There was nothing else for ten minutes.

"That's it," Lloyd said.

"This information, here, in this file, is all you have on them, correct?"

"Yes."

"Did they sign anything?"

Adams paused a moment. "Yes. The woman did. Janice has it."

"Janice has it?" Monique nodded to Chris, who quickly left the room for Dr. Rice's office. "Did anyone else see these people?"

"Janice did. She got the mask for them after I told her to."

Monique rubbed her temples. How could Rice not have mentioned handing over the Ghost Dance shirt and False Face mask? If these Natives were guilty of murder and assault, then Janice was in trouble.

"Janice just went up and took the items off display, and you handed them over? I cannot believe you did that."

Adams closed his eyes and took a deep breath. Monique thought he might jump up and bolt out the door.

Chris came back in and shook his head. "She's gone. Office is locked."

"You have a key?" Monique asked Adams.

Adams's shoulders slumped. "Yes." He rummaged in his top desk drawer, pulled out a wad of bronze and silver keys, and separated a silver key from the rest.

"Open her office for us."

Monique and Chris were breathing down Adams's neck as he opened Dr. Rice's office door. Adams stepped back, and Monique gave him the sort of subtle smile one sees prior to a crocodile strike. Monique stepped into the room and turned on the light. There were two metal filing cabinets against the wall, both with the lock buttons pushed in. "The keys will probably be in the desk," Chris said.

"Thanks," Monique said to Adams without looking at him. "You can wait in your office." Looking dejected and a bit frightened, Adams turned to go.

Chris found two small keys in the back of the top drawer. He tried the smaller cabinet and pulled out the top drawer. "Lots of files," he said.

The file they needed was in the back of the second drawer. The folder tab was clearly labeled "Repatriated Items." The rest of the drawer held files labeled for exhibits: "Cowgirls of Oklahoma," "Samurai," "1884 Classroom," "1890 Dentist's Office," "Surgical Instruments," "Cowboy's Campsite," and so forth.

Monique scanned through the forty or so pages until she found what she wanted: a page that listed one Seneca False Face mask and one Hunkpapa Ghost Dance shirt. The signature at the bottom was in elegant cursive handwriting. "And lo and behold, she lives in Norman." Monique handed the file to Chris. "We need to profile Wastannee."

"What's wrong?" Chris asked.

"Why?"

"You have that look."

"What look is that?"

"The look like your brain is about to overheat."

"I'm thinking that we might be dealing with a powerful woman. Traditionally, Iroquois women had important social, political, religious, and economic roles. It makes sense that an Iroquois woman would try and get them back."

"Is this Ginger Iroquois?"

"Wastannee doesn't sound Iroquois. But it could be a married name. I think it's Navajo, but hell, I don't know. Maybe she's Plains. She could be Southeastern and married into that name. I'm not sure about women's traditional roles among Northern Plains tribes or Nevada Paiutes who were more active with the Ghost Dance. Activists often stick together even if they aren't from the same group. As I said before, most spiritual leaders, female and male, are good, righteous people—but not all. Others were and are mean spirited."

"So you think these people came back and killed the guard?"

"All I can say is that wanting remains back is not bad or evil—unless they killed to get them. It's a real possibility that whoever killed the guard and wounded the other did so in order to take remains that they believed rightfully belonged to them."

"But they got what they asked for two months ago. Why come back and kill now?"

"Maybe there's more that they wanted in here and Adams turned them down. Or maybe Adams gave them the key to the Room and then tampered with the video. Hell, I'm beginning to see the possibilities. He's an anthropologist—maybe he wanted bones that he was afraid might be repatriated."

"But what good would it do to horde bones if a scholar has to reveal the source of their research?" Chris countered. "Would a person who would steal bones to keep them from Natives do so for personal and not professional reasons?"

"It's also possible that the descendant of a non-Native collector wanted the items back in the family. Those sorts of people exist, Chris. Many collectors keep Indian skulls and other bones on their mantles as a sign of their superiority over the heathens the Euroamericans conquered in the name of Christianity and democracy."

"A bone collector?"

"One kind."

"He wouldn't have had time to mess with the video," Chris said, "unless he got there earlier than Lester Martin did. But this makes me wonder about Rice," Chris said. "What if she wanted to help repatriate the remains and tried to take bones from the Room, got caught, and killed the guard?"

"Unlikely."

"Why?"

"Because whoever came to steal also brought a weapon. And scalped and stripped the guard. I don't think Rice is capable of that."

"So what's left?"

"The most likely scenario is that a Native, or group of Natives, wanted their ancestors back and took action to get them. Stealing would be logical. I might attempt it if I knew for certain that my ancestors were in a museum."

"You would do that?"

"Within limits, Chris. I believe all remains should be returned to their tribes for proper and respectable internment, but it would be absolutely wrong to kill to get them."

"Someone disagreed."

And not knowing who did accounted for the sick feeling growing in Monique's mind and body.

15

The officers searching the building had not returned from their break and first floor search by the time Monique and Chris had finished in Janice Rice's office.

"They sure are taking their time," Chris said.

"Every nook and cranny," Monique answered. "By this run-through, Weiser and Blount know to look into every corner and behind every fossil and geode." She smiled as she pictured one of them standing on the other's shoulders to look into the mouth of the whale suspended from wires in the Hall of Oceans.

Rachel and Louie were still looking for fingerprints when Chris and Monique got back to the Room. They had made it through two of the aisles, dusting the metal shelves and boxes as they went.

"How're you doing?" Monique called out.

"Living the nightmare," Rachel answered from somewhere out of sight.

"Nothing worth writing home about," Louie told her. "In fact, nothing at all. Every one of these boxes, at least to six feet off the ground, is covered in undisturbed dust. No prints at all. Not even mouse tracks."

"Any blood drops or splatters that might indicate where the guard's clothing is?"

"Zilch so far."

Rachel came from around the corner of the first aisle. She carried a bottle of water and drained the last of it. "I need more water," she said hoarsely. Her hair, eyebrows, eyelashes, and shoulders were covered in dust. "This fine shit is stuck in my throat."

"I'll get it," Chris offered, grabbing her bottle so quickly that she had no time to reply.

"He's certainly eager to help," Monique said as she watched him hurry out the door.

"And cute, too," Rachel replied.

"Then do something about it. He blushes every time you talk to him."

"Maybe I will."

"He likes pizza. So, did you find anything at all?"

"Nope. But if someone really got in here without using that door, we'll find out how. We've checked all the obvious places thoroughly—the door, the floor around the victim, the filing cabinets, the light switch. The only prints other than ours belong to Lloyd Adams—and even those are covered in thin dust—and Chris's partial because he turned on the light. We'll continue to go down the aisles. Then we'll go up the walls."

"Take a break outside," Monique told her. "This isn't a place to stay all day if you can help it."

"Don't I know it? Monique, you're aware that we're going to have to look in every one of these boxes?"

Monique winced. "I've been trying not to think about it." She already felt mentally fatigued, and this would be a tedious and onerous task. "We need to find those clothes."

"I'll ask Linda," Rachel said.

"We'll be upstairs. Call me right away if you find something. And keep this door closed until one of the officers can come down here to provide extra security. We don't know if the perps have left the building. Most likely they have, but we can't be sure."

"I'm carrying," Louie raised his shirt to reveal a .38 revolver in a holster.

"Good idea."

"Darn right."

Rachel turned her back to Monique. She also lifted her shirt to show her a small snub-nose pistol cradled in a small waist holster.

As Rachel started to close the door, Monique remembered the dropped call from Robbie that morning. "Wait. Call me and make sure the phone works."

Rachel dialed and waited a few seconds. No ring came through on Monique's phone.

"Shit," Monique said. "You have to be standing at least in the doorway."

"We'll be fine," Rachel said. "Don't worry."

"I know you will. I'm just concerned that there's some entrance we haven't found."

"I can handle it," Louie said.

"Me too," Rachel added.

"If you say so," Monique answered. "Remember, Rachel, you have to get close to the target to be effective with that pea popper."

"Yes, ma'am."

Monique gave her colleagues an encouraging smile as she closed the door. "Come on, Chris, let's see what's happening upstairs."

Lester Martin was coming around the corner of the "Cowgirls" exhibit when they entered the foyer. He was sweaty. "I looked everyplace again. All the classrooms, the labs, the closets. I opened the restrooms, looked, then locked them. I guess it's possible that someone could be hiding in the building, but I just don't know where. No place obvious."

Monique nodded. "Thanks, Mr. Martin. I agree. I'd like you to go down to the crime scene now. The forensic investigators are still in there. The door is locked, but they can get out if they need to. They're armed, but I want someone else down there so they aren't alone."

"I'm on it," Martin said and trotted toward the stairs. Monique wondered about his energy reserves. This had been a very long and difficult day for him. "Mr. Martin," she called after him. "Drink some juice or something else with sugar."

He gave her a thumbs-up.

Monique called Weiser and asked that he and Blount walk the outside perimeter of the building. Then she called Linda. "Where are you?"

"By the old cameras exhibit. Taz hasn't picked up the scent of anything, although she perked up by the stuffed chimps. They must smell pretty funky."

"Keep on, then."

They headed back to Adams's office to gather him for a look at the downstairs archive and labs.

"I'm getting to know this place," Chris said.

"Just like the good old days," Monique agreed. She was tired, hungry, and frustrated. The Mango Loco Monster Juice, water, and Ibuprofen in her stomach made an unpleasant combination. Even a few bites of an apple would sooth the burn in her guts.

As they reached Lloyd Adams's office yet again, Chris looked at his Fitbit. "Hey, 3.2 miles. And all inside this place, other than the walk from the parking lot."

Adams led them downstairs to a drab hallway that reminded Monique of a hospital corridor, with four heavy wooden doors, two on each side, and blank walls between them.

The battered old door he led them to at the end of the passage bore no identifying marks. Adams flipped through his keys to find the ones for the two locks on the thick door. After the second lock opened, he turned the knob. "Your officers left the lights on."

"What's in those other rooms?" Chris asked.

"The one next to this is an adjoining lab. The room directly across the hall is a library. That other has old computer equipment, museum pictures we took down years ago, extra tools. Things like that. This is my lab."

Monique hung back a bit, not eager to walk into yet another room of death. She felt the air blow out of this archive just as it had from the Room.

Chris went in first and stood with his hands on his hips as he looked around. "What's that?" he asked immediately.

Monique took a deep breath, walked in, and wondered the same thing. In the middle of the open space in front of the shelves of boxes was a table not unlike those she'd seen at the morgue. On top of a blue sheet was a skeleton, the bones old, dry, and yellow.

"It's a skeleton," Adams said.

"I know that," Chris said. "Guess I should have said *who's* that?"

Adams walked over, put his hand on a humerus, and ran his index finger down the length of the arm bone in an affectionate caress. Monique shivered.

"This is a female, probably Nez Perce." He touched a spot on the articulated skull. "I'm convinced that she died from this fracture to her jaw. See how the mandible was broken then healed crookedly? Her bottom and top teeth don't touch. She couldn't chew and probably starved to death."

Adams caught Monique's look. "You noticed that I put a blue cloth under her? I did that out of respect. I do that with all of them. And there's some sage right here." He held up a bunch of dried gray sage lying next to the bones.

Monique started laughing.

"What's funny?"

"You attempting to placate Natives so you can proceed with . . . this."

"Look, Detective. I'm not desecrating anything. I'm studying her for the good of mankind." Adams pulled another blue sheet over the skeleton, then smoothed the material.

Monique watched his every move. *Like a cat stalking a mouse*, Chris thought.

"So, Dr. Adams," Monique said. "This might be a Nez Perce woman. She broke her jaw and died because she couldn't eat. Great work. Humankind will benefit enormously from that knowledge. Who else you got in here?"

Adams peered at her over his bifocals. "The catalogue is over there in that filing cabinet," he answered quietly. He motioned to the cabinet that looked identical to the old one in the Room of Secrets.

"And is this the only entry into this particular room?"

"Yes. It's just like the room upstairs. Except the vents are underneath the floor."

She walked around the spacious area. The anthropology lab was about one-third the size of the Room and had about one-tenth the number of boxes. After Monique made the circuit she came back to the skeleton and Dr. Adams.

"Why are there fewer boxes in here?"

"These are remains that have been identified. They're new deliveries." He did not meet her gaze.

"But if you know who they belong to, as you seem to, then why aren't they back with their tribes?"

"They will be. We're in the process of notifying tribes, and they'll be shipped as soon as we have the resources to do so."

"But until that time you're looking at them?"

Adams shrugged. "Well, no. Just her." He motioned to the shrouded skeleton.

She shut her eyes and ground her molars. Judging from the lightning pain in her jaw, the back one was cracked and about to blow. At the rate she was cracking teeth, she might as well make an appointment for another three root canals.

"Okay. Let's see the other archive, please. No wonder you have two locks," Monique added as Adams locked the door behind them. "This is the place where you stash the goods."

He did not respond.

Adams used a key to open the metal door to the adjoining lab. This space was smaller than the first two, but the air was no less oppressive. A large table supported one small broken pot.

"And that pot is?" Monique asked.

"It was buried with an Arikara boy."

"Swell. Dare I ask if you have him?"

"He's in the lab. Under the other blue sheet."

"I see." Monique clenched her fists and stared at the floor until she could control herself. "What else is in here?"

"Mainly cultural items. Pots, bags, clothes. No bones."

Monique knew that he could pretend that the absence of bones made it okay, but many of these things would have been taken from burials and were sacred to the tribe who owned them.

"And what about another door?"

"Just this entry and the one in the hall. I never use that one."

"And there are alarms for both rooms?"

"Yes. If someone came in, the guards would have known it."

"Looks like the only thing they wanted was in the Room upstairs," Chris said.

"Apparently," Monique agreed. "And they knew it was there."

"I'm getting a headache," Chris said.

"It must be contagious."

"Let's get out of here for a while."

"You okay?" Chris asked Monique as they walked down the corridor to the vending machines in the Courtyard Café. Through the window they saw the peacock, tail feathers splayed, strutting in his enclosure.

"Fine. Just fine."

"You almost lost it in there."

"I did not." Monique fished around in her pocket for change, did not have enough, and instead used two bills to buy a Sprite. She opened the bottle and gulped half of it. She coughed as the carbonation went up her nose. "Here's some change. What do you want?"

"I have some quarters." Chris chose a guava Rockstar energy drink from the neighboring machine.

"Yuck," Monique said. "I had a Monster Juice earlier. Damn near killed me."

"Try a Red Bull."

"I tried a Diet Red Bull once. It tasted like cold urine, and I spit it out."

"You do know there's no caffeine in that Sprite, right?"

"I don't need any at this point. Look, Chris, that poor woman who lived a very long time ago clearly died a painful, horrible death. But how is knowing that going to help her descendants solve the problems they're dealing with right this minute? That woman was buried with good intentions by her tribe, and now she's an object on an anthropologist's table. The kind of obvious information Adams comes up with is good for an anthropologist's career, maybe, if he or she is applying for grants or is up for tenure."

"I understand that. But Adams wouldn't kill that guard to get tenure, or anything else."

Monique swallowed the remainder of her Sprite and belched. She pitied the swaggering peacock that had only prairie dogs and owls to observe him. "I don't think he killed that guard either," she said as she crushed her can and tossed it into the bin. "Let's go tell him he can leave."

The yellow tape draped across the doors on the outside fluttered in the afternoon breeze. Although black-lettered signs informed museumgoers that the museum was closed for the day, a dozen people hung around waiting for something to happen. Inevitably, a television crew was waiting for someone in authority to make a statement.

"Monique Blue Hawk!" a woman yelled. Monique sighed. Darcy McKnight from Channel 4 News was known to be relentless in getting information. She presented her newscasts with wide-eyed enthusiasm, as if every story was as exciting and tragic as a plane crash.

"Hell, it's Darcy," Monique muttered. She would never understand how anyone could get excited about disasters. Darcy hovered around accidents and misfortunes like the Angel of Death.

"Can we have a statement, please?" Darcy asked. Her heavily sprayed blonde hair remained perfectly still in the stiff breeze blowing across the parking lot. "Is it true that there was a murder in the museum this morning? And another guard was seriously injured?"

"How does she know that?" Chris asked, quietly.

"Oh, she has ways," Monique answered. "Let me do this."

They walked to where Darcy stood, her fake smile revealing teeth that looked like symmetrical Chiclets. Monique flinched when Darcy stuck the microphone an inch from her mouth.

"Go ahead," Darcy said with her huge smile. "What can you tell us, Detective Blue Hawk?" The afternoon sun was bright, but the camera operator's assistant aimed a spotlight at Monique's face anyway.

Monique forced herself to ignore the pain in her head and jaw as she composed her thoughts. "This morning one individual was found injured and one dead in the museum. Their identities will remain confidential until the next of kin are notified. The museum will remain closed the rest of the day while investigators work. That is all I can tell you at this time. Thank you."

Darcy looked disappointed. "Are the victims security guards?" she asked hopefully.

"That information is confidential right now, Darcy. You know what that means."

"And didn't one of the guards have his throat cut?" she asked breathlessly.

"That's all for now." Monique turned so she and Chris could hightail it to their cars.

"Geez. What a vulture," he said as they scurried across the lot.

"Really? I hadn't noticed." She looked toward the street and saw Channels 6 and 11 careening around the corner. "Quick. Get in my car before they catch us. Let's go get some lunch. I'll bring you back after they're gone."

Once they were safely inside, Chris spoke up. "Something I've been meaning to ask: what's a Ghost Dance shirt?"

"The Ghost Dance started on the northern plains in the 1880s," she told him. "A Paiute named Wovoka claimed that God spoke to him and told him that if believers danced, chanted, and prayed in a certain way the whites would disappear, the buffalo would return, and the dead Indians who had fallen would return to life. Some of the dancers wore shirts that they believed were bulletproof—the Ghost Dance shirts. That's the short version. Anyway, the dance didn't help Big Foot's band at Wounded Knee."

"You mean, as in 'Bury My Heart at Wounded Knee'?"

"Same place. Ghost Dancers wore the shirts."

"Why would they think that dancing would solve their problems?"

"They didn't just dance. They prayed. Just like most people pray today when they want something good to happen or they're afraid something bad might. When they were faced with losing their lives, their land, their culture—hell, with losing everything—they turned to what they thought would save them."

"Religion."

"Yes. Religious movements have popped up throughout Native history. Handsome Lake, Kenekuk the Kickapoo Prophet, Tenskwatawa the Shawnee Prophet. They all said pretty much the same thing. That if the people behaved a certain way, danced and prayed in a set pattern, then life would become as it used to be before the invasion."

"That sounds a bit simplistic."

"No. The Shawnee Prophet said that the Shawnees had to give up all things brought by the Europeans. A lot of the people didn't like that idea since they'd become used to needles and thread, knives, and other metal things. Plus guns and whiskey. Why give up the good things that made your life easier or more pleasant? Of course, dependency on these things was a curse in itself."

"How can knives, clothes, and guns have been a curse?"

"In order to get them the Natives had to have something to the white people wanted—something to trade. Tribes started competing with each other, fighting and sometimes making a mess of the environment. In the Northeast tribes sided with the French or the British, depending who was in power, and they fought with each other for the Europeans' favors. In the Southeast, Choctaws hunted white-tailed deer almost to extinction to get deer hides to trade."

"Do tribes still dance the Ghost Dance? Is that why those Indians wanted the shirt?"

"Probably in some places they do. They don't advertise it, that's for sure. People who do this dance are traditionalists with high hopes that their world will change. A lot of Natives want to believe that bison will return and things will become as they once were."

"So, what you're saying is that if the Ghost Dancers are successful, then all the white people would have to go someplace else."

"That's right."

"Ummm..."

The other two news vans made a beeline for the detectives.

"Let's eat. Chris, I wouldn't worry about the Ghost Dance. You're not going anyplace."

16

Monique and Chris stopped at Subway for sandwiches on their way to the office to decide on their next move. Chris went to make a few calls while he ate. Monique just wanted to sit at her desk for a few undisturbed minutes, shoes and jacket off. For the third time that day, she considered removing her vest, anticipating how wonderful a deep, unconstricted breath would feel. She left it on.

Monique's little office looked more like a cubicle with a lid than a proper workspace, but she liked it because it had a window. She could look outside at the big black jack oak and the squirrels and nesting birds that made it their home. Unlike Drs. Rice and Shimura and their carefully planned office décor, Monique preferred to add and subtract objects as the mood hit her.

Just last week she'd brought in a ficus tree to put in the corner to replace the Norfolk pine that she took home and planted in her front yard because it was getting too big. She hung a satellite photo of the Grand Canyon in place of the one of Saint Mary Lake at Glacier National Park. Pictures of Steve and Robbie came and went with the seasons, as did the small lamps she bought at Target. Colorful linen runners covered the tacky metal desk and filing cabinet, and a multicolored rag rug brightened the depressing green-and-white linoleum floor. The humming mini-fridge that she bought on sale at Walmart held a dozen drinks, six or so yogurts, and a few mozzarella sticks.

A knock on the door sounded, and she looked up to see Dan Pickles, an older officer with gray hair and a heavy brace from his left hip to his foot. She winced every time she looked at it. Pickles had split his patella two weeks ago at Lake Texoma when he jumped in to SCUBA dive and hit a rock outcrop. He was on desk duty while he healed. Whether he liked it or not was hard to tell since he was always smiling.

"Afternoon, Monique," he said in his usual cheerful voice. "You got a call."

"Thanks, Dan. Who?"

"Your cousin Dustin."

Dustin was probably wondering if Robbie planned to come trick-or-treating this year. It had become something of a family tradition. Dustin and his wife, Benda, lived in a tidy neighborhood where everyone decorated for Halloween. A few families took it too far every year. She'd seen a decapitated Barbie head cemetery in one front yard and a full-blown *Night of the Living Dead* scene with bloody and deformed mannequins in another. Every year, horrified parents complained about the fake intestines and splattered brains, but that only emboldened the families to take things to the next level. Last year there were vampire babies and torture racks. Monique was curious to see what grossness they had planned for this year. The important thing was that kids could always count on entirely too much candy. Dustin and Benda always asked if Robbie could come visit their youngest daughter, Ever. Thinking of Benda and Ever always brought to mind the family joke that Ever had stolen Benda's *r*.

"He sounds excited," Dan said. "It's the third time he's called today."

"Excited happy or excited upset?"

"Excited scared, I'd say."

That sounded intriguing. Dustin was a big, loud guy who hunted, cut down his own trees, and regularly pounded the heavy bag set up in his garage. What could have him spooked? "What line?"

"Four."

"Thanks," she said and pressed the button. "Dustin?" She rummaged in her top desk drawer for an Ibuprofen.

"Monique?" he answered loudly and quickly.

"It's me, Dust. What's up?"

"I was in the hollow last night, Moni. Me and Zach."

"Ah. The Hollow of Horrors. Haven't been there since you made me sit in a tree stand with you all night to listen to Nature's creatures. You were hoping I'd get scared and cry," she teased, "but as I recall, you were the one who cried." That had been about thirty years ago. It was a dare, actually. Dustin had said that women can't handle being in scary places, so she'd challenged him to go with her and stay overnight in a tree stand. He'd started backpedaling after he realized Monique wasn't going to back down.

They had arrived at Andrew's allotment at dusk, and by dark they were sitting uncomfortably in two tree stands chained to twin cottonwoods. The screaming began as the last of the light faded away. Bullfrogs with voices like bellows started it, then a large cat shrieked and a pig squealed, a very strange sound, deep and rolling. The noise grew so loud Monique almost screamed from the pain and fear. Only her determination to out-last Dustin had kept her from running. After twenty minutes it faded away. It was a terrifying night that made no sense to her. She had not seen a bullfrog in the creeks and streams during the day and wondered where they hid. Then she thought about the big cats and giant pigs as she and Dustin rushed out through the muck and mire. She'd been so scared that she crawled into bed with her parents that night.

"Zach got a twelve-point buck," Dustin told her.

"Great," she said, wondering what was so scary about that.

"I'd hoped to get out of the hollow sooner, but it got dark before we found him. And when we did, he was all mangled, Moni. I've never seen anything like it." He breathed hard and swigged some liquid that, knowing Dustin, was probably Pearl Beer.

"Did it fall on something? Did a limb fall on it?"

"No. Something or someone bad ripped it up. Deliberately. Its antlers and one of its eyes were gone."

"Something bad," she repeated. "There's a lot of bad somethings in the hollow." She took a large bite of her sandwich.

"Yeah. Moni, listen. There were owls there. At least two big ones, and—"

"Owls?"

"Yes. Great big ones."

"You mean big like great horned owls?"

"Bigger. And one had yellow eyes. And I mean *yellow.*"

Monique knew where he was headed. Dustin believed there were boo-giemen and giant owls in the hollow. While many Natives from many tribes believe hearing an owl hoot signifies impending death or another catastrophe, she tried to be rational and assumed that a hoot means the owl is calling another owl. But that did not mean she would ignore the hoot if she heard one. Like many other Natives who have not decided if they believe their tribal stories, she would probably race home to make certain her family was alive.

"Dustin, coyotes could have torn up the deer."

"No. Coyotes can't break joint bones that fast and easy. Besides, there weren't any coyote tracks. And someone sawed off the antlers and cut out the backstrap. Perfectly, like a surgeon."

She watched the pigeons through the window as she thought about that. She heard their muffled coos as they unloaded their droppings on the tree and on her windowsill. White splatters dotted the ground and branches. "What did Zach hit the deer with?"

"An arrow directly into the heart and both lungs. A truly great shot." He paused. "Monique, I know we didn't tear it up. And I'm pretty sure that a pig didn't either. And there were owl feathers on the buck's head.

Andrew went out there this morning to retrieve Zach's bow, and he didn't
see pig tracks anywhere near it. But that's not why I called you."

Monique knew by now that he wasn't calling to invite her to Oktoberfest.

"A flock of owls attacked us. We ran into the trees, and they went away,
but my God, it was a nightmare. Zach's scared to death." More slurping.
"Owls, Monique. Huge ones. And something tore up that deer."

She looked out the window again. A strong gust of wind rustled the
dying leaves on the oak. Some blew off the small branches and floated
away.

"Andrew brought back the owl feathers."

"You brought back owl feathers into your house? Are you nuts? Why
not just pray for bad luck?"

"We called Leroy to come over. He's gonna look into all this. And I
was thinking maybe someone at the museum could identify the feathers.
You know. To make sure."

"Good idea."

"Can you come, too? I mean, Zach will really appreciate it."

"I'll talk to Leroy. Don't worry."

"They tore it up, Monique. Something is wrong."

"Dustin, I—"

"You need to get here."

Chris walked in just as she said good-bye and put the phone down.

"Ethan Lewis is out of surgery and in intensive care," he told her.
"Also got Ginger Wastannee's address. South Edmond. Not too far."

She continued to watch the swaying branches.

"Monique? You okay?"

"Great."

"Long day."

Monique took another giant bite of her revitalizing sandwich—her
favorite turkey, cheese, lettuce, tomato, olive, jalapeño, mustard, and oil
and vinegar, sprinkled with oregano—then wiped her mouth and stood.
"And it's a long way from being over. Let's go."

17

The detectives drove twenty-five minutes through heavy traffic to Ginger Wastannee's house in south Edmond.

"You think she did it?" Chris asked during the drive.

"It's possible. Activists can mean well and act right, or they can have bad attitudes and try to make a point by behaving badly."

Chris stopped his car in front of the Wastannees' mailbox. The house was on a quiet street with sidewalks. Ginger had landscaped with thought. Fruit trees now losing their leaves lined the sides of her house, and tall pecan trees in the backyard towered over her roof. Oval flowerbeds surrounded the tree trunks. Birdhouses and chimes hung from the branches. Ceramic planters in the front were full of colorful kale and chard.

Monique and Chris got out of the car and walked up the sidewalk, which was lined with path lights that probably looked nice at night but would make for a tough edging and mowing job. The porch had a swing big enough for two and more wide-mouth urns. Ceramic rabbits placed around the cement planters looked up at the detectives.

Monique rang the doorbell, which sounded loud even outside on the front porch. They waited half a minute before a burly Native man answered. He looked like a bouncer. He had very thick, long curly hair, which was tied back in a high ponytail. A hearing aid was visible in his right ear, and Monique could see a red-and-black tattoo peeking above the second button of his shirt. His crooked nose meant he had been in at least one fight.

"Hello," Monique said. The two detectives held up their badges. "I'm Detective Blue Hawk, and this is Detective Pierson. We're looking for Ginger Wastannee."

"Yeah, she lives here." He looked from Monique to Chris and back again.

"Good. We need to talk with her."

"What for?"

"It's a police matter, sir," she said politely. Monique was willing to be nice for two minutes, but that was her limit. "Perhaps you could ask her to come to the door so we can talk." She had not gotten to the "otherwise" part yet.

"Just a minute." He shut the door and locked it.

Another sixty seconds ticked by before the door opened again. Ginger stood behind the screen this time. Monique assessed her as she considered how to conduct the interview. She knew that many Natives had been abused by police, or at least their family and friends had been abused, and they wore a perpetually angry look. They were suspicious of most people, law enforcement for sure. They also looked sideways at white people whom they believed were responsible for their problems in the first place. But they reserved their really angry looks for sell-out Indians.

Ginger had that look now. Monique was not a sell-out. A police detective, yes, and proud of it. She was not going to put up with any bullshit this woman might throw at her. Monique stared back at Ginger.

Chris looked from one woman to the other and wondered which would break the impasse first. Monique had sweat on her upper lip that was not there a minute ago.

"Yes?" Ginger asked coolly. Her long, dark hair was mussed, and she wore an oversized flannel shirt and sweatpants. Perhaps she had been sleeping.

"You are Ginger Wastannee?"

She nodded. Monique introduced herself and Chris again.

"What do you want?" Ginger looked back at her companion, whom Monique could see through the screen lying in a recliner. He drank something from a can. She hoped it was not a beer, then scolded herself for stereotyping.

"We understand that you talked with Dr. Lloyd Adams several months ago, and he released a False Face mask and a Ghost Dance shirt to you."

Ginger paused for a count of five. "Yes, he did. It was legal. I have copies of papers I signed."

"I know. I saw the originals."

"So what about it?"

"I want to ask you a few questions."

"Why?"

"I can tell you inside."

"You can tell me outside."

"If you don't want to talk inside your house, then we can talk inside the police station."

Ginger stared at Monique. Chris thought Ginger looked like a hawk on a telephone pole examining its prey.

"All right. Come in," she said.

Ginger opened the door and motioned the detectives into her den. Monique liked it. The room was clean and bright and had artwork on the tables and walls. Pots, carvings, drawings, and sketches dominated, while two wooden credenzas with glass fronts displayed beadwork, small carvings, fetishes, and old photographs. The furniture looked dated and well used, but the place smelled of flowers and meat roasting with garlic and onions. The smell made her mouth water. She hoped Steve would have dinner waiting for her.

"Have a seat." Ginger motioned to a long sofa that faced the television, the same direction the chairs faced.

They sat and Chris took out his notepad.

Monique casually crossed one leg over the other. "Sorry to bother you," she said, making it clear that she really was not.

"Tell me again why you think you need to see me?" Ginger asked.

"As I mentioned, we understand that you had some items repatriated to you from the museum." She paused in case Ginger had a comment. She did not. The man slightly turned his head to listen.

"Records show that you and other Natives visited the anthropological archives several times in the past few years. To have displays removed. And to request some items be repatriated." Monique paused again, and again Ginger said nothing. Neither woman broke her stare at the other. "According to the documents we have, Lloyd Adams gave you some items without going through proper procedure."

"Those items are already with the tribes, and there's no way you can get them back," she said. With that statement, she established her unyielding stance. Then she added, "They belong to those people, not to the museum."

Monique fully expected her to say that and in fact heartily agreed. "I'm not concerned about the repatriated objects."

Ginger's eyes narrowed.

"Then what *are* you concerned about?" the man asked.

"Who are you?" Monique asked him, finally taking her gaze from Ginger.

"Ethanny Puma."

Monique snapped to his name immediately. Ethanny Puma was a well-known Muscogee artist. No wonder the house was full of art. "And you live here?"

"We're married," he said dryly.

"I see. Fine. I know your work." Before he could respond, Monique turned back to Ginger. "What we are interested in is the date of your last visit to the museum."

"What do you want to know for?"

Bad grammar aside, as long as she decided to play tough, then Monique would too.

"All right. We're investigating the murder of a security guard that occurred this morning at the museum. In addition, a second guard was seriously injured."

Ginger's mouth fell open, and she gripped the arms of her chair.

"And there was a theft. The missing items are from the archives that house skeletal remains and possibly sacred cultural objects. The guard was murdered in that room, and the wounded guard was found on the floor in the hallway where you once had an argument with Lloyd Adams. Or I should say, at least once that we know of. We have you on tape."

Ginger's eyes widened. She looked surprised but not guilty. Monique's intuition was pretty good, but still, she knew she could be fooled.

"You said murdered?"

"Yes. Quite horribly. He was completely scalped." She let that settle in for a few seconds. "The items removed from that room were very old and not of value to the anthropologists, although they may have been to some Natives." They weren't sure what had been taken yet, but that seemed like a good bet. She hoped Ginger wouldn't ask for specifics.

Ginger stared at Monique as if she had sprouted another eye in her forehead. The challenge was gone. "What makes you think I had anything to do with this?"

"I just told you."

"Look, I've been in that museum three, four times. The first time was about twenty years ago. I was told that there were skulls on display, and I went to see for myself. Then I met several times with the museum administrators and attended a Board of Trustees meeting one night to talk about why it's offensive for museums to display skulls, even if they're plastic."

"Who went with you?"

"Some members of American Indians Against Desecration. A few other interested skins from the area. We argued our points, and the skulls were removed. So were the Ghost Dance shirt and the mask."

"And then?"

"A couple of months ago I went back because I'd heard the items were back on display. After all this time." She shook her head. "I demanded their removal, and the men with me asserted their tribes' right of ownership."

"So the last time you were there, Lloyd Adams gave you the items." Monique reached into her pocket and took out a folded copy of one page of the file with the names on it.

"Yes."

"Where does Edwin Left Hand live now?"

"Last I heard, Rose Bud. He's campaigning for Tribal Council."

"Lin Short Horn?"

"Pine Ridge."

"Bryan Smith?"

"Akwesasne. There's a water pollution problem."

"Billy Longhair."

"Montana someplace. I have his email address."

"Jake Lynx?"

"Jake's working with Bryan in New York."

"None of these men are in town?"

"Not that I know of. And I would know if they were."

"Anyone else go with you the other times you protested? And that you may not know their whereabouts?"

"Well, Ash Kinley may be in jail. He drinks a lot, and I never was sure where he lived."

"What about you, Mr. Puma? Have you ever been to the museum?"

"Only once. I don't like museums. I just do their art shows."

"Where were you last night and this morning?"

"Wait a second here." He sat up straight and put down his drink. It was a V8. "I think I need a lawyer."

"That's up to you. But you can save the expense if you have an alibi." He leaned back into the recliner. "I was in my studio. Out back."

"And you?" Monique looked at Ginger.

"At work. I go to work in two hours. Night shift."

"And work is?"

"The hospital. I'm a nurse."

Monique's eyebrows shot up then dropped. "And your nation?"

"Assiniboine." She paused a few seconds. "And Cree." The pause meant she primarily identified as being Assiniboine.

Monique tuned back to Puma. "Anyone who can vouch for you being in your studio?"

"UPS dropped off a package at nine o'clock this morning."

"That's too late in the day to be useful."

He looked thoughtful. "Uh, I ordered pizza around eight last night, and I know the delivery guy. He can vouch for me."

"Too early."

"I know!" Ginger said. "I called him at two this morning to remind him to make sure George was in. That should be on my cell phone list."

"Who's George?"

"The cat."

On cue, a large Siamese meowed and strode into the room. She looked at everyone and chose to jump on Chris's lap, picking the one person in the room who was not a cat lover. Chris tentatively patted the purring cat's head.

"The problem with phone calls is that we don't know if Ethanny answered from here."

"Y'all," Ethanny said in a quiet voice with his hands spread out like Jesus addressing the masses. "I had pots in the kiln, and there's no way I leave the property when they're baking."

"Where's the kiln?"

"In the backyard. In the kiln shed. Wanna see?"

"Actually, yes."

Chris stood slowly, and George landed gracefully on the floor. The two detectives followed Ethanny and Ginger through a neat and savory-smelling kitchen. Beautiful watercolors of peppers and other vegetables and fruits covered the walls. Bowls of apples, oranges, bananas, and potatoes sat on the tiled countertop. A large clear cookie jar filled with Fig Newtons reminded Monique that she had not had any in a long time. Next to the Newtons sat a blender and a fancy coffee machine. Loaves of fresh-baked bread and a nice Acoma pot with dried flowers in it sat atop the refrigerator. The atmosphere was homey and warm—a look she'd love to imitate when she had the time and money.

They passed through the laundry room slash mudroom with shelves of boots and wooden racks that held up coats, muffler, and sweaters. More pots and framed sketches adorned the walls along with homemade Christmas ornaments of birds with tiny sprigs of pine needles in their beaks, Santas with full toy bags, and angels with trumpets that might have hung by wire from the ceiling all year long.

The room at the back of the house was clearly an addition. Tables held pots and sculptures, some covered with moist wraps and in the process of taking shape. Sketches leaned against the walls, and shelves bent under the weight of paint and clay supplies. Ethanny had enough supplies in here to open an art store.

"This is where I do my work," he said.

"And the kiln?"

"Out back." He opened the back door and gestured for them to exit.

"Could a neighbor have seen you?" Monique asked Ethanny as they stood on the redwood deck.

"Oh, yeah. Hadn't thought of that. We have a very nosy lady on this side." He motioned to a small gray house next door. Its yard was bare except for drying grass. A small white dog sat on the back porch, looking lonely. "That old busybody looks out the window pretty much full time."

Chris nodded at his partner. That would be easy enough to check out.

Two friendly goats greeted them when they left the deck. The male had long horns that curved backward, long salt-and-pepper-colored hair, and impressive testicles. The brown-and-black female's sides bulged as if she had watermelons in her gut. George ran to the goats and touched noses with both.

"They're little for goats, aren't they?" Chris commented.

"They're pygmies," Ethanny said. "She'll have twins next month."

Monique was not fond of goats. They stank. These didn't seem to smell bad, though. Ginger and Ethanny had fenced off a garden to protect it from the goats, which had eaten every other blade of grass in the yard. Two large pecan trees shaded the rest of the yard. The flagstone sidewalk and brightly painted metal lawn furniture made up for the lack of ground cover.

"The buck had a bath this morning," Ethanny said as if reading Monique's mind.

The goats tagged along behind them to the kiln, which looked like one of the big, round clay ovens that southwestern tribes use to bake bread. It had a door that opened like that of a regular oven. A shingled roof supported by four wooden logs protected it from the rain. Ethanny had built a small tin shed next to the kiln. The doors were open. Rakes, hoes, and the usual yard tools leaned against the walls.

The buck touched Monique's hand with his nose and bleated. She scratched his head, and he seemed satisfied. The doe investigated Chris.

"I keep the wood under here," Ethanny motioned to another door underneath the upper door. Stacks of pine and oak sat next to the fence. "When I have pots baking, I check them often, day or night, depending on when I put them in."

Monique and Chris looked around carefully. Nothing they saw seemed to indicate that the Wastannee or Puma was vicious. Except for seeing a pregnant pygmy goat, Monique found it all unenlightening.

"Ginger, tell me something. How did you really get the mask and shirt removed from the display?"

She shrugged. "Like I said. I asked for them."

"And Dr. Adams gave them up—just like that?"

"Pretty much." She averted her eyes to the blue jay shrieking on the fence.

"You did more than that, Ginger," Monique said quietly. "Chi-ikhana-li."

"What's that?"

"I said I know you."

After a few moments of the kind of eye contact that would send most people running in the opposite direction, Ginger finally asked, "What nation?"

"Chahta. My uncle's an *alikchi*—a doctor. Like you."

She nodded. "My father was a doctor. I'm learning to be one."

"You've done more than learn a little, I'd say."

She nodded again. "No harm was done. You have to understand the importance of those items to my friends."

Monique's face stayed impassive.

"Sorry," Ginger finally said. "You do know."

"Yes, I do. And as I said, right now I'm not interested in your repatriation efforts except for how they might connect with this case. I'm trying to figure out who got into a locked room that has no other entry. The surveillance video shows no one entering besides the guards and only the one injured guard exiting."

"I wouldn't know about that."

"Whoever did it took something from the archive. We believe it was some very old, as yet unidentified bones. In a box in the back of a shelf behind many other old boxes. The perps knew what they wanted and went right to it. No one goes in that room."

A breeze blew strands of hair across Ginger's face. A few pecan leaves flitted to the ground. A goat bleated.

Monique scratched the persistent buck's head as she continued to stare at Ginger. "You got any ideas?"

"Only that I had nothing to do with what happened this morning. I don't do that. The people who went with me would not do that either. You say you don't know what kind of bones were taken?"

"We have only an empty box to go by. We're still searching for information about where and when they were found. We're sure that they are more than a hundred years old."

Monique considered how much to tell Ginger. She rarely told her husband about her cases. But she would wager that this woman would keep
the information to herself.

"It's not a full skeleton. Just uh, parts."

"What else?"

"There is only one way into the room. No one is on video. No tracks
on the dusty floor."

Ginger cocked her head and blinked.

"The guard was scalped. His moustache was taken. His throat was cut."

Ginger looked at the bluejay perched on a low branch. It did not move,
nor did it make a sound. It listened.

"I can think of a few people who want remains," Ginger said.

"Other than the obvious descendants or tribal members?"

"No, it wasn't them."

"Who, then?"

Ginger leaned in and tapped her temple with her forefinger. She whispered, "I think you know."

18

Monique sat in the car and drank a warm tangerine Diet Rite while Chris paid a visit to Ginger and Ethanny's nosy neighbor.

I think you know. What did that mean? What was she supposed to know? Ginger was a special, powerful person who would always know more than she would say. Yet she seemed to think Monique knew the answer. Monique closed her eyes and listened to a squirrel fuss on the branch above her.

As she continued to mull over the connection between murder and bones, the woman in pink curlers, a short-sleeved flowered bathrobe, and green slippers told Chris that yes, she had seen "that Indian" outside working in his shed. She seemed unaware that it was a kiln.

"Always out there, yes, sir." She talked fast in a loud, thready voice like a person with laryngitis who insists on speaking through inflamed vocal cords. "Back and forth, back and forth. Carrying things. He takes things out and leaves them. Carries things into the house."

"And you saw him last night around what time?"

"Eight-ten exactly. Carrying a pizza box and a clay pot on top of it. Then he was at it again at two in the morning, and then around four. Like I said, back and forth."

"Does he make a lot of noise?"

"Nope. Quiet as a mouse. That's what makes me nervous."

"So, you stay up all night and watch him?"

"Well, of course not. I mean, not usually."

"How do you know he's out there if you can't hear him?"

"He has a light that comes on and off."

"I see. Where is your bedroom located in the house, ma'am?"

"Right on the side where I can see him."

"She had her chair in front of the window and binoculars on the side table," Chris told Monique after he returned to the car. "She watches him day and night."

"Is there a husband?"

"Not that I could tell. But she has at least a dozen cats." He shuddered. "Man, the stink in there."

"Lucky for Ethanny he lives next to Gladys Kravitz," Monique said.

"Ha! I'm glad I'm not that lucky."

"I don't think that Puma's a part of this."

"Ginger?"

"Nope. I think she senses something, but she's not going to be any help." Chris yawned loudly. "God I'm tired. What time is it?"

"Eight-thirty. Let's get out of here. We need to call in and see if they found anything at the museum." That meant Chris was supposed to do it. "And while you're at it, get another team in there for the night."

"Anything else you wanna do?" he asked.

"Eat an elk steak. Drink a bottle of wine. Watch a movie and have a massage."

"You don't always have to be literal. I mean on the case."

"Not tonight. I'll go home and think about it. You do the same."

"You know, it's interesting," he said. He looked out the windshield, his eyes focused on something far away, deep in thought.

"What's interesting?" Monique hoped he had thought of something she had not.

"I petted that goat, and my hand doesn't stink."

19

Monique could smell dinner as she rolled down the window and pulled into the garage. "Thank you, Steve!" she yelled.

From the aroma, she knew that he had put the pinto beans he soaked all night into the crock pot along with salsa, garlic, peppers, and chicken broth. After a day of cooking, the beans would be soft and filled with savory flavors. She took off her shoes and left them next to the driver's door. Her keys and purse stayed in the car, so all she brought in was herself, her clothes, and her weapons.

As she walked through the door leading to the kitchen, the wonderful smell of slow-cooked legumes and spices greeted her. True to form, a pan of cornbread and grated cheddar cheese sat on the counter.

"There she is," Steve said. He wore her apron with KITCHEN BITCH on the front. She walked into his hug.

"Ugh," she muttered into his shoulder. "What a day."

"Later. Eat something."

"I gotta go back early," she said as she took off her jacket. "Let me get this vest off." She walked down the hall and stripped off her clothes and vest, put her weapons in the cabinet, then put on a T-shirt and shorts. She returned and washed her hands in the sink. Steve handed her an empty bowl, knowing that she always put together her beans in a particular way.

She put in a layer of cornbread first, then the beans, a layer of cheese, and on top of all that a dollop of salsa and some chopped jalapeños. The salsa was made from tomatoes, onions, and peppers from her garden, along with black beans and corn from the farmer's market. There were several dozen jars in the pantry, but those wouldn't last until Christmas.

"Hey, Mom," Robbie said. He no longer ran to her as he did when he was small. She put down her bowl. He gave her a quick, teenaged boy hug. "What happened today?" he asked. He really wanted to know, but Monique was aware that the answer might be more than he could handle.

Monique felt like crying at the warmth of her home, the hugs of her men, and the smell of savory beans.

"Mom, what did you do?" Robbie pressed.

"A little of everything," she hedged as Steve and Robbie looked at her expectantly.

"We saw you on the news," Steve said.

Monique took a cold Miller from the fridge, opened the can, and chugged three quarters of it. "Ah, that was good." She offered the can to Steve. "You want the rest?"

"Yuck, no." Steve did not drink beer; it gave him gas. He preferred a shot of vodka with lemon juice. "I'll rinse my hair with it, though."

"No way," she said, then snatched away the beer and carried it and the bowl to the sofa.

"Mom, come on," Robbie said. "Tell us."

She ate quickly while her husband and son watched her. "All right," she said finally. "A security guard was killed this morning. Another was badly injured."

"You said that on the news," Robbie said. "Where? And how was he killed?"

"Down in the basement. By the offices. Visitors don't see that area."

"Were they shot?" Steve asked.

Monique took another sip of beer. "No."

"Mom."

"Robbie, you don't need to hear about this."

"Yes, I do," he begged.

"They were stabbed."

"Stabbed how?" Robbie asked.

"I don't know everything yet, son."

"Who did it?" Steve asked.

"That's what we're trying to figure out. I'll have more to tell you when I get home tomorrow. Promise."

"Was it by the dinosaurs?" Robbie asked.

"No, honey. It was in the basement. We never went down there when you were little."

Robbie ate his beans. "Can I get a scorpion? Dad said to ask you."

"What? No. Why would you want one?"

"They're cool. And they eat crickets."

"You need to stick with pets you can commune with."

"Pet Haven has baby bearded dragons."

"Let's talk about this later, okay, honey?"

"Yeah, okay." Robbie's enthusiasms usually faded quickly. He finished his bowl and put it in the sink. "Homework. Night."

"Night, sweetie." She stared at the wall.

She and Steve watched *Cuomo Prime Time* on TV for a few minutes, then Monique said, "Can you please turn on *Saturday Night Live* on the DVR? I could use a laugh."

Steve instead clicked to the Weather Channel and turned to face her. "Is it bad?" he asked.

"Very."

"You want some wine?"

She normally did not drink on a work night, but the beer called to her. "Sounds really good, but no. Beer's enough."

"You look tired," Steve said. "I'll put the food up. There's enough for three days."

"Freeze some for the weekend. My mind's tired."

"And stressed."

"Maybe. Some." Nevertheless, she went through the day's events while he listened. Steve remained still when she told him about the scalping and mysterious Room of Secrets.

"Remains. Bones. Scalping. Moni, you shouldn't be messing around with remains. Or burial things. Call Leroy. You need to do everything right."

"I'm going to, believe me. First chance I get. I have to go in early tomorrow morning, but I'll call him as soon as I can." Being around thousands of body parts whose spirits are not happy about being stored in boxes called for some real healing.

"I'll clean up the kitchen," Steve said. "You sit and finish your beer. Want some dessert?"

She shook her head, then sat with her eyes closed and listened to water running and dishes clattering in the kitchen. In a few minutes Steve returned with his dessert bowl of yogurt, bananas, raisins, and Cool Whip. He sat down in the lounge chair and asked the question that had haunted her all day. "How did they get into that room?"

"I don't know."

"It shouldn't be that hard to figure out. The killer didn't walk through the wall. There's something peculiar about this."

"And what makes you say that? It's a perfectly normal case," she added, sarcastically.

"Don't be flip. It's not any normal person who's after the bones. There's something evil here."

"Murder itself is evil, Steve."

"Whoever did this is clever and sneaky."

"That's a given."

"Do you think it was Indians who wanted remains back?"

"That's what I thought at first. Or maybe white collectors. But that's not why Ginger Watsannee and the others were there the last time they came in. They wanted masks and shirts."

"There are Indians who'll go to extremes to get their tribes' bones, you know."

"Without a doubt." She closed her eyes.

"Go to bed," Steve chided. "You're not going to catch the killer tonight."

Monique took a quick, hot shower then changed into her nighttime uniform: sweatpants and T-shirt with socks that she always pulled off in the middle of the night. She turned down the covers and opened the bedroom window to say hello to Rover, who bounced up and down in delight. There was no breeze. She could hear a car one street over. Her neighbor whistled for his dog to come in. A siren wailed in the distance.

Then came a hoot. It seemed to come from a rooftop to the north. Then another hoot came from the south. Monique listened without breathing for a few seconds, then quickly shut the window and turned on the fan. Like many other Natives who hear owls hoot, she tried to rationalize that she imagined the hoots. No one wanted bad news. She was home and safe, but nebulous and uneasy thoughts stirred through her head.

She stroked Foogly until both of them fell asleep. Steve came to bed after watching *The Daily Show*. Monique woke at the sound of his whirring Sonicare, but she was too tired to open her eyes.

He gently rubbed her back and whispered, "You'll figure it out, Moni. You always do." She fell asleep again.

20

Monique and Chris met in the front of the museum at 7:10. Her stomach could not tolerate fully caffeinated coffee, only half-caff, but this morning she drank two cups of robust coffee made from a box of latte mix flavored with vanilla that Steve's mom gave her. She had downed several handfuls of granola, and she knew the crumbs had fallen all over the kitchen floor. Steve pestered her again about eating cereal out of the box.

"Get a dang bowl, why not?" He asked as he swept up cereal particles by the laundry room. "Be a normal person and eat it with a spoon."

She never did eat cereal with milk. But she sometimes compromised and smeared peanut butter on a banana, then rolled that over cereal in her palm. Some cereal still fell to the floor, but she had caught most of it. She also was careless with bread.

"And put the twisty back on the bread bag while you're at it. Thank you."

She sighed at thinking of Steve's frustration over her morning eating habits. She saw nothing wrong with just folding the bread bag and putting it back on top of the fridge, or leaving eggshells out where they could dry so she could put them in the garden. Steve was a neatnik, and they perpetually argued about kitchen cleanliness.

Monique was in no mood to fight. She had been awakened at five o'clock by a distant scream. Through the hum of her fan, it sounded like a woman. She sat up in bed, cocked her head, and listened but heard nothing more. Foogly and Steve did not stir. The scream hadn't sounded like a cry of distress. It sounded more like an assertion. She went back to sleep and didn't wake up until Foogly patted her on the face. She looked at the clock and leapt out of bed. "Damn! It's six-thirty." As she made coffee, she mulled over that scream. As she left the house for work, a sleepy Robbie came into the garage and hugged her. "Love you, Mom," he said.

"I love you, too, hon." Robbie started back inside, then hesitated.

"What's wrong?" she asked.

"I dunno. Something woke me up early."

Monique inhaled. "What do you mean?"

"I thought . . . I thought I heard a lady scream. But I'm not sure if I really did."

"Oh, sweetie. You probably just heard a cat."

That seemed to placate him. "Yeah, you're right. See you tonight."

"We'll talk about what to name the scorpion and chameleon." He waved and went back into the house.

What did we hear? Monique wondered. Driving into work, she felt nervous and fidgety. *Probably the coffee.* When a large red leaf blew across her windshield, she gasped. "Damn it! Get a grip."

She sat in her car until Chris arrived in the parking lot. Several vehicles in the back lot presumably belonged to the security guards and other employees. Monique noticed that Rachel's silver Explorer was parked there as well. The museum would not open to the public for another two hours, and the main front lot was empty.

"Morning, Monique." Chris wore a blue shirt with a brown stain. She was too distracted to give him grief about it.

"Our teams searched the museum again last night," he told her. "No one is in there."

Monique nodded. "The museum's going to open to the public today."

"I hope it's safe."

"You and me both," Monique said.

"But . . . great day, huh? No clouds. No wind."

"Yeah. Great," she answered.

Lester Martin met them at the front door with a sad smile, clearly depressed by the loss of his friend. "How y'all doin' today?" he asked.

"Fine, thanks," Monique lied, thinking she'd be feeling much better if she'd had time to run this morning.

"Jus' great," said Chris.

"Y'all find anything yet?"

"No, not yet," Chris said. "Getting close, though."

That was the only information Chris could share. No telling who Martin spoke to.

Once again they followed Martin through the exhibits, and once again Chris slowed at the tyrannosaur versus triceratops exhibit and grinned like a true dinosaur geek. By Monique's count, this was at least the fifth time he'd seen them, but it didn't seem to get old. Monique felt crabby and didn't look at all. They kept going until they reached the offices.

Lloyd Adams stood at Mrs. Willis's desk waiting for them. He looked tired and dehydrated. *Like he shrank overnight*, Monique thought. Dark smudges under his eyes threatened to grow into full-blown circles. On the other hand, Monique would have been surprised if he had looked rested.

"Good morning," Monique said. She didn't care how he was, so she didn't ask. The feeling must have been mutual because he didn't ask her either.

The door to the Room of Secrets was propped open. Inside, Louie stood on the top rung of a ladder examining boxes on the top shelf. Monique stuck her head in and said hello.

Louie waved and went back to dusting for prints. Rachel was over dusting the east wall, standing on her toes to reach as high as possible. Dusting a wall seemed an odd thing to do, but you never know where you might find something of interest.

"Will it take long today?" Adams asked. "I really have a lot of work to do." She noticed that he held a flashlight.

It would serve no purpose to act bitchy. "I hope not. Ready to take a look at some files?" she asked.

Martin emerged from Adams's office with the keys, handed them to Adams, and nodded to Monique and Chris.

Adams stopped at a door with a smoky glass window in the center. Boxes of paper sat atop a scarred old oak chair that barred the entry. The three had to move the boxes to reach the lock, which looked like it belonged in the museum as an antique. Adams pushed the door open, and decades of dusty air poured out. All three sneezed in unison.

"You've gotta be kidding," Monique wheezed.

Adams felt for a light switch and instead found a string. He pulled it, and faint light glowed from a dusty, bare overhead bulb. Thick layers of dust covered an assortment of wooden filing cabinets and the few boxes sitting on the floor. A small, lonely desk with metal sides and a warped wooden top stood against the wall opposite the door.

Monique removed her jacket and hung it over the back of the oak chair outside the office and rolled up her sleeves. Adams stared at her right forearm, for the first time seeing her tattoo, a complex montage of colored corn, the universal symbol of tribal subsistence and fertility. Or, as she explained to those who asked, "Indigenous woman power."

Monique coughed. The dust in the air was worse than when she cleaned her old wood-burning stove. "When was this room used last?"

Adams cleared his throat. "I haven't had reason to come in here for, well, I don't remember the last time. Nine years, maybe. Even then, I mistook it for a broom closet. The files pertaining to some of the unidentified remains and artifacts should be in those cabinets." He stepped to one of the three aged wooden cabinets, leaving clear footprints in the dust.

"You mean no one has been interested enough to look in here? You just walk past it every day?"

"Well, yes."

Chris coughed and took out his notepad. "Where would the file be for card 7514?"

"Maybe in that one?" Adams pointed to the sixteen-drawer file cabinet closest to the desk, though Monique had a feeling he was guessing. He put his hand on a dirty handle and pulled, then harder, to no avail. The top drawer would not open. He yanked again. No one had looked at these files in a long time.

"Okay, wait," Monique said. "My grandma has a cabinet like this. There's a catch on the side. Here, Chris, you move this latch forward while I pull." She pulled open the long drawer, and voila, a neat line of yellow file folders emerged. They began reading the labels on the tabs.

"This drawer has stuff about pot sherds," Chris said.

"Let's check the next one." Monique opened the drawer below it and scanned the file tabs. "This one is, too." After a quick glimpse into the other drawers, she said, "The other drawers have information about baskets."

Adams sighed dramatically and went to the next wooden cabinet in line. Its metal runners needed oil. "Perhaps it's this one, then." He opened the top drawer, releasing a cloud of dust, and shook his head. "Carvings and fetishes."

"Damn," Monique said.

The three sneezed, and Chris looked at his watch. "You don't think we'll get, like, black lung disease?" he asked.

"We're in a closet, Chris," Monique reminded him, "not a coal mine."

The dust-covered light bulb flickered. It was thinner and longer than the light bulbs in Monique's house, and she wondered how old it was. The dust caused her sinuses to swell, and she longed for a squirt of Afrin. As

she looked around the room and pondered her next move, she noticed a
short, dark wooden door almost hidden behind one of the cabinets.

"What's behind that door?"

Adams sighed again, grabbed the cabinet, and began wrestling with
it. Alternately pulling and pushing, they got the cabinet out of the way.
Adams tried all his keys, but nothing matched the lock.

"I have no idea what's in there," he finally said.

"Wait a sec." Monique went to the three-drawer cabinet, opened the
top drawer, and moved her hand across the underside of the top. She felt
underneath all the drawers. Next she felt the undersides of the drawers
in the cracked old desk and found a key taped there. "Ah ha!" She handed
the key to Adams.

The short wooden door opened surprisingly easily. Adams shined his
light inside the little room and looked for a light switch. There was none
on the wall. Instead, another chain hung from the ceiling next to the bulb.
He pulled it, and weak light emanated from the almost-dead, dusty bulb.
They could barely make out a tiny room the size of two bathroom stalls,
which housed a three-drawer filing cabinet, a broom and mop with broken wooden handles, and an empty metal bucket.

Chris stuck his head in the room and sneezed again. "Is this the jackpot?"

Adams glanced at them before trying the cabinet handle. It rolled open
to reveal a dozen file folders lying at the bottom of the drawer. He lifted
them out, and Chris and Monique moved aside so he could read in the
light from the outer room.

"Here we go," Adams began. "Right on top. This one, file 46, contains
document 7514. That's the one we want. All right." He quickly scanned
a yellowed paper and said, "The items that were stored in the middle of
the row in the Room were found in the southeastern United States." He
muttered something else.

"What?" Monique asked impatiently.

"Oh. They're very old. The box we're concerned with in that row came
from Mississippi. From Nan-ee Why-ya."

Monique sniffed. On top of keeping her ancestors' remains piled away in boxes in a dusty, forgotten room like so many specimens, Adams could not even properly pronounce the name of her tribe's place of emergence into the world.

"Nah-neh Way-yah," she corrected.

"Sorry," Adams said.

"What's Nahnee Wayyah?" Chris asked.

"The place where many Choctaws believe we emerged out of the Earth," Monique told him. "Or I should say from caves that are near the mound. The mound is real and still stands in Mississippi. Some say it contains the bones of thousands of years of Chahtas."

Chris knew better than to question her more about that in front of Adams. "Hmmm," he mumbled.

"You're saying, then, that those boxes contain Choctaw remains?" she asked Adams.

"Yes, ma'am." As Adams continued reading to himself, his eyes widened. After a few breaths, he put the file on the dusty desk and took off his glasses.

"What?" Monique asked. She picked up the file. The old typewriter's keys had struck the paper so hard that the imprint of the letters almost went through it. The paper itself was dry and yellow around the edges. A corner had been dog-eared and would break off if she touched it.

"The date at the top of the first page is December 1, 1940," she said. "Here it says in double-spaced type, 'Third review of the specimen. Fully articulated skeleton of unknown species." She looked up at them. "An unknown species? Discovered in 1940? I'd think that science would have been acquainted with every species found in North America by then— except for maybe some insects in faraway jungles."

Adams studied his shoes. Chris waited for her to continue.

"*Four feet, two inches in length. Teeth retracted halfway in, or possibly out, of maxilla and mandible. Protuberance of horny substance from maxilla and mandible. Elongated, asymmetrical ear apertures. Skull small and rounded. Depressed fracture in the frontal bone above the right orbital cavity."*

"What does that mean?" Chris asked Adams.

Adams chewed his lower lip but didn't answer. Monique heard his wheezing. She skipped down a bit and read excerpts: "Vertebrae in pelvic region fused. First and fifth phalanges missing." She paused to reread the descriptions to herself, then proceeded reading aloud more slowly. "Elongated second metacarpal. Wrist and hand bones fused. Right foot is that of a normal human. Left foot phalanges are small and fused into three bones. Pelvis indicates female." Her sinuses swelled, and her temples throbbed. "Then it goes into a list of which bones are normal human bones and which ones are hollow."

"Hollow? You mean like bird bones?" Chris asked.

Monique kept her eyes on the paper. "From what I recall from anatomy, humans aren't put together like this."

"No," Adams said quietly. "No, they are not."

She looked back at the faint print and rubbed her forehead, smearing her face with dust. "Small, rounded skull with elongated, asymmetrical ear apertures," she repeated.

Then she put her hand on her left ear. "It also says that two fingers are missing and one finger is very long. Teeth are partway in, or out, of the jaws. A 'horny substance' may be present where the teeth are."

"It's a cryptid!" Chris said eagerly.

She set the file down. "I don't know what it is, Chris. It sounds like its part human and part bird."

Adams hacked a dry cough. "This thing got hit in the head. Perhaps that was the cause of death."

She shrugged. "Maybe. It's more important to figure out what it was than what killed it. And why others would kill to get it." She went back to reading. "Prior to that is a page from March 21, 1898. It says that this 'appears to be the remains of a man and a bird.' Then before that is only part of a ripped page dated 1889."

Chris stroked his chin. "Maybe the remains in the box were mixed? Maybe some bones from a bird and some from a person got accidentally mixed in together?"

"That seems logical, but that's not what this says. These bones are from the same skeleton." She turned to Adams. "Did you know about this?"

"I already said that I've never seen those files, and I never saw the specimen." Adams answered as he leaned on the doorframe, sweating.

"How could a specimen like this end up on a museum archive shelf? It's unique, not something to be stored away and forgotten."

Adams shrugged. "That last report was done just before the war. My understanding is that the curator at that time was young. He went to war in 1942 and died at Tarawa when the U.S. invaded the Gilbert Islands. An interim curator who didn't know what he was doing ran the museum for a while. Things were quite chaotic. Items came in and were misplaced. He misidentified dinosaur bones and even put some together incorrectly with wire and cement. All that had to be completely redone. It took decades to clean up the chaos and get everything sorted out."

"It doesn't sound like he got his hands on these bones."

"No. I expect he would have put them on display if he had."

"That would have drawn quite a crowd," Chris offered.

Adams ignored him. "Maybe this information was filed before that curator arrived and only a few people knew the specimen and papers were here. It could be that the specimen was shelved, then the file was put in this room by the curator who died in the war. The last time it was examined was, when did you say? Late 1940?"

Monique nodded.

"Makes sense. The box was way in the back of that shelf. No one would look there. He probably assumed he'd get to it later, but the war broke out, he died, and it was forgotten. Then other items came in, and it got pushed to the back of the shelf."

"But you said no one even goes in there."

"They don't," Adams said quickly. "What I mean is, in most archives, items that aren't considered important get pushed to the back. Items used frequently end up at the front."

"Does the file say who dug these bones up?" Chris asked.

Monique flipped to the first page of the file then went forward until she found a letter still in its envelope tucked between the pages. She took it out and gently unfolded it. The page began to split in the creases. "This is dated August 15, 1888. Elegant handwriting. It's addressed to a Professor Parley."

"He was the original curator," Lloyd said. "The museum had opened the year before."

Monique read aloud:

> The son of a neighbor who recently passed on gave this box and its contents to us. We have opened it twice, and only twice. The first time was to view the contents and once again last year. The young neighbor reported that his father received the box from another man in Arkansas twenty years before that. The Arkansas man says he had the box for thirty years. During that time he loaned it to a man who put the contents on display at a county fair in Arkansas. He said he acquired it from a Choctaw who had traveled the removal trail. The Indian man said they came from a place called Nanawaya and was very happy to give it up. We have retained the box now for ten years.
>
> We have looked to no avail to find a home for the box. While we were compelled to be rid of the contents by burying them, or casting them into the river, some force prevented us from doing so. My husband has died. I feared that he became ill last summer after he handled the contents. He continued to waste away until the Lord took him home. Our house burned last month. The box survived while everything else burned around it. This is most unnerving. I am moving to my sister's home in Connecticut.

I beseech you to accept this as a gift and hope that it is something a museum curator such as yourself might find useful and curious. If you are not interested, then perhaps you can give this box to a local church for burial.

Cordially,
Mrs. (Lucinda) Frederick Robertson

"I understand why she wanted to get rid it." Chris asked. "I certainly wouldn't want this thing in my house."

All three started when someone knocked at the door.

"It's just me, Rachel. We found the guard's missing belongings."

21

Jenn bit into her blanket to start a tear. She ripped a fingernail in the process of pulling off a strip and gasped in pain. She managed to tear two more strips, then she braided the three pieces and knotted the braid at both ends.

She tied one end of the braid around her neck, then tied the other end to one of the wooden cage poles. She leaned forward, legs straight and hands behind her back, but the pressure around her throat made her gag. Crying in frustration, she grasped at the rope around her neck and stepped backward to relieve the pressure. This wasn't going to work. If she was going to kill herself, it had to be quick.

Tears ran down her cheeks and alongside her nose. She was drooling, too, but she did not bother to wipe it away. She took a deep breath and thought about another way to do this. She put her hands on one of the wooden poles and reached up. She could not feel the top.

She picked up the potty and placed it at the base of the pole. Holding onto the pole she stepped on an edge, then put her left foot on the opposite edge, careful not to flip it. She was five-seven, and holding her arms over her head added at least a foot and half. She stretched and felt a large knot of thick rope at the top that kept the cross pole in place.

Jenn smiled and stepped off the potty. She made loops at both ends of her braided rope. The knots kept slipping, but that didn't matter. She threw one end of the rope over the cross-pole. She balanced on the potty again and put one loop through the other loop and pulled it taut. Now she had a noose hanging from a pole. She would have to stand on her toes on the potty to get her head through it.

She heard one of them approaching, his bare feet slapping the hard cave floor. Quickly Jenn put her head through the noose and felt a few strands of hair pull out. "Ouch," she said. She moved her hair to the side. "Pulled hair," she said. "How stupid."

"Nooooo!" the man shrieked when he saw what she was doing. Jenn jumped up as high as she could off and away from the pot, and in the split second it took her to fall the short distance she heard a high-pitched wail. Then she felt an intense pain in her neck, saw a bright white light, and everything stopped.

Outside the cave entrance, a squirrel lay curled in her soft moss-and-leaf nest inside the cavity of an old oak. Shells of pecans and walnuts lay around her. The squirrel had injured her leg running from an owl a few days before and had not left her nest since barely making it back inside the tree. The predator had pecked at the entrance and squawked at the squirrel, but it could not reach her. All the other squirrels and birds that had made nests on branches were either dead or had abandoned the hollow. The squirrel chirped in alarm at the anguished scream that emanated from the cave. It panted, furry sides heaving, as it listened to the harsh voice diminish into rolling waves of sobs until it was drowned out by the more comforting banshee wails and shrieks of the denizens of the hollow. After a few moments the almost ear-splitting vibrations diminished. Wind blew through the tree branches. Leaves rustled. The squirrel heard no sounds of predators and after a few minutes fell into a fitful asleep.

22

Peterson Murray ate the last bite of his blueberry Eggo and swallowed some warm sugared coffee.

"You gonna mow the grass today, honey?" Doreen asked. His wife stood at the sink with her hand out, waiting for his mug. "Grass still looks nice and green thanks to the rains. Don't you think so, honey?"

"Yeah. Nice and green." Although he liked a green lawn, he always felt some relief after it browned in late fall and stopped growing for the winter. Three acres of mowing should not have been tough for a guy on a twenty-five-horsepower lawn tractor with a sunshade, but when that guy never exercised, it felt like a huge chore.

"Grass is gettin' tall," she added.

"Tall. Yeah."

"Won't take too long. Then you can help me move that sofa over in front of the television."

"Yeah. Okay."

"You feelin' okay, darlin'? You tossed around a lot last night. That hollow give you a nightmare?"

"I didn't go in the hollow yesterday. I just picked up some pecans and talked with Andrew a while." Peterson realized there was only one way to escape Doreen's chatter. He had to mow the damned yard. He put on his flap hat and slowly moved to the mudroom where he donned old running shoes before heading outside. He squinted in the bright sunlight and felt the clear, cool air through his T-shirt, and thought that maybe he needed to put on a windbreaker. He squinted and went back inside for sunglasses. He took a deep breath and thought about what he would do after mowing.

Today was his third and last day off from the Red Bud R.V. Repair Shop and Campground. Other than watching some television or maybe seeing if the catfish were biting, he couldn't think of much else to do. But if he didn't come up with activities on his own, Doreen would have him on the roof, in the basement, and in the attic.

One thing was sure: after what he heard coming out of the hollow yesterday afternoon, he was not going back there anytime soon. He and Andrew had planned to scout for turkeys in the hollow. Peterson arrived before Andrew and Sistina returned from Home Depot. He exited his truck and walked a few paces to look down into the bowl. He scanned the forest before him. Many trees, including strong bois d'arc—what locals refer to as Pawnee or Osage Orange—grew around the hollow and along the edges of the grassy ranch. The five acres of pecan trees closer to the house supplied enough fall pecans to pay for Andrew's family summer vacations. The three hundred rocky, hilly acres of grass and trees surrounding the hollow were home to turkeys, quail, deer, and a multitude of birds. So many white-tailed deer lived on Tubbee's land that the bolder coyotes often killed them in Andrew's driveway.

Peterson continued to listen and stare into the darkness. No breeze moved the tall grass, and no birds flew over the treetops. A hawk cried far to the south. Something felt wrong. Even if he could not see any animals, he should be able to hear them or sense them. Nothing. His heart hammered against his ribs, and the few hairs on his arms stood up as if he were shivering. He knew as surely as nuts on a boy squirrel that something was watching him. Not a hog, not a coyote, and not a bird. Peterson knew the stories. Some Choctaws argue that the Old Ones with magic and dark powers stayed behind in Mississippi after Andrew Jackson's Indian removal policy forced the tribe west. Others, such as Peterson's grandparents, believed that the weary and sick Choctaws who arrived in the southeastern part of what is today Oklahoma were not alone. The Old Ones had shadowed them. And they were still here. Mostly unseen, but clearly present to those who looked closely.

Peterson had on occasion felt the presence of Shampes, the huge, hairy, and elusive creatures of Choctaw folklore that had followed the tribe west. In popular culture they are known as Bigfoot or Sasquatch, although other tribes also have legends of large, hairy manlike beasts. Andrew complained that the Oklahoma Monkey Chasers, an organization dedicated to finding and documenting Bigfoot and other creature oddities, asked Andrew's permission to explore the hollow to see if Bigfoot lives in the mysterious tangle of woods. Andrew turns down every request. Others say not to waste their time, that Bigfoot lives further east, over by Beaver's Bend State Park, or dwells around Boggy Creek by Fouke, Arkansas.

Peterson felt certain that other ancient entities were here as well, hidden in caves or deep in the forest. Creatures such as Nalusa Falaya, a black being who lures hunters away from their campfires and into the darkness, and Kashhotapolo, the man-deer who appears to lone hunters in the deep woods. Andrew's white friends laughed at the stories of strange creatures in the hollow but had no intention of asking Andrew if they can check for themselves the veracity of the tales.

Peterson knew one of those beings was watching him. When he turned around to walk back to his truck, a single scream shot out from the gloom so loud that he fell to his knees and his ears rang. Then all became silent.

When Andrew arrived, he found Peterson sitting cross-legged, shivering and facing away from the hollow.

"What the heck?" Andrew asked. "You sick?"

Peterson shook his head and held up a finger for Andrew to wait. He wiped his forehead, looked back at the trees, and then started talking.

"They're in there," Peterson whispered. He stayed where he was on the grass. Andrew crouched next to him.

After listening to Peterson's story and his theory as to which entities probably live on Andrew's property, Andrew told him it probably was a new wild cat that he heard because he had seen some big tracks around the edge of the forest.

"Maybe," Peterson said in a low voice, but he knew that no feline had made that screech. He had the feeling that Andrew had doubts as well but did not voice them.

Today, walking toward the garage to get out the lawnmower, Peterson could not shake his apprehension. Something was happening. The dreams he had had since childhood had grown stronger. One in particular frightened him. It featured a short gray woman with hair that stuck out in all directions, as if she had been electrocuted. She screamed and shrieked into the darkness in Chahta anumpa—the Choctaw language—but her words sounded strange to Peterson, like a corrupted version of the language he had been speaking all his life.

The gravel crunched beneath his feet as he neared the garage. He bent down to grab the handle of the double garage door, bending his knees so as not to hurt his back, and made a decision. "Enough of this," he said aloud. "I have to stop watching *American Horror Story*." He was halfway through season two, *Asylum*, and was certain that some of those story lines were contributing to his bad dreams.

Peterson picked up a stick and threw it for his brown Lab, Worf. The dog did not move as it watched the stick sail through the air.

"We need to start jogging, y'all," Peterson said to him.

The zero-turn Cub Cadet started smoothly. Peterson put the mower into gear and rolled out of the garage to the front of his house. He mowed straight lines until the yard was neat, then he raised the blade and started on the taller grass and weeds that surrounded the area where his kids played.

When he reached the pond, he stopped and looked, expecting to see red-eared sliders sunning on the logs. He saw not a one, and in fact hadn't seen any for the past month. That was odd. Turtles had always lived here, and now there only were two large snappers. Come to think of it, the Canadian geese had not been around either. "Where'd y'all go?" he asked aloud.

Peterson had completed a little under an acre when he felt once again that someone was watching him. He stopped the mower and cocked his head. He looked around and saw nothing but his house, lazy Worf asleep in the shade, and the blackjack oaks that grew thickly along the western edge of his property. He started the motor again. As he shifted with his right hand, something knocked off his cap.

Peterson looked around and saw his hat on the ground at the edge of the trees, thirty feet away. "How'd you get over there?" he asked his hat. There was no wind, not even a breeze. He sighed and got off the mower to fetch his hat. He looked back at Worf, but his dog was gone. *Must have gone in the garage*, he thought.

As Peterson bent to pick up his hat, he heard a faint laugh coming from the oaks in front of him. He looked up, and in the shadows he saw the yellow eyes from his dream looking back at him. Stunned, Peterson hesitated only two seconds before turning to run back to the house. Before he could yell for his wife, a hand clamped down hard over his mouth and another arm wrapped around his waist and yanked him into the bushes.

23

Lloyd Adams locked the door to the dusty old closet. Monique brushed
the dust off her shoulders and wondered if she had spiders in her hair.
It felt like something was crawling around up there. Chris had gray
dust in his ears and nose, and Monique figured that she did too.

Monique felt like she was floating down the halls with her arms folded
tightly around the file, thinking hard about Nanih Waiya. She had thought
about the mound often—ever since she was five and her parents took her
and her brother, Brin, fishing at Lake Eufaula. She remembered watching her father stringing fishing poles and baiting hooks, happily chatting
about bass, perch, and how he planned to pan-fry the fish.

One year they stayed a few weeks at Lake Eufaula in their camper.
Monique remembered that she wished she could sleep in a tent because
her father had a cold. He coughed and snorted so loud it shook the whole
camper. One July night it rained hard, the drops beating on the trailer
from all directions like sticks pounding a drum. She and her brother huddled together, scared of the noise.

That next morning the kids ventured outside to eat their Bavarian
Kreme Dunkin' Donuts and Tang—and stepped right into piles of dead

locusts, drowned by the heavy rains that had pummeled the camper. The lake was still, and millions of tiny insect bodies floated on top of the water. Monique's mother stood there under the cheery blue sky, looking out at the lake.

"Goddamn, what a mess," Monique's mother said before taking a bite of her gooey doughnut and turning back to tend the fire. She'd had to use damp wood, and thick smoke billowed to the northeast. Several filleted bass and a catfish lay on the wooden cutting board, ready to cook in metal baskets. Canola oil, bacon, and eggs sizzled in the skillet. *Breakfast of champions.* The daily doses of saturated fats, cholesterol, and sugar had stopped her father's heart a year after that trip and had given her mother the diabetes that helped to eventually kill her. Monique did not think about food much in those days. From her perspective, both her parents seemed hale and healthy. After her father's death, Monique read *Back to Eden* and cleaned up her diet. Her mother, however, could not keep away from sweets, carbs, and Pepsi.

Monique preferred to remember her mother as she was at the campsite that summer, her dark skin glowing against her pink warmup suit as she told her children, for the hundredth time, her favorite Choctaw creation story.

"Our people—we were called Oklas then—first emerged from the ground, a place in Mississippi that Choctaws call Nanih Waiya. We were locusts." Her mom moved to the right a bit to avoid the smoke.

Now her children were old enough to ask questions.

"Locusts?" Monique asked. She was an inquisitive kid and always talked back to adults. "We were bugs? Like these on the ground? They stink."

"No, dear," her mom said. "They were different then."

"Like how different? How do you know that?'"

"Shut up," said Brin. He was still mad at her for pushing him off the bed while they were jumping on it the week before. He'd hit his head on the corner of the dresser and required five stitches in his eyebrow. Monique still regretted that incident. Fifteen years after that fall, the day

Brin turned twenty-three, he went out to meet some friends at Brick Town in Oklahoma City. Monique and her mother had called him at his apartment in Norman late into the night in attempts to wish him a happy day and to make sure he came to his post-birthday breakfast the next morning. The handsome and amiable newspaper photographer did not walk through his mother's front door at 8 a.m. Instead, the police arrived to tell them that he had been stabbed to death and left behind the garbage bin at his apartment complex. His death hastened their mother's demise and was the catalyst for Monique's law enforcement career.

Monique persisted. "Were the Choctaw locusts bigger than regular locusts?"

"I don't know, dear. Anyway, the Choctaws and Chickasaws were all one group then. The locusts, our ancestors, lay on the ground to dry themselves, then they got up and marched away and eventually turned into people. The group was led by the two brothers who were created by Nanishta, Chahta and Chickasa. They led the group to find a place to settle."

Monique wiped white sugar from her mouth. "You mean that's where Choctaws and Chickasaws come from?"

"I'm getting to that, dear. As one version goes, the people came across a red pole that was supposed to tell them which way to go, but they couldn't decide if it was standing straight up, which meant to stay where they were, or if it was leaning toward the north, which meant to go that way. Those who thought it was straight stayed put and called themselves Choctaws while the others kept walking and became Chickasaws."

Monique recalled that she looked at the ground at the dead locusts and had a hard time understanding that story. There lay some locusts, but they were soggy, stinky, and decomposing.

Her mom put two fillets in the pan. "Won't take long to cook," she said.

"Good. We need to leave. These bugs smell terrible."

Brin swallowed the last of his Tang. "That's like that movie *Quatermass and the Pit*, where the Martians looked like locusts. And they fell apart in the air."

"I saw that movie, too, son," Mom said.

Monique was not surprised. Her mother knew more movie trivia than Roger Ebert.

"Those were ancestors of humans," she continued. "They left their imprint in our ancestors' minds, and that image is what we think Satan looks like. So when an old Martian ship was found under the subway in England, the Martian custom of killing off inferior Martians resurged in our human memory, and the people in the movie started killing each other. That movie has nothing to do with our creation story."

Monique still wondered about that. Mythologies intrigued her. The crazier the better. How did they start? Did one person make up a story, and it got repeated aloud down through the generations, morphing until it was written down? There was more than one Choctaw creation story, so clearly not everyone agreed on a common tale. Add in Christianity with Adam and Eve, and there was a third version. If this human-bird skeleton really existed, was this deformity, part bird and part human, how a story began? And then there was Mothman. What if . . .

"You okay?" Chris snapped her back to the present.

"More or less. Just thinking. Trying to figure out what happened." She took deep breaths like a diver about to look for pearls.

"I hope I can sleep through the night," Chris said. "You have bad dreams?"

"No. I just don't sleep well," she lied. "This case is getting to me. I need to meet with my Uncle Leroy to be cleansed. I can only imagine how sick I'd get working in this place all the time."

Adams turned and looked at her but said nothing. He had heard this kind of talk from Indians before.

"Let's figure this out once and for all," Chris said as they got back to the Room. "The perps could only have come in through the door, but there's nothing on the video showing they did."

"There sure doesn't *seem* to be any other way in," Monique agreed. "No other doors, no windows, no trap doors in the floor."

"Someone used a key, I tell you," Lloyd argued.

"But there's nothing on the video," Chris repeated. "Maybe they somehow stayed out of the way of the camera?"

"No. The camera had a wide range. We're missing something," Monique said. "The answer has to be another entry point in this room."

"And if there isn't?" Chris asked.

She had no response to that. "Where's Louie?" she asked Rachel, who was waiting for them next to the filing cabinet.

"I'm in the back," his disembodied voice shouted. They followed Rachel past five tall metal shelves and hundreds of boxes to where Louie stood at the base of a ladder, examining the bottom shelf.

"The clothes and things are in that box up there," he said.

Monique looked up to the top shelf where boxes were stacked four high. The shelf was about twenty feet above her head. Each shelf below the top one was packed just as tightly. "Way up there?"

"Yup. I decided to come back here and work forward toward the door. I gave the top boxes a quick look and found the items in that wide one." He pointed to a box that stuck out a bit over the shelf. It appeared to be the same shape as the plastic one she had at home to store tubes of wrapping paper.

Monique hated to state the obvious. "That means the perp would have climbed up there."

"Sure doesn't look like it," Louie answered. "Not using this ladder, and not climbing up from shelf to shelf."

"No?"

"How else could he have done it?" Chris asked. "Did he throw them up there?"

"No. The top is on the box, and it's pretty snug. They had to use a ladder somehow," said Louie. "The problem is, there are no marks showing the ladder was moved from where it is now. There'd be tracks on the floor and on the shelf where the ladder moves along the shelf." Louie pointed a latex-gloved finger at the floor. "Mine are the only footprints. And up at the top the dust came off easily when I moved the ladder. I'm not finding any evidence of hands or feet on the shelves or boxes."

No one spoke for a few seconds.

Monique chewed her lower lip and looked up, then along the floor. "Ropes from the ceiling, pole vaulting, drones," she offered.

"They climbed," Chris said firmly.

"They didn't," Monique said.

"But there is no other way. They climbed. You know Occam's razor, the simplest explanation is—"

"Don't," Monique interrupted. "I hate that." She turned to Chris. "Do not suggest that I cannot make multiple assumptions here."

"Hey, I didn't mean—"

"Chris," Monique said in a low tone, "the evidence says otherwise."

"Uh," began Louie, "in order to get to the top boxes on the top shelf, you'd have to step on some boxes. As you can see, they're made of thin cardboard and would collapse. They're all covered in dust, and I can't find a single print of any kind."

"They're so close together that you can't even get a toe between them," Rachel added. "No way a person got up there by climbing. Sorry, Chris."

Chris flushed and examined his fingernails.

"And behind this shelf is what?" Monique asked. "Another shelf, right?"

"Yes, ma'am. Two shelves, back to back." Louie answered. "More boxes stacked just as tightly. No way up there, either."

"He's right," Rachel said. "I did a quick search and didn't find prints on this entire section."

The group stood silently, gazing upward.

"Monique," Rachel said. "Come here and take a look."

Monique followed Rachel around the edge of the shelf. "Look at the distance between aisles," Rachel said.

"Six feet," Monique estimated.

"Correct. You'd think that a person could jump from one top shelf to another."

"You'd think."

"But it didn't happen. In order to leap from one top shelf to another in the adjacent row, then you'd need take-off room. You would have to move some boxes. As you can see, those boxes behind the box with the clothes are stacked five high."

"And on each side," Louie interjected, "boxes are stacked the same. I already looked. None of the boxes have moved like they would have if a person ran into them jumping from one row to the other."

"So what you're saying is the clothes were dropped into the box from above?"

"There's no other explanation."

"Is that ladder in here all the time?"

"Yes," Louie said. "And like I said, it hasn't been used in a long time. The top four rungs were covered with dust. I cleaned them off as we climbed up."

"Is there a way someone could have placed dust on these things to make it look like no one has disturbed the room?" Chris suggested.

Rachel smiled. "I did hear of a case in which a perp dumped the contents of a vacuum cleaner all over his murder scene to throw off the scent. But that's not the same thing. Someone could gently blow dust over an object or a small area, but in order to fool us, the dust would have to be uniformly distributed throughout the room. That would be impossible to do. No one would have time to cover the entire contents of this room to the extent they'd have to in order to make it look realistic. Plus, we'd see evidence of someone putting the dust down."

"And they'd have to get out somehow after spreading the dust," Louie said. "There aren't any tracks in the dust anyplace in this room. If they backed out while spreading dust, it would be out that one door. And they'd be on the videotape."

Monique rubbed her chin absently. "You're right. Let's get those clothes down."

"Any chance they don't belong to the guard?" Chris asked.

"Yeah," Monique said. "Maybe they're old clothes stuck in the box a century ago and put on the top shelf. That would answer the riddle." It sure would make life easier.

Louie climbed the ladder and retrieved the box. Chris reached up to help take it when Louie got halfway down the ladder.

"No," Rachel said. "Let me. I have gloves on, and we're not finished looking at this thing yet."

She took the box, looked underneath it, and held it up so Louie could look as well. "Hang on," he said, and dashed to the door where his satchel sat. He returned with a roll of brown paper. He unrolled a large piece, and Rachel set the box down on it and opened the top.

Inside was a shredded security guard's uniform shirt stained with sticky blood. The nametag that faced upward, as if it had been placed there on purpose, read RECTOR. A large owl feather lay next to it.

Monique gasped and jumped back.

"What?" Chris asked. "Monique, what is it?"

"An owl feather," she whispered.

"I also found a few other things while I was just at the top of that shelf," Louie said.

"Like what?" She heard her blood sprinting in her ears, rushing like spring rains in a creek. She wondered if she had tinnitus.

"Two feathers in between two boxes on the shelf where the clothes were."

"What?" she asked, even though she heard him perfectly.

He held up another paper sack. "Two big brown ones."

Chris looked up and around like he expected to be attacked by an owl. "There are birds in here? Where?"

24

"Are those owl feathers too? You're sure?" Louie asked Monique.

"Yes."

"How'd they get in here?" Chris asked.

"You sure that's not a turkey feather?" Louie persisted.

"Yes," she insisted. "Positive."

Louie looked at the feather a few seconds. "Hey," he said, thoughtfully, "you know that weird thing that looked like a dust bunny that was next to the bones? I'll be back." He went to his bag and pulled out the evidence bag with the oval object. "I think I know what this is." He took out the mass carefully and set it on the baggie on the floor. He took out his knife and gently cut it lengthways. The others crowded around to watch.

"What is it?" Chris asked.

"It's an owl pellet."

Rachel leaned in close to see. "A what?"

"Owl pellet. Owls don't digest their prey's fur and bones and other hard stuff. They compact it into a pellet in their gizzard and throw it back up. Saves wear and tear on their guts. See?" He pulled the mass apart. "This stuff inside the pellet is actually fur, not dust. And this looks to be a tooth. Dang, a sharp one, too. Like from a raccoon or some other carnivore."

"Raccoon? Can an owl eat a raccoon?" Chris asked.

"A baby," answered Monique.

"But it would have to pull the tooth from the jaw."

"True. I don't know then, Chris."

"How did that get in here?" Chris asked. "How old is it?"

Louie held it up, sniffed, and winced. "Not old at all."

"So, clearly, an owl has been in here," Rachel said. "Hey, maybe it was a trained owl. An owl could have put the clothes up there."

No one replied.

"How'd it get in?" Chris asked again.

"The same way the robber got in and out," Monique answered.

"I still don't see any way besides that door," Rachel said.

Monique stood silently as her colleagues discussed the feathers and pellet. The room seemed to shift when she raised her eyes.

"Hey, you okay, Monique?" Chris asked as he took her arm.

She looked at him, then at his hand on her arm. "Fine, Chris. I'm thinking."

"You were swaying." He let go of her arm but kept watching her.

"There's another possibility," Monique finally said.

"What?" Chris asked.

"Follow me," she said to the group. They arrived at the filing cabinet. "Up there," she pointed to the vent. "That air duct."

"We considered that from the start," Rachel said. "And we all agreed it's too small."

"Yes, it is," Lloyd Adams said from the doorway. "Although it is hinged at the top to open upward. And it connects to hundreds of feet of ventilating system that goes through the walls."

Everyone turned and looked at Adams.

"Look, I know I'm not supposed to be in here, but I needed to use the restroom and heard you talking."

"All right," Monique acquiesced. "Come in."

She went to stand under the vent, and Louie went with her.

"What do you see?" she asked Louie.

He shrugged. "An air vent."

"Look closer. Look at the vent cover and around it on the wall."

Louie squinted. "I think those are scratches on the paint. And those may be scratches around the opening of the vent on the wall."

"Taz went right over here yesterday," Monique said, "and Linda dragged her away. Rachel, we need to find out what's in it."

"Okay," Rachel said, "but that vent's no doorway. Not even Melinda could get into that."

"I agree. It would be impossible for a person to fit through that opening," Adams said defiantly. His arms hung at his side, fingers clenching and flexing.

Louie and Rachel brought an extension ladder over and set it under the vent opening. Then they raised the top of the ladder until it reached the bottom of the vent, twenty-three feet from the floor. Rachel climbed while Louie held the ladder steady. She reached the top and examined the vent cover for a few seconds.

"Eee-yoo!" Rachel exclaimed. "Stinks like a dirty wet dog in here."

Monique inhaled sharply. "Where're those other feathers?" she asked Louie.

He held up a paper sack. "In here."

"You okay, Monique?" Rachel asked from above. "You sound like you stepped in dog doo."

"Fine," she answered. "It's just a little warm in here."

"If you say so." She pulled up on the vent cover. "It's hinged at the top like Lloyd said."

Rachel held up the vent with one hand and shined her penlight into the hole with the other. "Dark," she said. Then, "Lookie here." She put her arm into the opening and pulled out a long, brown feather.

"Are there birds nesting in there?" Chris suggested.

"We've seen no evidence of droppings," Louie answered. "Plus, what would they eat?"

"I want to get up there," Monique said suddenly.

"Hang on a second." Rachel pulled an empty evidence bag from her pocket and slipped the feather inside, then started down the ladder. "Be my guest," she said when she reached the bottom.

Monique glanced into the bag at the feather before she started up the ladder. The top rung stopped at the vent. She shined her pen light around the walls of tunnel to see that scratches covered the metal back about four feet. At that point the vent took a right turn.

"There's some white stuff in here," she told the others. "And there's also what looks like a few chunks of yellow chalk."

"Don't touch anything," Rachel said.

"I won't."

As long as she had a view, Monique figured she might as well look around at the vista of box tops. Some boxes stood up higher than others, and for the most part she saw only flat brown tops. One thing looked out of place, however. A white lump on top of a box on the second shelf row from the door.

"There's something over there, on top of the second shelf." Monique pointed to the white object. She came down the ladder to allow Louie up.

"What is it?" he asked as he climbed.

"Dunno. You tell me."

Louie took a long look, squinted. "Can't be."

"What?"

He didn't answer as he scurried down the ladder like a spider monkey. He ran to the rolling ladder for the second row, pushed it twenty feet down the row, and then climbed up. Monique, Rachel, and Chris watched as he fumbled with the item on top of the box.

"Man," he yelled down at them. "This is wild. It really is."

"What is it, Louie?" Rachel asked impatiently.

"A human pelvis."

25

"I'd like to talk with Dr. Wright about this," Monique said quietly.

"Clarence? What for?" Adams asked incredulously.

"We need some advice."

"From Clarence?!" He snorted.

She ignored him. "Louie, give me those feathers."

"Sure thing," he replied. "You think he can tell us something about them?"

"I don't know. Maybe the age of the birds, the types of owls."

"You think that's important?"

"I'm beginning to think it's very important." Monique grabbed the files on the way out the door.

"Dr. Adams, Go back to your office, please," she said. "And stay there. I may have some more questions."

"I can't imagine why," Adams said, his voice dripping with sarcasm. "I mean, Clarence knows everything."

"No. But he does know some things," Monique said as he turned to leave. She stepped out into the hall to call Wright and put him on speakerphone when he picked up.

"It's me," Wright answered cavalierly.

"Dr. Wright, this is Detective Blue Hawk. I'd like to ask you a few more questions."

"Detective Blue Hawk," he said. "If it's about the crimes in the Room, I've already told you everything I know." A television blared in the background, and clearly he had something in his mouth. She pictured him sitting in his underwear eating chips and dip and throwing the empty bag on the floor.

"There's one more thing I need to know."

"I told you already. I don't associate with Lloyd or any of those anthropologists."

"That's not what I want to ask you about."

"What, then?"

"I'm calling from the museum. Be here in twenty minutes." She hung up.

Monique and Chris went back into the Room and walked slowly through the aisles as they waited, inspecting the corners, the walls, the shelves—looking for anything they could have missed.

Chris watched his partner as she paced the floor, looking up and down, occasionally rubbing her temples. Her intensity had set in, and he knew not to walk too close when she was like this.

"Maybe a trap door?" Chris suggested.

"If there is one, it's under thousands of pounds of shelf metal and bone boxes. No way, Chris."

"Then the security tape is wrong."

"I don't think so. It's the vent."

"I just don't see that as the ingress and egress point."

Monique continued to wander the Room, inspecting the walls, peering into the small spaces below the bottom shelves and between the boxes. As she'd anticipated, there was nothing new to discover.

Steps sounded from the hallway. "Where are they?" a loud voice boomed. Clarence Wright had arrived.

Monique and Chris walked out into the hallway, avoiding Ethan Lewis's blood on the floor, and she motioned Wright to his office with her forefinger. The three entered and sat in the places they had the day before. Wright was dressed in an Oklahoma Sooners T-shirt, jeans, and flip-flops. She shuddered. Monique loathed the OU Boomer Sooner phrase and the Sooner Schooner mascot, and she did not need to be reminded of the loss of tribal lands at the hands of opportunistic whites. "I have some feathers for you to look at."

Wright shrugged. "Hit me."

She passed him the paper sack. Wright opened it and dumped the feathers onto his desk. "Owl." He did not hesitate. "You can tell because they're combed at the ends. For silent flight."

Monique looked at Chris and raised her eyebrows. If nothing else, they were learning a lot of science trivia. "We know they're owl feathers. Can you tell us what kind of owl?"

He touched one. "This one is great horned."

"You sure?"

Clarence stood and retrieved a box from a shelf. He sat, opened the box, and took out a handful of feathers. He held up a white one. "This is a snowy owl. They aren't common in Oklahoma, but they've been spotted here. And this one is from a screech owl. Dunno if it's a male or female. If this belonged to a barn owl, then I could tell. Females have spots on their feathers." He picked up another feather from Monique's bag. "This other one is also a great horned owl. Maybe the same bird, maybe not."

"Male or female?"

"Can't tell great horned owl gender from feathers. You can tell from their calls, though. Males have deeper voices. But females are bigger."

"Can you tell the age from the feather?"

"Nope."

"Health?"

"I can look under a microscope for mites and wear. But these look to be in pretty good shape."

"Can you train an owl?"

Wright laughed. "To do what?"

"Well, to carry an object and drop it someplace."

"No. No way."

"Why not?" Chris asked.

"Lots of reasons. They're stubborn as hell. Independent. Great horned owls are apex predators, and they do what they want. And they're nocturnal. Maybe you could train them to catch a rabbit or something, but it comes back to if the owl wants to. Why? What do owls have to do with what's happening right now?"

"We thought that maybe someone used an owl to move the guard's clothing to the top of one of the shelves in the Room."

Wright looked at her as if he thought she was simpleminded. "Nope," he said.

"Thank you."

"That's it?" Wright put the feathers back in her bag. He started to stand.

"Please, stay seated. This poster on your wall, the one with the crazy-looking woman with wings?"

Chris turned to look at it. Then he whipped his head back around at Monique.

Wright looked surprised. "What does she have to do with anything?"

"Just humor me. Who is she?"

"I don't understand. Why?"

"I want to know."

"Okay. Her name is Louhi. She's a Finnish legend. Also known as the Dame of the North Farm. She wanted the magic mill, the Sampo."

He waited as if he expected them to be familiar with the term.

"The Sampo," he started, pleased that he was being asked to speak about it, "was the mill that continually ground out salt, grain, and money—the things people most needed and wanted. You know."

"Go on."

"One version of the story from the *Kalevala* says that Louhi promised Väinämöinen one of her daughters in exchange for the Sampo. You see, Louhi really, really wanted it."

"Who's Väinämöinen?"

"He was the son of the goddess Luonnotar. He was wise because he had stayed in his mother's womb for thirty years."

"Right. Please get on with it."

"So, yeah. Thirty years in the womb absorbing wisdom or something."

"I get it." Monique rubbed her left temple. "Proceed."

"Väinämöinen didn't want to give up the Sampo, so when Louhi's men tried to take it, he played a song that put them to sleep. Then he stitched their eyelids together."

Monique nodded. Chris uncrossed then recrossed his legs.

"Anyway, that pissed off Louhi, and she caused a storm. Väinämöinen had power of his own, though, and he made rocks spring up in front of Louhi's ship, and the ship crashed into them and broke to bits. Louhi took the pieces of wood from her boat and made wings. As you see from that picture, she also created scythes for her hands—you know, talons—and swept down on the ship like, well, a big bird. She grabbed the Sampo and took it with her. At some point, the mill fell into the sea. No one knows if she dropped it accidentally or if the magic mill had a mind of its own and wished to return to its owner."

"And then?"

He shrugged. "It's still grinding out salt."

"Not money?"

"Not that I know of."

"So, that is the source of sea salt?"

"I guess."

"So Louhi wasn't a bird?"

"Some people tell the story as if she turned into one. I think this is more interesting. I mean, how can you just make wings and start flying?"

Monique didn't know which was crazier: Wright telling the story as if he believed it or her listening to him.

"You should read the *Kalevala*."

"Which is?"

"It's a Finnish epic. It tells of Louhi and the Sampo. There're several versions of that story, by the way."

"You say that you're a cryptozoologist, right?"

"That's right."

"What do you know about bird-men?"

Wright cocked his head.

"Bird-men," she repeated. "Men who are part bird."

"You makin' fun of me?"

"Not at all." Monique's head was pounding. "Look, Dr. Wright. We found something odd here. A file description of a—well . . . of a half-human, half bird."

"What?"

"We found information about this thing in one of the files, although the skeleton actually isn't here. It's—"

"No shit? What file? Where did you find it? Can I see it?"

She handed the file to Wright. "Careful, it's very old."

He took the brittle file and laid it on his desk. He took a pair of white cloth gloves from a side drawer and gingerly opened it and began reading eagerly. She and Chris watched him for a few minutes as he read the file with his mouth open.

"Damn!" he dropped the papers on his desk. "I mean hot damn!"

"We found it in an old broom closet at the end of the hall," she said. "The one with the thick glass on the door."

"That closet? Man, I've been asking about that on and off for *years*. Lloyd always says it's just an old broom closet that doesn't have anything in it. I asked if I could use it for a second office, but he told me it doesn't have ventilation."

"It doesn't. It stores brooms and mops and a filing cabinet that contains old files. The one you're holding documents the bones that were taken out of the Room when the guard was murdered."

Wright read through the file again quickly. "Half bird? This is wild. And this thing is gone? None of the bones are left?"

"Yes. Gone. That's what the thieves were after. The only evidence is an empty box and the file in your hands." She did not mention the pelvis.

Wright reread a few passages, scratching his head and making comments like "Holy shit" and "Incredible."

Monique shifted in her seat. "You have any ideas what this thing might be? Have you come across legends of animals that might fit that description?"

"Let's see. There're all kinds of stories about weird birds. There's one that a lot of people have seen. Most describe it as big and definitely a bird with long wings and a pointy beak, like a pterosaur. They lived during the Jurassic and into the Cretaceous, about sixty-five million years ago, you know?"

Monique did not but nodded yes to keep him going.

"They had a wingspan of almost thirty feet. Then there's Quetzalcoatl, the feathered serpent, from Mesoamerica. It had a wingspan twenty feet wider than that. People have seen them in Zambia, Namibia, and even in Texas in the 1970s."

"That's impossible," Chris said.

"No," Monique answered.

"No what?" Wright asked. "It's not impossible?"

"No," she said, "it's too big for what we're looking for."

Chris looked at her incredulously. Wright's eyes darted back and forth between her and Chris.

"Well, there's the Thunderbird."

"What does that look like?" Monique asked.

Chris cleared his throat to get her attention. She was starting to sound like she believed all this crap. Monique waved him off.

"Thunderbirds cause thunder, you know," Wright told her. "They flap their wings and then *pow*. Thunder."

"How big?"

"Well, like regular thunder, I guess."

"I mean how big is this bird?"

"Reports from Pennsylvania in the 1960s say seventy-five feet across."

"Come on, that's incredible," Chris said.

"Yes," Wright agreed. "A kid in Alabama saw a smaller one that was fifteen feet."

"That had to be a condor," Monique said.

"No way. Condors aren't in Alabama. There're from Peru and are hardly anywhere else. Those birds are endangered, and you just don't see them much. They've been released in Arizona and there are only a few there. There's no way one got that far east."

She drummed her fingers on the desk. "Okay. What else?"

"Umm. Giant owls in England."

"Owls," Monique repeated.

"Yeah. Some kid saw one about ten years ago. It was huge—the size of a man. He said it had bright eyes, and it smiled. The feathers were silver, and the claws were black."

"A human mouth?"

"I don't know. But sounds like it."

"Can you find that report?"

Wright looked around his office, eyebrows knitting in concentration. "Hmmmm, yeah. It's here somewhere. I'll look for it."

"Please do that. Any sightings in this country?"

"Actually, there *have* been sightings. Lots of reports of Indians seeing them up in the woods of the Northwest and around the Ozarks and Alleghenies. Some of us believe they may actually have seen the Mothman."

"Mothman?" Chris interjected. "Like in the movie with Laura Linney?" He looked at Monique and gave a thumbs-up.

"Exactly." Wright beamed.

"Explain the Mothman," Monique asked.

"Oh, wow," Wright exclaimed. "He's cool."

"Cool how?"

"The Mothman seems to have been first sighted in Clendenin, West Virginia, in the 1960s. There were some guys working in a cemetery, getting ready for a burial, and all of a sudden a person burst out of the trees and flew off."

"A person?"

"They were specific. A person with wings. And it was brown."

"Go on."

"Then later that year, other people saw it. One couple said it had glowing red eyes and passed their car along a road at a hundred miles per hour."

"Come on," Chris exclaimed. "Really?"

"Look, buddy. I'm only reporting the facts."

"Dr. Wright," Monique prodded. "Continue."

"Others who saw it said the eyes were red and as big as dinner plates. And it seems that the Mothman appears before disasters and death."

"Considering the roles that owls played in tribal cultures, this Mothman might actually be a large owl," Monique mused.

"No. The man-bird thing described in this file is less than five feet. It's not the same thing. Mothman is big. Seven feet tall at least, according to people who've seen him."

"Is there a Mothwoman?" Chris asked.

"Never heard of one," Wright answered.

"But maybe there are other owl creatures a little smaller than that," Monique continued intensely, homing in on the pattern that was becoming evident to her.

"Monique," Chris said, "you're starting to scare me."

"Chris," she replied threateningly.

He put his hands up in surrender. "Okay, okay."

"What other bird things do you know about, Dr. Wright?"

"Not many. Like I said, I'm mainly interested in Bigfoot."

"What about that giant shark?" Chris asked.

"The megalodon? Oh, yeah. He's around, for sure. Scientists say they died out almost two million years ago. But some teeth that have been carbon-dated are only eleven thousand years old. Scientists also say the megalodons only lived in coastal areas like great whites, but hey, they're down in the deep trenches now, below the thermocline. They're there all right. Big and hungry."

"Sounds like it."

"There're a couple of movies out about megalodons, but the sharks look fake."

"Dr. Wright," Monique said quietly, putting an end to the shark discussion, "thanks for the information. If you think of anything else about bird-men, you call me."

"Will do."

"You can go home now." She held out her hand for the file. Wright closed the folder and reluctantly handed it back to her before leaving the office. Monique and Chris watched as he walked down the hall to the elevator.

"That was very bizarre, Monique," Chris said. "You sound like you've been nipping the cooking sherry."

"That's a sexist thing to say, Chris."

"I didn't mean—"

"Men say that about housewives and upset women. Do not say that to me again." She turned to look at him. "Ever."

Chris looked at his feet. "I said that to my ex once. She hit me."

"Consider yourself lucky this time."

"I'm sorry."

Monique's shoulders slumped. She was not in the mood to argue any more. "I feel like we're surrounded by souls who need to go home."

"I do understand that. I'd be more comfortable in a cemetery at midnight than I am here. What's up with that bird lady on the wall?"

"I'm not sure about that either. It was just a wild thought. My people have stories . . ."

They heard panting in the hallway, and a second later Taz appeared around the corner. Linda appeared next.

"We came back to give it another try." She scratched Taz's head. "We looked everywhere again, and she wasn't interested in much at all this time."

"You went into the Omni and the planetarium?"

"Yup. Well, I should say she looked up and seemed curious about the big dome ceiling. She sat and whimpered some. But she didn't find a scent to follow—not in the offices, closets, or displays. We did find this, though." She pulled a baggie from her breast pocket. It held an owl pellet. "I don't know what the heck it is. Maybe a spider egg sac or something?" She handed the bag to Monique. "Taz growled at it. I had to reprimand her so I could pick it up. And when I put it in my pocket she barked at me."

"It's an owl pellet," Chris said quickly. "Owls throw up bones, beaks, fur, and claws from their prey so they don't have to pass all that through their systems."

"Gross. How did that get into the planetarium? Do they have an owl show in there now?"

Taz pulled on her leash until she reached Monique, then put a paw on Monique's leg and looked up into her eyes. "Good girl," Monique said, surprised. She reached out tentatively, stunned that Taz had approached her. "She seems awfully subdued." Monique continued to rub Taz's ears, relishing the opportunity to pet the dog that no one other than her handler dared approach.

"Yeah, she's not as energetic as yesterday."

"Did she eat?"

"Not much."

Taz let out a deep howl, the kind of sound a dog makes when a siren is hurting its ears, then turned to the door. She pulled hard on the leash.

"Geez, Tazzy." Linda reached out for her dog to comfort her. "Maybe we should call it a day," Linda managed to say before Taz began dragging her down the hall toward the exit. "Taz, Taz, what's wrong?"

"Interesting. Tough old Taz acting like a scared puppy," Chris said. "That's funny."

"No," Monique said. "It's not."

26

Monique's cell phone rang just as she was about to take a break in the bathroom, hoping to sit on the cool floor and think in private. "He is? Thanks! We're on the way."

She stood and walked outside. As she expected, Chris was standing in front of the caiman pool. "Good news," she told him. "The guard is awake."

"Seriously?"

"Yeah, he's alive. Let's get there while he's conscious."

Monique drove with full lights and sirens, dodging and weaving through traffic like she was a stunt driver for *Fast and Furious*. Chris gripped the ceiling handle, yipping when she took a corner at forty-five. The tires squealed, and the car fishtailed and slid into the opposing lane.

"Jee-suus, Monique!" he screamed. "Slow the hell down."

"Hush," she said.

They squealed into the Mercy Hospital parking lot and screeched to a halt. Monique set the brake, pulled out the keys, jumped out, and sprinted for the door. Chris staggered after her, pale and weak-kneed. Monique looked behind her and locked the doors with the key fob. As soon as the desk attendant told her where the guard's room was, she jogged down the hall; Chris struggled to keep up with her.

Ethan Lewis was heavily bandaged and even more heavily sedated, but the security guard's eyes were open. As best they could tell, anyway, through the swelling that distorted his face.

An unsmiling nurse with sleek hair parted in the middle and pulled back into a severe bun hustled around the bed checking his catheter and tucking in the covers.

"At the very least, he'll need surgery to repair the deep tears in his scalp," Nurse Ratched said. "He had significant lacerations across his forehead and cheek. He'll need plastic surgery for that, too." Ignoring Lewis's shocked blink, she continued her ham-fisted description of his wounds. "He'll have terrible scars, so deep that no amount of dermal abrasion will smooth out his skin."

Monique looked at Ethan Lewis and hoped he was so out of it that he didn't understand what the nurse was saying. But she also hoped he was conscious enough to tell them what he had seen. The nurse left the room, and Monique approached the bed. "Mr. Lewis," she said softly. "I'm Detective Blue Hawk, and this is Detective Pierson."

He seemed able to focus on the detectives' faces, but there was no telling how much he understood.

"We're investigating the events at the museum yesterday morning. Can you tell us what you saw in the Room of Secrets?"

His eyes stayed on her. "Sam? Where is he?" He swallowed hard.

"Mr. Rector's being taken care of," she said. She was not lying. He was being taken care of in the morgue.

"Sam called me," Lewis said with a quivery voice. "The alarm inside the Room went off, and he said he was going in to see why."

"Where were you when he called?"

"I was a floor up in the west corner. I told him to wait for me, but he said not to worry, it was probably a mouse. I got to the door and heard him screaming." Ethan Lewis began crying as men do, with heavy breaths and few tears. Chris watched and took a step back. This situation was out of his comfort zone.

Monique waited for Lewis to calm down. The guard swallowed with difficulty, clearly dehydrated. His lips were dry and cracked, and Monique had the urge to smear lip balm over them. "I opened the door and something yanked me in. Then the door slammed shut. I just saw feathers and birds. They were everywhere. I had my arms over my face, but I could see Sam on the ground. Something was tearing his clothes off."

"What was tearing his clothes off?"

"It was a man. A man—with feathers. He was sitting on Sam's chest tearing at his clothes." Lewis was sobbing openly now. "Oh, my God. What were those things?"

Monique took the guard's hand and squeezed. Chris retreated until his back hit the wall. "That's what we're trying to find out."

"They were flying around. Just hovering. One had yellow eyes, then they turned red."

"The men?"

"Yes. The men. And the birds. I think. Both of them."

"Then what happened?"

"I don't remember. At least two flew at me and started slashing with their feet. I'm not sure how I got to the door. One had a hold of me." He squeezed Monique's hand very hard, still gasping for breath.

A tall woman with short, curly blonde hair came in holding a chart. She had on a white jacket, and her attitude screamed doctor—that and the nametag that read DR. VARTEL.

"And you two are?" she asked.

"Detectives Blue Hawk and Pierson," Monique told her.

After one look at her patient, Dr. Vartel said, "He's had enough for today, I think."

"Probably," Monique agreed. "May we speak with you outside?"

Vartel nodded.

Monique turned to the wounded man. "Thank you, Mr. Lewis," she said with another hand squeeze. "We appreciate your help. Rest now. You're safe."

Monique and Chris stepped outside and waited while the physician checked on her patient. As soon as Dr. Vartel emerged and closed the door behind her, Monique asked, "What cut him?"

Vartel paused a few seconds then said, "Hard to say exactly. The wounds were made by something sharp, but the cuts are jagged. As if whoever did this had an unsteady hand. The lacerations meander."

"And he's due for more surgery?"

"Yes. His scalp is torn, and I don't like the looks of it over his ear. And the laceration through his eyebrow may have severed a nerve. All the cuts were deep, and one looks infected. We've given him antibiotics, but we don't know what type of bacteria we're dealing with yet."

If he had been cut and punctured by talons, Monique mused, he might have a variety of microorganisms under his skin. But she was not going to start that conversation.

"All right." Monique handed her a business card. "If you find out, let me know immediately. And you should talk to that nurse, by the way."

"What do you mean?"

"She's a bitch." Monique relayed what the nurse had told them in front of the injured guard.

Dr. Vartel sighed. "She's competent and perceptive, but rough."

"No shit, she's rough," Chris said.

"Well, besides that, have you any leads?"

"Maybe."

"You people always say that."

"Perhaps, Dr. Vartel. What I will say is that I will find the perps. And I always do find them. Have a good night."

27

Monique and Chris wound their way through the bowels of the hospital's basement, the same route taken by those who die in a hospital bed. It is a dreary trek, although Monique knew that Melinda came through an entrance straight from the parking lot into her office and did not walk through the maze.

They arrived at the swinging doors that said PERSONNEL ONLY. A guard sat at his desk, reading the paper and eating popcorn. Rusty Wagner nodded. "Detectives."

In the two years she had known him, Monique had never seen Rusty outside this environment of death. "Hello, Rusty. Is Dr. Batters in?"

At his nod, they walked up to the heavy metal door labeled MORGUE in white-stenciled letters. Monique pushed the door open, and the odor of death assaulted her. The smell of Rusty's buttered popcorn vanished. Bright lights illuminated the morgue suite where Melinda and her assistant worked on an individual who did not need anesthesia.

"How're you, Monique?" Melinda said without looking up. "You and Chris should gown up. Next to the lockers."

As always, Monique ignored Melinda's greeting. She took off her jacket and hung it in a locker, then selected a gown marked "Medium" from those hanging on the hooks attached to the wall. Chris took off his jacket and revealed a shirt with yellow pit stains.

"Chris, go get some new shirts already."

"I have new shirts," he said. "I just hate to wear them. They'll get dirty."

"That sounds like my son when he says, 'Mom, why should I have to make my bed when I'll just mess it up again?'"

"Aprons are in front of you. Same place as always," Melinda told them. "Gloves and masks are in that box on the table next to the sink."

Chris and Monique donned Latex gloves, then made their way to where Melinda had just completed her study of a young Black male with deep facial lacerations and a flattened skull. He might once have been handsome. A woman stood next to the table, clothed in medical whites.

"This is Louisa Wahtahnee. My assistant."

The young woman pulled down her mask. She looked to be about twenty-eight, with dark hair, eyes, and skin. Monique could tell she was from a Plains tribe. Louisa waved but did not hold out her hand. It was covered in blood and red chunks of something. "How're you doin'?" she asked loudly.

"Good as can be, considering," Monique answered. "How long have you been here?"

"Couple of hours."

"No, I mean with this office."

"'Bout a week. Just starting my residency."

Chris pulled his mask up over his mouth and nose as he walked to the table. He had to bend over because Melinda had the table at its lowest setting. "So, uh," he began, "residency. Cool. Why did you want to be a pathologist?"

"Well, my family owns a mortuary business, and I grew up around that sort of thing. We provide services for tribal citizens. I'm not too keen on just getting people ready to bury. I'm not a cosmetologist." She laughed. Chris was not sure how to react, so he laughed, too.

"I want to know why people die, and forensic pathology is the way to do that."

"Louisa is a standout student," Melinda said. "Double major in biology and chemistry, then got her medical degree at Johns Hopkins. Hopefully I'll have Louisa here for her three year pathology residency before she goes on to her fellowship in forensic pathology."

"Wow," said Chris. "I'm impressed."

"What tribe?" Monique asked.

"Comanche."

"Lords of the Plains."

"You bet," she grinned, the skin around her eyes crinkling above the mask.

"So, what happened to this guy?" Chris asked.

"Car wreck," Melinda answered. "Inebriated. Not wearing his seatbelt. After his car hit one tree, he was ejected through the windshield and hit another tree. Head first. Caved in his skull."

She pulled the sheet up over his face. They moved to the next table. On top lay another body still in a bag. "This is your guard, Samuel Rector. Everything will be recorded, of course, and you can review it whenever."

Melinda unzipped the bag to reveal Rector's corpse, covered in dried blood. Louisa maneuvered the bag down the body so she could begin photographing.

Melinda began. "The subject is a white male. Appears to be between twenty-eight and forty years of age. His height is . . ." she pulled out her measuring tape and handed one end to Chris. He held it at the man's head. She rolled it to his right foot. "Seventy-four inches. Weight one hundred eighty-four pounds."

Monique noticed what looked like small feathers stuck in the dried blood on his chest. "What are these?" She reached for one, but Melinda caught her arm.

"Uh-uh. Don't touch."

Louisa took several photographs of the feathers and then took a metal bowl from a side table and began picking them off with forceps.

"They look like down feathers," Monique said, "like from a turkey's breast." But she knew these were owl feathers.

"Did he go hunting before work?" Melinda asked.

"If he did, he went in the dark. And I highly doubt a bird flew down his shirt."

Louisa and Melinda pulled off the remaining feathers and the remnants of the guard's clothing, and put a few stray hairs in separate containers. Melinda took the bags off his hands next and looked for debris under his nails, commenting on every detail. Louisa then took a long hose and gently rinsed the blood off the corpse.

"My God. He looked better with the blood," Chris said.

Melinda continued speaking. "No scars, no tattoos, no obvious deformities."

Monique furrowed her brows as she continued to inspect the guard's torso. "These are stab wounds. They don't look very deep," she said.

"Detective," Melinda chided, "I'll do the dictating." She proceeded. "The victim has multiple stab wounds."

Louisa began counting them and stopped at forty.

"Damn," Chris commented.

"We spoke with the other guard, Ethan Lewis, just before we came down here," Monique said. "He said he came into the Room and saw someone sitting on this man, ripping his clothes."

"That someone was doing more than tearing fabric. There are ten stab wounds in the mid left pectoral," Melinda continued, "around the nipple. Eight are clustered under the left clavicle. The remaining twenty-two wounds are on the upper sternum and to the right of the sternum."

"Looks like the assailant got into a rhythm," Louisa assessed. "Up and down, up and down in one area, then slightly moved and stabbed downward in another cluster, then moved a bit more to his left. If he—or she—was sitting on this man's abdomen I can see how that's possible."

Melinda paused and looked at the chest to make sure she had seen everything. No one else spoke.

"All right," she began again. "Louisa, lift his left arm and rotate the hand. Thanks. No defensive wounds on his left arm or hand."

They repeated the process for his right arm.

"Was he conscious when he was stabbed?" Monique asked.

Melinda shook her head. "Don't know yet." She moved to his head. "The cut to his throat appears to have sliced through the carotid arteries. Actually, it severed everything—esophagus, trachea, muscles." She leaned in to look closer. "The wound extends to the cervical vertebrae."

Chris whistled. "Almost decapitated."

"Indeed," Melinda agreed. "But not quite."

"Cause of death?" Monique asked.

Melinda held up her hand. "Not so fast."

"What is all that tissue around his neck and coming out his mouth?" Monique asked. "It looks like, like, well I don't know what. It's all bunched up at the top end of his throat. You said it was his esophagus when you first saw him, right?"

"The corners of his mouth are torn, and something appears to be in there, for sure," Louisa said. "And it looks like the same tissue that's around his lips is the tissue we see protruding from his neck wound. Coming out of his throat. Looks like esophagus to me. Or part of it, anyway."

Chris gagged and swallowed hard.

Melinda stared at the wound a moment without blinking, then shook her head. "Let's come back to this. Going on, the scalp has been removed. A jagged incision under the eyebrows . . ." She leaned in and looked closer. "And deep scratches on the, uh, above the right orbit."

Monique looked at Louisa. The young Comanche's right eyebrow was arched. Monique had never heard Melinda flustered.

"The laceration extends through the pericranium." Then she whispered, "All the way to the bone. The pericranium is ripped. This was not incised. It was . . . torn." She looked at Monique.

"Okay. And . . . ?"

"Cut and torn," she repeated.

Louisa said nothing.

"I thought they just took the top part," Chris said.

"Who is they?"

"Well, I mean. Indians scalped, right?"

"That's how we did it," Louisa said as if she had seen it done firsthand.

"The only scalping I've seen was after a man got his ponytail caught in a power drill," Melinda said.

"Holy cow," muttered Chris.

"I was leaving for the afternoon and went through the ER to pick up Thin Mints from a nurse who was selling them for her kid. Medics wheeled him in right in front of me. His scalp and hair were in a cold pack on his chest. Surgeons tried to reattach it."

Chris swallowed. "Did they?"

"Don't know. I should ask."

Melinda touched the dead man's top teeth with a gloved finger.

"The labium superius oris is missing," Louisa said.

The ravaged face appeared to sneer.

"I see remnants of a moustache," Melinda said.

Chris started to sweat. Monique knew that some people enter an autopsy suite intending to make sage commentary while cavalierly watching bodies being dissected. It does not take long until that idea fades, and you just try to hold on to your lunch and stay upright.

"Then the upper lip was, well, ripped off from right to left, exposing the superior jowl fat."

Monique looked at Chris. Sweat was running down both sides of his nose, and his skin was ashen. "Step outside, Chris."

"I'm fine."

"No shame if you gotta puke," Louisa said. "Just walk away for a second."

Chris swallowed and walked to the sink. He leaned over it and rested his arms on the edges.

"Making the chest incision," Melinda continued.

Choking noises emanated from the sink. The women ignored it, and Monique watched as Melinda wielded her small scalpel. *Such a small tool,* she thought, *to do so much damage to a body.* Melinda quickly made the basic Y incision from the right shoulder across to the left and down to the groin. Monique knew there would be no blood, so she was not concerned about spurting. Still, she remained fascinated by how easy it was to hurt human flesh.

Chris returned, and Monique looked at him. "Chris," she said, "you're leaning."

He jerked his head up. "What?"

"Sure you're all right?"

"Never better." He swallowed and shuffled his feet.

Melinda dropped the scalpel into the metal bowl, pulled up the skin above the man's clavicles over his face, and drew back the skin over his ribs and draped it down toward the table. The gray skin looked to Monique like the hide of a dead deer. Except that deer hide was thicker, hairier, and a bit more yellow. The ribs, whitish gray underneath dark reddish bits of flesh, reminded her of the wild hog her cousin Dustin brought her and Steve last year. They hung it up by its hind legs from the rafters in the garage with a bucket underneath. She told them to put down a tarp because she didn't want blood stains on the garage floor. Dustin had already gutted the massive sow, so he and Steve proceeded to skin and meticulously excise portions of the animal. The two men cut and talked until 3 a.m. and finally got what they wanted from the 180-pound monster. After they were finished, what was left looked like a zombie hog.

Crack! Monique snapped to attention when Melinda used the bone cutter to cut through the ribs. Chris held up a hand and staggered back to the sink. Monique closed her eyes and took a few deep breaths.

By the time she looked back down, Melinda had pulled back the ribs and opened the chest cavity, and her hands were buried inside. Monique thought of the scene in *The Thing* when the guy's open chest suddenly snapped shut and severed the doctor's arms.

"Earth to detective," Melinda said.

"What?" Monique asked. She realized that she, too, was sweating.

"This is a real fucked-up mess in here," Melinda said in a quiet voice.

"I don't know how you do this every day," Monique agreed. "Bodies everywhere. How many more in the freezers?"

"I don't mean in the room. I mean in *here*." Her hands occupied, she nodded to the body cavity.

Louisa stared at the chaotic innards of the dead museum guard and said, "Wow."

"Is it supposed to look like that?" Monique asked.

Melinda looked inside the cavity, moving her head around like a heron scouting for frogs. "Just a minute."

Melinda lifted the skin above the clavicles, laid it back over the chest, then used a pair of scissors to cut a vertical incision up the left side of the guard's neck.

She worked fast, asking Louisa for a retractor and a probe. "Veins and arteries are torn," Melinda said. "In addition, the esophagus is ruptured and was partially pulled up into his mouth. Some of the tissue was caught behind his incisors and canines, as is a chunk of trachea cartilage. The lungs are partially in his throat because they were pulled out. His stomach is displaced as well."

"What?" Monique asked. "What do you mean?"

Melinda kept looking and probing.

"All right. We counted forty stab wounds, but only two made it through to his lungs. It appears as if the person doing the stabbing either didn't have much strength or wasn't trying very hard." Melinda was speaking to herself.

"And?" Louisa.

"Hang on." Melinda moved back to the open chest cavity. She asked for the same tools and appeared to be performing surgery. "I've never seen, or even heard, of this before."

Chris swallowed heavily. "You mean the scalping?"

"No," she answered almost distractedly. "This man's heart is lacerated."

"Lacerated?" Monique asked. "You mean, because he was stabbed? You must have seen that before."

"No. I mean his heart, lungs, trachea, esophagus, and tongue all were cut multiple times. From the inside."

"Is that possible?" Monique asked. "I mean, surely all that came from him being stabbed?" Both Chris and Monique were perspiring profusely now.

"No." Melinda leaned closer, her face almost touching the corpse. "And it appears that part of his heart is missing."

"What?"

"A small section has been cut away. The heart is very tough, so it makes sense that whatever they used couldn't do more than take a sliver. See?" She held the organ up and turned it.

Monique swallowed. "Yeah, Okay."

Melinda put the heart in the tray then slowly pulled the retracted skin toward her face and inspected the underside. Monique feared Melinda might actually put her nose on the cold flesh. Saliva flooded her mouth, and she knew she was seconds away from heaving.

Instead, Melinda drew back, put the guard's abused skin back into position, and straightened. "Only two stab wounds perforated the chest. What happened here wouldn't be an easy thing to accomplish. But it could be done if a long, slender knife or something like it was pushed down his throat. There are lacerations on the stomach. The base of the tongue is also cut multiple times, as if a knife sawed up and down."

"What the holy hell are you talking about?" Monique asked. She licked her lips. Salty tears touched her tongue, and she flinched.

"Something was put down this man's throat. Something long, thin, and sharp. It lacerated the—"

"Before his throat was cut?" Monique asked.

"Yes. Then, somehow, the esophagus and lungs were pulled upward. Multiple times. Stomach through the esophagus, lungs through the trachea."

"That is unbelievable," Monique stammered.

"Strange, yes, but not beyond belief."

"What's the significance of pulling out someone's innards?" Chris asked.

"What's the significance of any of this?" Melinda countered.

"Damn and shit fire," Chris said.

"Indeed," Melinda said. "Something pulled these tissues up through the man's throat. I have absolutely no idea why."

"How could anyone do that?" Monique whispered.

"Some tool with a claw. Somebody stuck it down his throat, grabbed tissue, and pulled it—"

"Jesus God, Melinda," Monique said quietly.

Melinda stepped off her stool. Monique looked at her, trying to fight back the hot tears rolling down her face.

"He was dead before his throat was cut," Melinda said. "Whatever was shoved into his mouth suffocated him. If not that, he would have died from internal blood loss after the arteries were severed."

"Thank you." Monique turned and methodically took off her morgue gown.

"I need to think about this," Melinda said as Monique and Chris prepared to leave. "How about you give me until tomorrow? I suggest you two go home and have a drink."

Monique closed her eyes.

"Take a hot bubble bath," Louisa added. "That's what I do."

"I don't think even a shot of Midleton whiskey would do it," Chris said, "if I could afford to buy it."

28

onique and Chris drove through Taco Bell for tacos and other meaty, cheesy, crunchy selections that had the same ingredients and tasted pretty much the same. She knew that fast food was destructive to her system but occasionally she would relent and eat a few tasty tacos.

"I can't believe it, but I'm hungry," Chris said when he picked up his tray of tacos and a burrito.

"I thought I was, but now I'm not." Nevertheless, Monique chewed a small mouthful of bean burrito and stared out the window at the patrons going in and out of the liquor store across the street.

"Weird, huh? I mean, you'd think I'd be sick or want a drink."

Monique took a bite of the taco she held in her other hand, and pieces of the crunchy shell rained down on her lap.

Chris gulped down two more tacos and a bean burrito. He wiped his mouth.

Monique looked on in amazement. "You sure flipped a switch."

Chris shrugged. "Getting out of there made me feel completely different." Then he paused. "Monique."

"Yes."

"Why and how did they do that to that poor man?"

She shook her head. "Melinda will tell us more when she's finished." The case had become so odd and so disturbing that she was not quite sure how to evaluate their progress.

"Okay. Let's talk about something else. You were upset when we found that index card. What's the deal? What's Nanih Waiya?"

"I told you. It's a place—the place where some Choctaws believe we emerged from the Earth and became people."

"So, like God creating Adam and Eve? He made Adam from clay. The Earth part is the same."

She put her taco and burrito back in the bag and took a large gulp of Diet Coke. "All right. There are several versions of how Choctaws came to be."

"You mean were created by God?"

"Yes. But not in the way the Bible says. And the first Chahtas didn't call him God. The stories don't resemble the Adam and Eve version, and none say we came from Africa or Mongolia like a lot of anthropologists like to argue."

"How did they get here then?"

"Up through the ground, from what I'm told. We were locusts, then dried off and turned into people."

Chris did not know what to say to that. He unwrapped a stick of gum. "You go to church?"

Monique gave him her small smile, the one she used when asked questions like this. "I don't have to go to church to believe in God."

"I know that."

"Christian Choctaws have a hard time with that creation story. The emergence from the ground is one thing, but the idea that we descended from locusts is too much to accept. I question our creation story and still wonder how Choctaws could have been locusts. Of course, lots of tribes believe they started as animals. Or they had animal helpers to guide them."

"Animals?"

"Most tribes have animals that play prominent roles in their creation and survival. Tribes in the Northeast say Turtle Island."

"I've heard of that."

"The world is on the back of a turtle. Some say Grandmother Turtle. I once saw a bumper sticker that read, 'When Grandmother Turtle dies, the world ends.' That was in reference to pollution that is killing the natural world. That makes sense to me, but my tribe doesn't use that concept."

"Huh," Chris breathed as he thought about it. "Turtle."

"Some tribes had thirteen-month calendars based on the thirteen scutes on a turtle's shell."

"What's a scute?"

"You know—the large pieces on a shell." Monique googled turtle shell and showed him a picture.

"So, where did the bones in Nanih Waiya come from?"

"Well, there are other versions of the creation. Some Choctaws say that we didn't come from Nanih Waiya, we came out of underwater caves off the west coast as humans. After we moved east, we created the mound as a place to house the thousands of bones of loved ones we had carried around with us since our creation. That version said the Oklas traveled for forty years or so before settling in Mississippi. Christians don't like that story either because there's no mention of Adam and Eve."

Chris nodded. "We all have our gods and legends, I guess, and most of us just take it on faith. What do you think that thing was in the archives?"

"I don't know. Some mutant, maybe. Clearly, someone knew it was in the Room and wanted it."

"But Adams said no one has access to the files, so how would someone have known the bones were there? That room hadn't been touched in years."

"Maybe there's more than one copy of the card," she said. "Actually, that would explain a lot." And it would certainly take away the gnawing feeling that something even nastier than a homicidal creep was responsible for the murder and the theft.

"Taz was acting strange."

"Maybe she doesn't like blood."

"K9s are trained to tolerate it," Chris countered, "whether they like it or not. She sensed something there, and I think we missed it. Whatever it was."

But Monique knew what it was. Taz had sensed evil. She had sensed it herself in that room. She was going to need Uncle Leroy's help to end this.

"Where do we go from here?" Chris said.

"Back to the museum. We know the perps are not in the building. Probably they left before Martin got there and found Lewis. But we do know that there were birds in the Room *with* the perps."

"You think the birds got in through the vent?"

"That's the only way."

"But we still don't know is how the people came and went."

"Let's go see if we can figure it out."

They drove back to the museum and hurried through the entire building once more, this time with the building plans in hand. There were no secret doors or windows, nor any underground passageways. They looked behind the stuffed longhorn cattle and inside the antique whiskey barrels.

On their way back to the basement, Monique looked into the koi pond area. The caimans looked to be asleep, so Chris climbed into their enclosure and looked behind a faux boulder.

As he moved to inspect the foliage, Monique called to him with some urgency, "Uh, Chris?"

He turned around to find the three fifty-pound reptiles lined up in a row and facing him. Chris paused in surprise, then sprinted to their left, jumped into their shallow moat, and hurdled the metal fence. He slipped on the marble floor and fell on his side.

"Wish I'd recorded that," Monique said, offering him her hand. He stood and looked down at his wet trousers and shoes.

"Got extra pants in your car?" he asked.

"Actually, yes, but I don't think you can squeeze into them. Good thing you didn't hurt one of those cute little lizards." They looked back to see that the caimans had moved to the edge of the bank and were watching them intently, mouths agape.

"Thanks a lot."

"Let's check on Rachel and Louie and then call it a day," Monique said wearily.

"I think I could find my way from the dinosaurs to the alligators in my sleep by now," Chris said. His wet shoes squeaked as he walked.

"Caimans are not alligators. Still, be careful what you wish for, my friend," Monique answered. "You don't want to dream about any of this."

Rachel and Louie were just finishing up their investigation of the Room and the hallway. Both of them looked tired and discouraged.

"Nothing on those boxes or the bones on the Room floor," Louie told Monique. He looked at Chris. "Hey, you're wet."

"Yes. Yes, I am."

"All righty." Louie was covered in dust and looked tired. "Looks refreshing, actually."

"Please say you got *something*," Monique said.

Louie frowned and shook his head.

"You always get something."

"No prints, no sweat, no skin oil, nothing."

"But in saying you got nothing," she said, "you're telling me that the perps didn't touch the boxes or the bones. That tells me something." He nodded. "No data can be good data," she reminded him. "Evidence comes in many forms."

"Well, we're done." Rachel took off her gloves. Louie closed their cases. "Let's get outta here."

"I'll see you tomorrow," Monique said.

"Tomorrow? Why?" Rachel asked.

Monique nodded toward the vent.

"Seriously?"

"Serious as scalping."

29

onique said good night to Chris in the parking lot and started home. She knew a few things for certain: the people who did this were willing to kill to get what they wanted, they were skilled, and the feathers were from owls. She mulled over the autopsy findings as she drove. Her cell phone rang when she was only a mile from home.

"Hey, honey," said Steve. "Where are you?"

"Almost there."

"Can you stop and get some almond milk? I thought we had enough for breakfast, but it's all gone."

Monique sighed. "I guess." She hated being asked to stop at the store when she was tired and wanted to get home, eat, and fall asleep. Why hadn't he gone for the milk himself? She was not in the frame of mind for an argument, though, and now that she thought about it they also needed bread and bananas. An extra ten minutes wouldn't matter.

Walmart was the closest store. She pulled into the lot, turned off the engine, and watched a shockingly obese woman in stretch shorts and a tank top put bags into the trunk of her tortured Mazda. The immense woman's belly hung down below the leg-line of her shorts. Monique wondered if the woman had checked her clothing before venturing into public.

She got out of her cruiser and locked it. The day had turned to a cooler, humid evening. She scanned the sky and saw no stars. Faint light flashed in the southeastern horizon. She would check for storms on the weather app to see what might happen tomorrow.

Although she was tired, the big store always tempted her. As much as she disliked box stores that paid low wages for overworked employees, she frequented them for just one or two items. The problem was that she often went in for milk and came out with enough food for the Chinese army. Sure enough, she suddenly felt the urge to buy. Maybe it was stress or her apprehension for what the investigation might turn up. Therefore, she picked up some limes with the staples because limeade sounded good. She got a sack of potatoes because a large spud covered in cheese and salsa would go nicely with the limeade. The trail mix would be perfect on her dessert yogurt, and so on.

In front of the checkout she spotted a large tropical plant so she added that to her cart as well. The croton was so tall that she had to peek around it to see where she was going. After paying for her supplies—which filled the entire cart instead of just one sack—she made her way back to the car. The lot was emptying fast.

Monique pushed the cart with a loose front wheel through the lot. She had almost reached it when she smelled wet dog. Then she sensed someone behind her.

She turned to see three very odd-looking men—if they were indeed men. Their heads appeared to be almost round, like the Walmart Price-Chopper's happy face. Their eyes, with yellow irises and dilated black pupils, were enormous. The muted parking lot lights allowed her to see that one of them had creeping crud on his skin. One wore striped Adidas tights, an inside-out white T-shirt, and untied Nikes. He looked like he had stolen the clothing from the women's locker room at a gym. Another man wore black pants and a black turtleneck. He looked like a beatnik, or maybe a pumpkin-head version of Mike Myers's *Saturday Night Live* character Dieter.

The tallest of the three wore a green polo shirt and tan shorts with an expensive leather belt, but no shoes or socks. He grinned and showed yellow teeth. He held a large knife.

"You're gettin' nosy, Missy Monique." He mispronounced her name, calling her "Moe-nicky."

"About what?" she asked as she moved her cart to keep it between her and them.

"You know," the beatnik said. Monique caught a whiff of his breath—a combination of rotting meat, coffee, and macaroni and cheese. As she looked at them, their features began changing; they were growing hair and beards right in front of her. The tallest man's pursed lips kept extending outward. He appeared to be morphing into something.

Monique shoved her cart at them and went for her gun. In the split second that took, the man with the knife slid around the cart and slashed at her face with the large, shiny blade. She moved back quickly enough to avoid a knife swipe across her cheek, but he came at her again and sliced the knife across her chest. Her torn blouse fluttered. He swiped again and caught her forearm before she managed to get her gun out of the holster.

She had never screamed for help in her life, but she screamed then. Two young men four rows over who were loading an outdoor grill into the back of a truck stopped what they were doing and looked her way.

"What the hell?" the taller of the two said. He turned his gimme cap around on his head so the bill faced backward. He reached inside his truck and pulled out a tire iron and a baseball bat, throwing the latter to his friend. The two charged toward Monique and her three attackers.

"Hey! Hey, you!" the one with the tire iron yelled at the men.

The three assailants turned toward the young men running toward them, then backed away into the next row that was darkened because of a broken light bulb. Monique fleetingly noticed that the men shrunk a bit. One man said in a ragged voice that sounded like he was missing a few vocal chords, "We gotta go, Mac."

"Another time," Mac said to Monique in a whispery voice even more ragged than his partner's. His yellow circle eyes widened and flickered red, and he and the others disappeared into the darkness, leaving behind a stink reminiscent of a dirty chicken coop.

"You're bleeding, lady," one of Monique's young saviors said as he reached her. "Whoa, you're really bleeding."

"Where'd they go?" the other man asked. "They just disappeared." He held his tire iron in both hands, looking around the lot for movement. "They got away, man."

Her arm felt warm, and now that she was able to focus on it, it had begun to sting. She looked down to see that her shirt had been sliced open. Her vest was in full view. The material of her jacket and blouse were cut along the length of her unprotected lower arm. The widening pool of blood at her feet explained why she felt lightheaded.

"Ow," she said calmly. "Make sure my gun is in the holster. I'm a police offi . . ." she trailed off as she fell backward and hit the ground. She saw one of the young men talking on his cell phone before she closed her eyes. She opened them again to sirens and lights and realized she was in a speeding ambulance. The siren wailed loud enough to warn everyone for blocks around that it was approaching.

"Detective," said the medic. Monique had seen him before, at the museum. He and another woman had carted off Ethan Lewis the guard. "You're okay," he assured her. "You have a cut on your arm, and you hit your head. The loss of blood made you faint. It's under control." He smiled, and a flash of insight told Monique that he said that to all his patients regardless of their condition.

"I have two—"

"We have your weapons up front."

Every time Monique tried to sit up, she was gently pushed back down. As she watched headlights come and go past her, she realized that the cut on her arm was no small scratch. She felt weak and could not think straight. It didn't take long to reach the hospital. At least it didn't seem long.

A flurry of people surrounded her and wheeled her into a room with bright lights. She recognized the emergency room. She had come here last summer because of a persistent migraine that Tylenol with codeine couldn't touch. Ironically, emergency rooms are not the best environments for people in pain. The noise, lights, and bustle make a migraine considerably worse until you can get a shot of Demerol. Monique felt herself fading again. She forced herself to focus. A cool hand touched her wrist, and she looked up to see Tall Blonde Lady Doctor looking down at her.

"So we meet again, Detective," Dr. Vartel said.

Somewhere in the distance, muted as the morphine drip took effect, she heard Chris Pierson yelling, "Where is she? What the hell happened?"

30

"That's all I can tell you," Monique said to Chris and the tall Captain Hardaway. Her stomach threatened to heave from whatever pain-killer they had pumped into her IV. Her ears rang, and she knew the persistent throb in her arm ought to hurt, though it didn't.

She had been out more than two hours. Someone had braided her hair to keep it out of the way. A few strands hung down over her left eye, but she was too tired to push it aside. She moved her tongue around in her mouth and knew she needed a Listerine swish. Dr. Vartel had come to tell her it had taken twenty internal stitches and forty external stitches to close the long slash in her forearm. The damage to the extensor carpi ulnaris muscle would heal if she kept her arm and hand still, though she would sport an impressive scar. More immediately, the thick bandage would drive her crazy after she awoke fully.

Steve sat outside the door with Robbie as Monique spoke with her colleagues. The officers who arrived at the scene first had talked with the two college students who had come to her aid in the parking lot. They had stayed by her side until help arrived, but they couldn't tell the officers much. They saw three blurry men running across the parking lot who seemed to dissipate in the darkness. That was about it. No one except Monique could give detailed descriptions of the men with round heads.

She knew her story sounded ridiculous when she told it to Chris and Captain Hardaway. Chris looked at her as if he thought she was nuts. He had been doing that a lot lately. *And he knows me pretty well*, she thought. *Maybe I am.* Captain Hardaway had rubbed one hand over his crew cut as he listened. When she was finished, he smiled and gently squeezed her shoulder. "You get some rest," he said. "We'll talk later." Monique knew he thought she had hit her head *very* hard.

Fortunately, she knew she would make sense to someone. After saying good night to Chris, Steve, and Robbie and assuring them she would sleep tight, Monique lay in bed thinking about what to do. Steve returned an hour later, saying that Robbie was spending the night at a neighbor's house. He demanded that the nurses fix a bed next to Monique's so he could stay with her.

"Foogly's gonna pee on the bed without you there," she told Steve groggily.

"I put her in the laundry room."

"Fine. She'll pee in there."

"Her litter box is on the floor."

"Doesn't matter when she's mad."

Around two o'clock a nurse brought her a pain pill and an antibiotic and told her the next check would be in two hours, at 4:00 a.m. The nurse looked at Steve who lay with his arms around his trusty bear. She did not say anything or change expression. She simply glanced at Monique, then left. As she drifted toward sleep, Monique planned to call her uncle Leroy Bear Red Ears. Because of what Leroy knew about Choctaw history, culture, and especially cosmology, odd stories featuring round-headed men might make complete sense to him.

Monique drifted off, awoke, then fell back asleep. She awoke again and found herself standing in her driveway. She was satisfied with the oil level in her new dually truck. The 2019 Chevy came equipped with fog lights, lift kit, and enormous all-terrain tires. The front end of the truck faced her garage so she could easily access any equipment she might need from the array of tools she had collected over the past twenty years.

The day was a bit cool, so she wore a postcolonial Choctaw dress: calico skirt with a white apron and high-collared button-front shirt. She'd styled her long hair into one long braid, and she wore moccasins with leggings that Steve's sister gave her for Christmas. As she walked into the garage for some Windex, she heard a footfall behind her. She turned to see three strange men with owl faces walking down the driveway toward her like a row of gunslingers, their round heads bobbing from side to side on wide shoulders. The men stared at her with golden eyes. All wore colorful Hawaiian shirts and Bermuda shorts. She had seen them before, but she couldn't remember where or when.

One stepped forward while the others stood their ground and grinned, revealing brown-yellow teeth.

The man had a whispery voice and spoke through a beak. "My name's Mac Crow. I need you to come with us, Missy Moe-nicky."

Monique dropped the oily rag. "Like hell."

Her father had always told her that using curse words reveals the speaker's laziness and that she should use a dictionary to better express herself. "You can always think of a better descriptive word," he would say. Much to her parents' dismay, Monique still preferred to curse when she needed to make a point.

She grabbed the gas can under the tool bench, unscrewed the top, then threw purple gas on the owl men. A lighted match that burned with a pink flame materialized between her fingers, and she threw it. As the men burned, Monique ran to safety through a back door that was made of wired-together femurs.

When she looked through the green-tinted kitchen window into the lilac-colored night sky, she saw three owls fly in front of the full red moon, their smoldering wings trailing green smoke. They looked back at her with shining red eyes. Owls cannot smile, but these did.

Monique's eyes popped open. It took her several minutes to calm her breathing and orient herself. *I'm in the hospital. That was a dream. It's morning.* She remembered that Steve had left a couple hours ago. He made sure that Monique ate a few bites of oatmeal and took her meds, then left to pick up Robbie and take him to school. She had fallen asleep again listening to Kate Bolduan on CNN. Most times when she had bad dreams, she recovered quickly, but this was different. She still smelled the wet-dog odor of the owl men in her room. She felt their hot breath.

She drank some water and immediately felt thirsty again. She sat up and straightened her arm. The stitches pulled painfully at her skin. "Damn!" she exclaimed.

Monique looked around the room and decided she felt better. "Time to go," she said aloud. She pulled back the thin covers and looked down. A large owl feather lay on her lap.

31

Monique called Leroy. "Those were the Crows," he said. "Wicked men who can change from owls to men. They've been around our tribe since the beginning. They prey on us, Monique. They always have, and they will as long as they are living."

"Why us? Where did they come from? They're witches, aren't they?" Monique asked between deep breaths that she hoped would keep her from crying. She had swallowed half a Tylenol 3 and felt relaxed but a bit paranoid. Monique feared that her people would think she was witched and refuse to talk to her anymore.

She looked at the door. Her doctor had vetoed her decision to leave the hospital, so she was stuck here at least one more day. But the call to Leroy couldn't wait. Steve had left the room the talk to the nurses and get some coffee in the cafeteria. She was worried that he might walk in and hear the conversation. If her burly, aggressive husband knew her attackers were witches, he would have the family in Mexico City by midnight. Steve was well aware that witches existed. He had never encountered one, but he knew that, like other malevolent beings, witches are around nonetheless.

"Why us? I don't really know. Crows have always done this to Chahtas." Her uncle referred to Choctaws in the old way.

"So Crows are . . . what? Are they also Choctaws?"

"A family that has always been around."

"Always," she repeated.

"Yes. The owl men were the lazy ones in the beginning who wouldn't help the Oklas find food or build homes. And yes, they're witches. And they can change shapes. Many tribes have shapeshifters who can take the form of animals. Sometime birds, sometimes wolves or coyotes. The Crows can change into owls. And even when they're men, they still look like owls."

"How do we get rid of them?"

"It isn't easy. Only certain people or animals can kill them."

"You mean you?" Monique asked hopefully.

"No," he said regretfully.

Monique heaved a sigh. If a Chahta doctor could not kill the Crows, then who could?

"Nanishta allowed the Crows to exist, but they couldn't live forever," Leroy said. "He made the bargain that the evil ones could live but would die at the hands of someone they tried to kill. And didn't."

"Huh?"

"Throughout history, various members of the Crows have been killed— but only by people they had attacked but failed to kill. These people didn't die, and so they lived to fight and kill the Crows."

She had a moment's hope. "I don't believe that," she said. "What about the security guard they wounded? Could he help?"

"No, Monique. He doesn't know our ways. The owl men showed what they can do at the museum. They took another's hair, ears, and moustache. And something else, I wager."

Monique thought of the missing sliver of the guard's heart.

Leroy continued. "They're sneaky and slippery as a pocket full of pudding and can fit into small places. That's how they got into that room in the museum. They're not easy to get rid of, Ibitek." He paused. "You are the one, Niece."

"Yeah, they did try to kill me. Why?"

"You're getting too close."

"How could they know what I'm doing?"

"You are not listening, Monique," Leroy said softly. "Someone they intended to kill but couldn't can kill them."

She gasped with understanding. That would be *her*.

"That is why you have to get yourself here to me," Leroy said. "And to make you feel better about what you must do, know that the tribe passed a law in 1834 stating that the penalty for witchcraft is death."

"Oh, for God's sake. That law was revoked."

"So? The meaning and intent were clear. We always knew they were among us. And someone must be able to fight them."

Monique tried to think. Steve would never allow her to see Leroy if he knew she intended to kill witches. Most Natives aware of their culture are all too familiar with evil—witches, though, can be unpredictable. They don't broadcast how they intend to hurt you.

"In a few days, Monique. You have to come. Go to sleep now. Heal your arm. You will need all your strength to deal with these witches. Sleep."

She did. But as she was drifting off, she wondered why Leroy knew so much about them.

32

"I know who did it, Chris. I know who killed Samuel Rector and attacked Ethan Lewis. Although I still don't know why they wanted to steal the bones."

"Who?" Chris demanded. He'd arrived almost immediately after she called him at 8 a.m. It was plain that he hadn't changed clothes from the day before. He had slept in them.

Monique had debated showing him what the Crows left her, then thought better of it and hid the offensive feather under the sheet. "The Crows," she said.

"What crows? I thought it was owls who killed them."

"The Crows. It's their family name. Men who can change into owls."

"What drugs did they give you, Monique? Are you high?"

"No. It was owl men."

Chris made a face.

Monique barreled through her explanation before she stalled out. "They've been around our tribe since our beginning. They prey on us."

"Us?"

"Choctaws. Many tribes are plagued by evil beings and witches. We have the Crows. They have always picked on us Chahtas." She repeated what Leroy had told her. "The owl men wouldn't help the first Oklas find food or build homes. They let everyone else to do the hard work. They're witches and can change into owls." She knew she was babbling.

Clearly bewildered, Chris said, "Well, what do they want? Why did they attack the security guards?"

"I'm not sure yet. Leroy is going to explain it when I see him."

"Monique . . ." Chris shook his head. "You hit your head and lost a lot of blood—"

"Let me finish. Leroy says some evil is obvious, but you have to learn to spot it before it gets you. You and I are in the depravity business. Don't you think that's true?" She had asked Chris that question before.

"Sometimes, yes," he agreed. "But people can't change shape. Men can't turn into owls."

"They do. I don't know how, but they do."

"And what about the bones they stole at the museum, the skeleton the document described as a cross between a person and a bird? Was it one of those owl men you're talking about?"

"Yes. That's what they wanted."

"You won't get very far with this explanation. You know that, right?"

"Chris, a lot of tribes have shapeshifters. Always have."

"Fine. I'm not going to argue with you. But why'd they come after you?"

Monique let out a breath and tried to straighten her wounded arm. The bandage felt too tight, and the stitches itched. Her fingers didn't move like they should. At the back of her mind she worried they never would. "I've been having weird dreams for several months," she told him. "I don't recall much about them when I wake. Every time, though, I feel unsettled, like someone is trying to communicate with me. This morning I had a real doozy. The same men who attacked me at Walmart were in it." She told him about the owl men coming after her in the garage and how she defended herself by lighting them on fire.

"It makes sense that you would dream about people who attacked you," he said patiently.

"But these dreams have been going on for months."

"Do you keep a dream journal?"

She sighed. "Yes, I have a dream book by the bed. Pages are empty except a few vague recollections. This time I clearly remember every detail of those owl men, right down to their yellow nails and sprouts of what didn't look like hair on their chests."

"Sounds like you're high."

"You think?"

"So, fire is how to get rid of them?"

"I don't know why I dreamed that. Maybe because the gas can was right there. Only certain people or animals can kill them."

"You mean Leroy?"

"No. He said he couldn't."

"What about Steve? He's a big guy."

"Steve absolutely believes in witches, but he knows better than to confront one. Leroy told me that they can only be killed by someone they tried to kill but didn't."

"Tried to kill and didn't?"

"Someone who survived an attack. That's the deal Nanishta made."

"Nanishta's God, right? God makes deals?"

"Chris, I only know what I've been told."

Chris paused to swallow half the contents of his Odwella bottle. "Okay. So, what about those remains at the museum?"

"Obviously, the bones were important enough for them to take."

"And you think that the Crows got in here in the form of owls and took some bones?"

She sighed. "Yes. I do."

"And what about the sliced-up organs? How'd they do that?"

"Melinda told us how they did it."

"You can't get your hand and arm down someone's throat, Monique." Chris sat back and crossed his right leg over the left.

"Scully did it to Spock in *Hannibal*."

"What?"

"Gillian Anderson played a psychiatrist in the television series *Hannibal*, and she killed a the guy who played Spock in the new *Star Trek* movies by cramming her hand down his throat. Look, never mind. Think about what Melinda told us. Who said it was a human hand and arm?"

Chris looked at her, slack-jawed. "You mean they used a tool?"

"No."

"Not a tool? You think they changed into something that had an arm that could reach down into his chest?"

"You got a better idea?"

"I just told you. A tool."

"Like what?"

"A long metal rod with a claw at the end."

"What about talons?"

"Talons? . . . You mean claws?"

"Yes."

"How would . . . ?" He massaged his right ankle.

"You don't have to know everything right now, Chris."

"But owls? No one is going to believe this."

"Not everyone has to."

33

"The pelvis was too big to fit through the vent," Monique explained to Leroy on the speakerphone in the den the next afternoon. The doctors had tried to keep her one more night for observation, but Monique insisted on being released late morning.

She leaned back in Steve's lounge chair eating sorbet and blueberries as she talked to her uncle. Steve sat at the kitchen table peeling a tangerine as he listened.

Her arm hurt. Still, it was better than injuring a leg. At least with an arm injury, she could run and get in a decent workout. She had felt off-kilter earlier, no doubt because of the pain killers. Oxy made her sick, so they gave her Percocet. Maybe that caused her to hallucinate. She refused her tablet after she had reached under the sheet to retrieve the owl feather and found it missing. Somehow, some way, those owl men got into her room. Or did they? She vowed not to take any more pills. Monique needed a clear mind in order to understand why these men from tribal legend had appeared and why they had broken into the museum to take the bones.

"Owls in vents," Steve said. He laughed without humor.

Monique continued to wonder if the feather had been a drug-induced dream. On the other hand, she had felt it, smelled it. It was real. So where did it go?

"They had to take the skeleton out in pieces to get it through the air vent," Leroy said, stating the obvious.

She blinked and sat up. She would think about the feather later. "Yes, that's the only way. But they couldn't get the pelvis through the opening. There were little dents in the metal where they tried to pull it through. When they gave up trying, they dropped the pelvis on top of a box on a top shelf. Maybe they planned to come back for it."

"Then they dragged the bones through the vent and outside," he said.

"Yes. Turns out they followed a connecting vent to the Omni Theatre and exited through a window in an unused office. They had to worm their way through wires and cables."

"They got ahold of building plans," Leroy said. "They knew the layout."

"I think so. The dog handler, Linda, told me earlier that her German shepherd didn't have a clear scent but did pick up a smell that disturbed her around the Omni Theatre. This morning my partner, Chris, took a team into the theatre and discovered more feathers near an adjoining office window. They also found an open vent we'd missed. Evidently, that vent led to a duct that connected to the Room of Secrets."

She heard Leroy take a drink, no doubt from the glass bottle of distilled water that he always kept nearby. He refused to drink or eat out of plastic. Then she heard him unwrap something, probably a sugar-free Double Bubble. "We found the dead guard's clothes in a box on a top shelf," she went on. "There weren't any prints that would indicate someone climbed the shelf. I got a call this morning from the forensics team who've been trying to figure this out. Louie says all they found were light scratches in the dust on the boxes that were opened or overturned."

"Feather marks."

"I believe the dead guard had his throat ripped by talons and was cut and stabbed by someone who had a sharp blade but not much strength."

"That would be right," Leroy agreed. "They can change in flight. But they can't move well if they have not changed completely. The men and owls are strong only if they have completely changed into one form or the other. In order to hurt the guard without leaving footprints, they would have needed some man-strength, but they also had to be part owl to hover above the floor."

"That's why there weren't any footprints in that room."

"Yes."

"The dead guard's organs were cut up. Someone managed to lacerate them by going through his throat."

"What?!" Steve dropped his tangerine. Monique had been hoping to keep that little detail from him.

"Mmmm," Leroy responded.

"Who in hell does that?" Steve said, alarmed.

Leroy heard him. "Tell Steve to calm down, Monique. Tell him I said so."

Steve looked at Monique, his mouth open.

"The guard was killed in that manner to scare anyone who saw him," Leroy continued. "The Crows do things like that for fun."

"How could that be fun?"

"Just because. They have no morality. Same reason people torture people and animals. These entities are different and infinitely more dangerous. They can change from humans to owls," Leroy repeated. "That means they become things that are in between a man and a bird. Thinner arms, longer fingers. Talons are very sharp. They can easily slice open a scalp."

Or tear it completely off, Monique thought. "I understand what you're saying, Leroy, but can't there be another explanation?" she asked.

"You sound like Dustin," Leroy admonished her.

"Dustin tends to see things simply. There's no room in his religion for witches. But," she added, "he knows something is out there, and he's frightened."

"The Crows are real, Monique. They're not cryptids."

"You know about cryptozoology?"

"Are you suggesting that I don't do my research?"

Monique thought he sounded professorial. "Well, I didn't mean . . ."

"You know these are real. You've seen them in your dreams before they met you at Walmart."

"Dreams aren't real, Leroy."

"They can enter your dreams, Monique. They get into mine if I let them."

"How do you keep it from happening?"

"I'll teach you, but not now. We have more pressing issues."

"We do, yes," Monique said tiredly. "Where did the Crows come from—this time, I mean—and where do you think they are now?"

Steve sat with his arms folded, staring at his naked fruit.

"I think you know, Monique," Leroy said quietly. She held her breath. Ginger had also said that to her. Then Leroy seemed to change the subject. "There are stories about witch holes in Doaksville."

"Doaksville?" Steve asked. "That's a ghost town."

Leroy heard him. "You could call it that. At one time it was our capital. Doaksville was a trade center. Fort Towson was close, and the trade line went to Fort Smith and other places. After General Stand Watie surrendered, it just faded—"

"Leroy," Monique interrupted, "why are you talking about witch holes? What are they?"

"Holes in the Earth. Some elders say they are bottomless, others say they're two hundred feet deep. Most say that they sometimes glow. Witches would sit on the edges of the Doaksville hole and brush their hair. When someone approached, they jumped in."

"You believe that? Witch holes? Are you sure they weren't just wells?"

"They aren't there anymore," Leroy continued. "I looked."

"So you don't believe in them."

"I didn't say that."

"Are you saying that the owl men came from a witch hole?"

"Yes."

"Where do we find them?"

"I can only guess. But I think I know," he said again.

"Where? Tell me."

"Chalakwa Ranch."

"What?! Andrew's land?"

"Yes. There has to be a place in the hollow. In the center of that land. You've been there."

"Yes. But—"

"I think there is an entry into the Earth there."

"You mean like a tunnel or a witch hole?"

"In this case witch holes lead to the tunnels."

"For crying out loud!" Steve yelled. "A witch hole on Andrew's ranch? You cannot be serious!"

"You sound like John McEnroe," Leroy said. "Calm yourself."

"Steve, we need to talk this through, and you're not helping," Monique said.

"I think maybe the tunnels are connected," Leroy said. "You ever hear of the Hollow Earth Theory?"

"No. What's that?"

"Many cultures around the world believe the Earth is hollow," he continued, "or at least is riddled with underground passages and caves. Some have stories about people who live underground; others say that strange creatures live in the Earth below us. There are holes that some say are their sites of emergence, like in our Nanih Waiya creation story."

"Right," Steve snorted. "Underground worlds. Like in *Journey to the Center of the Earth*."

"Please hush, Steve. Is that possible?" Monique asked Leroy.

"Who knows? There are enormous caverns underground that seem to support the theory. The largest, Mammoth Cave in Kentucky, is a little over three hundred fifty miles long. Jewel Cave under the northern plains is about a hundred thirty miles. Lechugilla Cave in the Southwest is about a hundred and ten miles. There's another cave in Zapoteca that the Spanish missionaries found. They thought it was the entrance to Hell, and so they walled it up with boulders and dirt. It was located where they did human sacrifices. The Spanish thought it was an evil place."

"Sounds like it," Steve interjected.

"They thought it was necessary." Leroy said. "Those people accepted it as part of their lives. Anyway, something new is happening here, Monique. The hollow is changing, and the owls are part of it."

"New how? It's always been a peculiar place."

"The voices, for one thing. There have always been the night screams, but in the last few days there is another voice. A female. Andrew has heard it. I heard her this morning after I spoke with you. Something evil has moved in. The pigs, snakes, mice, frogs—all the creatures—are coming out into the grass to get away from it. Andrew drove around the property yesterday and ran over more tarantulas with the ATV than he has ever seen before." He paused. "Monique."

"I'm still here."

"The bones missing from the museum are from a being who lived a long time ago."

"Yes, we know that. The skeleton was found at the end of the colonial period. But there's no telling how long those bones have been in the ground. We don't know exactly how old they are."

"They belong to one of the First," he said calmly.

"What do you mean by the 'First'? First what?"

"One of the Eldest. A female. The one called Hatak haksi."

"Evil? The evil one?"

"Yes. She began the Crow community shortly after creation to serve her. Throughout all the years since, she has committed ever more evil deeds that have made her what she is."

"You mean 'was,' don't you? What she *was*?"

"No. Chahta thought he killed her, but she is alive again."

"Chahta? Leroy, Chahta was one of the first Oklas to emerge from the Earth. There's no way of knowing how long ago that was."

"Yes," Leroy agreed patiently. He spoke about the Old Ones as if he had seen them last week. "She was buried. Now you say that she was found by white people who dug around Nanih Waiya many years later, and they kept her bones in a box."

"Right. The box was passed from person to person until 1888 when the museum took it from a woman who was trying to get rid of the bones. After her husband died."

"They were bad luck," Leroy said. "You knew that."

"Yes. I guess so."

"Somehow the Crows recently found out where she has been resting. They came to get her. She is alive again."

"How is that possible?"

"It just is."

Monique looked at Steve and his mangled tangerine. His face reflected what she was feeling.

"Monique, listen to me," Leroy said. "The Crows will not just go away. As I've said, this is not the first time they have bothered us."

"You call this 'bothering'?!" Steve yelled. "How about 'tormenting' or 'destroying'?"

"Steve," Monique warned.

"What do they want?" she asked Leroy quietly. "They have the bones. What're they going to do now that she's, uh, reanimated?"

"They desire power and revenge. These entities are inherently mean-spirited."

"No kidding. They sure got me good."

"Yesterday she and the others attacked Peterson Murray. At his house."

"Oh, no!" Monique sat up. "Not Peter."

"Damn!" Steve shouted. "That's enough!" He slapped his palm on the tabletop. Foogly jumped off his lap and sprinted across the den to the windowsill. Steve crossed the room and sat on the arm of Monique's chair.

Monique and Peter had attended elementary and junior high together. He was a chubby, happy kid who had grown up to be a kind, happy man.

He and Doreen had three vivacious daughters, all of them jokesters like their dad and pretty like their mother.

"He was out on his riding mower early today," Leroy said. "They swooped down on him from the trees and tried to cut his throat and take his ears, but they just got part of one. Partially scalped him."

"What . . ."

"His dog alerted Doreen, and she found him under some downed branches. Back in the trees. He was airlifted to Norman. You just missed him. There are other things coming out of the hollow too." He described the wall of insects that hit his house.

"But why Peter?" Her eyes burned. Steve put his arm around her.

"Because he heard her voice and knows she is in the hollow. He told me the night before they came for him. After we spoke, I went to hear her myself."

"Was Peter in the hollow when he heard her?"

"No."

"Then how could he know what she sounds like?"

"Chahtas have memories. You do too, Monique."

"Me? How can that be?"

"These are real memories. They're in your head. And mine."

"But I don't recall anything like that."

"You do. You remember sights and sounds of the Old Ones."

"No, I don't. I'd know if I did."

Leroy did not respond.

Monique chewed her lower lip as bits of her recent dreams flashed through her mind and the memory of the scream she and Robbie had heard echoed in her ears. "Shit. Go on."

"Our knowledge is passed down through the generations through stories, of course, but they also are in our blood, but most Chahtas don't pay attention. We only see and hear when our bodies tell us we have to. Like when times are dangerous. Some of us are more sensitive than others."

Monique sighed. "Okay. I might have heard her in my dreams."

"I expect you have. She gets around."

"She screams."

"Yes."

"And Peter heard her, too." *And so did Robbie*, she thought.

"Yes. He told me he had listened to her for almost a year, but this time she was louder. Clearer."

Monique held the phone and stared out her window at the magnolia tree in the front yard. Kids played in the leaves across the street. Just like any day. "They won't come into our homes, will they?"

"Doubtful. You could try what the Muscogees do."

"And that is?"

"Put an owl feather on your door sill."

"Why would one of their own feathers drive them away?"

"Not sure. Or you could get a spitz."

"A what?"

"An Eskimo dog. One of those white fluffy ones."

"My God. Why a spitz?"

"They're the only dog that witches can't charm."

"And how is that?"

"I don't know. It's a Muscogee story."

"Leroy, that is completely random. Those dogs came from Europe. Why would they use spitzes?"

"I said I didn't come up with that."

"I think I'm out of my depth."

"We all are."

"I need to lie down," Monique said. "I'll call you in a few hours."

"Yes. Rest, and call me later," he said. She knew it was his way of saying, "Call me when Steve isn't around."

Monique disconnected the call and sat back in the lounge chair. Steve still hovered above her, his arms folded now and jaw muscles clenched in anger. "You're staying right here, Monique."

She looked up at him innocently. "And where could I go with my arm like this?"

"You know what I mean. I'm going to take a shower. You stay here."

"I will."

As soon as Monique heard the water running, she called Leroy back.

Leroy answered immediately. "Is he there?"

"In the shower."

"He means well, you know."

"Of course. What do you want me to do, Leroy?"

"Come here so we can deal with them. You've seen the Crows. And, well, you know the reason."

She drummed her fingers on the armrest.

After Monique hung up with Leroy, she called Chris and told him to meet her in her driveway at 7:30 the next morning. Armed to the teeth.

34

"I'm taking Robbie to school," Steve said, "and then going on to work."

"Thanks, honey. I'll see you later."

"Call if you need me," he said.

"I will."

"Bye, Robbie!" she called to her son in the kitchen. "Have a good day."

"Do not go anyplace," Steve added.

"I won't," she answered.

Steve stood at the bedroom door and looked at his wife for a few seconds.

"What?" she asked.

"I mean it. Stay here."

"Oh for God's sake, Steve." She kissed her palm and blew him a kiss. "Go."

He flared his nostrils before turning to go.

Twenty minutes later Chris parked his car on front of Monique's house. He hoisted his pack from the backseat and came up to Monique as she was throwing gear one-handed into the back of her truck.

"You sure about this?" he asked. For once he was dressed in clean clothes: flannel shirt with a T-shirt underneath, jeans, and decent boots. A day in the dirt would take care of that.

"You drive," Monique said as she got into the passenger seat.

"And we're off to?"

"East of Ada. My cousin's place. It's his family allotment. Gird your loins because it's like nothing you've ever seen."

"Why?"

"It's heavily forested in the middle. And I mean dense. Trees, bushes, creepers, and vines, and bogs in unexpected places. It's always dark, even in the daytime. Every kind of animal found in Oklahoma lives in there. At night it gets insane. Wildcats, coyotes, birds, and things we've never been able to identify start screaming. You can't listen without covering your ears."

"Sounds like a great place to spend some time." Chris laughed.

"This is no joke, man. The forest is a very dangerous place. It's marshy in places. Snakes everywhere."

"Lions, tigers, and bears?"

"Maybe even ligers."

"Ligers?"

"Barnum and Bailey's circus wintered southwest of Ada, around Loco, a long time ago. Folks say some of the animals escaped and reproduced, and their descendants live in the Oklahoma woods."

"I still don't know what a liger is."

"Obviously it's a cross between a lion and a tiger."

"Can that happen?"

She shrugged. "People say it did. The old-timers say you can hear them scream at night."

"A liger," he repeated. "Cool."

"Don't get your hopes up."

"Maybe I should call Clarence."

"No need. I'm just kidding you—about the ligers, anyway. Big cats like lions and black panthers have been seen in the east. More than a few in Illinois. Mountain lions, of course, in the west. California, Arizona. Nothing about ligers."

"Dang."

She snickered. "You disappointed?"

"No."

"Don't lie."

"Okay. A little disappointed."

"Chris, if things go like I think they will, you're gonna see things even more bizarre than a liger."

Monique waited until they were on the outskirts of Ada before she used her cell phone to call Steve at his store. If she had told him ahead of time that she planned to help Leroy kill the Crows, he would have barricaded her in the bedroom. She had already made plans for Robbie to go home with a friend and spend the night, so he was safe for the next two days.

"You're what?!" Steve shouted. "Get your butt back here," he said. "These are not people to mess with."

"You heard what Leroy said, honey. It has to be me. Now listen, Robbie is going home with Darrin for the night, but you need to get him tomorrow after lunch. I'll be home by tomorrow night. Chris is with me. And several others on the force, so don't worry. I'm just an advisor and will wait in the car," she lied. "We have an arsenal."

"Monique, turn around right now. I mean it. I'm—" Monique hung up before he could finish and then turned off her phone to spare herself the incessant ringing. She predicted Steve would start after her as soon as he could get someone to cover the store—within an hour at most—so she told Chris to step on it.

They stopped long enough to get gas and buy sandwiches from a truck-stop Subway, then they got gas and some water bottles at a 7-11. They arrived at Leroy's shady place around nine. The old man's house sat on the west slope of some hills amid a creek, cottonwoods, and pines. Through his kitchen window, Leroy could see miles of farms in addition to most of the dance grounds.

The spiritual leader greeted them in jeans, a long-sleeved Levi's shirt, and striped Teva sandals. His hair hung loose around his shoulders except for one thin braid in front of his right ear. He shook Chris's hand and hugged Monique hard. "Come on in. You must be tired."

"What's that smell?" Monique asked.

"Dead insects and some birds." He motioned to the dark piles that lay like heaps of decayed leaves around the base of his house. "This is what I told you about on the phone."

"What is it?" Chris asked.

Leroy explained the clouds of insects that had bombarded his home the day before. "I need to bury it. Or burn it. But not now. Come in."

"Steve's probably on his way," Monique warned.

Leroy laughed. "I'll talk to that Pawnee." He handed around cold cans of grapefruit La Croix, and they sat on his sofa. Lorraine jumped on Chris's lap. The detective reluctantly scratched the cat's head.

"So, what are we up against?" she asked.

His smile slowly dropped until his mouth was a straight line. "I'm not sure. We know that they took the bones of the Evil One from the museum. And now the hollow is getting loud and afraid."

"Afraid?"

"Yes. Everything that lives there is afraid. The small ones like lizards and frogs are fleeing even though predators wait at the edge of the trees to eat them. Coyotes don't stay in their cover, and neither do the other night animals like *shawi micha shukvta*. They're all out in the grass during the day. That's dangerous for them, but they'd rather be in the open than in there with the Crows."

"Chris, *shawi micha shukvta* are raccoons and 'possums," Monique explained before turning back to Leroy. "What do you think they're up to?" Monique's head pounded. Her arm ached. Truthfully, she did not want to do anything but put up her feet, eat, drink beer, and take a nap.

The old man sat back in his rocker and put his hands on the armrests as he looked out the living room window. Sparrows and finches swarmed around the feeders like feathered mosquitoes. "I haven't been through the hollow completely," he said. "But I know that the stream that flows into the hollow has stopped flowing out. The bogs haven't gotten bigger, so there must be a hole in the ground it's flowing into."

"I've only been into that hollow twice and didn't care for it at all," Monique said to Chris. "I don't recall much except that it's dark, stinky, and noisy. Mud and vines cover the ground, and there're things crawling everywhere."

The phone rang, and Leroy reached over to answer it. "Hello Dustin. Yes, there're here. Come on over. We need to get started." Leroy hung up without saying good-bye.

"Right now?" Monique asked. She had hoped to sit a while, chat, and perhaps work out another strategy.

Leroy smiled at her, reading her thoughts. "I need to change. We indeed have to deal with this now." He stood and shuffled to his bedroom.

35

ustin arrived within twenty minutes, and after a cousin-type hug and a hearty handshake for Chris, they all climbed into Leroy's Bronco and drove to Andrew's house.

"Sure you got everything?" Monique asked Leroy as they piled out of the car.

He reached over and squeezed her good arm. "Yes." He picked up his bag and slung it over his shoulder. Monique looked at his tired face and thought that for the first time he looked older than his seventy years.

"So do I," added Dustin. He carried a pistol in his shoulder holster, another two in hip holsters, his .30-.30 slung over his shoulder, and a large hunting knife big enough to skewer a bison in a leg sheath.

"Me too," said Andrew, walking out of his house onto the driveway. He had loaded himself with a variety of weapons. He was dressed in camouflage, including a Mossy Oak–patterned cap with a face screen that he'd rolled up over the bill. The hollow was home to millions of tiny annoying insects. He knew exactly how to dress for a bug-infested, smelly, mucky trek through the hostile woods.

Monique hoped her Levi's, T-shirt, Kevlar vest, and denim jacket would be adequate protection. The vest would be heavy and hot, but it had already saved her life in an encounter with these people, and she didn't begrudge the discomfort. Her hiking boots were only ankle high, and she hoped that the muck wasn't deep. She had a can of Deep Woods Off in her pack along with a sweatshirt. Her Glock, a .357 Ruger revolver as a backup, a six-inch blade, and the bear pepper spray she bought at Glacier last summer were all where she could reach them in a hurry. Monique felt confident that she could handle any human predator she ran across, but who knew who—or what—she would run into today?

"You damn well better have on your vest," she said to Chris.

"Are you serious?" he answered. "Hell yes, I do."

"Y'all don't have to come," Leroy said, putting on his red-and-white Bacone College cap. Dustin, Andrew, and Chris stood with their packs shouldered and rifles ready to hunt bear.

"Nothing can keep me away," Andrew said. He looked like a dark, husky Soldier of Fortune.

"Looking forward to it," Chris added.

Leroy did not seem impressed with their weaponry. "Okay, then. But do what I say and don't go tromping around by yourselves. And keep your weapons ready. Guns don't work if you can't pull the trigger."

The group loaded into Andrew's brown Suburban and drove across the bumpy dirt road lined with knee-high grass. Dustin got out and opened the gate that led to the adjoining allotment, then closed it after the Suburban had passed through.

After another slow ten-minute drive, they reached the edge of the hollow. A small herd of white-tailed deer stood in the shade of the cottonwoods, and three coyote heads peeked up over the grass.

"Cool!" Chris exclaimed. "Deer."

"Yes, they are," Leroy agreed. "They normally aren't out in the day."

"Look at those birds in the pecans." Dustin pointed to a murder of crows. "No noise."

"And lots of vultures circling," Andrew observed.

"Lots of dead things to circle," Leroy answered.

"This many wild animals visible in one spot isn't normal," Andrew said.

When Andrew turned off the ignition, Leroy reached over and took his arm. He turned so he could see the others in the backseat. "This isn't a hunting trip. At least not like you're used to. We aren't looking for animals. There's purposeful behavior here." He pulled down the bill of his hat a smidgen. "And foul. Stay behind me at all times." He got out of the SUV, laid his pack on the hood, and unzipped a pocket. He took out what appeared to be a leather burrito and unrolled it to reveal several yellow-and-black-mottled feathers. He handed one to each of his charges.

"What's this from?" Chris asked.

"Yellow-bellied sapsucker. His name is Biskinik. He brings news." Dustin put the feather in his hatband. Andrew put his in the top zippered compartment of his pack, and Monique put hers in the breast pocket of her jacket. Chris stood twirling his feather between thumb and forefinger as he admired it.

Leroy snatched it away and put it in Chris's hatband. "Do not lose this."

Next Leroy took out two tins and opened them. The first contained thick red gel. He took off his cap and drew a line down his face, slightly to the left of the midline, from his scalp to his chin. Looking in the car's side-view mirror, he painted the left side of his face back to his ears. The other tin contained black gel, and he painted the right side of his face before handing the tin of black to Dustin and the red one to Monique.

"Put it on like I did. You're telling the Crows that you're not afraid to draw blood and that you plan to send them to the dark soul-eater."

Dustin stared at the paint as if it might be poison. "The soul-eater? You mean Satan?"

"The one we used to call Nalusa Chito. Although some use that name to refer to the big beast in the woods."

"So, which is it?" asked Dustin. "Soul-eater or hairy thing?"

"Nobody has seen the Old Ones clearly," explained Leroy. "These are confusing names from stories that began long ago."

"And you're guessing they're true. Or that one of them is true."

"I'm not guessing. If he eats your soul, you can't be happy after this life."

Dustin looked at the paint with renewed interest. "Will this help?"

"As sure as socks fit a rooster."

"What? That makes no sense."

Leroy shrugged. "That means I don't know, but paint won't hurt. Put it on."

Dustin tentatively began painting his face, like a thirteen-year-old shaving for the first time.

"Get a move on," Leroy admonished him, and Dustin quickly finished painting.

The group passed around the tins. When they were finished, they looked like a pack of overzealous Washington Redskins fans. They adjusted their clothes and packs, and Monique retied her boots in an effort to stall.

Although Monique's arm was in full ache mode, she was not about to take any pain medication. Going into the hollow clear-headed was bad enough. Going into it feeling loopy could be fatal.

"All of us have headlamps, and I have a bright spotlight," said Leroy. "Turn them on if you need them. If you get separated from the group, stay in one place, turn off your light, and be quiet. Don't try to come out of the hollow alone. Clear?"

"Yeah," Monique said.

"I guess," said Chris.

"I don't plan on getting lost," said Dustin.

They followed Leroy across the grass, swatting away flies and mosquitoes. At first Monique watched the ground to avoid stepping on scurrying spiders, frogs, and lizards. Small birds burst upward in front of them, and the deer bounded off a few paces then stopped and stared. The coyotes did not move.

"Look at that," said Dustin. About seventy feet away to the south, a hairy rock with legs moved through the grass. Another one trailed twenty feet behind it. The rocks snorted, and the group smelled a pungent, musky scent.

"B.O.," Monique said to Chris. "Boar odor."

"Boars." Chris repeated. "Cool."

"Yup. Pigs," said Andrew. "Big ones. The one in front's about four hundred pounds. I call him the Hulk. The sow's Gargantua."

"They'll stay away," Leroy said without stopping.

The group walked closer to the thick trees. The late afternoon sun felt warm on their backs.

"Try and enjoy the sun," Andrew said. "It will be just a memory once we get in the hollow."

They reached the edge of the grass and looked into the quiet darkness. Monique had the impression of activity stirring deep in the shadows just beyond her view. She took a deep breath, moved into the gloom, and stepped onto something firm that suddenly gave way.

"Uck," she yelped and looked down.

"What? Are you okay?" Chris was bringing up his rifle.

"It's just a pawpaw," Leroy said. "A really ripe one. Smell it?"

"Sweet," Chris said.

"Very," Leroy agreed.

"Why is it that when I want a pawpaw I can never find one?" Monique asked.

"There's a tree right there," Leroy pointed. "Now you know where to look."

A crow cawed as it flew over their heads and streaked toward the light.

"Even *fala chito* wants out," Leroy said. "Some Oklas think ravens are malevolent. But not as bad as owls. Let's go. The fruit will be here when we return."

"Do you believe that?" Monique asked.

"Of course. No one is going to take them. But you'll have to hurry because they ferment fast."

"No, I mean do you believe ravens and crows are evil?" Many tribes had taboos against animals. Owls, mainly, but Navajos and some Pueblo tribes also avoided snakes and lizards. Other Natives wouldn't eat fish.

"Nah. I put out leftovers for them when I feed the chickens."

The little group followed Leroy down into the hollow. As soon as they entered the forest, thick branches at the edge of the mire blocked the sunlight and the temperature dropped from hot to cool. Monique thought she might need her sweatshirt soon.

They walked behind Leroy in the dim humidity for twenty minutes. He did not take them in a straight line. That would have taken them quickly to the other side of the hollow. They zigzagged around, across game trails, along creek banks, and through patches of odd mushrooms while Leroy stopped occasionally to listen and search the ground for tracks. There was no birdsong. No crickets chirped.

A coyote yipped mournfully somewhere in the distance. There was no answer. Leroy stopped and cocked his head.

"A coyote, right?" Chris asked.

"Yes. Interesting," he said.

"What?"

"Nothing. Stay quiet."

Monique's feet felt wet. She looked down and saw that she was standing ankle-deep in brown muck that had worked its way over the tops of her boots and inside her socks. The air was cool, and she began to feel an uncomfortable clamminess settle around her armpits and groin. She held her injured arm next to her body.

"You ever thought of putting a road in here?" Chris asked Andrew.

"What for? Everything we cleared would grow back overnight. Not worth the work. Game trails are good enough."

Monique pulled her right foot out of the sticky ooze. "Well, this game trail is a gunky mess." After twenty paces she stepped forward onto something crunchy. "Now what?"

The others shined their lights at her feet. "Bones," Andrew said.

"I know that. I mean, why are there so many piled up here?" Andrew spotted his light at the base of the tall tree in front of them and revealed two four-foot-tall piles of grayish bones among the poison oak that grew up the rough tree trunk. Huge, sickly gray mushrooms poked up through plants.

"What the heck?" Chris asked.

"Owl vomit," Leroy said.

"I thought they vomited pellets."

"That's the tidy way."

Monique tried and failed to visualize an owl that could throw up so many bones. "Well, seems to me either there's a giant owl in here with a heck of an appetite, or there are a bunch of smaller owls yakking in the same place. Or did men eat these animals?"

"Men and owls," said Leroy. "The bones are from small animals mostly, but you can see some larger broken bones mixed in. Looks like they've been chopped up to make swallowing easier." He pointed the toe of his boot at a long leg bone. "Even coyotes and deer aren't safe here anymore." He lifted his canteen and took a swig, then held it out to Chris, who waved it away.

Monique pulled out her iPhone to take pictures.

"Put that away," Leroy told her, "and pay attention to where you step."

"Owls don't eat coyotes and deer, do they, Leroy?" Dustin asked in a high-pitched voice, remembering his own encounter a few nights ago.

"No," Leroy answered. "But men do."

"Are you saying men ate these animals and barfed up the bones?"

"Something like that."

"Oh, for God's sake."

"Don't say that," Leroy said. "Drink this."

Dustin took a sip and made a face. "What is this?"

"Cedar tea."

"You can make tea out of cedar?" Chris asked.

Dustin handed Chris the canteen.

"I did."

Chris took a sip. "There's more than cedar tea in here."

"Hell yes, there is," Leroy answered.

"I taste tequila."

"Good for you." Leroy stopped and looked around and up into the tree tops.

"What do you see?" Andrew asked.

"The Crows are here."

"How do you know?" asked Dustin. "I don't hear anything."

"Look up there." Leroy pointed directly overhead. A large owl sat there, its eyes half closed but watchful. Andrew picked up a wet stick and threw it. The owl's yellow eyes opened wide as it spread its wings and flew into the cover of the trees, dodging and twisting to avoid branches. Its wingspan looked to be at least five feet. The bird's harsh yell did not sound owl-like.

"That sounds like a man," Monique said.

"It is a man," said Leroy. "Sort of. We'll follow it."

Chris took a long pull from Leroy's canteen.

"Even great horned owls don't have wingspans that wide," Monique said.

"No, they don't," agreed Leroy.

The big bird stopped occasionally to look over his shoulder, giving the humans trailing him time to slog in pursuit, panting and snapping branches. The liquid in their water bottles sounded like water sloshing in horses' stomachs.

"The owl's going up the slope," Andrew panted.

"It knows we're following," Monique said.

"Oh, it sure does. It's not worried," Leroy said.

"Should *we* be worried?" asked Chris nervously.

"Drink some more tea," Leroy answered.

The bird disappeared into a dark hole in the hillside.

"It's a cave," Dustin said as he drew closer. He turned on his flashlight and shone the light around the entrance to reveal a pile of large stones that resembled a chair.

"What's in there?" Chris asked Andrew.

"I didn't even know it was here," Andrew answered. "I've lived here my whole life and didn't know about it. That brush to the side hides the entrance. And something really stinks."

"You were right about the hole, Leroy," Monique said. "Maybe there's a tunnel entrance in there?"

"Something hacked the plants away," Leroy said.

"Something?" she asked. "You mean someone, right?"

Leroy ignored the question. "Wait. We need to back off and think about this." The group retreated through the muck to the center of the hollow.

"How could I not have known that cave was there?" Andrew said. "I thought I'd been everywhere on this property."

"It was kept from you," Leroy said. "Don't worry about it now."

"Did you know about it?"

"Yes."

"Then why didn't you—"

"How's your arm?" Leroy interrupted to ask Monique.

"Still attached." She now regretted not taking half a Percocet.

"Good." Leroy motioned everyone in closer and spoke softly and quickly. "Spies are all around." They huddled to hear Leroy's whispers.

Chris slapped at a mosquito on his neck. "Spies?"

"I had an itch about this," Leroy said. "The cave has a strange feel."

"It smells terrible, too," agreed Dustin.

"Yes. Death is in there. You remember our old stories? How we were created?"

"Sure. I know several," said Andrew. "One says Nanishta made us out in the west someplace, then the tribe followed the sacred stick for forty years, and we stopped in Mississippi."

"I learned that we emerged from Nanih Waiya as locusts," Monique added.

"I don't believe that one," Dustin said.

"Doesn't matter if you do or don't, boy," Leroy said, looking into the darkness. "Regardless of how we got to Mississippi, a common theme in all our creation stories is the caves. We came from caves underwater in the west, or we came from caves near Nanih Waiya in Mississippi. There's another story that maybe you don't know. A long time ago, years after creation, we were attacked by the Nahullos—large men with white skin and, at least some people say, horns on their heads."

"You mean like devils?" Dustin asked. Monique knew her cousin was a devout Christian and greatly concerned about Satan. He'd probably faint if he visited Bob Shimura's office.

Leroy shrugged. "I don't know. Probably they were just big ugly white folks." He paused, looked around, then spoke faster. "There is another deity, Hashtali, who we called Sun Father. Hopainla, the messenger of Hashtali, showed the Oklas an opening close to Nanih Waiya that led to underground caves where they could hide from the Nahullos. There was fresh water and plenty of room because the caverns stretched for more miles than the Oklas could follow. They brought in their animals and supplies and planted and harvested crops outside at night. They lived underground for almost a hundred years."

"Underground for a hundred years?" Monique had not heard that one. "Is this part of that Hollow Earth Theory?"

Leroy nodded.

"You can't live underground for years without sunlight," Monique said.

Leroy ignored her. "After that time a brave young man showed the Oklas how to shoot poison darts at the Nahullos. The Oklas ran the Nahullos off, and then the tribe came out of the ground. Another emergence. Hashtali sealed the entrance after they came out."

"Maybe that's where the emergence from Nanih Waiya story comes from," she said. "And the time they spent in the caves would have been exaggerated over the years." She felt Chris moving closer to her on one side and Dustin pressing in on the other. Everyone was trying to huddle for security.

"The point is," Leroy said, "that I think those caves really did exist in the east, and they connect underground all the way out here. And they may continue on farther west. The cave we just found is an entrance to that system."

"No way," Chris objected.

"Oh, yes, there is a way."

"Chris, we'll talk about the Hollow Earth later," Monique said.

"You mean the Crows live in there and move around from place to place?" Andrew asked.

"Well, they can hide in the caverns for a long time, anyway. There's another story about a group of people who lived underground in the mud. We called them the Shakchi. They were little and bent and hairy, and they would steal away Okla women to mate with them."

"Devils," Dustin said.

"No. They weren't malicious. Their population had decreased, and they needed women to reproduce. To make a long story short, they eventually came to the surface, got caught by the Oklas and were told to come above ground and live normally. The Shakchis plucked out all their hair to look presentable and then intermarried among the tribe."

"Are they here in the hollow, too?" Dustin asked. He looked around nervously, trying to catch the breath that kept running away from him.

"No. They all came out long ago. Now, if the Shakchi could live under the ground, so can the Crows."

The humans were huddled so close now that they could hear each other's heartbeats. The hollow was silent, rank, and very damp. Monique could barely see water moving slowly through the muck and moss at her feet. They were standing at the edge of a bog.

"But they can't just pop up out of the ground and take people," Dustin said. A bird called from the tree above him, then a sudden breeze swept away his voice.

"Why not? Why do you think the Crows can't be like the Shakchi? Their numbers dwindled while the First One was sleeping. Now that she is awake, they need human females to increase their tribe. She demands it. I think if you checked missing persons reports you would find that several young women have gone missing from this part of the country recently."

"Gross," Monique said. "This is just—"

"The good news is they don't take women very often," Leroy interrupted. "The bad news is that Crows live a long time."

"I don't believe this stuff." Dustin said, still breathing hard.

"Then why are you here?" Leroy asked him.

The bird twittered again, this time louder.

Dustin pushed his toe into the muck before replying. "Just in case. I have to protect my family."

Leroy slapped him on the back. "What a coincidence. Me too. Now let's go. Biskinik is warning us."

Monique looked up and saw the sapsucker hop on to a low branch. Having passed on its message, it leaped into the air and flapped toward the grassland and fresh air outside the hollow.

"So it's back to the cave?" she asked.

"Maybe not," answered Leroy. He looked over her shoulder and focused on something behind her.

36

Monique heard a moan that sounded like the noise Robbie had made as an infant when he belched. She slowly turned. Standing there in the beam of Leroy's spotlight was a short, stocky, nearly transparent man. Although he wore no clothing to mark him as such—or any clothing at all—he was clearly an Indian. He stood motionless, his arms hanging at his sides.

"Who are you?" she asked.

"He won't answer," Leroy said. He put a hand on her shoulder.

"What's wrong with him?" Chris asked, touching the butt of his Colt.

"He's a *shilombish*," Leroy said. "He's dead."

"Oh, shit," Chris said. "Not ghosts, too." He took a step back, but Leroy caught his arm.

"Stand still. I heard a yelp when we first arrived," Leroy said. "So did you. I thought it was a coyote, but when none answered back I knew it was a *shilombish*. Coyotes know not to answer one when they call."

"What the hell is going on?" Dustin was on the verge of hyperventilating.

Andrew took a step toward the ghost. "No, stop," ordered Leroy. "He's here for a reason."

Chris looked ready to bolt, but Leroy still had a grip on his arm. "Why is there a ghost here? Who is he?!"

"I think he is someone the Crows murdered," Leroy answered. He squeezed Chris's arm again, and that calmed him. "Listen. Each of us has an inner soul called the *shilup* and an outer soul, the *shilombish*. When we die, the *shilup* leaves the body right away, but the *shilombish* stays for a time near the spot where the person died, or sometimes where he lived."

"You sure about this?" Chris asked.

"No, I'm not, Sonny. Now be quiet. Before it can go to heaven, the *shilup* must face the Guardians. The *shilup* has to cross a slippery log that stretches across a deep chasm. The Guardians throw rocks at the *shilup* as it tries to cross. Good souls are able to cross over. Bad souls will fall into the deep canyon and into a whirlpool of foul water filled with reptiles and dead animals. They stay there forever, hungry, tired, and jealous of those who cross."

"What a sec," said Andrew. "I thought *shilup* is a ghost."

"That's what it means now. Over time, the word changed meaning. Back then what we knew as 'ghost' was *shilombish*. Anyway, the *shilombish* moans or cries and then fades away. This is a *shilombish*. I'm not sure why it's here, but I do know they don't fade as quickly if they were murdered."

"What happens to them if they're murdered?" Monique asked.

"Hey, wait a minute!" Dustin cried. "Where's Jesus in all this?"

"Dustin," Leroy said gently, "how do you know Jesus isn't here with us now?"

"The Bible doesn't mention these things."

"It doesn't discuss a lot of things."

"Our tribal stories can't be true." Dustin eyes focused upward, searching for owls and Jesus.

"And these stories weren't created in a vacuum," Monique added. "There's meaning to them."

"Yeah," Dustin said, his eyes wide and panicky, "but I didn't think all of them are true. With these creation myths, what people think happened in the past is more important than what actually did happen. Right?"

"Maybe," she said. "Are you saying you don't believe in all the Bible stories? The Garden of Eden? The parting of the Red Sea? Jesus walking on water?"

"No. But that's not the point. They're supposed to teach us lessons."

"So you're a Christian, but doubt the Bible stories. I'll have to think about that."

"Do you believe in God, Dustin?" Leroy asked.

"Yes."

"Jesus?"

"Yes."

"Then you're okay. Deal with it. This isn't the time for a debate on the Bible. I'm much more concerned about something else right now." He paused for a moment then added, "I heard a coyote howl a few nights before Pete was assaulted. There's another *shilombish* out here."

"More than just this guy?" Chris pointed to the wispy ghost.

"Oh, no," Dustin moaned. "Who?"

"No idea," Leroy answered. "Can't worry about it now."

The group jumped back simultaneously when the ghost abruptly turned toward the cave and pointed. It approached the opening without seeming to take steps, like a Halloween ghost on roller skates, and disappeared inside. Shortly afterward, a shriek like the one Monique had heard in her dreams stormed out of the cave and through the hollow. There was no wind at all, but the branches and bushes bent away from the noise.

Everything was quiet for a few seconds, then a pig squealed. The humans stood transfixed as a family of wild hogs ran toward them, their eyes yellow and angry, tusks shiny and discolored. They grunted and snorted like bulls running at Pamplona. At the last second, the four pigs maneuvered to pass the humans. They crashed through the brush and disappeared into the darkness. Next came a raccoon, then a bobcat. Neither gave the people a look. A stream of animals followed, ranging in size from buzzing insects to chattering squirrels to frantic deer. The life remaining in the hollow had decided to evacuate. After a minutes-long eternity, the group could hear only distant howls and yelps and the *shilomish*'s moans echoing from the cave.

"Oh, my dear God," Chris breathed into the silence.

"Hang in there," Monique said hoarsely, as much to herself as to him.

"So many animals," Dustin said.

"This was only a few of them," Andrew told him. "Most have already left."

"All the time I've been hunting in the hollow, these animals have been here," Dustin said quietly, "and I never knew."

"Of course," Leroy answered. "If they didn't know how to hide, hunters would kill them all."

Leroy bowed his head and began to chant. The others stood close to him, wishing he'd hurry but also hoping that Heaven would open and send a miracle to save them.

Suddenly the ground shook violently, and Monique widened her stance and bent her knees for balance. The canopy above them began to sway. Leaves and twigs fell to the ground. The swaying turned to shaking. Loud cracks sounded below their feet like pond ice breaking. Large branches broke free and crashed to the muddy earth.

Dustin grabbed Monique's hurt arm, and she yelped in pain. "Sorry," he said. "We gotta move."

Leroy put his hands to his mouth and yelled over the snapping trees. "We have to get away from these cottonwoods! Move, everyone, now!"

An enormous old tree fell across their path and landed with a series of snaps and swooshes of green vines. A branch flew through the air and hit Dustin's hip, knocking him down. Leroy grabbed the mud-coated man under his armpits and hauled him to his feet.

Chris watched dumbly as a tree toppled slowly toward him. Monique sprinted to him and pushed him out of the way with her shoulder. "Wake up, Chris! Let's go!" she yelled.

The ground shook again, and more trees fell. Another enormous groan sounded near the bog as a hole appeared. A maelstrom of muddy water swirled down the hole like dirty tub water.

"Back up!" Leroy screamed. They backpedaled until the cracking stopped. Except for falling branches and rushing water, the hollow stilled.

Monique watched water from the stream behind them rush forward toward the hole. More trees fell as the Earth groaned and the crack grew wider, then abruptly stopped. The small group stood still, afraid to move. Leroy stepped forward cautiously, and the others followed. Monique looked down into a crack in the world. Her jaw dropped in surprise, and she drew in a sharp breath.

A gentle glow rose upward from the depths, softly lighting the upper part of the cavern about a hundred feet below them. Water from the Chalakwa Ranch creek continued to tumble over the edge as a thin waterfall.

"The Old Ones," Leroy said. "The Guardians hold the lights."

Monique squinted and barely made out figures standing on a ledge that stuck out from the inner circumference of the chasm.

"Oh, man," Chris said as he took a step back.

"Oh, sweet Jesus!" Dustin wailed. "That's Hell, isn't it? It's real!"

"Well, down below the lights is the unhappy place," Leroy said. "I guess you can call it that."

"Is that a witch hole?" Monique asked.

"Not at all," Leroy answered.

"Who were you praying to?" Monique asked.

"God. Who else?"

"But you said it was Nanishta. Or the Sun guy Hashtali," Dustin argued.

"Supreme being, Dustin, whatever you want to call him." Leroy waved his hand in dismissal. "Get with it."

Raspy breathing sounded above them. Branches snapped as a body fell from the treetops and landed in a heap a few feet away. A few feathers drifted down behind it. The lump took form as it struggled to stand.

With the dim glow from the chasm as an effective backlight, Monique watched the lump change into a deformed woman with long, tangled gray hair, a round head, yellow eyes, and filthy fingernails so long they would qualify for Ripley's Believe It or Not. She was incongruously dressed in a sleeveless print housedress that looked like it had been pilfered from a farmyard clothesline. The Evil One looked around at the group, her weird eyes darting from one person to the next.

She wobbled, holding herself upright with broken branches. Pointing a long fingernail at Leroy, she said in a raspy voice, "*Chi hohchifo nanta?*" They saw only one tooth in her mouth when she spoke. Dead, dry leaves fell from above and landed on her wild hair.

"Don't tell her," Monique said to Leroy.

"What?" Chris asked.

"She wants his name."

The hag turned her attention to Monique. "*Minti*," she ordered.

Horrified, Monique shook her head. "*Keyu.* No. I'm not moving."

The hag smiled, showing her single tooth, and abruptly pointed to the cave. Monique smelled smoke.

"Smoke," Dustin said. "Something's burning in the cave."

"Don't think about that now," Leroy told them.

"She has sensed you before," a man's deep voice said from behind them. Monique turned and saw a nude Mac Crow standing ten feet away, blood around his mouth. His face looked the same as it had a few nights before when he had attacked her in the Walmart parking lot. Monique flinched and looked away.

He took a bite of the crushed marsh rat he carried in his right hand. She could not see his feet; they were covered in muck.

"You have poor table manners," Monique said. She felt strangely calm.

He dropped the rat and wiped his bloody hands on his filthy thighs. "She smelled you when you wuz in the museum. She lay in the dark in that box."

"Those were bones," Monique said.

"Yes," he smiled. "Bones. You gotta start with bones."

"The bones were gone when I arrived."

"I don't mean this week. I mean when you was a kid. Then again when you brought your kid. She knew you wuz there."

"Almost forty years ago," Mac said, just as Monique calculated it had been thirty-six years since the first time she'd been to the museum. "She smelled him, too." He pointed to Dustin.

"Me?" Dustin looked gobsmacked.

"She remembers the smell of everyone who came through the building. And now we know your kid too. Scared ya good the other night, huh?"

Dustin inhaled sharply.

"Did ya like what we did to your buck? We made him look good, right?"

"Hush," Leroy said quietly to Dustin. "Don't talk to him."

"Don't matter," Mac said. He talked like a friendly neighbor discussing lawn fertilizer. "We get put back together no matter what."

Monique thought she heard a faint chanting coming from the crevasse. Mac heard it too. He barely turned his head to get a handle on the source.

"How did you know she was in the archives?" Monique could not help but ask him.

Mac Crow blinked his large eyes. Another shape landed next to him. A man. He must have transformed in the tree branches. The skin on his round head was cracked and oozy, just as it had been in the Walmart parking lot. She had to force herself to avert her eyes from the rest of his naked form. Some things cannot be unseen. Monique hoped his skin disease wasn't contagious.

"We always knew she was there," the oozy one said. "We knew when she went over the trail. She stayed with some family for a time. We kilt the man. Then his lady gave the box to the museum. We followed."

"You remember Bubba," Mac said, gesturing to the second man. "His condition runs in the family." Monique wondered if he meant his skin or his ability to shapeshift.

"Why didn't you take her before now?" She really wanted to know.

"No need. We knew whur she wuz," Bubba answered.

"And here's Jeter. You remember him too, don't ya, Miss Moni-key?" Another Crow landed next to Bubba. Except for a disc player hanging on a leather belt around his waist, Jeter was as naked as the other two. He pulled out his earbuds, and in the quiet, the others heard Curt Corbain of Nirvana screaming "Right na-ow" cranked to eleven.

"You gotta be shitting me," Chris muttered, transfixed.

Mac ignored him. "She stayed safe in the museum," he continued. "All dry and quiet until we was ready." He noticed that Chris looked toward the cave.

"She just made sure you don't see what we had in there," Mac explained. "All burnt up now."

Salty sweat stung Monique's lacerated arm, and she felt the tackiness of the face paint on her neck. Her nose itched, but she was not about to scratch it. "How deep is the cave?"

"All the way to where we came from." He turned to look at Bubba as a long knife appeared in his right hand. Without warning, the three owl men rushed forward. Andrew didn't have time to pull up and aim the rifle hanging over his shoulder. "Shit!" he yelled, shrugging off the rifle and reaching for his knife.

Mac rushed Dustin with his own knife and slashed at him. The blade connected, and Dustin screamed.

Bubba had two knives. The point of the knife in his right hand faced backward, the point of the knife in his left hand pointed upward. He did not move either knife as he came for Chris. As Chris pulled his Colt from its holster, Bubba's right hand sliced horizontally, and the blade caught Chris high across the chest—above his vest. Chris staggered backward into a tree. Monique saw blood spread across Chris's shirt before she was forced to tend to her own adversary.

Jeter came at her holding both arms out, intending to choke her. Monique was momentarily puzzled because skilled fighters don't telegraph their moves so obviously. She sidestepped out of his path, and he changed direction just as quickly. She pushed his arms away with the basic inside-to-outside block taught in most self-defense courses and she felt her stitches pull free. "Damn" she yelped.

He hit Monique hard in the left temple with his left fist, and she fell on her ass into the muck. She kicked upward with both feet and connected with Jeter's lower body. Oddly, she met little resistance. His bones felt light, like they were made of PVC pipes. Jeter screeched like the mutant owl he was and fell backward into the mud as he tried to stand.

Panting heavily, Monique stood, took several steps back, and picked up a baseball-sized rock from the mud. She threw it at Jeter and hit him square in the forehead. His head jerked back, and blood ran down the left side of his face. Fighting Jeter seemed too easy. Shouldn't witches be tougher in combat? She pulled out her pistol to fire into his gut. As she aimed, she heard Leroy talking to her.

"What?" Monique turned to him and yelled. "What did you say?"

"I'm not talking to you," he said. "I'm praying. Pay attention to what's in front of you."

She turned back to see Jeter crumple to his knees. At first she thought she'd hit him so hard with the rock that he passed out. But she realized that he was shrinking. Morphing into an owl. She took off her jacket and threw it over Jeter. He continued to transform, then became stuck in the jacket.

"Are you stupid or what?" she asked as she picked him up, surprised at how little he weighed. Where had his body mass gone? The owl inside the jacket struggled to get free as she sprinted to the edge of the crack. Old Hatak haksi shrieked and hissed as Monique threw the bundle toward the blue lights. The graceful Guardians turned their faces upward, and one caught the bundle, then tore the bird from the jacket and put it down on the log that spanned the chasm. Immediately Jeter the owl began to elongate. His leg bones became longer, then his arms and spine. Next his ribcage expanded. The beak retracted and his head inflated. "Dear Heavenly Father," Monique whispered, "what the holy hell am I seeing?"

Monique turned to see Dustin and Mac rolling through the mud and vines, each trying to get a good grip on the other. Dustin's bloody face had picked up goop from the forest floor. Andrew was faring a bit better, having cut Bubba numerous times with his long knife as the Crow tried to stab Chris.

Monique turned back to look down at Jeter. He had changed into a human again. "Push Bubba to the edge!" she yelled to Andrew.

Andrew crouched low and slashed his knife side to side, making Bubba step backward closer to the chasm. Like someone posing for a photograph at the Grand Canyon and the picture-taker keeps saying 'step back . . . a little more, little more,' then they fall hundreds of feet to their deaths, Bubba kept stepping back and then stopped. He grinned. "I know whut yur about," he said.

"You son of a bitch!" Monique yelled. Then she took three quick strides forward and kicked Bubba in the chest. As Bubba fell backward, Monique fought for balance at the edge of the precipice. Andrew grabbed Monique's T-shirt and pulled her back to safety.

They watched as Bubba seemed to float downward. As he was about to pass the Guardians' ledge, hands reached out and caught him. One Guardian placed him on the log behind Jeter.

Hatak haksi screamed again.

"Andrew, help Chris!" Monique yelled before turning to see what Mac was doing to Dustin.

Mac Crow sat on Dustin's chest with the knife poised to plunge into his throat. Monique fired three shots, missing Mac twice and hitting him once in the neck.

"Ow," Mac said. "That hurted." He stood to face Monique, blood gushing from his wound. Hatak haksi creeped towards Mac, still screaming in her unearthly voice. Leroy stood to the side, his lips moving in prayer.

"That face paint don't look so good on you," Mac said.

"It's a facial," Monique answered. The blood still pumped from his torn carotid artery, and he made no effort to stop it. She motioned with her chin to the hole. "You're going down there, Mac."

"Nah. Not me. I been around for centuries, and I never even been close." His eyes darted to the side to take in the light emanating upward. Blood still flowed from his wound. His shoulders began to slump. He dropped the knife.

"*Inla!*" Hatak hatsi shrieked.

"Yeah," Monique said. "Change."

Mac put one foot forward and put his arms out for balance. He closed his eyes and tried to change, but he succeeded only in altering part of his head. Monique watched in fascination as his mouth transformed into a beak. It opened, and he tried to hoot. He staggered toward Monique. She moved to put him between her and the rift. As he reached for a branch to steady himself, Monique took advantage of his posture and charged him. She careened into his chest with her right shoulder as he straightened. They both fell backward into space, down toward the Guardians' lights.

"Monique!" she heard Leroy yell as she plummeted. She landed on her backside, almost in a sitting position. The pain in her coccyx was excruciating. She moaned and rolled over onto her left side, then onto her back. Hot streaks of fire shot down her left leg and up along her spine to her neck. She could feel that all the stitches in her lacerated arm had ripped free. She breathed in tiny gasps, whimpering in agony.

When she was able to open her eyes again, Monique found herself lying on the ledge. A dozen hazy faces looked down at her, faces that looked like wispy brown cotton candy. The Old Ones. She looked into eyes that shifted from clear to dull gray and back again. They looked like old full-bloods one second, then shadows the next.

Panting, Monique used her good arm to push herself upright against the chasm wall. The three Crows were nearby, lined up on the log that spanned the chasm. The Old Ones whispered and chanted, then pointed to the log. Mac stood behind Jeter and Bubba, his body still half-transformed. Jeter was the first to attempt to cross over. He stood at one end of the log, naked and ugly as all get-out, and took one tentative step. Rocks flew up at him from all directions, but Monique could not see who threw them. He had taken only two steps and had already gotten pelted worse than Steve's new Chevy truck in a hailstorm. He faltered and cried out as the rocks kept coming, then lost his balance and fell downward into the darkness with a scream. Five seconds later Monique heard a small splash.

Next to try and cross was Bubba, who had the same luck. He managed to take a step before a rock struck him in the forehead, snapping his head back. Then another sharp rock hit his shoulder with enough force to make him fall.

Mac did not make much of an effort. His head had not changed back into human form. He tripped and fell as he tried to take the first step. Apparently an owl's depth perception did not work with a human body.

With the Crows gone, the Old Ones looked to where Monique lay with her back against the wall. One Elder looked slightly transparent, although his skin was clearly dark. His gray hair fell to his ankles. He wore cured leather pants and no shirt. The stitching up the legs looked like sinew, an old-fashioned method the Choctaws had not used for a long time.

"*Hikia,*" he said. "Stand up." His voice was so quiet she could barely hear him. When she tried and failed, he grabbed her arm with a strong, warm grip and pulled her to her feet. Monique staggered to stand. Her backside and arm burned. The Old One put his hand on her lower back, and the pain immediately subsided. He stroked her injured arm with light fingertips, and the pain disappeared. Then he looked up to the edge of the chasm. "*Chukka ia,*" he said. "Go home. Do not go into the cave." Then he put his hand on her back again and pushed her toward the wall so she could climb.

The Old One's touch had somehow given her strength, and Monique climbed upward easily, using the rock outcroppings as handholds. When she arrived at the top, a bloody Andrew grabbed her good arm and yanked her up and out. She lay on her back looking up at him.

"Holy shit, Andrew. You won't believe what happened." She jumped when the jacket she had wrapped around Jeter flew up and over the edge and landed on her legs. "What the heck?"

"It's all good," Leroy said as he pressed a bandana over Andrew's bloody lower lip and chin.

Then Monique saw Hatak haksi. She stood in the same spot, still hunched over, leaning heavily on the two branches that she used as crutches.

"Why doesn't she move?" Andrew asked Leroy.

"She can't."

Monique stood. Her pain was gone, but she felt lightheaded. She took a few steps toward the witch.

"Be careful," Leroy said. "Don't get close to her."

The witch hissed like a cat and fell forward, screeching incomprehensible words. Monique walked to within five feet of her and looked closely at the crone for the first time. Her legs looked bow-legged but human. Her ribcage and drooping breasts also looked human, but something was very wrong. Then she realized what it was. "She has no pelvis, and part of her backbone is missing." Monique fought back a flash of nausea.

"Her pelvis is still in the Room," Chris said from where he leaned against a tree. The light was fading. Leroy shined his light on her partner, and Monique saw that his shirt was red. She hurried over and ripped it open to see a deep gash from right clavicle to left.

"So much for wearing a vest, right? I'm okay," he insisted.

"You're in shock."

Monique folded the jacket and pressed it to his wound.

Chris remained still while she held the heavy cloth against him to stop the blood. "Her lower half is held together by soft tissues," Monique said, "but there are no bones between the lumbar spine and her femurs."

Leroy stepped closer to the witch, who continued to scream.

Dustin came up behind Leroy and looked at the hag. "You've got to be kidding," he said.

"After all you've seen, you question that?" Leroy asked him.

"They couldn't get the pelvis through the air duct," Chris said.

"But they got her skull through," Andrew mumbled.

"Yeah," Monique agreed. "But the ceiling is a maze of ducts; they twist and turn and the pelvis didn't fit."

"How'd she get in the tree?" Chris asked.

"Watch," Leroy said.

The witch continued to scream as she collapsed into herself, her bones compacting and twisting in the impossible transformation. As her head shrank, her hair seemed to grow backward into her skull. When several inches were left, the hair changed to feathers. Her arms shortened, and her metacarpals fused. Her metamorphosis finished, she lay on the ground because she had no pelvis to support her weight. Her big brown wings flapped, and she rose with difficulty.

"Oh, Lord," Chris moaned. "Now I know what that document in the file meant."

"Andrew," Monique said without looking at him. "Give it to me."

She held out her hand to receive the rifle. She quickly aimed and shot Hatak haksi in the chest. Feathers exploded outward, and the owl dropped a bit but still hovered.

Monique aimed and shot again. The bullet threw Hatak haksi backward and down into the chasm and into the arms of the Guardians.

Monique hurried to look down. The Old Ones placed Hatak haksi on the log and waited for her to change back into a human. She, too, had to try to cross the log. The owl woman did not want to change, but the Old Ones compelled her. She whined and cried as she altered her shape, then lay still, staring at the Guardians.

"You think they knew each other back in the old times?" Monique asked Leroy.

"The Old Ones know everyone."

Hatak haksi pulled herself a few yards with her hands, and then the rocks came. Despite being struck in the head numerous times, she made it to the center of the log. Stones of all sizes rocketed upward, hitting her repeatedly, until she finally fell.

Her scream faded away, and the night became silent.

"One more to go," Leroy said.

The male *shilombish* emerged from the cave and floated toward the chasm. It jumped down and settled easily onto the end of the log next to the Guardians. They pointed to the other side. The *shilombish* floated across and into bright light that momentarily blazed like a flashbulb. Then he was gone.

The Guardians looked up and waited. At the sound of a howl behind them, Monique, Leroy, Chris, Andrew, and Dustin turned to see a nude blonde woman, her body opaque and ghostly white, gliding toward them.

"Who is that?" Chris asked.

"I have no idea," Monique said. "Leroy?"

"Don't know," he said, surprised.

The woman sailed past them, her waist-length white hair floating behind her, her head bent at an unnatural angle.

"I think she must be a woman the Crows captured," Leroy ventured.

"She's so young," Chris said.

"They like them young," Leroy answered. He put his arms in front of his friends. "Move back," he said.

The female ghost looked up, and in a flash her essence shot toward the sky.

"Where's she going?" Dustin asked.

"Heaven I guess. I don't know."

"Well, where'd the man go?"

"Same place, I expect. They just took different roads."

"Why didn't she see the Guardians?" Monique asked.

"Why should she? She's not one of us. And look, it seems there were more."

They turned to see two more nude female forms drift past them, one short and curvy, the other a bit taller. Both had very long hair, and both were obviously Native. The wrists and forearms of the first female were lacerated, but there was no blood. The second woman's neck was deeply cut on the right side. Both floated into the chasm.

The group moved forward to watch.

"Why are they dead?" Monique asked. "I thought the Crows needed them."

"They killed themselves," Leroy answered. "These women are much older."

Chris disagreed. "They can't be more than twenty-five," he said.

"No. I mean they are from a time long ago."

The two female forms silently and quickly made their way across the bridge. They, too, vanished within bright lights.

"Jesus help us," Dustin cried. "Look!" He pointed to the other side of the chasm.

A dozen ethereal shapes, all young, nude Native women with long hair, floated into the chasm. Monique could barely make out their images. Behind them drifted several male shapes. As Leroy's group looked down, the ghosts crossed the bridge and vanished.

The Old Ones looked up. Monique glanced at Leroy and saw him smiling down at them. Then she looked back to the Old Ones and watched as they extinguished their lights.

The ground suddenly shook and grunted. "Get back!" Leroy warned.

Monique and Andrew helped Chris stand while Leroy supported Dustin. They all moved into the forest away from the chasm. The forest floor heaved upward, and the sides of the canyon moved toward each other until the crack disappeared. Branches cracked and fell as the ground thundered. Rocks and soil made adjustments then became still.

The stream flowed to the center as it always did, and a small pool began to form. The overflow continued and made a rivulet.

A coyote yelled from the edge of the hollow and another answered from the opposite side of the bowl. Caws sounded as crows flew through the treetops. Pigs grunted in the brush, and a turkey gobbled in the distance.

"It's done," Leroy said.

"There's still some light. Animals will be coming home," Andrew said.

"And we need to leave," Leroy said. "Get your gear. This may get crowded."

"They're in a hurry," Monique said.

"The animals have made too many adjustments recently," Leroy said. "They have been waiting to come back here."

As they turned to leave, the squirrel peeked out of her hole in the tall oak. Her nose twitched as she took in the smells, the breeze, and the sudden lack of discord. She flipped her tail and climbed confidently out onto the branch to watch the two-leggeds until they moved out of sight.

The small group followed Leroy back the way they had come, through the muck and the vines and up the sides of the rocky bowl. It was slow going. Chris could barely walk, and Dustin had a laceration across his biceps and a knife puncture in his thigh. Monique could only imagine what they all must look like.

A pale pink light showed through the trees along the western horizon, and a crow cawed.

"*Fala chito!*" Monique called out. "Good evening, raven!" It cawed again and considered the group as they emerged into the fading light.

"Monique!" a man in the distance yelled.

"The Pawnee is here," Leroy said. "What are you gonna tell him?"

"I'll think of something," she said.

37

Steve Blue Hawk stood by a truck Monique did not recognize, his hands on his hips and a pistol tucked into his belt, as he watched the unlikely group file out of Andrew's Suburban. He could tell from the blood that all of them were injured, but they were so filthy it was hard to tell how seriously. Andrew was so coated with mud and debris that he looked like a chocolate-and-nut-covered banana.

"Hi, honey," Monique said serenely.

"What's on your face?" Steve asked as he bear-hugged her. "And what's the matter with Dustin?"

She looked at her cousin. His torn lip looked a lot worse in the light, and the bandana was not a very absorbent bandage. Worse, his pants were completely soaked with blood.

"Had a little altercation," Dustin mumbled through the bandage.

"What happened to Chris?" Steve started forward to help get him to the car.

As Steve moved toward Chris, Lester Martin, the museum security guard, walked out from behind the white truck. He had a rifle in his hands and a pistol in his belt holster.

"Mr. Martin?" Monique asked. "What are you doing here?"

"Always wanted to see the hollow," he answered, "and I figured your husband could use some backup. We drove out together."

"How'd you know where we were?"

"I know Peter. I heard he was hurt. I called the police station and found out you'd been injured too. Then I called the hospital. When they said you'd gone home, I called Steve at his shop."

"How'd you know he has a shop?"

Martin smiled. "I've ordered parts for my truck from him. He was on his way out the door to come after you when I reached him."

"Good grief," she said.

"Why are your clothes all torn?" Steve interjected. "What's with all these animals screaming and flying around? What're you doing now? Where're you going? What—"

"I'll explain it all. I promise."

"You lied. Where're all the officers?"

"Uh . . ."

"Steve," Leroy said. "You're about to bust a gut. Slow down. We got rid of the Crows. They're gone. We're safe. Monique's safe. We need to get Dustin and Chris to the hospital, so let's get going. Follow us."

"I thought *you* were a doctor," Chris said weakly.

"I am. And the doctor says we're goin' to the hospital now. Give me the keys, Andrew. I'll drive."

Monique hugged Steve before she got in the backseat of the Suburban with Dustin and Chris. She found a box of Kleenex and held a wad on Dustin's lip. It was the cleanest thing she could find. The only other possibilities were a dirty oil rag and a pair of smelly socks on the floorboard, which she used to put pressure on his thigh wound.

Chris sat on the other side of Monique, holding a towel on his chest and resting his head against the seat back. "Leroy, who were those dead people?"

He shook his head. "Among the many the Crows got ahold of. There's nothing to do about them. They're at peace now."

"Hey, Monique," Andrew said as they got under way. "Something I've always wanted to ask you and Steve."

"And what's that?"

"Are there really blue hawks? I've never seen a blue hawk."

"I don't know if there are or not," she answered. "But after what I've seen today I wouldn't be surprised."

"You're right about that," he replied.

"The stories are real," Dustin mumbled. His mouth started bleeding again.

"And we've seen proof that there's life after this one," Monique added, applying more pressure to the tissue. "What a gift."

"I'm gonna need stitches," he mumbled.

Leroy looked in the rearview mirror and assessed his cut. "Yes, you will. And looks like you'll need some in your hand," he said as he glanced over at Andrew. "That cut's between your thumb and forefinger. Can you move them?"

"Sort of."

Leroy did not reply.

"Leroy, fighting the Crows was awful, but it wasn't that difficult," Monique said. "I thought we'd have a harder time."

Her uncle looked back at her. "We were in the hollow almost seven hours. And I wouldn't call it easy. Look at yourself, Monique."

Monique inspected her right arm and was surprised to see a dozen cuts. A few fingernails were torn to the quick, and Dustin said she was bleeding from her right ear. Her left arm had bled so much after the stitches ripped out that the thick gauze wrap was soaked with it. Her jeans had numerous rips, as did her T-shirt. The back of her neck stung. She put her hand to the pain and brought away more blood.

"It was harder than you think," Leroy said. "Adrenaline helps when you know you might die. You are the only one who could kill them, and therefore you had extra strength. You'll never be that strong again."

"But I didn't kill them. I just pushed them into the chasm. You said I had to be the one."

"Well, prophecies sometimes aren't all that clear. You did get all of them to the bridge. I think we can consider that dispensing with them."

They rode in silence a minute.

"Another group of Crows, led by one called Jackson, came after another family." Leroy's statement startled everyone.

"What? When?" they all said in unison.

"A big family scattered around McAlester."

"What happened?"

"The Crows had tried to kill that family back east. Then they followed them over the trail and kept trying for many years. The witches were finally killed around 2000."

"And they were killed by someone they tried to kill and didn't?" Monique asked.

"Well, some*thing*," Leroy answered. "A horse."

"A horse killed them? Seriously?" Andrew asked.

"It was one of the family's breeding horses. The Crows had impaled the stallion in the head decades before and left a gaping hole, but didn't kill him. Archie—that's the horse—trampled them to death. There are surely more Crows out there," Leroy added, "but Hatak haksi is dead, so I think they will do no more harm."

"What in the name of Carl Kolchak are you talking about?" Andrew asked.

"That's a story for another time."

"My lip!" Dustin yelped. "Y'all are crazy!"

"Crazy. Yes." Monique sighed and leaned back on the headrest, then suddenly sat upright. "Leroy, what are we supposed to do with the pelvis?"

"Nothing."

"Shouldn't you destroy it?"

"No need. She's gone and will not be coming back. Ever. Let the anthropologists play with it."

"Can we come back and dig down to where the ancestors live?" Monique asked.

Leroy looked over his shoulder at her. "Why would you do that?"

"Because I want to talk to them. I have questions."

"We weren't supposed to see them yet."

"You mean it was like a near-death experience? When a person dies, sees the light, and then comes back to life?" Dustin asked.

"Something like that. Don't speak of them."

"Don't worry about that," Monique said.

"Besides, they won't be where we saw them."

"Where are they?"

"How should I know? The Earth is a big ball. Maybe deep in the tunnels. Maybe up there." He pointed his finger towards the sky.

Monique opened her mouth to ask what the ancestors did all day but thought better of it.

She held the tissue to her cousin's mouth and considered dozens of sharp pains and dull aches. She did not remember where the injuries came from. Leroy was cut across both shoulders and blood dribbled out his nose. Dustin sat covered in mud, and blood seeped from the wound in his right leg. Chris gasped every other breath.

"Maybe you're right. I'll remember all this in my dreams."

"And so will your descendants," Leroy said. "For the moment, however, we have to consider what we're going to tell the police."

"I'm all ears."

"Good. All of us must be on the same page. There are some things they must not know. Listen . . ."

38

The ragtag bunch that arrived at Ada Mercy Hospital around 8:00 p.m. looked like they had been in battle. Indeed, Monique thought "post-combat" was a good word to describe them.

Lester Martin entered the emergency room entrance first to find attendants who could help with wheelchairs and stretchers. Chris and Dustin were taken into separate rooms for evaluation. Both needed surgery: Dustin for the deep puncture in his leg, which had nicked his femur, and Chris to have a pectoral muscle reattached.

"Sorry, partner," Monique told him. "You'll be in a sling for a while."

"Fine by me," Chris said. "I need a vacation."

Monique required stitches in her arm to replace the ones that had torn. Leroy had four cuts, each deep enough to require two stitches. Andrew's pinky was broken and might need surgery if his hand remained numb. All of them needed a weeklong soak to wash away the smell of peat and decay.

Monique knew she had to explain to the three Ada police officers, the county sheriff, and the Choctaw officers how the group had come by their injuries. Leroy told her to stay calm and that whatever explanation she created, they would believe her.

She explained that Andrew was her cousin, and he had called her about poachers on his allotment. He found cut barbed wire and several deer stands on his property. The rugged and intense Sheriff Williamson put his hands on his belt.

"The tribe deals with problems on allotments," he said.

"Tribal police takes too long," she countered. "No offense," she said to the female officer from the Choctaw Nation.

"None taken," said the stout woman who looked like a dark-skinned version of Scarlett Johansson. She stepped forward and offered her hand. "Charlotte Harris," she said as they shook.

"Here's the deal," Monique said to the officers. "You have to understand that Andrew cares deeply for his land. Not every family got to keep their allotment. Many Indian families sold theirs off for just a few dollars in the 1920s because they didn't know any better."

Officer Harris nodded her head in agreement.

"We were in the vicinity, so that's why we took a look. My partner, Chris, came with me. I thought that after we dealt with this issue that he might get the chance to hunt some hogs sometime, which everyone agrees are serious pests, you know?"

"They wiped out the melons at Rush Springs in Marlow this year," Andrew chimed in. "No watermelon festival."

Everyone knew about that disaster. The officers nodded.

"Anyway," Monique continued, "Leroy and Dustin came along because they know this allotment well. We took down the deer stands." She knew that could be substantiated because Andrew regularly took down poachers' stands and stashed them in his shed. "Andrew suggested we check out a cave he knew about near the center of the forest because it seemed a likely place for poachers to hide out. When we entered the cave, we found signs that several people had been staying there. There was a gas stove and camping gear. We also found a map of the Norman Children's Museum and a box of human bones. Old ones, I mean. As you know, there was a murder at the museum a few days ago and some skeletal remains were taken. At that point, we realized this was the hideout of the perps." She rubbed her neck wearily and sipped from her water bottle.

Leroy took over the narrative.

"As we were leaving the cave, three men ambushed us. They had knives. We had guns, but we didn't have time to get them out. It was pretty much hand-to-hand fighting."

"Yeah," Monique said. "Look at us, right? And right in the middle of all this, the ground started shaking. The trees started crashing down. I think it was one of those fracking earthquakes. Uh, maybe around 5 p.m. The shaking was pretty intense, and there was an explosion in the cave. Maybe a lamp hit the ground. I don't know."

A few officers looked at each other, clearly skeptical.

Leroy continued before anyone could ask questions. "Then a crack opened up in the ground about twelve feet across. Right where we were fighting. I couldn't see the bottom of it. Monique almost fell in, but I grabbed her shirt and pulled her back. It was complete chaos. The three guys who ambushed us fell into the chasm."

"And where is this chasm?" the lantern-jawed sheriff asked. Monique had a fleeting thought that perhaps he was related to the Williamson who was falsely convicted of the rape and murder of an Ada girl some thirty years prior. Now was not the time to ask.

"Like Leroy said, it was in the middle of a hollow on Andrew's allotment," Monique replied. "But it's closed up now."

"Closed up? How?" asked an older police officer whose nametag read SILVER.

"Well," Monique said, "after they fell in, the rumbling started again, and the sides just closed together. And the men were gone. We didn't have a chance to try and pull them out."

The officers looked at one another and then back at Monique.

"That's the craziest damn thing I ever heard," Silver said.

Monique shrugged. They had been in the hospital almost all night, and she felt exhausted. "We can go out there," she offered.

"We will," Williamson said. "It'll be light in a few hours. You clean up as best you can."

"Y'all okay with those injuries?" Harris asked.

"We can manage," she replied.

"Yes, ma'am," Leroy said in a strong voice.

"Meet us here in an hour," Williamson said.

Monique smiled. The last thing she wanted to do was return to the hollow. Her arm felt stiff, and when the anesthetic wore off, it would feel like a hundred bee stings. But they had to get this over with.

At 9:30 a.m., Monique sat in the front seat of Sheriff Williamson's car, and Leroy sat in the backseat. Andrew rode in the backseat of Silver's cruiser, and Steve and Lester Martin followed. When they reached Andrew's house, there were two Choctaw Nation police cars parked in front, and four officers standing in the dirt driveway wearing camo and full gear. All four officers strode toward the arriving convoy. Three were white men and the fourth officer was Charlotte Harris.

"Damn," Monique said, aware of her blood-covered clothes. As she exited the vehicle, a tall blond officer sporting aviator sunglasses and sunburned cheeks strode forward. He stopped and assessed her appearance. Monique regretted not having the opportunity to shower and change her clothes, but she pulled herself to her full five feet eleven and faced down the obvious leader of the group. "Officer—?"

"Thorne."

"I'm Monique Blue Hawk, homicide—"

"I know who you are," Thorne answered abruptly. He held out his hand.

They shook, then Thorne motioned to the others. He introduced a short redhead first. "This here's Gene Hammond." Hammond nodded.

"Ryan Taylor." The tall, thin man with a shaved pate saluted as if he was in the military.

Charlotte Harris smiled and said, "I briefed them on everything you said. And I'm familiar with this area. My family allotment is about twenty-five miles from here." Then she winked.

Monique did not react.

Leroy came up behind Monique. "We can take you there, officers," he said congenially. He turned and started for the trees.

After a pause, Thorne said to the other officers, "Let's go."

Monique had already warned Steve that he could not go into the hollow with them. He didn't attempt to follow, but he stood in front of Lester Martin's truck like a god of war ready to storm the hollow at the first sound of commotion. Monique suspected that the backseat held half the contents of their gun case.

Low-lying fog enveloped the hollow. Leroy and Andrew led the group into the dark forest. Williamson kept one hand on his sidearm. The four Choctaw police officers in tactical gear carried AR-15s on their backs. Thorne shone a spotlight through the mist, and the others held duty flashlights as they carefully made their way through the ground creepers and mud holes to the now-sealed chasm. Water flowed over the healed rift. Monique closed her eyes to avoid being blinded.

After fifteen minutes of treading carefully, Silver spoke. "It does look like some kind of natural event occurred here. Look at all these downed and broken trees."

"Right here, you say?" Williamson asked Leroy as he shone his light over the shattered trees.

"Yes. Right here."

"I smell smoke," Thorne said. "Where's that coming from?"

"I think up that way." Silver pointed up the incline to the cave entrance.

Monique walked behind the group. She watched Leroy put his hand on Officer Harris's arm. When she stopped, he leaned close and whispered to her. She listened, nodded, and then followed the others.

Tangled brambles slowed the group, but they pushed through. Taylor stopped to pull a boot from the muck.

"Oh, man," he said.

"Gonna need the hose after this," Hammond said.

Dwindling smoke and detritus odor mingled.

"Smells like homemade stink bait," Taylor said.

Leroy stopped before the cave entrance.

"The Guardian told me not to go in the cave," Monique said softly.

He nodded. "Stay here," he instructed Monique and Andrew. "I'll go in with them."

The Choctaw officers, Williamson, and Silver entered the cave after Leroy. Fallen logs, still smoldering, lay piled over unidentified melted objects.

"Is this a toy?" mused Silver as he nudged the plastic child's potty, now an unrecognizable lump of muted colors.

"Looks and smells like burned plastic," Hammond said.

Thorne walked over and pushed some of the debris away with his foot. "This was a very hot fire. Nothing's left," he said. He bent over and focused his light on a small object. "Although this looks like it could be charred bone."

A fetid smell wafted from the darkness. It hovered over their heads then settled onto their clothes. Several of the group winced.

Williamson shone his light into the darkness, illuminating a large pile of rocks at the base of what appeared to be a tunnel.

"Where does that go?" Williamson asked.

"It stops a few feet back," Leroy told them.

Harris walked a few feet into the cave and shone her light above the pile for a few seconds. She turned and said in a loud voice, "He's right. It stops. There's nothing here."

"Hmmm," muttered Williamson. "Maybe we should—"

"Head out," Harris finished for him. "I can come back tomorrow and look closer."

"I agree," said Thorne. He wiped his sweaty face with his sleeve and coughed. "Good idea."

The group started for the exit, but Williamson continued to shine his light around the cavern. "Hey, what's this?"

Everyone turned. His light illuminated an old campfire ring.

"Looks old," Leroy said.

"Yes, old," Harris agreed. "Decades, at least. Not of interest."

Williamson examined the old fire pit then turned to exit.

Monique watched the group emerge from the cave, Leroy in front.

"What's the fail-safe?" Thorne asked Andrew.

"The what?"

"The way out of these woods in an emergency. The way out when things go south. Isn't there a better path someplace?"

"Uh, there is no sure way out," Andrew said. "Trails change. If there's one here today, it'll be grown over tomorrow. Just go in a straight line until you get to the upward slope, then up and out. That's what I always do."

They had gone only about thirty feet back toward the house when they met an aggressive hog family that had decided to return to the hollow. The agitated pigs snorted and pawed the ground. The big boar grunted like an angry bear, shaking his head as if about to charge.

Thorne reached up and over his shoulder and had his AR-15 pointed at the pigs before Monique could register what he was doing.

"Don't shoot," Andrew said. "Just back off."

"They won't do any harm," Leroy said. "Let them go."

"Brad. Don't," Harris said.

Thorne lowered his weapon, breathing hard.

The group watched the pigs trot into the gloaming.

"Well, I believe we've seen enough for now," Williamson said.

Thorne sighed in relief. "Lead us out," he said to Andrew.

Andrew, Monique, Leroy, Steve, and Lester Martin watched the police cars drive away. "What now?" Monique asked.

"We need to go home and rest," Leroy said. "When Dustin and Chris are better, everyone needs to come to my house. We need to be cleansed."

"I better be gettin' back home," Martin said.

"Glad you came along, Mr. Martin," Monique said. "How did you know about this place, anyway?"

"Are you kiddin'? Everybody knows about it. Or they think they do." He gave her a small salute then got into his truck and drove away.

"Let's get going, Leroy," Monique said. "And maybe I can rinse off at your place before I get in our clean, shiny truck."

"Hey, no one will write a book about this, will they?" Andrew asked Leroy.

"No."

They were about to get in their vehicles when a small squawk sounded above them in the pecan tree by the driveway. They looked up. A little screech owl sat there, moving its head side to side, searching for mice.

"Is that another Crow?" Andrew asked. He aimed his rifle at the small bird, and Steve pulled his pistol.

"Well, it's an owl," Leroy answered. "But she's not a Crow. She's old and tired. We don't normally see owls this close to houses. She's nearing her end."

"I thought all owls were connected somehow," Andrew said.

"No. Not all owls are mean-spirited or heralds of doom. And they don't all know each other. Some just fly around looking for mice."

"Then they don't mean anything."

Monique looked up at the pretty little bird on the branch. Sunlight appeared through the trees. The hoarse cry of a great blue heron flying overhead reverberated in the stillness. A large yellow spider clung to the center of her elaborate web spun between the branches. The owl decided not to pursue her mouse hunt so she closed her eyes and folded her wings tight against her body. Monique sighed at the simplicity and beauty of her short life.

"Actually, Andrew," she corrected, "they mean a lot."

EPILOGUE

Word got out about the events at the Chalakwa Ranch, and the story spread quickly through the community—with four or five different versions, although many gossiped that Bigfoot was somehow involved. Everyone claimed to have felt the earthquake, and indeed, a geologist at the University of Oklahoma confirmed that a minor quake had occurred at 4:48 that afternoon, then another one forty minutes later.

Clarence Wright pestered Monique endlessly about the case. He badly wanted to write a paper about the bird person described in the file, but Monique would not allow him access to the hollow. He wrote down what he could recall of what he'd read, then proceeded to annoy elder Choctaws, asking for their creation stories and owl legends. He made his way to Leroy, who shut him down by speaking only Chahta anumpa. After the fifth call to Monique, she knew she had to do something. She asked Andrew to allow Wright into the hollow. "You covered the entrance to the cave with brush. What harm could it do to let him wander around?" she asked.

Wright arrived one morning outfitted for a week of camping. Andrew predicted that he wouldn't last until midnight of the first day. To his surprise, Wright did not emerge until the next morning at sunup. When he did, he was covered with muck, his clothes were ripped, and his gear was falling out of his pack. He gave Andrew a curt wave, got in his truck, and peeled out, leaving deep grooves in the grass. Monique did not hear from him again.

The Monkey Chasers likewise continued to beg Andrew for access until he relented and allowed the enthusiastic Bigfoot hunters to venture into the hollow.

"Want to bet how long they stay?" he asked Peterson. His friend's scalp had been reattached, but he was still waiting to see if his hair would grow back. His mangled ear healed, and Andrew teased that didn't look any worse than Khabib Nurmagomedov's cauliflower ears.

"Less than two hours," Peter said.

The two men stood at the fringe of the bowl, sucking on popsicles as they watched the eight intrepid searchers descend into the darkness. They braced themselves for the nightly song that still began on cue at sundown and burst outward like a grenade. Within minutes of sundown, the terrified explorers fled up and out of the deep woods and into their vehicles. Smiling, the two men walked back to the house toward the smell of venison stew drifting out the kitchen window. Like Clarence Wright, the Monkey Chasers never again asked to venture onto Andrew's property.

AUTHOR'S NOTE

The hollow at the center of Andrew Tubbee's Chalakwa Ranch does not exist. I patterned the tract after a desolate area located on North Mud Creek, southeast of Loco, Oklahoma. Hunters who are allowed on the private property, including my husband, Josh, and his cousin Terry, tell stories about the eerie cacophony of pigs, bobcats, coyotes, birds, and other shrieks they cannot identify that fills the air after dusk and before sunrise. Mist hangs over the thickly brambled and muddy forest, and the dense foliage keeps the area in perpetual shadow.

The Norman Children's Museum of Science and History doesn't exist either, but during my childhood I spent countless hours in the Fort Worth Children's Museum, now called the Fort Worth Museum of Science and History. My childhood memories of the museum are the basis for the story. Sadly, many of the beloved exhibits that I describe in this book are gone, as are the live animals and midnight laser magic shows set to the music of Pink Floyd.

As I have stated in other publications, I do not teach or write about sacred ceremonies, dances, songs, or prayers. There is nothing in this book about traditional Choctaw cosmological beliefs that cannot be found in books, the tribal newspaper archives, or online sites. As one can see from the dissimilar versions of creation stories, deities, and afterlife possibilities, Choctaws do not agree on religious dogma. In fact, in 2018 the Choctaw National Council passed a resolution, CR-01-19, declaring the Choctaw Nation a "Nation of the Christian Faith," to the dismay of the Choctaw citizenry, who had no vote in the matter. This statement illustrates the intertribal dichotomy of beliefs about colonization, patriarchal thought, and the impact of missionary intrusions into our culture. For those interested in Choctaw acculturation and intra-tribal factionalization, I explore ideological differences between tribal Nationalists and Progressives in *Choctaw Crime and Punishment, 1884–1907* (2010).

Monique Blue Hawk first appears in the 2011 novel *Document of Expectations*. The Crows I write about here are a branch of the family that I introduced in *Roads of My Relations* (2000). Owls are omens—either good or bad—in many tribal cultures. Among Choctaws who heed the old beliefs, owls are omens of bad events. There are a variety of other spiritual entities in the Choctaw pantheon besides *ishkitini*, but they are often referred to by different names. The backstories of these beings are vague and leave much to the imagination.

ABOUT THE AUTHOR

Devon Mihesuah is an enrolled citizen of the Choctaw Nation of Oklahoma and is a Chickasaw descendant. She is the Cora Lee Beers Price Professor in the Humanities Program at the University of Kansas. A historian by training, she is the author of numerous award-winning nonfiction and fiction books, including *Roads of My Relations*; *Ned Christie: The Creation of an Outlaw and Cherokee Hero*; *Choctaw Crime and Punishment: 1884–1907*; *American Indigenous Women: Decolonization, Empowerment, Activism*; *Cultivating the Rosebuds: The Education of Women at the Cherokee Female Seminary*; *Document of Expectations*; and *Recovering Our Ancestors' Gardens: Indigenous Recipes and Guide to Diet and Fitness*. She is former editor of *American Indian Quarterly* and the University of Nebraska Press book series, Contemporary Indigenous Issues. She oversees the *American Indian Health and Diet Project* at KU and the Facebook page, *Indigenous Eating*.